8<u>oo</u>

Dug's shield was reduced to an iron hub, fringed with splinters of smashed wood.

It still worked for slamming in Dumnonian faces. His hammer swung and smashed bone. A sword clanged into his helmet. He lashed out with his hammer and another Dumnonian fell. A face screamed and a backhanded hammerblow silenced it.

A small voice scrambled up from the deep in his mind and timidly suggested that he was tiring, that he couldn't possibly keep this up. Soon he'd make a mistake or meet someone stronger, better or luckier than he was. He'd done his bit, for now at least, and it was time to take a breather.

Dug snarled at the little voice to bugger off. He was busy.

ALSO BY ANGUS WATSON

Iron Age Trilogy
Age of Iron
Clash of Iron
Reign of Iron

CLASH of IRON

Iron Age Trilogy: Book Two

Angus Watson

orbit

Orbit
Hachette Book Group
1290 Avenue of the Americas
New York, NY 10104

Printed in the United States of America

ISBN: 978-1-62953-442-8

Orbit is an imprint of Hachette Book Group, Inc. The Orbit name and logo are trademarks of Little, Brown Book Group Limited.

The publisher is not responsible for websites (or their content) that are not owned by the publisher.

For Tim

Part One

Britain
61 BC

Chapter 1

Queen Lowa Flynn of Maidun knew she'd have to fight the moment she saw King Samalur the Tough of Dumnonia. She'd been fairly sure that violence would be required when she'd heard that he called himself "the Tough". Appearance and name aside, the fact that he'd marched an army five times the size of hers into her territory hardly heralded a friendly hello.

The boy king looked down at her from the low wall of the abandoned hillfort that he'd appropriated for Dumnonia's temporary headquarters. He was perched on the edge of the ornately carved wooded throne. He did not look tough, or, indeed, like a king. He looked like a spoilt child who'd spent a lot of other people's time and effort trying to look majestic. Fanning up and out behind his throne was a ludicrous, scallop-shaped wooden adornment the height of two tall men, laboriously etched and painted with hunting scenes. Lowa thought what a huge and pointless hassle it must have been for some hapless peasants to haul the thing all the way from Dumnonia.

The king's skinny legs dangled from the massive throne, clad in the finest tartan trousers. His boots, hanging a good foot above the platform, were tipped with polished ox horn. His bony, nobble-elbowed arms sprouted from a shiny brown otter-skin waistcoat. He wasn't much older than Spring, yet, below a bulbously arched nose and deep-set eyes, his smile shone with the unshakeable self-satisfaction that men didn't usually achieve until much later in life (and women rarely managed; some women that Lowa knew tried the look, but it was usually unconvincing).

Around his perched throne stood granite-faced guards adorned with the boar necklaces of Warriors, and next to them young, pretty female and male attendants. The former looked at Lowa with mild interest, the latter bathed their ruler with sycophantic smiles while regarding Lowa with the same disdainful rolling-eyed glowers that they might have given an elderly flasher.

Lowa sighed. Three days a queen, already she hated it.

She'd come to meet Samalur on horseback, bringing only Carden Nancarrow and Atlas Agrippa with her, intending to show how relaxed she felt about a gigantic army invading her territory. Having seen Samalur and his gang, she now knew that she'd made a mistake. She looked cheap in their snobbish eyes and that had weakened her negotiating position. Looking up to the boy king on the hillfort wall, she was below him physically as well, which didn't help. Perhaps she should have brought some sort of platform? Found a taller horse? She hadn't expected to be skilled at diplomacy, and she'd been right. Things were not going well.

"I have no quarrel with you, Samalur," she tried. "Quite the opposite. It will benefit both our tribes to unite against the Romans."

"The Romans?" His voice was high and haughty. "Do you know where the nearest Roman is? In Iberia. Should we unite to fight all the fish in the sea — because they're a lot closer!" Samalur giggled like the teenager he was, looking left to right at his court, who laughed along fawningly. His Warrior bodyguards smiled like men and women who'd been told to smile but weren't happy about it.

One of them wasn't laughing or smiling. Chief advisor Bruxon, the only one of Samalur's retinue who'd been introduced to them, was looking grimly at the grassy ground. He was about Dug's age with black-stained woollen clothes, a clean-shaven face and dye-blackened hair tied back in a short ponytail. He looked almost comically severe. Perhaps because he disliked his conceited ruler? Perhaps he might be useful in winning round or even unseating the young king?

"And don't think Bruxon's going to help you because he looks like someone's tricked him into drinking piss!" Samalur sniggered. He'd seen her looking at Bruxon and read her thoughts. Lowa was reluctantly impressed. "He always looks like that. But he's loyal to me. It was Bruxon's plan for me to kill my dad and become king in the first place! He tried to make me think it was my idea, but I'm cleverer than that, aren't I, Bruxon?" The advisor nodded resignedly. "So I'm also too clever to believe any of the crap that the druids spout about Roman invasions. They only do it to make themselves look important. That's why I don't keep druids near me. I killed all my father's. And do you know what's really funny? They bang on about seeing the future, but not one of them saw me coming!"

Laughter rang out from Samalur's throng.

"You don't need druids," the boy continued, "you can talk to the gods without them. I do. But I am part god, so that probably makes it easier . . . I'd recommend you kill all your druids, but you won't have time, since I'm going to kill you and take your territory. Tell you what; after I've wiped you and your army off the battlefield, I'll kill all your druids for you."

Lowa clenched her fists. "I would have agreed about druids not long ago, Samalur, but I've learnt differently. I know at least one druid who can see an invincible force of Romans coming to conquer us all with the same certainty that we might see rain coming across a lake and know that we're about to get wet. I've seen her do things that make me believe her."

"No, sorry, won't work, I don't believe her or you."

"Samalur, if our armies clash, thousands will die. Whoever wins, both armies will be weakened and we'll be more open to invasion. Not just from the Romans, but from the Murkans and anyone else who puts their mind to it."

"So surrender. I've given you my terms." Samalur smirked.

Even if the terms had been overly reasonable, Lowa could never have surrendered to the cocky little shit.

"You may outnumber us, Samalur, but our skill and experience is greater. We will rip the belly from your army like wolves savaging an aurochs."

"Take the belly. There'll be plenty left. We'll still win."

"Even if you do, a multitude will be killed. Your people will be weakened for generations."

"What are armies for if not to fight? I've got a huge army and I want to use it and nobody can stop me. Least of all you. You're not my mother. You can't be, I killed her."

Lowa put a hand on her bow.

"Lowa," said Atlas quietly, "we don't have—"

She held up a silencing hand. "All right, Samalur, I'll fight your army and I'll kill you myself. Wait here, we'll be back after nightfall."

As Lowa turned her horse, the laughter of Dumnonia's upper echelons made her skin prickle. She kicked her iron heels into the animal's flanks and galloped away.

"Lowa," Atlas shouted over the drumming hooves, "We need to go back. There are too many of them. We have to come to terms. It is not too late—"

"It is too late. Call a council the moment we return. We have a battle to plan."

Chapter 2

"I can't," she said, shaking her head then looking up.

Lowa looked seriously angry. Spring couldn't remember anyone ever looking so angry with her, apart from perhaps her father, King Zadar. It wasn't like Lowa at all. Being in charge changed people, it seemed, and not for the better.

"Spring, whatever you did to Dug and me in the arena, you're going to do it again to both of us and to as many other Maidun Warriors as you can, and we are going to tear this Dumnonian army to pieces."

"Lowa, no. I can't." Spring looked at the sling in her hands. She'd come into the woods ostensibly to hunt game, but really she wanted be alone. Finding out that she could use magic had thrilled, confused and upset her. Realising after the death of her father that her magic seemed to have left her had not cheered her any. She'd thought that getting away from all the noise of Maidun and walking on her own through the trees might make things clearer. So far it hadn't. She'd also thought she'd been careful to leave no trail, but Lowa had tracked her.

"You will try," said Maidun's new queen. "This isn't a game. The Dumnonians outnumber us massively. It is very likely that they will kill us all, Dug included. Do you want that to happen? I don't know what your power is or where it comes from, but I know what it can do. You have to use it to help us."

Spring wanted to burrow into the ground to get away. If she could have used her magic still, she would have created an island miles across the sea where she could have lived with Dug for ever, and perhaps a few other nice people, but certainly nobody who wanted to get involved in battles. "Can't Drustan help?" she asked.

"He's going to do what he can, but he says that compared to you he can't do anything."

"I do want to help, but I can't. I don't know what I did to you and Dug to give you strength, I just did it. It was the same the night before when I took Chamanca's outfit. I knew that I should take it, I knew that by touching it I'd make the leather strong and it would protect you, and I knew that I should put it in your cell. But I don't know how I knew. And I'm certain that I can't use my magic against the Dumnonians, totally certain, as certain as I am that I can't drink all the water in the sea. There's no point trying, I just can't." Spring's vision blurred with tears.

"But in the arena—"

"I know! I'm sorry!"

Lowa's lips were a thin white line. For a moment Spring thought she was going to hit her.

"So, when you put – for want of a better word – the magic into Chamanca's outfit that stopped the chariot's blade from chopping me in half, that was the first time you'd used magic?"

"I don't know if it was magic, or what it was."

"Was that the first time?"

"Oh no. It's happened loads before. Like when I met Dug he wanted to kill me, so I had to change his mind, but before that Ulpius wanted to kill me so I had to wake Dug up by going into his dream and getting him. Sometimes I just know things. Like I know the Romans are coming, and just before I met you I knew that Weylin would want a cart and I could rescue you and Dug by getting one. Sometimes I can do things, like when Juniper the dog jumped at me I stopped her heart, and sometimes I can make other people know things, like when I taught the girls to use the slings and then, like on Mearhold, I can make people fall in and out . . ." Spring reddened as she remembered that Lowa mustn't know about that. ". . .of boats, like I did for a joke once with one of the boys—"

"Hang on." Lowa took Spring's chin gently in her hand and looked into her eyes. "That's not what you were going to say." Spring tried to pull away. Lowa's fingers tightened. She leant forward. Her gaze speared through Spring's eyes and bored into her brain. "You missed something out, didn't you?" she said quietly.

"No."

"No?"

"No."

"On Mearhold. You used your magic for something that you're not telling me."

Spring tried to squirm away, but Lowa's grip was iron. "No, I didn't!" she insisted. With her lips pressed together by Lowa's strong fingers she sounded like someone who'd had their tongue split in two by liars' tongue scissors. "What could I have used it for?" She had used her magic to make Lowa fall out of love with Dug on Mearhold. At the time it had made good sense. She and Dug been happy before Lowa had come along. Meeting Lowa had resulted in Dug being savaged half to death by a horrible animal, not to mention Spring herself being stabbed and kidnapped by the awful Ogre, and who knew what more trouble this blonde archer was going to bring them? So Spring had acted to save Dug, and, if she was honest, because she wanted Dug to herself. However, when Spring had seen how much her actions had upset Dug, and Lowa, too, she'd realised that she'd made a mistake. She'd tried to cancel her spell, or whatever it was, but she didn't know if she had succeeded, and there was nothing she could do now that she had lost her magic. Besides, even if it came back, she'd learnt her lesson about mucking around with people's affections and she wasn't going to do it again. So she could have told Lowa what she'd done, but there was nothing to gain from it and plenty to lose.

Spring fixed her eyes on Lowa's and said, as firmly and seriously as she could through her squashed mouth: "I did not use my magic on Mearhold."

Lowa released her, but her stare did not let up. Spring squirmed and resisted the urge to tell her all just to stop those eyes poking about in her head.

"Enough of this," said Lowa, "I've got a battle to plan."

"I'll come to the battle. I'll do whatever I can to help. I'm good with my sling! But I won't be able to use magic. I'll try, I will, but I know it won't work."

"You do what you want." Lowa strode away.

Spring watched her walk off. She'd come to the woods to try and make herself feel better, but now she felt as rotten as she ever had.

Chapter 3

Dug wrinkled his nose at the endless Dumnonian army, stretching out of sight south and westwards across the grassy undulations of Sarum Plain. Opposite him, in the enemy line, horses stamped and blade-wheeled chariots creaked. Some hairy Dumnonian men and women shouted insults but for the most part they waited quietly like Dug. There'd be plenty of time for shouting once the Dumnonians charged. Assuming that they did charge. Dug didn't know the battle plan in detail, he knew only that he and the hundred men he'd been put in charge of were to wait until the enemy came at them. He looked down and saw that his knuckles were white from gripping his hammer. He relaxed his hand, filled his lungs then breathed out long and slow.

It was a cool, dry late summer's day under a white cloud sky, which was a plus. Fighting was more pleasant when it wasn't too hot. But why was he fighting at all? He could have carried on out of Maidun and be waking up now in some town like Bladonfort with a bit of a hangover, ready to start working on the next one. Instead he'd come back, had risen before it was light with thousands of other nervous bastards and was lining up for yet another battle. Great big badgers' arses, why? Because, he admitted to himself with a self-chastising shake of his head, he was an idiot who wanted to impress Lowa, even though she didn't even know he'd gone away, let alone that he'd come back, and she was too busy being queen to care anyway.

Talk was that the Dumnonians numbered a hundred

thousand men and women. Dug was sure that they didn't. That was what the shout had said, and everybody had accepted it. People always exaggerated army sizes and it wasn't as if anyone had popped over to the Dumnonian camp, asked them all to stand still and counted them. One thing was sure, though – there certainly were shiteloads of the nasty looking buggers – many, many, many more than the Maidun army had.

So it looked like Queen Lowa's reign was to be a short one. It was an odd twist of fate, mused Dug. If Lowa had waited less than a moon, then Zadar would still be ruling Maidun instead of her, the Dumnonians would have crushed him instead and would have avenged her dead sister and friends for her. But now Lowa was leading a formerly enemy army that she'd previously been a part of, against an army that she would have joined, had she known it was going to attack the army she was now leading. The world, thought Dug, was rarely straightforward.

The outcome of the battle would be, though, without even taking the massive difference in army sizes into account. Before it had even begun, Lowa had made some blinding errors, as Dug had noticed that new kings and queens were wont to do.

There was a ripple along the Dumnonian line and a couple of chariots started forward. Were they about to charge? Dug and the rest of the Maidun army tensed as one, but the chariots wheeled round to display a couple of naked, mooning posteriors, and returned to the Dumnonian lines.

Now, where was I? thought Dug. Oh yes, he'd been thinking that he should have gone to the war council and pointed out how rubbish the plan was, and not chickened out of it because he didn't want to see Lowa and that woman-stealing arsehole Ragnall together. Whatever advice Drustan, Carden, Atlas and the rest had given her, it had either been crap or she'd ignored it. He could see three glaring mistakes.

First rule when fighting a larger army was to find somewhere narrow to fight, like a valley or, better, a cliff-lined gorge, to ensure that fighting was never more then one on one. Yet Lowa had decided to meet Samalur on an open plain, where he would surely encircle her much smaller force and attack every soldier of hers with ten of his.

Second rule with a smaller army was surprise. Hit the enemy when and where they didn't expect it. Yet the Dumnonians had been camped in the same place for three days, and Lowa had announced that she would attack them there. It couldn't have been less of a surprise.

The third, and biggest, error was meeting Samalur in battle at all. An army that size would be able to feed itself for only a matter of days in enemy territory, so, had Lowa pulled her people up into impregnable Maidun Castle and closed the gates, the Dumnonians would have gone home soon enough.

The only good thing he'd heard that she'd done was to tell the Dumnonian king that they were going to attack the night before. With any luck he would have kept his troops awake in readiness, while the Maidun forces had slept. And, Dug admitted to himself, he didn't know everything. There might have been more to the plan than immediately met the eye. Whatever, it didn't matter. He just had to follow orders, give orders, and fight.

Down by his feet were two long spears and a large, hefty shield. They'd been sneaked forward once the ranks were already in place so that the Dumnonians wouldn't know they were there. That was pretty tricksy and should really muck up a chariot charge, so it was possible, he supposed, that Lowa had other schemes in place.

Another positive was that the breeze was an easterly on the Maidunites backs, rather than the more common southwesterly. That was a spot of luck, since their projectiles would go further than the enemy's, but it was hardly a gale, and there was no way Lowa could claim credit for the direction of the wind.

Dug's thoughts were interrupted by a rattling blare of bronze trumpets with wooden clackers in their mouths. They rang out first from the Dumnonian army, then from their own. The Dumnonian front line shuddered as one, then rolled forwards. Here we go. Dug felt the contents of his stomach lurch and asked Makka the god of war to ensure, if nothing else, that he didn't shit in his leather battle trousers. If he was going to the Otherworld today he wanted to arrive clean-arsed.

"Ready!" he shouted, looking around at his men and women, then added, "Arms' length between you all!" more for something to say than anything else – they were already well spaced. They looked back and him and nodded; some were wide-eyed with their lips parted in fear, some serious, some wild-eyed and froth-mouthed. They were mostly armoured in leather like him, a few wore iron helmets like his. Most were armed either with hefty iron swords or stout spears. He was the only one with a hammer. Very few, thank Toutatis, looked like they were going to flee before the fighting had begun, so that at least was a great improvement on some battles he'd been in. He looked back to the Dumnonians and spotted a large dragonfly, flying between the armies as if it was just another day.

From horseback in the centre, atop one of the burial mounds that clung on to Sarum Plain's uplands like a well-spaced migration of giant slugs that had died and solidified, Lowa watched as the Dumnonian chariots charged her right flank. She'd sent Atlas to the right with the infantry to encourage Samalur to line his heavy chariots there. The young Dumnonian king had obliged. With his massively superior force, Samalur had done the sensible thing and matched her battle lines on both sides, heavy chariots on the left, infantry on the right, light chariots and cavalry in reserve ready to zoom wherever they were needed. Numerically superior, the Dumnonians had no incentive to try anything more advanced than the classic "infantry attacks chariots, chariots attack infantry" tactics.

Dug was leading a section on the right, she remembered once again, about to be hit by thousands of thundering chariots and their crews of murderous, heavily armed Dumnonians. Atlas had told her that he'd come back to Maidun offering his services, and that he'd been given a company to lead. She was hurt that he hadn't been to see her on his return, but then again it wasn't long since she'd woken him up by having sex with Ragnall on the other side of the campfire. How could she begin to explain and apologise for that? She banished Dug from her thoughts. This was no time for childish romanticising.

Thinking of children . . . it was irksome that Spring wouldn't use her magic. If the girl had made Lowa feel like she did when she'd fought the chariot and Chamanca, she would have taken on the whole Dumnonian army herself. But Lowa believed that she'd been telling the truth about not being able to use her magic, because the girl was a terrible liar. Lowa was sure she'd lied about using her magic on Mearhold, and she had a fairly firm idea about what the jealous little brat might have done. That was something else she'd have to address if they lived through the day. Right now, she'd found another use for Spring.

Drustan had helped a little, magic-wise. By sacrificing an ox, so he said, he'd caused the wind to veer round to the east so that it was behind them. But that was it. He said that those who could use the gods' powers could only draw a limited amount. Lowa had asked him if there was anyone else. He'd said no. The gods had shown him that he was going to find a young person who was the greatest ever practitioner of magic. He'd thought that this was Ragnall, and he'd even tricked Ragnall into believing he'd lit fires with his mind in order to draw it out of him, but now he knew that the young man had no contact with the gods. The magic youngster foretold was Spring.

But now Spring had lost her magic. Had the gods deserted her, Lowa wondered, because the Maidun army was doomed to be annihilated by the Dumnonians, and gods don't like helping losers?

There was one way to find out.

She raised her arm and dropped it. The Maidun trumpets spewed their cacophony. Her army's left, her mass of heavy chariots, stirred then surged towards the Dumnonian line of foot soldiers.

On her right, the Dumnonian chariots charged the Maidun infantry. Javelins launched. Maidunite shields appeared like a sudden bloom of flowers. There was a great howl of disappointment from the Dumnonians as their missiles were deflected by the revealed defences, but they charged on, swords aloft, wheel-blades flashing.

At the last moment, all along Maidun's right flank, long spears sprung up like hair bristling on a wildcat's neck. The Dumnonian chariot line faltered as thousands of reins were yanked in panic, but it was too late. The horses and chariots hit the infantry's spears. A heartbeat later she heard the sound of a thousand wooden poles snapping under the impact of horses and people, followed by the screams of Danu knew how many Dumnonian horses and men as iron spear heads punctured their limbs, stomachs, faces . . . She thought of her own soldiers, kneeling behind shields as tons of man, horse, iron and wood smashed down around them. All along the Maidun line, horses' hooves would be crushing skulls and splintered chariot draught poles impaling the chests of her own people. That had been unavoidable. She prayed that not too many were killed, and that none of them was Dug.

The Maidun front line held. The Dumnonian attack crumpled as wave after wave of horses, chariots and charioteers crashed into and on to the broken pile of their fallen comrades.

On the left, Maidun's chariots stopped twenty paces short of the enemy line, as, Lowa thought with some satisfaction, the Dumnonian heavy chariots should have done. Maidunite javelins flew. The volley whumped harmlessly into thousands of Dumnonian shields. The Dumnonians shouted in delight, dropped their shields and charged. The Maidun chariots paused for a moment, then unleashed their second, unexpected salvo of javelins. That was much more successful, as were the third, fourth and fifth javelin volleys. Hundreds of Dumnonians fell. Their line dissolved in disarray. Some ran back to retrieve their shields. Some ran at the chariots. Captains screamed contradictory commands.

For centuries it had been the pan-tribal British custom to carry only one javelin in each chariot. You chucked that as an opener, then the crew-warriors dismounted for some proper mêlée fighting with swords, axes, hammers and the like. It hadn't been easy, but Lowa was glad she'd talked the charioteers into flouting tradition and carrying five javelins each. Hopefully now, if they survived this battle, some of the other innovations she had in mind might be more readily accepted.

On the right, her infantry dropped their pikes and dashed in to finish off the downed charioteers. The Dumnonians saw the line broken, rallied and came at them, but the Maidun soldiers rolled back into their line, retrieved their spare, unbroken pikes, held them aloft and retreated steadily, backwards and outwards, away from Lowa and the centre. The Dumnonian heavy chariots pressed, but, having seen what

happened to the first lot, held back from all-out attack on
those bristling pikes.

Another discordant trumpet blast honked from the Dumnonian
centre and their light chariots set off at a gallop to swing
around Maidun's right and attack the flank of the infantry.
Lowa gritted her teeth. She'd planned on Samalur doing
exactly that, but not so quickly. If the Dumnonian chariots
got round behind her right flank, then her plan was screwed
and they were all dead. It was going to be close.

On the left, the Maidun charioteers had exhausted their
javelins. Hundreds of Dumnonians had been killed or disabled, but that was only a tiny proportion of their force and
the battle there was far from over. On the same trumpet call
that sent Dumnonia's light chariots around their left edge,
thousands upon thousands of their infantry charged on the
Dumnonian right, armed with shields and heavy iron swords.

The Maidun chariots cantered away. Like the Maidun
infantry, they retreated both backwards and away from the
centre, spreading the width of the battlefield.

One Maidun chariot stopped and was soon left behind,
on its own between the two armies. A little warrior leapt
out, sword in one hand, ball-mace in the other. Even from
a couple of hundred paces away, Lowa recognised Chamanca
the Iberian, ex-bodyguard to Zadar, the woman who had
bested her on Mearhold and would have done again in the
Maidun arena had it not been for Spring's magic. The fastest
Dumnonian infantry reached the lone figure. A blur of
movement, the Dumnonians fell and the Iberian was left
standing. But there were many more Dumnonians coming.
Chamanca leapt for her chariot, but too late. The main body
of the Dumnonian infantry swept over and gobbled up horse,
chariot, driver and Chamanca. Lowa grimaced, then smiled
as Chamanca's chariot burst from the Dumnonian ranks,

with the Iberian aboard and shaking her fist at the pursuers.

Queen Lowa looked back to Spring, on horseback behind her, and nodded. The girl yelled a screeching "Fiiiiiiiii – errrrrrrr!!!!", louder than any trumpet or whistle. All along the rear of Lowa's battle line, men and women put torches to the tight bundles of thatch that sat on a long line of catapults.

Dug looked about, shaking his head in exasperation. Someone had taken his badger-fucking spear. "Remember where you put your spare spear, and make sure you pick up the same one again. Not someone else's." That's what he'd told them. But some wanker had taken his. It was unforgivable.

He saw a spare one and bent to pick it up.

"Oi! That's mine! Hands off!" shouted a young, square-jawed woman. "It's your plan, Dug! What's everyone else going to do if you don't stick to it? Come on Dug, leadership!"

It was Nita, Mal's wife. Mal, next to her, raised a "you see what I have to put up with?" eyebrow.

Dug nodded. He didn't want the spear, he was a lot happier with his hammer, but Nita was right. He was leader and he wanted to show everyone what to do with their spears. However, looking about, they seemed to have got the idea. They were marching steadily backwards in good order, long spears raised. Dug shook his head in gratified surprise. He'd never commanded men and women who did what they were told more than about ten per cent of the time. Say what you like about Zadar, but his troops knew how to follow orders.

"You all right there, Mal?" Dug had been glad to see a familiar face when his old mate Mal Fletcher had sought him out a couple of days before.

Mal winked. "We should have stayed back at base and guarded the tavern like you suggested. Thought I'd retired long ago, but this one," he cocked his head at his wife, "reckoned Lowa would need our help."

Dug nipped in behind Mal. Without a spear, he'd just be in the way in the front line. "Lot of trouble, that Lowa. Might get us all killed one day." It was rubbish banter and Dug knew it, but at times like this it was good to be distracted from one's surroundings.

"One day? Have you seen what's coming?" Behind and uphill of the pursuing heavy chariots, they could see the Dumnonian light chariots thundering northwards across the plain, perpendicular to the line of battle. The lead chariots had already swung eastwards towards them, aiming for the criminally exposed Maidun right flank. A flash off to the left caught his eye.

"Oh no," said Dug. "Look, she's gone and fired her bloody catapults too late. If they were meant to slow the light chariots, which I bet they were, then we're in trouble."

"She's lost it!" said Mal. "She's lost her mind and we're all going to die."

Nita slapped his arm with the flat of her sword. "Lowa knows what she's doing."

"Then why," said Mal, "has she used the one unusual weapon we've got that might actually surprise the enemy to bombard the gap left by the Dumnonians attacking us? What did she hit?" Mal stood on tiptoes to peer over soldiers' heads. "Yup, thought so, a grassy space where the enemy used to be. I'm sorry, Nita, but she really doesn't know what she's doing with those catapults."

Nita didn't have an answer.

Dug looked to Atlas to see if he'd seen what had happened. He had. Two hundred paces away along the front line, the large African had climbed on to someone's shoulders; Carden Nancarrow's probably, since those two were always together and Carden was about the only man in the army who could have born Atlas' armoured weight. The Kushite blew an iron whistle twice.

The Maidun line doubled the speed of its retreat, jogging

diagonally backwards, away from the pursuing Dumnonians and out from the battle's centre, spears brandished to keep the heavy chariots at bay. They were headed for a thickly brambled band of wood, which would protect their flank from the light chariots and their slingstones. Given the speed those chariots were coming, though, there was no way they were going to make it.

Dug was glad he wasn't on the far right. Very soon they were going to be hit hard by a hailstorm of lethal stones. Still, it didn't really matter whether he was there or not. If the far right collapsed under the onslaught, they were all fucked.

Dozens of balls of burning thatch crackled over Lowa's head.

She looked across to Samalur's position. She had a clearer view of him since both armies had split down the middle, hers retreating away from the centre, his following, leaving a gap in front of his central command position. Like her, he was perched on a burial mound, surrounded by a few guards and probably the same group of hangers-on from the day before. For an instant she was sure he was looking directly at her, but then he was obscured by smoke from the burning thatch.

Atlas' whistle sang out three times, the signal to pick up the pace again. It would be difficult for the ranks to maintain form at that speed, so it meant that something was going wrong.

Oh aye, thought Dug, as he saw over on the right the first of the light chariots come into range and unleash a volley of slingstones. Those holding pikes in the front rows – the ones holding the blade-wheeled heavy chariots at bay – didn't have shields. A lot of them fell. The heavy chariots charged.

"Now?" asked Spring.

"Now," Lowa agreed, putting her hand over the ear that was nearest to the girl.

"Horrrrr – sesssssss!!!" screeched Spring. She might not be able to use her magic, but her scream, louder than all the battle trumpets combined, was proving useful.

From their hiding place behind a low rise, Ragnall and two hundred other riders armed with swords and bows heard Spring and mounted. For the first time in a while the young man felt brave, confident and full of purpose. He roared a battle cry. That drew some disapproving glances from his mostly older and more sensible fellows, but he didn't care.

He was off. He was leading the charge.

Lowa saw then coming and sped ahead, followed by Spring. So Lowa was leading the charge now and Spring was at her shoulder. How annoying, thought Ragnall. Although also something of a relief. The first enemy stones and arrows were not usually targeted on the third rider from the front.

Up ahead, the catapulted bales burnt merrily, gushing smoke away from them, obscuring the Dumnonian army, then Lowa as she and her horse plunged into the fog, followed by little Spring on her mount. Ragnall willed his horse on. The beast complied. Ragnall took a deep breath. Gripping his horse with his thighs and his sword in his hand, he followed the new queen into the smoke.

They reached the trees and stopped retreating, but it was far from the end of problems for the right of the Maidun army. In fact, Dug realised with a snort of annoyance, it was the beginning of his.

The far right was now, as planned, protected from Dumnonia's chariot-mounted slingers by a stand of bramble-skirted trees, but the slingers leapt from their chariots and ran across to join the warriors from the heavy chariots. Together, the Dumnonian heavy infantry and slingers advanced at the now static Maidun line. Dug gulped. There were a lot of them and they all seemed to be coming at him.

Shields went up over Maidun heads as slingstones rained down. Soon those shields would be needed to stop swords. It was a nasty situation. Retreat was tempting, but if they fled the Dumnonians would part ranks and the bladed chariots would stream through and cut them down.

There was, Dug realised with a mixture of terror and disappointment, only one thing to do.

Atlas worked it out at the same moment and five blasts rang out on his whistle. It was the signal to charge. Dug shook his head. So it was time to attack. No choice in the matter. He shuddered. Just as he thought his growing fear might overwhelm him, it morphed into raging courage. It felt like a monster was growing inside him, expanding out from his stomach, widening his shoulders and burning in his head hot as a bone-fed furnace. His battle lust was coming, he realised with a mixture of shame and excitement, and it was time to bid rational thought goodbye for a while.

Dug gripped his shield in one hand, warhammer in the other, and sprinted at the broad enemy line. The ground flew under him as he pumped his legs. He ran full tilt, no thought of pacing himself. He didn't need to. He had all the energy in the world. Slingstones whistled past his ears. The front line of Dumnonian troops, a mass of bearded men, shaggy haired women, sharp iron weapons and flying stones, zoomed towards him.

A grin split his face and he screamed with joy. He smashed spears out of his way with hammer and shield. He swung the hammer, felling three of them. A sword came down. He whacked it aside with his shield and drove his hammer's top spike into the underside of the sword swinger's jaw.

Mal shook his head as he jogged towards the Dug-shaped breach in the enemy line. He'd seen it before, but it always amazed him when Dug, who was possibly the most workshy man Mal had ever met, burst into this rampaging ball of fury on the battlefield.

"Stay behind me!" he shouted to Nita as he knocked the first spear thrust aside and smashed his sword into a Dumnonian head.

"Will I fuck!" shouted Nita, pushing past him, her slim sword flashing in one hand, wheel iron whacking down in the other.

"Don't get too close to Dug!" Mal shouted at her unheeding back.

Chamanca licked blood from her lips. She was soaked in Dumnonian gore from her brief foray into their lines, but it wasn't nearly enough.

"Not so fast!" she shouted at her charioteer, cuffing the girl. The Dumnonian infantry had slowed its charge and the Maidun chariots were getting too far ahead. Chamanca wanted to be ready for any overzealous and speedy Dumnonians who ran clear of the main group. Killing a dozen or so had only enhanced her appetite. She yearned to champ her teeth into someone's neck. It had been ages since she'd sucked Weylin's life away, and Queen Lowa's rule wasn't going to provide as many blood-drinking chances as King Zadar's. Not that she didn't like Lowa. What wasn't to like about the brave, king-toppling, hot-bodied beauty whose blood had tasted so silky and skin felt so smooth when they'd fought on Mearhold and in the Maidun arena? But Lowa had rejected the Iberian's offer to prove her loyalty by biting the throat out of anyone who opposed her, and made it clear that she wasn't going to ask her to drink anyone's blood. Chamanca was going to have to take her sanguineous dining opportunities when she could. So it was somewhat annoying to be running away from tens of thousands of racing-pulsed Dumnonians.

The enemy kept coming in their annoyingly regular line, and her chariot bounced on. The shaking and jolting was doing nothing to improve her mood. If Chamanca had been commanding this side of the line she would have ordered a charge, despite Lowa's orders for this retreat, and despite the fact that she could see the insanity of attacking the multitudinous Dumnonians. Unfortunately, Lowa had not only put someone else in charge, but also told the other charioteers not to listen to Chamanca.

The only person Chamanca was allowed to be in charge of was her young driver. She cuffed her again, then hooked her blonde hair aside and ran her fingers down the back of her slender neck. The girl knew better than to complain or even turn round. Chamanca licked her lips.

Dug's shield was reduced to an iron hub, fringed with splinters of smashed wood. It still worked for slamming into Dumnonian faces. His hammer swung and smashed bone. A sword clanged into his helmet. He lashed out with his hammer and another Dumnonian fell. A face screamed. A backhanded hammerblow silenced it.

A small voice scrambled up from deep in his mind and timidly suggested that he was tiring, that he couldn't possibly keep this up. Soon he'd make a mistake or meet someone stronger, better or luckier than he was. He'd done his bit, for now at least, and it was time to take a breather.

Dug snarled at the little voice to bugger off. He was busy. He ducked a sword-swipe, crunched the handle of his hammer into someone's bollocks and his hammerhead into possibly the same person's face. He waded on, deeper into the Dumnonian ranks, hammer flailing, shield boss punching.

Ragnall galloped out of the smoke. Already there were arrow-stuck bodies on the ground and riderless horses panicking on the burial mound. The remainder of Samalur's guard were tightening around their king, swords aloft. Lowa was up ahead, drawing her bow, shooting down one of the guards, reaching into her quiver then nocking another arrow, drawing and shooting another guard, again and again. The movement reminded Ragnall of a waterwheel on a stream in spate.

Spring was trotting behind the queen, slinging out stones almost as quickly as Lowa's arrows, smiling like a girl on a pleasure ride. Ragnall heard an incongruous noise. Was Spring singing? She was.

A remaining slinger aimed at Lowa, but a stone from Spring send him tumbling from his horse with a surprised squawk. Ragnall wondered why Samalur's guard didn't contain more slingers and archers, then realised that it probably had done but Lowa and Spring had targeted these first.

Lowa reined her horse to a halt ten paces from the man-high mound. Ragnall drew up next to her. The two hundred others of the Maidunite cavalry arrived behind. There were perhaps ten Dumnonian guards left, concealing the young king somewhere in their midst.

He couldn't see any of the rest of the other hundred thousand or so of the Dumnonian army. They were all off chasing the two split horns of Maidun's forces. The plan had been a simple one, and far from original. With a few tweaks like the burning straw bales, it was roughly how Alexander the Great had beaten Darius of Persia's much larger force at Gaugamela. Ragnall had learnt about it on the Island of Angels. He'd been surprised at the war council when nobody else, other than his old teacher Drustan, had heard of the battle. Then he'd swelled with pride when Lowa had decided to use his plan. He was perhaps even more glad that Lowa had allowed him to take charge of her equivalent to Alexander's Companions – the cavalry who charged through the gap to take Samalur. He felt a little glow in his stomach, remembering that Alexander had taken one of his Companions as a lover.

Lowa turned to Ragnall and the other riders, smoke whirling around her. "Surround the mound." She said, then, louder. "Bruxon! Give us Samalur now, or you all die."

"You don't have a hope, Lowa! My forces . . . Aaaark!" Samalur's voice was cut off, the horsemen parted, and a severe-looking black-clad man whom Ragnall took to be Bruxon marched down the mound, dragging the king by the collar.

Lowa dismounted and headed towards them, bow in one hand, sword in the other.

Bruxon thrust Samalur forward.

Dumnonia's king stumbled toward Maidun's queen and fell to his knees. "Lowa . . ." he stammered, arms outstretched and palms upward. "We need to be allies. It's like you said. Together we can—" Lowa pulled her sword arm back. Samalur raised a protective arm and screamed: "No! Don't!!"

Lowa spun in a whirling blur. Samalur's hand and head flew up in the air. His body fell forwards, severed neck and wrist spurting. The gasp from his guards was overwhelmed by cheers from the Maidun cavalry.

Lowa snatched up the boy's head, leapt on her horse, shouted "Follow me!" and galloped away.

Ragnall looked round at the others. If they were surprised as him it didn't show. They heel-kicked their horses and sped after the queen.

"Stop!" someone was shouting at Dug.

The cowards were running!

"Stop!" They were getting away. He swung his hammer and missed.

"Dug, you arse! Stop!" Somebody grabbed his hammer arm. Somebody strong. Dug whipped round the dented, blood-covered shield boss to beat away the hindrance. He needed that arm. But something grabbed his left arm too.

"Stop!" came the annoying shout again. He tried to shake off his captors, but the little voice in his head which had been struggling to make itself heard for some time finally got through and persuaded him to desist struggling for the briefest of moments and take assess the situation.

Dug shook his head. His ears popped. It felt like a bandage was ripped off his eyes as reality whooshed back to him. Mal was holding one of his arms, Atlas the other. "Um?" He said.

"Thank Sobek for that," said Atlas. "It's over, you great fool. Look."

Dug looked around. The fighting had stopped. Some Dumnonians were heading back to their chariots. Many from both sides were sitting on the bloody grass, nursing wounds. Others, less fortunate, were screaming in pain, trying to hold their guts in or staring at their severed limbs. Others were bubbling their last. An awful lot were dead. Dug looked at his blood-smeared hammerhead.

"What happened?" he managed.

"Lowa," said Mal. Atlas was already off, shouting at the beaten Dumnonians not to stray too far.

"Lowa?"

"Lowa." Mal shook his head in exhausted wonder.

"Could you give me a wee bit more detail?" asked Dug.

"Sorry, battle took it out of me. We're not all Makka-driven madmen like you, Dug. We were fighting away, when there was this unholy scream and there was Silver – Spring, I mean – on horseback, next to Lowa." Now Mal mentioned it, the northerner did find the memory of a weird scream somewhere amongst all the rage. "And Lowa was holding up the Dumnonians' king's head," Mal continued, "shouting that the battle was over. Almost all the Dumnonians said fair's fair and put their weapons down. And that was that, more or less. A few idiots like you fought on for a short while, but most of them gave up like men who never wanted to fight in the first place. Lowa galloped off southwards, presumably to halt the battle over there."

"She's gone?"

"She's one of that lot." Mal pointed at a flock of cavalry galloping across the plain to the other side of the battlefield.

"Badgers' cocks," said Dug.

Chapter 4

Ragnall had drunk way too much alcohol once before. He'd behaved like a chump, been beaten up and woken the next day feeling as if he'd been poisoned and that everything he'd done or ever hoped to achieve was worthless. So he'd made the sensible decision to never get very drunk again, in much the same way, he reckoned, that a dog might pull apart a wasps' nest only once.

So he didn't understand, the evening following the battle, why all the people around him, Drustan included, had drunk so much beer and cider that they were telling the same stories over and over and wagging fingers at each other as if they'd discovered the secret of life, when in fact their observations were to philosophy what farting was to singing. Ragnall decided that he'd rather lie on his own looking at the sky than listen to another half-remembered story or quarter-cultivated pearl of wisdom, so he headed off.

He was nearly clear of the impromptu outdoor inn's rough tables and benches when a tough looking but cheerily drunken man grabbed him.

"Have a drink!"

"Thanks, but I've already got two over there," he lied.

"I see! You know when I knew that Lowa would be queen?"

"I don't." Ragnall tried to pull away, but the man held his arm. It seemed that he had a story and was determined to tell it. Ragnall decided it would be easier and quicker to listen than try to reason his way out of the situation.

"You know when I knew that Lowa would be queen?" the man repeated.

"OK, when did you know Lowa would be queen?" Ragnall asked.

"Boddingham," said the man.

"What?" said Ragnall.

"Boddingham," the man repeated, nodding his head vigorously. "When we sacked it. That's when I knew Lowa would be queen one day."

The peaceful summer night and the victorious laughter of the revellers melted away as Ragnall remembered riding home to Boddingham. His dead friends. The smashed palisade. His slaughtered brothers. Slaughtered by arrows . . .

He shook his head. "But Lowa wasn't at Boddingham. She told me she was off scouting that day."

"Wasn't at Boddingham? Lowa? Scouting? Lowa? Nah, nah, nah. You got that very wrong, mate. First over the palisade, that was her, moving as if she and that horse were one, shooting those arrows into man, woman and beast. I said to myself right then, she'll be queen one day, that one. She was like a goddess. You would not believe how many she killed that day. I told myself then and there that she'd be queen. Moving like she and the horse were one, she was. First over the palisade." The man was nodding enthusiastically.

"How many?" Ragnall managed.

"How many what?"

"How many people did she kill?"

"At Boddingham?"

"Yes!"

"I don't know. Maybe fifty? Maybe ten. Probably more than ten, less than fifty. A lot. Maybe fifty."

"I see. I have to go."

"Have a drink! I'll go and get you one. You look like you need a drink."

Ragnall stopped. "All right, I think I will have another

drink." He found a space on a bench and sat down to wait. The man tottered away.

After a while Ragnall realised that the man wasn't coming back and he got up to find his own drink.

Away from the noise of celebration, Lowa spoke to Bruxon the Dumnonian for a long time. Lowa asked most of the questions and Bruxon did most of the talking. She heard how Samalur's father, Vidin, had been a tyrant very much in the Zadar mould, perhaps worse, ravaging Dumnonia to enrich the few and win favour with the coming Romans.

Bruxon and a few others had plotted, rebelled and killed Vidin. They'd replaced him with his up-until-then studious son Samalur. It had been a mistake. Samalur was a good deal more intelligent than his father, but the moment they'd put him on the throne he'd turned his keen mind to merciless persecution. As well as all the druids, he'd killed anyone he perceived to be a rival, including three of his own brothers, two sisters, his mother and a slew of uncles, aunts and cousins. Anyone who wasn't a threat but had some power, he'd bought off with gold, land and slaves. Bruxon and the original plotters, those of them left alive, had been looking for a way to be rid of the young oppressor when Lowa had kindly done it for them. He apologised profusely for the battle, offered food, weapons and gold as reparation, and swore that Dumnonia would join Maidun as a more numerous but junior ally in battles against the Romans, or anyone else for that matter.

He also asked Lowa's permission to become king of Dumnonia. The tribe's leadership had always been rigidly hereditary, but Samalur had murdered his relations so thoroughly that Bruxon, a distant cousin of the royal line, had as good a claim to the throne as anyone, as well as the support of the more morally upstanding survivors of Samalur's rule. He swore that he'd treat his people well and prepare his armies for the Roman invasion.

Lowa was convinced. She considered telling Bruxon to wait for her decision, intending to discuss it with Drustan and Atlas. But some decisions had to be made quickly. It was for decisions like this that tribes had a sole ruler. So she sent Bruxon off, demanding that he and his army return home immediately and that he report back to her in four moons with the promised reparations.

Chapter 5

Nearly a moon after the battle on Sarum Plain, Lowa was walking down from Maidun Castle, bow in one hand, arrow-stuffed quiver bouncing on her back, on her way to win the archery competition. She'd considered the long-distance running race, which she might have won, and the mêlée scramble, in which she might have learnt something while not winning, but in the end she elected to enter the one event in which she'd definitely triumph. Now that she was queen, winner was a more appropriate look than plucky loser.

Lowa had organised a few days of competitions, eating and drinking to mark the victory over the Dumnonians and the beginning of her reign with something that people would remember. More than that, she wanted her newly appointed captains – Atlas Agrippa, Carden Nancarrow, Mal and Nita Fletcher and more – to see others' abilities and choose their own officers.

Even more than that, perhaps, she wanted a break from the mind-knottingly tiresome and convoluted arse ache of running a realm. Zadar had left her with a thousand problems, not least how to reduce the crippling taxes that he'd claimed from tribes under his boot and free all the slaves he'd collected, while still feeding, housing and arming the army. The obvious answer would have been to disband the army, for a few moons at least, but that wasn't an option. Even if the druids – including Spring – hadn't all insisted that the Romans were coming, she still had the Murkans in the north to ward off. If they heard that Maidun was uprooted, they'd be on her like a starving dog on a dropped bucket of offal. But they didn't matter so much. The Romans were coming and she had to be ready. The Dumnonians' reparations would begin to plug the hole left by the removal of Zadar's evil income, but not nearly enough. She should have demanded more.

She could feel the party atmosphere humming from Maidun Camp, even that early in the day. The network of muddy tracks that linked the makeshift sheds and tents of the camp's ever-growing population (another problem she had to deal with) was even thicker than usual with people running hither and thither with cauldrons, sacks of food, weapons, barrels of booze and all the other equipment essential for a day of games. On the flat land over to the west the football tournament had already started, with teams of ten trying kick an inflated bladder past the other team and into a goal-bucket. She'd never been a fan of football herself, or of any other team game for that matter.

She saw Drustan emerge from the throng and head towards her, across the open land surrounding the castle towards her. She hadn't seen him since after the battle on Sarum Plain, when she'd sent him away with Carden, Ragnall and a squad to free slaves from the ports and holding camps dotted around Zadar's territory.

"Lowa, might I have a word?" said the druid.

Surely "Queen Lowa" would have been more appropriate, she thought, but at least he hadn't shouted "Oi!" at her from a distance, like Spring had the day before.

"The slaves?" she said, without breaking stride.

"Most of them are home or on the way there," Drustan said, following. He had to half jog to keep up with her. "A few are too injured or sick to move, so I left those in situ, as well as a few to look after them. But that's not why I need to talk to you. Please can you stop walking? I do not want others to hear this."

Lowa stopped. They were on the track down from Maidun Castle, perhaps thirty paces from the edge of the Camp and the crowds, near where Lowa had crawled for hours, climbed into the castle and been caught by Drustan, on her way to assassinate Zadar. Funny, she thought, how time could move on so dramatically while geography stayed the same.

There were a few flapping ears on the road, so Lowa walked off it and leant on the rough wooden fence of a corral. A few horses sauntered over, with muzzles raised in "how about plucking some of that better grass on your side of the fence for me?" enquiry. She ignored them.

"I heard about your agreement with Bruxon and the Dumnonians," said Drustan, leaning on the fence next to her.

"Oh yes?" she asked, pushing away the nose of a persistent horse.

The druid paused for an almost awkwardly long time, then said: "You made a mistake."

"Oh?" said Lowa. "And what would you have done? Executed all the able-bodied Dumnonians so that their crops rotted in the fields and the young and elderly starved? Or taxed them into weakness and starvation? We'll need the Dumnonians, fighting well and willingly on our side."

"We will, which is why we need to know what they are doing, and why leverage over them would have been useful. You should have appointed their king, or at least forced a few advisors on Bruxon. You should have also demanded child hostages from him and their most influential families. Instead, a few days' ride away, is a man we do not know commanding an army much larger than ours. You had an opportunity to have control over that army and you threw it away."

"I trust Bruxon." Lowa realised how lame it sounded as she said it.

"Because he looks trustworthy?" Drustan's blue eyes

sparkled at her from his tanned, wrinkly face, wreathed in curly white hair. Her solo decision to be lenient towards the Dumnonians had made good sense at the time, but shortly afterwards she'd asked herself the questions that Drustan was asking now.

"Decisions made quickly and alone are wrong more often that those made with long thought and good advice," said Drustan. "I understand why you acted alone, but there are ways of consulting those close to you, while still having onlookers think that all commands come directly from you, formulated solely by you."

"Yes," said Lowa. "None of the great kings and queens that the bards tell us about are nearly as renowned as the committees that advised their every move."

"Every one of those kings and queens had advisors, Lowa. When Cran Madoc holed Grang Bilton's boats before the attack to retake Caer Madoc, do you think that was his idea?"

"Yes."

"It was not. The plan was constructed by a group of people, as are all the best plans – like your battle with the Dumnonians. You listened to your advisors, Ragnall particularly, with impressive humility before the battle on Sarum Plain, showed great sense in choosing the most feasible plan, and won a marvellous victory. The bards will tell of it for the rest of time, but history ignores inconvenient and boring details, so the story of the council before the battle will die with people who were there. It will suit history much better to say that you were the great warrior queen and the plan was yours. Ragnall will not get a mention." Drustan reached down to pluck some grass, which he fed to a grateful horse. "But I stray from my point, which is that the indulgence you showed to Dumnonia may yet sink Maidun. Hopefully not."

Lowa knew he was right. The stupidity of her impulsive clemency made her feel a little sick with shame. The druid took her sleeve and looked her in the eye. "All I ask is, please, next time, think long, and talk to people before you make major decisions."

Drustan walked away, leaving Lowa leaning on the fence. Was he meant to request permission to leave her presence, she wondered? She didn't want to be a dick about it, but it was important that she had respect, and part of that came from how people saw other people interacting with her. Should she get petitioners and supplicants to kneel when they spoke to her? Probably not, but some show of fealty was surely apt? Most people, she realised, did treat her with a hefty dose of deference. When she'd had Mal and Nita Fletcher brought before her to thank them for their roles in the rebellion and give them positions of command, they'd pretty much crawled with abasement.

The difference, she realised, was that they hadn't known her well before she was queen. Perhaps her reign would be more successful if she got rid of all those who she'd been close to in her pre-regal days – Atlas, Carden and others. Of course she wasn't going to kill them, but there were other ways of getting people out of the way.

Thinking of people she knew well, if Drustan was back from sorting out the slaves, it meant that Ragnall was back, too. She didn't want to see him. She'd enjoyed some times with him, liked him quite a bit, and was grateful for his plan for the battle of Sarum, but his seemingly unconditional affection bugged the crap out of her. What had once been puppyishly appealing now made her want to punch him in the face.

"Hurray! Hurray! Hurray! Whoooo-oop!" Spring jumped up and down along with the rest of the crowd in the arena, apart from Drustan, sitting next to her, who clapped politely. They'd all known Lowa – Queen Lowa – was going to win the archery, but still that had been an amazing shot.

Amazing. Although she couldn't help but feel sorry for the squirrels.

"Is there a squirrel Otherworld?" she asked, sitting back down next to Drustan.

"What do you think?"

"That answering a question with a question is a cop out, and that there probably is an Otherworld for squirrels. Their souls have to go somewhere when they die. Perhaps they share ours? They're not going to like it much when Lowa gets there."

"You're certain that the Otherworld exists?"

Spring looked at kind, clever old Drustan, then down at the ring. Since the slaves that used to do such things had all been freed, members of Lowa's cavalry – whom everyone was calling the Two Hundred because it sounded like an improvement on Zadar's Fifty – were clearing arrows and rodent corpses ready for the wrestling. Spring was looking forward to the wrestling most of all. Dug was going to fight. He hadn't intended to, but the prize for first place had convinced him. It was enough gold, he'd said, to get his seaside farm started somewhere miles away up north. Spring had told him she'd use her magic to make him win, and then it could be their farm and she could come and live with him. He'd said no, she mustn't use magic to help him, and she couldn't come north with him because everyone needed her here. She'd come up with the brilliant idea of him getting his seaside farm in the south, then she could live with him and be near Maidun if they needed her. And the weather was better, and the people nicer. Dug has said that farms cost much more gold in the south, but he hadn't said no, and he'd definitely looked as if he was considering it. He'd still forbidden her to use her magic, though, and had said quite emphatically that she couldn't be more wrong about people being nicer in the south.

It was a good thing he didn't want her magic, because she

didn't think she'd be able to give it to him. She wasn't as
certain as she'd been before the battle on Sarum Plain, but
she was pretty sure the magic wasn't with her today. She'd
felt that it might have been the day before, when she'd gone
boar hunting with Dug, but she'd had nothing to do with
it. Funny how it worked.

"Drustan," she said, pulling on his woollen poncho, "what
did I do that time in the arena to Dug and Lowa? How did
I do it? How does magic work?"

Drustan paused, looked like he was about to speak, then
paused again. Spring sighed and looked around. Most of the
other spectators were taking advantage of the gap in proceed-
ings to nip out of the arena. The tramp of their feet beat a
cheerful rhythm, overlaid by the music of laughter and
good-natured shouting. The air was sweet with the smell of
cider and roasting meats. Zadar was dead, the Dumnonians
were defeated and the sun was shining. These were happy
times.

Still no answer from Drustan, though. Spring was about
to poke him to check he was alive when he said: "I don't
know." Then he was quiet again.

Spring shook her head a little, not so much that he would
see. She'd hoped for a better answer than that. Especially
when it took so long in coming. She looked down at the
arena. The first two wrestlers were walking on. Neither of
them was Dug. Both of them were bigger, younger and fitter
looking than him. Dug, she was sure, could have beaten both
of them at the same time.

"What I think I know," Drustan continued eventually, "is
that magic comes from the gods."

"Which gods? Where are the gods? How many are there?
How did I get magic from them?"

Drustan looked at his hands and Spring's head bobbled
with impatience. It seemed to her that she and the druid
moved through time at different rates. She reckoned she

could fit in ten years' worth of doing stuff before he'd even begun to think about lunch.

"Many lifetimes have been spent pondering those questions," Drustan said finally and slowly, "and many more will be. Fruitlessly, in my opinion. I'll tell you what I think about the answers, then I will tell you what I know about your magic."

"Okay!" said Spring. She had time. While Drustan had been talking, Spring had also been listening to a woman in the arena shouting out the rules of the wrestling, and announcing that Dug Sealskinner would be given a bye to the third round, since he'd fought so well in that very arena just recently against Tadman Dantadman. Atlas Agrippa the Kushite had also been given a bye, since he'd won the last wrestling competition. Well, Dug hadn't been in the last wrestling competition and Atlas wasn't going to win this one, thought Spring.

"So, where are the gods?" said Drustan. "Perhaps they are all around us, in the air. Perhaps they are the air, the water and the earth. Perhaps they are fire. Most likely, I think, is that they are on a different world, watching us. I suspect that world is separated from ours by something other than geography. The world of the gods is perhaps like the world we see in the reflection on a lake. It is there, but we cannot go there, nor imagine how we might. Our physical essence simply does not work there. Their world is close to ours, however and perhaps, to bring the analogy back on itself, it mirrors ours."

Spring nodded as the crowd clapped politely, and wondered why adults so often took such a long time saying: "I don't know."

In the arena the first fight had been won by one man throwing another out of a circle twice. That was the game. Get the other one out of the ring, best of three wins. The first fight had been a two-nil, one-sided affair, hence the crowd's less than wild celebration of the result – all apart from one knot of ecstatic cheerers whom Spring took to be the victor's friends and family.

"How many gods are there?" Drustan continued. "A lot. There is so much utter evil and so much absolute good in the world, and so much in between, that it must be the work of many gods, as differing in personality as we are. If there were only one god, as some will have you believe, then that god must be raving mad."

"OK," said Spring. This next fight looked like a good one. It was Chamanca the Iberian against a large but worried-looking man.

Drustan seemed to realise that he wouldn't have Spring's attention, and paused while the Iberian used her attacker's momentum to send him flying out of the ring twice. He hobbled off, clutching his whacked balls to much laughter and cheering from the crowd.

"Now, what do I know about how you use your magic?" Finally, the bit she wanted to hear. "It is not like a spigot in a beer barrel, which you can turn on and off at will."

"Yes." Spring hoped he was going to tell her what it was, not just what it wasn't.

"It is connected to the gods."

"Uh-huh." That was a bit better, but hardly a surprise.

"It is linked to love and death."

"What?" He'd only gone and told her something she didn't already know! Why hadn't he started with this bit?

"There are two types of magic, it seems, both of which are stronger in you than in anyone I have heard about since ancient days."

"How are they linked to love and death?"

"Patience, Spring. I call the two types passive and active. Passive is thoughts and abilities that come to you. So, for example, you are unusually good with a sling. It seems to me that that is a passive magical ability. Chamanca's speed when she fights is another example as is, possibly, Lowa's prowess with a bow."

"I'm not that good with a sling. I'm not much better than Ragnall."

"He is much older, he is trained and he was the best with a sling on the Island of Angels. You are ten years younger, have perhaps a tenth of his strength and you haven't been trained by the Island of Angels' best. You should not be nearly as good as him, let alone better."

"Hmmm. That's an ability. What about the thoughts?"

"Have you ever simply known that someone you love is in trouble?"

"Yes, and something told me what to do. A voice in my head, but not like a voice. More like a feeling. But it didn't grow like a feeling, it was just suddenly there."

"That's it." Drustan nodded. Around them the crowd clapped as more fighters began or finished. Spring didn't know, she'd stopped watching.

"Tell me," the druid continued, "are the Romans coming?"

"Yes."

"Will they conquer Britain?"

"Yes."

"Definitely?" The old man seemed disappointed.

"No. Almost definitely. You know those days when it gets dark, cold and windy suddenly and then it rains?"

"Yes."

"But sometimes, almost never, but sometimes it gets dark and cold and everything, but it doesn't rain?"

"Indeed."

"It's like that. I'm not certain they're going to conquer us, but it looks a lot like they will. Now tell me about the active magic!"

"Active magic," said Drustan, "is where you are unlike anyone else I've met or even heard about, not just now but through all history."

"Yes?"

"I said it was connected to love and death. Nobody understands why, but if you kill something, you can perform stronger . . . let us call them spells. So when Lowa fought the chariot, I gave her strength by killing a rat. At least I thought I did at the time. I realised soon afterwards that it had been mostly you."

"It was. But I didn't kill anything?"

"No. That is what makes you different. Felix, you see, is a more powerful druid than me, and I think he has a better understanding of magic. He seems more willing to . . . experiment with its darker properties. He converted Elliax into a strong power source by making him consume his wife. I don't think that Felix been planning to sacrifice Elliax, or Anwen for that matter, to kill Lowa. I imagine that he created those magic sources for a wider purpose. However, confronted by your magic, he had to use them. And yet your magic still triumphed. What is both terrifying and exciting to consider is how powerful your magic might be if you mixed it with sacrifice."

"I'm not going to do that. I'm never even going to kill a fly for magic."

"I hope that you never have to. Especially because the more you love your sacrificial victim, the more powerful the magic."

"But you used a rat!"

"I liked that rat. I caught it on Mearhold and had been looking after it since. It saddened me to kill it. I suspect that a human sacrifice would produce stronger results, but I decided a long time ago that I will never sacrifice a human, no matter what is at stake."

"I see. I won't either. And no animals, too. So why didn't Felix kill someone he loved?"

"Nobody likes killing people they love. And perhaps he loves only himself, so that would not have been practical. I do not know."

"Oh yes. I see. And when Lowa wanted me to use my magic against the Dumnonians, why couldn't I?"

"I do not know that either. Magic is complicated and contradictory, like everything else in life. Things are only simple, Spring, in bards' tales. Possibly you'd exhausted your quota, possibly the god or gods that you draw on were busy elsewhere that day. But, look, your fellow Dug is in the fighting ring. He seems to be upset about something."

Dug nodded hello to Atlas. The Kushite was built like a particularly heavyset ox, but that wasn't why Dug had had to complain to the referee.

"You've made a mistake," he said, "I shouldn't be fighting him yet."

"I'm not surprised you're scared. You can back out if you like. We'll just call it a lose." The referee was a short, proud-chested man perhaps five years younger than Dug and ten years older than Atlas.

"I'm not scared." The prospect of fighting Atlas didn't exactly fill him with joy in fact, but that wasn't the point. "But I shouldn't meet Atlas until the final. I'm telling you this for the sake of the crowd, not me."

"As I said, you can back out. Otherwise, I'd like to get the fight started." The referee walked to the edge of the circle.

Great big badger's bollocks, thought Dug. It would have been easier to explain the point to a sheep. "Atlas, don't you agree? We were both given a bye so it's crazy that we should fight each other before we fight anyone else? For the sake of the crowd?"

A crooked but bright white smile cracked Atlas' purple-black face. He'd probably, thought Dug, been a handsome man before Lowa had rammed a venison bone through his face. "It doesn't make any difference to me," he said in his booming voice, rolling his colossal shoulders.

"Right, so if you don't mind?" said the referee, smirking happily at Dug.

"All right, all right. It's the wrong way to do it, but it's your competition. If you want to do things wrong it's your lookout." Dug walked into the circle, still muttering to himself.

There were two ways, Dug reckoned, to fight someone bigger and stronger than you were. First was to use their weight against them, which meant being quicker or more skilled, or, optimally, both. Second was to go absolutely badger-shit crazy and overwhelm them with a furious onslaught. Problem with the latter is that people tended to get hurt, and most often it was the person going badger-shit. So Dug pretended to lunge at Atlas a few times, then stepped back towards the edge of the circle, as if inviting Atlas to have a go at shoving him out.

Atlas came fast, but Dug was faster. He stepped to the side, stuck his leg out and reached for Atlas' leather jerkin.

Two heartbeats later Dug was in the air, upside-down, being carried out of the ring. As he thought about grabbing Atlas' legs, the African dropped him, and he had to put his hands out to avoid landing on his head.

Dug lay face down on the dirt listening to the crowd's laughter.

So, plan two. Dug leapt up, roared and flew at the African, fists windmilling. Atlas stepped aside and put a foot out. Dug tripped, spun to try and slow his momentum, got tangled up in his own feet and fell backwards. He thumped down on his arse, painfully, just outside the circle.

This time the laughter was much louder.

Badgerfucktwats, thought Dug as he walked out of the arena, cheeks throbbing with embarrassment, trying not to limp on his sore knee. He heard one person cheering. It was Spring, waving and whooping. That made him a wee bit happier. He waved back.

As he headed for the ring's exit, the one he'd charged through the other day to rescue Lowa, movement caught his eye. Someone had closed the door of one of the cells built into the ring wall from inside, someone who looked a lot like Lowa. He was still avoiding her. He'd been keeping busy on purpose, because every time his mind wasn't occupied it came back to her, to her face, her smell, her voice . . . and that boy Ragnall's white arse pumping up and down on her while she moaned with pleasure.

However, without thinking, he walked over to the cell door and opened it. He'd been seeing Lowa everywhere where she wasn't recently, so he didn't expect to find her in there.

"Hello," said Lowa. She was sitting on the cell's rude bed, her unstrung bow propped next to her. The light from the opened door made her white blonde hair shine. She smiled, a little sadly.

"Hello," said Dug, leaning on the door. "Well done in the archery."

"Thanks. I saw your fight. Tricky one, that Atlas."

"Aye. Big bugger got me twice in a row. If they made it best out of five . . . he'd have had me three times in a row. There's always a bigger fish. Although maybe not a better archer."

"I'm sure there will be soon. Spring's started learning, and with the way the gods love her . . ." Lowa looked at her feet.

Dug looked at her feet too. Very nice feet they were, even cased in leather. The silence was heavy for a couple of heartbeats, then both started talking at the same time.

"Dug, I wanted . . ." said Lowa

"What are you doing . . ." said Dug

"In here?" asked Lowa, as if relieved not to have to say whatever it was she'd been about to say. "This is where I was held when Zadar had me fighting in the arena. I was

just sitting here thinking how much things have changed
and wondering what to do next."

"Aye, Lowa the fighting slave to Lowa the queen." Dug
liked using her name. It made the encounter more real, which
was good, because he couldn't really believe he was there,
talking to her. It was such a precious moment, so important,
that even as it was happening he felt it was already over and
he was remembering it.

"I never thanked you properly, Dug, for saving me from
Tadman."

"I just beat up a big bastard. It was Spring really. Her
powers. I could have done with them today. I wanted that
prize money to get a wee farm."

"You don't need the prize money," said Lowa. "I'd thought
I'd see you, but I didn't, then I was going to send somebody
to tell you and I didn't get round to it. Sorry. The point is
that all Tadman's wealth is yours now because you killed
him in battle. He had no family, no friends even, so his
fortune is indisputably yours. It was a large one, gained in
the same way you gained it from him. It's more than enough
to set up the largest farm you could dream of."

"Oh. That's good."

"Yes, it is . . . Where will you . . . ?"

"I was thinking way up north, where I lived when I was
young."

"Ah."

"But Spring has this idea that I could get somewhere in
the south, not too far from here. That way she could live
with me some of the time, and spend the rest of it training
with your army. I'm not . . ."

"Definitely south, near here," interrupted Lowa.

"Why?" said Dug, stifling the urge to run over to the bed
and kiss her. It may have been his imagination, but her pale
skin seemed to flush a gentle pink. She paused, then said:
"It will be good for Spring to have you around. And it's

warmer and lighter in the south. Better for crops and animals, too. And it'll be more peaceful, I hope."

"And will you visit?" Dug dared. He felt as if he might faint.

Lowa looked up. Her eyes shone. A sad smile grew on her yew-berry-red lips.

"Dug, I'd—"

Dug felt a large presence next to him at the door. "Lowa, sorry to butt in, but you're needed." It was Atlas. "Big fight in the stands between the charioteers and some freed slaves. They'll stop when they see you, but if you don't hurry people will be killed."

Lowa's smiled hardened. "All right, I'm coming. Dug, see Drustan – he knows all about Tadman's belongings and where you can pick them up. Oh – and you'll need a couple of strong leather leashes. Actually bear poles will be better."

"What?"

"I'll catch up with you later!"

She rushed past and Dug was left standing in the doorway, alone. He walked in and sat on the bed for a while. The room still smelt of her. Just when things had been looking good, she'd dodged out. Yes, she'd had to go, but she'd seemed relieved at the interruption. If he did stay in the south, it would be for Spring's sake. He had to forget about Lowa.

Chapter 6

Lowa sat by Zadar's expansive hearth, her hearth now, sharpening and polishing arrowheads. She'd cleaned out some of the less tasteful decorations from the ruler's oversized hut – the pots containing the heads of defeated enemy rulers steeped in cedar oil had gone, for example – but rows of excellently crafted shelves were still packed with bronze torcs, silver crowns, gold bracelets and other purloined treasures. She supposed she should find their rightful owners, or at least their rightful owners' heirs, and return them. There was so much to do. For now, though, she'd focus on polishing her beautiful arrowheads.

She'd always put people who complained about the loneliness of command in the same full-of-disingenuous-crap sack as people who said how miserable their riches made them, but now she was beginning to see their point. Her days as queen had so far been nothing but one hassle after another. She didn't know how to deal with most of the hassles, she had hardly any time to deal with the ones that she could see solutions to, and she had nobody to talk to about it.

All would have been much more bearable if her sister were still alive. Lowa didn't want help, ideas or even advice, she just wanted someone who'd listen. Dug would have been as good as Aithne, but she'd gone and fucked that up and now he was going away to the far north and she'd never see him again. She wondered what she could do to make him stay, to make him forgive her, then dismissed the idea. She didn't deserve him. And she'd seen the look on his face when she'd

clumsily suggested he stay in the south. The very idea of it
had made him look ill. No, she'd lost him.

"Queen Lowa!" A shout from outside. A visitor, no doubt,
come to complain about nothing, or to put forward some
self-interested proposal that they'd say was for everyone's
benefit, or to warn her about something she was already
aware of . . . but perhaps it was Dug.

"Ragnall Sheeplord would like to see you," the voice
continued.

Badgers' cocks, thought Lowa, but yelled: "All right!"

The large hut's door opened and Ragnall stomped in. Lowa
smelt that he'd been drinking.

"Ragnall. Thank you for helping Drustan—"

"You killed my brothers." Ragnall stood in the centre of
the hut, shaking, pointing at her as if his finger were a
weapon.

"Yes," said Lowa, holding his gaze. "I was acting under
orders. I have since rejected those orders, and killed the
person responsible for them."

"You're not even going to apologise?"

"Of course I'm sorry. Does it help if I say the words? If
so, here you go – I'm sorry. But look, Ragnall, I was a soldier
following orders. I'd expect people to do the same for me
without question. That's why we have rulers. If you hate the
orders, you get rid of the ruler. So that's what I did. That
was my apology for everything."

Ragnall was staring at her open-mouthed. She was being
too harsh, but she didn't care. How dare he come here to
whinge? Everyone had lost people. She'd lost everybody.

"You should beg my forgiveness . . ." Ragnall managed.

Lowa looked at him and saw privilege and entitlement
looking back. He'd had a life of getting his own way and
now that things had turned sour he wanted an apology? She
felt the frustration of the previous few days rise. She thought
of twin girls she'd seen after the battle on Sarum Plain,

wailing with grief, clearly mourning a dead parent or perhaps two. She thought of her crew, her sister, murdered by Zadar. Rage boiled up like a storm surge. Even as she drew in the breath to shout, she knew that Ragnall wasn't the real target for her anger, or even a legitimate one, but out it came all the same.

"Beg you!?" she raged. "Take your head out of your arse and stop whinging about the past. Either get over it and fuck off or stop whining like a bitch and do the only thing you can do to a queen when you disagree with her. Try to kill me. Come on."

Ragnall stared at her. His gaping mouth slowly closed. His wide eyes narrowed into hard slits. His fingers reached for the hilt of the sword at his waist.

Lowa took a step towards him, lifting the arrow that she'd been polishing. She'd have his thoat out before his sword was halfway from its scabbard.

Ragnall's face crumbled. He lowered his head with a long, low moan. The moan became quieter but higher pitched until it sounded like a distressed seabird keening out from deep in his throat. His whine was cut off by a snotty snort, then his head bobbed with regular, sucking sobs that made him sound like a bereaved seal.

Oh for Bel's sake, thought Lowa.

"Here, sit down," she said, leading him to a chair. She handed him a scrap of linen and sat across from him. Now she felt bad for shouting at him. She felt bad for killing his brothers, too – one brother anyway, she was pretty sure she'd killed only one of them – but she couldn't let herself go down that path. She'd killed so many people. If she started to feel bad about it, she would fall apart. She had to believe that destroying Zadar and his regime absolved her, and that she could make further amends by ruling justly, by fighting off the Romans and saving more lives than she'd taken. The alternative was suicide and that did not appeal.

Ragnall's blubbing reduced to snivelling and she said: "By bringing down Zadar together, we have avenged your brothers, your parents and everyone that his regime killed. And I mean 'we'. It couldn't have happened without you."

"I didn't do anything. It was all you and Drustan and Dug and Spring," Ragnall cried. He bubbled more snot and blew his nose into the already sodden rag.

"You saved Drustan's life. It was your idea to take the boat which let us escape from Mearhold. Dug wouldn't have known I was in the arena if you hadn't thought to get him and persuaded him to come. Without your plan, the Dumnonians might have beaten us on Sarum Plain and all would have been for nothing. We certainly wouldn't have beaten them so easily, so at the very least you saved thousands of lives. You have done a lot. I would not be alive, let alone queen, if it weren't for you."

"I suppose so."

"And I need you to do more," Lowa continued. "I have a mission for you and Drustan. But first . . . look, I shouldn't have been so harsh. You've had a bad time, and I understand why you're angry. Why don't you stay here for a while and tell me all that you remember about your family?" She'd heard somewhere that talking about the dead could help people get over their grief.

"OK . . ." sniffed Ragnall. "My first memory was seeing my father climbing down a ladder. I remember being worried that he'd fall through the gaps of the ladder, even though . . ."

Oh for the love of Danu, thought Lowa, pulling her face into a caring smile.

Dug walked slowly across Maidun Castle's torch-lit lower expanse. The evening was warm, the journey was generally uphill and he knew that if he walked quickly the sweat would come and wouldn't stop. He did not want to be sweaty for the task ahead.

He'd seen Drustan that afternoon and almost fallen over when the old druid had told him how much wealth Tadman Dantadman had amassed through killing people. Dug was surprised that there was anyone left alive. Lowa had taken half to fund the army, but the remaining half still made him a very rich man. He could have bought a gold-plated farm by any coast and filled it with sheep made of silver. He'd made some half-hearted objections – he didn't deserve it, it could be put to better use – but Drustan had insisted that it was all his and he hadn't complained for long. The only downside, Drustan had said, was that he'd also inherited Tadman's two pets, two large war dogs named Sadist and Pig Fucker. He hadn't met those yet, but he didn't like the sound of them.

It was a strange but excellent feeling, knowing that he'd never have to toil for food or shelter again. It was like a smothering weight that he hadn't known was there had been removed. He felt more generous towards everybody, not materially perhaps, but certainly in spirit.

So he moseyed cheerily across Maidun Castle and up to the eyrie, half-singing breezy greetings to everyone he passed.

He'd made up his mind. Forget the farm. There was only one place he wanted to be, and that was with Lowa. Maybe she had been dismissive the other day, maybe she hadn't. He needed to know. She definitely had liked him – loved him even? – so there had to be a chance that she still did. He loved her, so he had to risk it. He'd tell her about Spring's spell, that it wasn't her fault she'd shagged Ragnall, and that he'd forgive her if there'd been anything to forgive, but there wasn't. If she was pregnant with Ragnall's baby that might add some complications, but they could cross that bump when they came to it.

"Sorry it's late," he said to the guard at Lowa's hut, "but could I see Lowa, please?"

"Hello, Dug! How's it going?"

"All is wonderful, thanks. You?" He peered at the woman. He didn't think he knew her. Since he'd defeated Tadman in the packed arena and become a wee bit famous, a lot of strangers now acted as if he were an old friend. It was disconcerting.

"I'd let you straight in," said the guard, "but she's got someone with her."

"No matter. I'll wait."

"I don't know how long she'll be. Might be all night." The guard winked. "It's a young man – a fine-looking fellow."

"Oh?" said Dug.

"Name of Ragnall. Lovely manner about him." She nodded enthusiastically at Dug's blank look. "Very well-spoken, he is, very well-spoken. A real young hero, quite the match for Queen Lowa."

Dug had taken a hammerblow to the guts once. This felt very similar, perhaps a little worse.

"Has he been in there long?" he asked.

"Ages. And I've heard some fascinating noises." She made a long moaning sound, then giggled smuttily. "You're welcome to wait, though?"

"No, no, that's fine. I'll come back." Dug smiled. Without thinking, he turned and walked away. He was vaguely aware that the guard was still talking.

Ragnall sat back, feeling a great deal happier and much less drunk. It had helped, telling Lowa about his family and Anwen.

"I am sorry, about how I was," he said.

"Don't worry." Lowa put a hand on his knee. "You have losses to grieve. And I think you're fairly new to heavy drinking? Not that many people ever learn how to do it without regularly making dicks of themselves."

She really was a very decent woman. Firm, but fair. He remembered her naked body pressed on to him, his hands

on her back and buttocks and her thighs, her eyes looking
into his. She certainly was firm and fair. He told himself to
focus. There was something important he wanted to ask her
. . . oh yes.

"You said that you had a mission for me and Drustan?
More slaves to free?"

"No. Something quite different. I want you to go to Rome."

"Rome?"

"Yes. Big place. Easy to get to by road, apparently."

"Rome." Visions flooded Ragnall's mind. They said there
were a million people living in just the one city, buildings
the size of hillforts, and flocks of beautiful, degenerate
women . . . "Why Rome?"

"If we're to fight them, I need to know about them. I also
need to know when they're going to get here. I'd like you
and Drustan to pose as a prince and his tutor who have
travelled to see the city – which is exactly what you will
be, so that shouldn't be too hard. When you've found out
all you can about the Romans and their invasion plans, come
back and tell me."

The idea was exciting, but there was one massive reason
he didn't want to leave Britain.

"What about us?" he asked.

Lowa grimaced. That, thought Ragnall, was not the
response he'd hoped for.

"I like you very much and I enjoyed our time together,
but it was a fling, Ragnall, just a fling. I'm sorry."

She looked sad and vulnerable. Underneath her iron skin,
she was just a person like him. She hadn't wanted to kill his
family, Zadar had made her. She had been in love with Dug,
and he'd used magic to make her betray him. She still thought
it had been her own decision. She was hurt and consumed
by self-loathing. He knew what betrayal felt like from the
side of the betrayer, and he didn't want her feeling like that
because he'd tricked her. He had to tell her.

"You should know something, before I go to Rome. I have some druid powers. Nothing like Spring or Drustan, but I'm learning."

He paused. Lowa was looking at him, seemingly unmoved by his revelation, waiting for him to get to the point. He couldn't hold her gaze.

"On Mearhold I put a spell on you to fall out of love with Dug and fall in love with me. It was my magic that made you betray him."

Lowa looked at him for a long while. He looked at his hands and waited, half expecting her to fly at him and ram the arrow that she was holding through his eye. He deserved it.

"So you raped me," she said eventually.

"What!? No!" It was worse than an arrow through the eye, because as soon as she said it, he knew it was true.

"You made me have sex with you against my will?"

". . . Yes."

"What else would you call that?"

She was right, but she wasn't right. It was hardly like grabbing someone by the hair on a village raid and dragging them behind a hut. It wasn't the same at all. "But there was no violence," he stammered. "You enjoyed it!"

Lowa sat quietly, letting him stew in the misery of realisation. She was right. It was just as bad as if he'd forced her against her will, because he had forced her against her will. The only difference was that he'd used magic instead of a knife point. It didn't sound so bad in all the stories, but it was. "Love potions", the bards called them.

"I'm sorry," he said.

"I forgive you." She was half smiling.

"But I . . ."

"It's done, it's over. Don't tear yourself to bits about it. Just don't do it again, and make sure you do a good job for me in Rome."

"I will! I'll do the best job. I'll . . . leave no Rome unturned!"

"While you're there, you might use some of that magic on your sense of humour."

He looked at her. She seemed happy. Was he really forgiven? She was a wonderful woman. He couldn't blame her for following Zadar's orders, especially when it was her who had ended the tyrant's rule. And how could he not forgive her when she forgave him so easily? He would do the best possible job for her in Rome, and when he came back he'd be older and wiser and very much his own man, and maybe she'd want him again? Although, after he'd met the women of Rome, would he still want her?

Part Two

Rome and Britain

Chapter 1

Ragnall put himself away, but continued to stare down at the pool he'd urinated into. A small shark broke the surface then flashed away. Three small rays flapped past like lazy birds. A spider crab, golden torchlight gleaming off its spiky red shell, picked its way delicately along the tank's rocky floor.

"This is nothing!" A man arrived next to him, hoisted his purple-fringed toga and urinated with a stream that would have pleased a horse. "I take it you've never been to one of Licinius Lucullus's parties?"

"I haven't," Ragnall replied, wondering where to look.

"Shame! The man is building some disgustingly eastern gardens in Rome – they're going to be simply marvellous, they really are – but his horribly over-the-top showpiece is his villa at Naples. It's not far from one of my places actually. He's had thousands of his slave-johnnies rebuild Mount Athos to bring saltwater to a whole string of simply amazing lakes. They are enormous. They make this little piss pond of Caesar's look like a rock pool. A bloody rock pool! Simply amazing. Although again, nastily Persian. Xerxes in a toga, someone was calling him the other day. Bit unfair, but he definitely has gone a smidgen native after his jaunts out east. Those boy-shagging desert-johnnies like their ridiculous gardens, but I doubt they have anything that comes close to Lucullus's little inland sea. He had a dolphin when I was there, but I suspect he's eaten it by now. Wonderful chef he has, wonderful."

The man finished urinating, dropped his toga carelessly and turned to Ragnall. Like most Romans, he was short – a good foot and a half shorter than Ragnall. Small dark eyes peered from his smoothly fat, melon-shaped face.

It seemed that a reply was required, although there'd been no question.

"Sounds . . . god-like," said Ragnall, and he meant it. Rebuilding a mountain for nothing but display and entertainment, surely, was something that only capricious, wasteful gods would do. In Britain, he'd thought it was stupid when eccentrics gave the best bits of meat to pet dogs, but remoulding a mountain to house pet fish was another level. Were the fish even pets, he wondered, or more like farm animals? Romans didn't piss on their pets, surely? Or their farm animals for that matter . . . "They won't eat these fish, will they," Ragnall asked, "after everybody's—"

"Pissed in their water? Depends how drunk the chefs get, what!"

Ragnall chuckled hesitantly.

"But probably not, no," the man continued, "they'll all die this evening of piss poisoning and be thrown into the main drain."

"Seems a waste."

"A waste?" The Roman's face creased into such a look of disgust that Ragnall took a step back. "A waste? A few fish? You're not some bloody actor making me part of a clever new play are you? You're meant to be taking a piss, not taking the piss! Ha!"

"No, I'm from—"

"The provinces? Yes, you do have a touch of the barbarian brush, don't you? That would explain it. Sorry for calling you an actor, old fellow. Waste! A few fish! Ha ha! Just the other day Caesar had a villa built – in Campania, I think it was – then he had it knocked down – razed completely – without ever seeing it."

"Why?" Ragnall asked.

"Why?" The man snorted a laugh. "Why? By Jove, you really are very provincial."

He walked away, leaving Ragnall next to the fish-churned piss pond.

He washed his hands in a water-filled giant clam shell held by a topless, dark-skinned woman with sparkling black eyes, a shaved head and very pronounced cheekbones, which he took particular notice of while endeavouring not to look at her chest. She didn't acknowledge him in any way. Her eyes seemed to be focused on an entirely different reality. The whole toilet experience had made Ragnall feel very uncomfortable. The sooner he found Drustan, the better. If the rest of the party was anything like its loos, he'd be better off at the side of his unflappable mentor.

Drustan had used some magical persuasion and a good deal of charm to get them into the birthday party of Julius Caesar, the man whom nearly everyone Ragnall had met was talking about. He shouldn't have left Drustan so soon, but he'd been bursting. He'd been drinking a lot of water, partially because it was always as hot in Rome as the very hottest days in Britain, and partially because man-made rivers supported on arches – aqueducts – carried the most delicious cool mountain water right into the middle of the city where anyone could drink it for free.

Magical persuasion was something he couldn't do, thought Ragnall, as he dried his hands on a wondrously soft animal fur, baby goat perhaps, held by yet another topless, oiled slave, this time a male one who was alternately tensing each pectoral muscle of his shaved chest.

He would never be able to persuade anyone to do anything with magic. He was magically barren. On the voyage from Britain he'd failed again and again to light a fire with his mind until eventually Drustan had confessed that he'd cheated that first time, and lit the fire that Ragnall had thought he'd lit. His tutor had done it to encourage him, he'd said, since he'd thought he might be the powerful saviour druid that had been foretold. Instead, Spring was the druidical messiah and Ragnall had no magic at all.

He didn't blame Drustan and he couldn't miss something he'd never had. In fact, it was something of a relief, since it meant that he hadn't used magic to make Lowa have sex with him, so he could in no way be accused of having raped her. She'd dropped Dug and shagged him purely because she was selfish and unkind.

A while later, it had come up in conversation that Drustan had told Lowa about Ragnall having no magical ability, well before he'd confronted her in her hut. So she'd known it wasn't rape! But she'd persuaded him that he had raped her, and used that to make him forgive her for killing his family, and to go to Rome. She was more than unkind, he thought. She was evil. He wasn't sure yet what he was going to do with all these revelations. He had lots of ideas. Returning to Britain and reporting to Lowa as if nothing had happened was not one of them.

He shook his head as he walked out into Caesar's garden and the noise of a hundred conversations. To cheer himself up and clear Lowa from his mind, he reminded himself how he'd amazed Drustan by learning to speak Latin in the couple of weeks it had taken their ship to reach Ostia, Rome's port. Apparently people spent years studying to be as good as he was. Indeed, a week after their arrival he was already more fluent than Drustan, who'd been speaking Latin since he was a boy. So he may not be some weirdo magic maker, but he was a great deal cleverer than most.

And better looking, he added to himself, as a glamorous older woman peeled away from the throng of partygoers, grabbed his arm and spoke very close to his ear.

"Wotcha," she said "I'm Clodia. Clodia Metelli. What's your 'andle?"

Her rough accent was a surprise. She wore precisely applied make-up, a blue tunic that shimmered expensively in the breeze, a golden necklace of knuckle-sized precious stones and a heady perfume that wafted an aroma of young flowers and wealth, but she spoke like the street-wretches and rag traders from the Aventine Hill, the poorest quarter of Rome where he and Drustan had found the cheapest lodging.

"My . . . ?"

"'Andle. Handle. Name."

"Oh sorry, I'm Ragnall Sheeplord."

"What a name. From Britain?"

"Yes! How did you—"

"Got some British slaves. You sound the same. Come with us then, Ragnall, I wanna hear why you're talking to me and not carrying a tray of drinks. Talking of drinks—"

Clodia whipped two golden glasses from a passing slave's tray, beckoned with a tilt of her head for Ragnall to follow and walked away through the crowd. Her flowing tunic clung to her rear, which swung mesmerisingly below a narrow waist. Ragnall had a quick look about for Drustan and didn't spot him. He shrugged and hurried after Clodia.

They passed a group of older, sensible-haired, clean-shaven men in red leather shoes and finely made togas with broad purple stripes. They were looking with undisguised distaste at a gang of young men dressed in transparent, loosely belted tunics. The more youthful fellows all had similar goatee beards. They were looking back at the older men, talking under their breath to each other, all scratching their heads with one finger as if it was a secret sign, then giggling. One of them pointed out Clodia and Ragnall and they giggled all the more.

The women, mostly standing in small clutches separate

from the men, wore brighter, full-length variations of
Clodia's dress, though few of their clothes, if any, looked
as finely woven as hers. They'd adorned their necks, ears
and fingers with coloured stones and while Clodia's locks
hung down in simple tresses, many of the other women's
hair was piled high in elaborately curled, twisted and
knotted towers.

Gliding deferentially through the clumps of men and
women were more dark-skinned, oiled, lithe slaves, carrying
drinks and platters of what was apparently food.

"Truffle-stuffed mare's vulva?" asked a slave girl with an
impish smile and a coquettish shake of her hips, proffering
a plate of glistening brown lumps at him.

"No thanks," he replied.

These slaves weren't as dark-skinned as Atlas and the
towel holder by the fish pond, more a paler bronzy-brown
like Zadar's former bodyguard Chamanca, so Ragnall assumed
that they were Iberians like her. The party, after all, was to
celebrate Julius Caesar's recent military successes in Iberia,
as well as his fortieth birthday.

They passed a pair of enormous yellow and brown animals
with bizarrely long necks that Ragnall took to be giant deer
from some far-off land, and reached a quieter area that was
draped in fruits and vegetables so preposterously ripe-
looking and unblemished that they might all have been made
of polished wood. Ragnall stuck a fingernail in an apple to
see if it was real. It was.

Clodia sat down on a rough wooden bench that looked
out of place next to all the newly cut stone. A split in her
dress fell open, revealing a tanned thigh. She crossed one
leg over the other and patted the bench next to her.

Ragnall sat down.

"So. What brings you to Rome?"

"I've come with my tutor. We've heard so much about your
city that we wanted to visit and see if the stories were true."

"Your Latin's brilliant."

"Thanks. So's yours."

Clodia smiled. "I'd heard Britain was, like, all hairy barbarians dressed in smelly skins and that, too stupid to scratch their own arses?"

"I thought you had British slaves?"

"They'd been broken in and trained when I got 'em. So, are the British grunting hirsute idiots, got up in stinking rags, or not?"

Ragnall looked down at his toga. He'd become completely accustomed to it in a very short time. He wondered how he'd ever felt happy wearing anything else.

"Actually that's not far off."

"Who are your slaves in Britain? Is there some island further north that's got even stupider, hairier people?"

Ragnall thought of Dug. "People from the north of our island are less intelligent, and there are islands further north that I've heard of, but I've never met anyone from them. We don't have slaves. We just sell them to Rome – well, some of us do."

"Fuck!" Clodia's eyes widened. She had unusually large eyes, set high up on a broad-cheeked face below a narrow forehead. She wasn't a typical beauty – she looked nothing like the ubiquitous statues which were presumably considered the peak of female attractiveness in Rome, but something – the challenge in her gaze perhaps – blasted away any attempt to appraise her looks rationally and made Ragnall's throat constrict with lust.

"Who does all the shit work?" she continued.

"Shit work?"

"That awful messy business of agriculture. Washing pots and pans. Clearing up other people's stink. Things that decent people shouldn't have to do."

Her accent, Ragnall noticed, had swung from a market-trader drawl to a well-bred staccato that better suited her looks and outfit. "I suppose we all do those things. Well, I don't, but—"

"So 'ow come you're different?" And her accent was back in the gutter. Odd, he thought.

"I . . ." Why was he different? He thought of his family, about the people of Maidun, of the druids and other children on the Island of Angels, and he looked around the crowd of increasingly drunk, braying Romans. These people didn't look better than his people, but they'd certainly created something much better. They'd been in Rome almost a moon and still he found it hard to walk around with his mouth closed. The massive buildings were minutely and intricately decorated. Mosaic floors were so skilfully made and beautiful that he could have spent a whole day looking at each of them. The painted statues were exquisitely lifelike. Overarching all was a fiercely vibrant hum of activity; people scurrying hither and thither, merchants shouting their wares, politicians shouting their ideas and the relentless demolition and construction of buildings. And there was the size of the place. A million people lived in Rome, they said. A thousand thousand people all in one tight space, yet somehow they managed to gather everything they needed every day and take out everything they discarded. How, by Danu, did they do it? The systems that must have been involved were so vast and complex that it made him feel dizzy to consider them.

What was more, even though the city was more spectacular, luxurious and shinier than he'd ever imagined even the halls the gods might be, it felt strangely safe. More than safe, he felt comfortable. It was paradoxical. It could not have been more foreign, yet he felt more at home here than he ever had in the excrement-stinking circles of dilapidated huts that passed for settlements in his homeland.

"I think I'm just different from the rest of the British," he said, turning to look at Clodia. Her eyelashes raised questioningly. "Perhaps I'm a Roman soul born in a foreign body? I certainly couldn't ever be a slave."

"No. Slaves are born, not made."

"There are so many. Why don't they—"

"Rebel?" Her coarse accent had vaporised again. "They do. But they don't rebel against the idea of slavery as you might think, they rebel against the fact that they themselves are slaves. Every time they rebel successfully, they make others their slaves. But they always end up slaves again – because that it is what they are. There was one exception to that, one who nearly did make a difference, a wonderful Thracian named Spartacus. But he . . ." She sighed sadly, "He made the mistake of taking on Rome. He did better than most, and it did look for a while like he might free all the slaves. But, if my romantic side is a little in love with him, the practical part is glad he didn't succeed. I rather like my slaves. I never have to do anything mundane and they remind me that I'm free . . . But I'd like to learn something about you. Tell me, what has struck you most about Rome since your arrival?"

"The buildings are colossal, and there are so many. I walked from—"

"Yawn."

She wanted a clever answer, Ragnall thought. Well, let's see how she likes this: "All right. Here's a big difference. In Britain, the women rule as much as the men do. They fight in the army. In the household, men and women share the work. Men are not in charge of women, and women are not in charge of men. Yet I've heard that Roman women, even rich ones like you who say they are free, are actually no freer than slaves. I've heard you have no power. I heard a man say that women were decorations and not much more. Is there any truth in that?"

Clodia pursed her lips and wrinkled her large nose. "Some truth. We are not men's equals in Rome's eyes. Immigrants distort the picture so it's not particularly obvious, but there actually are far fewer Roman women than men because so many baby girls do not pass infancy."

"Why not?"

"It is the parents' right to kill them and many do not want a girl. Girls are more likely to bring shame than honour to a family." She smiled wryly. "As I have proven. Women cannot be any sort of official, so cannot curry favour or win battles. Look at our host, Julius Caesar. He has won awards and positions all his life, saturating his family in so much glory that they walk around smiling like sex pests in a gymnasium. Just this month he forsook a Triumphal march celebrating his Iberian victories so that he could be eligible for the vote for next year's consuls. Everyone is saying what a hero he is, and how much he is sure to achieve. No woman has ever been able to draw such adoration. The Roman way won't allow it. Women are kept down in other ways, too. Girls are given away as wives, often to much older husbands, and are expected to remain faithful, yet men are seen as lacking virility if they haven't fucked all their slave girls and any number of their friends' wives."

"Sounds oppressive." Ragnall considered putting a consoling hand on her smooth leg, but thought better of it.

Clodia, seeming to notice the tiny movement in his arm, took his wrist and placed his hand just above her knee, then carried on. "It is what it is, and we must move within its constraints. It need not be oppressive. Like a head slave who enjoys power and respect in his little kingdom, women can rule a family, and more. We can create and destroy men without them realising that we are controlling them. But yes, we must do it clandestinely and without acknowledgement."

As she'd been talking, her aristocratic tones had dissolved into yet another accent, still refined, but quieter and sadder. That seemed odd, but not as odd as the fact that his hand was still on her knee. Perhaps it was a Roman thing. He tried not to think about it, but even thinking about not thinking about it caused stirrings under his loose toga that weren't going to remain invisible for long.

"And Roman men are free," Clodia continued, "perhaps freer than any men have ever been. But that freedom will destroy them. A handful of men now hold power – Crassus, Pompey, this fellow Caesar and a few more – and it will not end well. A few years ago Sulla nearly took it all for himself. These men, I sense, are even more greedy, and they seem to be friends. If they unite in some unholy threesome, it would be disastrous. There were rumours ten years ago that Caesar's magician was working with Crassus, and that the six thousand rebel slaves who died on the Appian Way were crucified for him to perform some dark spells, but then the magician disappeared. Now he's back. I don't like it. We have an oracle called Sibyl, a soothsayer like your druids."

"You know about druids?"

"I talk to my slaves. Sibyl has predicted Rome's future. Do you know what she said?"

". . . No?"

"That Rome's own sons will rape her – a brutal, interminable, gang rape. Her words, not mine."

"That doesn't . . . sound good?"

"Ha ha!" Clodia's face illuminated with a broad smile and her world-weariness fell from her, Ragnall thought, in much the same way that her blue dress might fall on to the rug-strewn stone floor of her undoubtedly opulent bedchamber.

"Enough misery!" she continued. "To business!"

Without taking her eyes off his, or his hand off her leg, she placed a cool hand on his nearest, bare knee, and curled long fingers around it. Her middle finger traced light circles on the knee's inner declivity. It sent shivers of lightning up his thigh, into his torso and out along his other limbs. The erection that he'd been struggling to subdue burst into life like an excitable dog freed from its lead.

"You," her hand slid maddeningly slowly up the inside of his thigh, that finger still rotating gently, "are a very attractive young barbarian and I intend to have," she glanced at his crotch, widened her eyes and licked her lips, "a large part of your foreign body inside my Roman soul."

She looked at him coolly, as if waiting for a reply.

He opened his mouth. No words came.

She smiled and removed her hand. "Visit me. Soon. Ask anyone where Metellus Celer's house is." She stood up and walked away.

"Who's Metellus Celer?" he managed.

"My husband," she called back, without slowing or turning.

Ragnall stayed sitting. A toga might suit him better than the British jerkin and trousers, but it was no good for concealment. It was almost as if Clodia had known that, and created his erection to spear him to the bench so that she could get away.

"You're a barbarian."

Ragnall started. A man melted from the display of fruit and vegetables. Had he been there the whole time and witnessed the entire exchange? The intruder was in his mid-thirties, about the same age as Clodia, but the height of a twelve-year-old back in Britain. Perched on a long neck with a pronounced Bel's apple was a triangular head, flat across the top with a pointed chin. The uppermost parts of his ears stuck out, but were tight to his head at the lobes, like a pair of minute wings ready to flap into action. Save for people living on the streets, he was by far the messiest man Ragnall had seen in Rome. His toga was splattered with food stains and his tightly curled hair had not seen a comb for many a moon.

"I'm from Britain." Ragnall realised he could now stand up and did so. "You'll have to excuse me, I'm just off."

"In Rome, we introduce ourselves when our betters address us."

Ragnall stopped. "I am sorry. It's just that I'm here with my mentor and—"

"I am Cato. Marcus Porcius Cato Uticensis." He reached out a hand.

"I'm Ragnall. Ragnall Sheeplord." Ragnall gripped the little man's upper wrist and Cato gripped his, weakly. They released. Ragnall preferred this Roman hand-wrist shake to the British man-to-man greeting of the hug, which he found awkward and often smelly.

"How quaint. You should watch your step with Lady Copper Coin."

"Lady Copper Coin?"

"Clodia. Her nickname comes from the copper-coin whores of the Aventine, although Athena knows it would be a rich streetwalker who managed to sleep with as many men as dear Clodia."

"Why should I watch my step?"

"Each year we elect two consuls to rule. This year her husband, Metellus Celer, is one of them."

Ragnall knew about consuls and the other Roman ranks – aediles, quaestors, senators, tribunes and more. Drustan had drilled them into him on the voyage. Consuls were top of the heap, which meant that they could have people killed on a whim.

"Moreover," Cato continued, leaning in conspiratorially, "she herself is dangerous. The first thing you should know is that she's a phony. She's the eldest daughter of the Claudian family, one of Rome's oldest and richest clans. Her name is really Claudia, but she changed it to Clodia to sound more plebeian, as if there was something good about that. Did you notice anything odd about her accent?"

"It changed . . ."

"She affects common parlance, then forgets. Pathetic. Is there anything that makes one's skin crawl more than a posh person pretending to be a pleb? What's worse, she seems to have made it the fashion." He spat this last word with venom. "All the young are doing it now. Along with their silly little beards and their stupid finger signals. Sickening."

"I liked her—"

"Really? Not long ago, a young fool like you liked her. He made the mistake of leaving copper coins by her bedside when he left in the morning. Most likely it was a tip for the slaves or possibly a joke." Cato smiled. "But Clodia took it as an insult. So what do you think she did?"

"Didn't see him again?"

"You're right, she didn't. But she went a little further. She hired a gang. They beat him and raped him in public."

"What? You can't rape a man!"

"You can and they did."

"How do you rape a man?"

"Same way as a woman, but from the other side."

Ragnall thought it through and his jaw dropped.

Cato seemed to enjoy the effect he was having. Ragnall didn't like him at all. "I have to go," he said.

"Stay away from her!" Cato called after him. "She'll be your end!"

"There you are! I thought you'd been kidnapped," said Drustan when Ragnall found him. "Meet Cicero." The man who had been in conversion with Drustan held out an arm. Ragnall had heard of him. Cicero – Marcus Tullius Cicero – was a former consul and Rome's best, or at least most famous, lawyer. He was taller than Ragnall had pictured. The grey hair that remained on his half-bald head was combed and lightly greased into small, regular, forward-reaching curls.

"You're Ragnall Sheeplord, the British prince," said Cicero.

"Your tutor has told me about you. Welcome to Rome." He had a quiet, measured voice which didn't quite match his gangly, long-limbed figure. "Now, it's apposite that you should mention kidnap, Drustan. I was just telling your tutor, Ragnall, about two potential pretenders to the power currently held by Crassus and Pompey. The one, Clodius the Beautiful, comes from the greater family. The other, Julius Caesar, whose party we have the honour of attending, is the greater man. I have told Drustan the story of how Caesar had to divorce his wife – poor, dear Pompeia – after Clodius was suspected of sleeping with her."

Ragnall wondered if anyone was ever faithful in Rome.

"But the better stories, tales of honour and shame that explain the difference between the two men exquisitely well, come from when both, on separate occasions, were captured by pirates. Now, Ragnall and Drustan, I hope that you will indulge my joy of storytelling by lending me your ears for a grain or two of the hourglass?"

Cicero looked from Ragnall to Drustan. The two Britons nodded enthusiastically. Ragnall had never felt so drawn into a conversation, even though it was more of a monologue. By his childish nodding, Drustan felt the same. Ragnall's chest swelled to think that one of Rome's most important and famous citizens would even acknowledge him and his tutor, let alone take the time to tell them a story.

"Before you start," he asked, "is Clodius the Beautiful related to Clodia Metelli?"

Cicero smiled knowingly. "You have been using your time in Rome well. He is her brother. Now, the story. Ragnall, you are about nineteen years old?"

"Twenty."

"When Gaius Julius Caesar was a year younger than you, he won the civic crown for high gallantry, for saving others' lives while storming the walls of a city that all had said was impregnable."

"Ragnall himself won a battle for our queen in Britain last year, when he was nineteen," said Drustan.

Ragnall beamed. Cicero looked him up and down appraisingly: "I'm sorry, I had no idea I was talking to a hero. Perhaps you will follow in Caesar's footsteps? But on with my tale.

"Six years later, when he was twenty-five years old, Caesar took a ship to Rhodes, headed for the oratory school of Appolonius Molon, where all the greatest orators have their skills honed by the greatest teacher. You are not a thousand miles away from his most successful graduate." Ragnall was confused for a moment, then realised that Cicero meant himself. "At the time, before Pompey's purges, Our Sea teemed with pirates. The pirates were not Roman, but they were created by Rome. You will have noticed many slaves in Rome?"

Drustan and Ragnall nodded. The city teemed with them. In the smarter areas like the Palatine Hill, there were more slaves than citizens. On the poverty drenched streets of the Aventine Hill, where Drustan and Ragnall lived, there weren't so many. There, it was mostly moon-eyed, formerly rural Italian families apparently driven from their farms by large-scale landowners who had replaced them with slaves.

"The pirates grew fat from the slave trade," Cicero continued. "On the island of Delos a decade ago the pirates sold ten thousand slaves every day. And to whom did they sell their slaves?"

"Romans?" asked Ragnall.

"Give the boy a prize. And why did nobody crush the pirates, or at least make some sort of effort towards preventing misery and murder from flourishing quite so virulently across Our Sea?"

Ragnall had no idea. He looked at Drustan, who said: "Because Rome gained more than it lost from the pirates, and Rome had destroyed all the other powers in the

Mediterranean – Your Sea – that might have checked the pirates' expansion."

"Exactly! You have a brilliant tutor, Ragnall." Ragnall thought he saw a blush bloom in Drustan's cheeks. Surely he was mistaken?

Cicero lent in and continued in a voice that was just above a whisper: "So, it was no surprise when Caesar's boat was taken by pirates on the way to Rhodes. Outnumbered, he would have been a fool to fight. The pirates, in turn, would have been fools to kill him, or to sell him on Delos. One could ransom a high-born Roman like him back to his family for much, much more than his slave price.

"The pirates returned to their base – some well-hidden cove – and demanded twenty talents for Caesar's freedom. Young Julius told them that he was worth fifty and sent some of the crew from his ship to collect that sum. For the next few weeks he stayed with the pirates, not as a moping captive, but living as one as them. He joined with their sports and their carousing. He read them passages that he'd written. He insisted that they were quiet when he wanted to sleep. He began to teach some of them how to read.

"All the time, he told them that after he was ransomed he'd return and crucify the lot of them. They must have thought he was joking."

"He wasn't?" Ragnall asked. The rest of the party had disappeared for him, enveloped as he was in Cicero's tale. He pictured a young man standing on a hot shore, making impertinent demands from fierce cutthroats. Could he really have been that confident and capable, or was he a brilliant blagger who'd spent every moment in captivity terrified for his life?

Cicero continued. "He was not joking. The ransom arrived – fifty talents – and Caesar was freed. He sailed to the city of Miletus, and, with no authority beyond his own boldness, with no funds other than promises, in a foreign city miles from home, he raised a small army and commandeered four ships.

"He returned to the pirates' base and, using his knowledge of their habits and defences, captured them all with no casualties on either side. He sailed the pirates in shackles to Asia and handed them over to the Roman governor there. The governor dithered, which didn't suit Caesar at all, so he carried out his own justice, as promised."

"He crucified them?"

Cicero's eyes widened. "Do you know what it is to be crucified?"

"Is it painful?" answered Ragnall.

"It is the most unbearable torture, which we see all too often in the Roman world." Cicero shuddered as if at a bad memory, then gathered himself. "So what would Caesar do? He'd given his word that he'd crucify them, and a Roman keeps his word. However, these were men who, Caesar knew, had been led to a world of piracy by the policies of Rome, and, moreover, had treated him well and become his friends."

"A tricky one," said Drustan.

"What did he do?" asked Ragnall, grabbing a cup of wine from a passing slave.

"He had all of their throats slit, then he crucified their corpses."

"A man of honour and clemency," said Drustan.

"Indeed. Now, let's compare that with Clodius' tale." Cicero grinned a surprisingly naughty grin for such an eminent statesman. "This is not such a noble saga. Perhaps five years after Caesar's brush with pirates, Clodius was on his way home from a war in the east, one in which he'd ignominiously stirred up trouble in the ranks, because he didn't think the general, Licinius Lucullus, was pillaging his conquests sufficiently."

"Fish-tank Lucullus?" asked Ragnall.

"The same. Having betrayed Lucullus, Clodius was captured by pirates on the way home. As we've seen, it was embarrassingly common at the time. Clodius said that the king of Egypt was his friend and would pay up without quibble, and his captors demanded the standard twenty talents.

"The Egyptian king, a very rich man, did indeed know Clodius. He sent back a messenger with two talents and a letter saying that Clodius was worth only one talent, but he was feeling generous."

Drustan chuckled.

"How did he get away?" asked Ragnall.

"His nickname 'the Beautiful' is less fitting now than it was. He is still a fine-looking man, but he was an exquisitely attractive youth. He claims that he persuaded the pirates to free him with his fine oratory. Everybody else says the price for his freedom was his virginity, shared by all the pirates. Having heard him speak, I suspect that everyone else's story is the more likely one."

"The pirates were women?" It didn't seem a bad deal to Ragnall.

"None of them were women." Cicero raised an eyebrow.

". . . Ah . . ." said Ragnall.

"So while Caesar's escape is a tale of honour and bravery, Clodius paid for his release, with, if you'll pardon the expression, his arse." Cicero chuckled.

"I keep hearing about . . . love between two men," said Ragnall. "In Britain, if two men want to make love, that's their lookout and not really anybody else's. Here it seems to be a form of punishment?"

"No, no, it isn't normally. I believe that there's nothing wrong with consenting adults doing whatever they want to each other. Most educated Romans share that view, but the official line and the average pleb do not. Moreover, homosexuality is illegal in the army, exactly where perhaps it

shouldn't be, given the lack of women. Of course it happens
in the army and it is mostly ignored. In town, it's tolerated
but one is expected to carry it out with decorum. If you're
discovered, you won't be beaten or ostracised, though.
Roman citizens are more homo-amused than homo-phobic,
so you might be teased, possibly to an unpleasant degree,
but no more. There's a story, in fact, about Caesar, when he
was about your age, Ragnall, and his long stay at the palace
of Nicomedes, the king of Bithynia. People still call Caesar
the queen of Bithynia sometimes, behind his back. If you'd
like to find out what crucifixion feels like, then try calling
him the queen of Bithynia to his face. Ah! And talking of
the man . . ."

Ragnall followed Cicero's gaze.

Above the throng in the garden, walking slowly from the
shade of a veranda to the cheers and applause of the partygoers, was Julius Caesar.

For a Roman, Caesar was tall, perhaps a hand-span shorter
than Ragnall. Facially, he looked a decade older than his
forty years, but he had the figure of an energetic thirty-year-
old. His leanly muscled, hairless calves led into a baggy,
loose-belted, long-sleeved toga. Dark but sparkling eyes
shone from a strong, large-featured face crowned with a
wreath of oak leaves. Under the wreath, Ragnall could see
that he'd combed greying hair forward to disguise a receding
hairline. Despite all the affectation in his appearance, the
man was immediately and potently striking. Ragnall had
recently heard the expression that some men filled up a room
with their presence. Caesar filled the outdoors. All conversation ceased and all eyes turned towards him. Ragnall felt
himself staring, open-mouthed, but he couldn't drag his
attention away.

Finally, Drustan broke the spell with a fear-filled whisper.
"Turn round, keep your head down. We have to go. Now."
Ragnall had never heard the old druid so perturbed. He

turned, full of concern, and saw dread in the old man's eyes. He followed his gaze.

There at Caesar's side, smiling at the throng, was King Zadar's chief druid, scourge of Britain and the man who'd killed Anwen, Ragnall's fiancée. There, next to Rome's man of the moment, was Felix.

Chapter 2

Spring rode down the track to Dug's farm, her pony's hooves clopping loud in the still evening. She saw he'd built – or, more accurately, hired labourers to build – yet another little building since she'd last been half a moon ago. She guessed it was the chicken house he'd been planning.

Dug had once told her that exchanging coins for goods and services was a silly Romanisation. Things that you exchanged for other things should be useful, he'd argued, and coins weren't. However, now that he had a lot of coins, he'd had a dramatic reversal of opinion. He'd exchanged a vast amount of coins in the last few moons, mostly for building materials and labourers' time. The track had been converted from a muddy rut into a well-drained road, hemmed in by regular wooden fences. On her left, four shaggy ponies trotted towards her across the field that ran down to the cliff edge. On the right, a smattering of scrubby-coated brown sheep had noticed her as she'd crested the hill, but had apparently found her uninteresting and returned to their grazing.

Six moons before, the farmhouse itself had been a small, smelly, tumbledown hut. Now it was a large, tidily made home, comprised of four mud and straw roundhouses joined by three wooden halls, all topped with a thick thatch to keep it cool in the heat and warm in the cold. This main building enclosed three sides of a square, stone-flagged court-yard with a well, a cook fire and a new potter's wheel which had never been used and, Spring reckoned, probably never would be now that Dug had discovered that you could exchange coins for pots. At the nearer end was Spring's room, hers the whole time, even though she usually lived with Lowa on Maidun Castle. It was big, taking up all of one of the roundhouses, with two shuttered windows, one looking out to sea and one over the courtyard.

Arranged neatly behind the house was a clutch of outbuildings. As well as the new chicken house, there was a grain shed on stilts, stables, a sty, pens and a strange, empty conical building that Dug's farmworkers had built one day when they'd run out of useful work but Dug had wanted to get his coins' worth out of them.

The farm buildings rested on the side of a shallow, dry valley, which stretched two hundred paces from the house before being brought to an abrupt, grass-fringed stop at the top of the sea cliff. A hundred paces from the rest of the farm was the long cluster of mini huts that contained Dug's bee colony. It was the part of Dug's new farm that he was least happy with. He liked honey, but some unscrupulous man from a tribe of bee worshippers not far to the north had persuaded him that he needed many more bees than he actually did. He was thinking of getting rid of them, because the dogs kept getting stung. Those dogs . . .

As if they knew she was thinking about them, Pig Fucker and Sadist's broad faces poked up from behind a large trough, ears aloft. They saw it was Spring, woofed happy hellos, lolloped up the road and looped round to trot either side of her for the final few paces. They were huge, almost as big as her little horse, and identical apart from their colour. Pig Fucker was a sleek black Sadist and was the colour of a tawny owl.

The dogs were another big change. When Dug had inherited them from Tadman they'd been chained monsters, snarling and snapping, absolutely furious with the world. They were still monsters, but the worst they'd ever do to

Spring was slobber on her face, which she hated. Dug didn't seem to mind when they licked him with their big gooey tongues, which was disgusting, especially considering his beard. What's more, Sadist and Pig Fucker were not nice names and they no longer suited them – Dug had a boar and four sows, for example, and Pig Fucker hadn't been near them for ages – but Dug had insisted that you couldn't change a name. She'd pointed out that she did it the whole time – her real name was Sabina and he was happy to call her Spring, for the love of Toutatis – but he'd been adamant. Sadist and Pig Fucker they remained. So Spring called them Sadie and Pigsy, unless they were naughty.

She dismounted by the stable, tied her pony to a rail, stroked the dogs for a few heartbeats while avoiding their mouth foam and corded dribbles of saliva, then headed round to the courtyard, wondering why Dug hadn't walked out to greet her as usual. It worried her a little. She'd had a recurring nightmare recently of Dug floating underwater, dead. She told herself not to be silly, and the stomach rumble-inducing smell of chicken cooking over a fire did make it seem unlikely that anything could be wrong. Probably he was at a crucial stage of cooking and couldn't leave the chickens unattended.

The first thing she saw in the courtyard was a man who wasn't Dug, leaning against the well. He was in his early twenties perhaps, clad in tight black trousers, a black smock and a black hat. He had a heavy iron blade at his waist, a pinched face, trimmed, dark facial hair and eyes like a weasel's, one of which was surrounded by a fresh and nasty looking ring of bruise. His whole bearing screamed that he was up to no good. She started, then relaxed when she saw that his hands were tied behind his back.

"Hello?" she said. He scowled back.

"Welcome!" Dug stopped turning the spit that held two delicious smelling chickens over the cook fire, and stood up from his chair. "Caught this fellow after my chickens."

"I was just looking at them," whined the man.

"You don't need to put them in a bag to look at them. We talked about that," said Dug.

The man darted his little eyes from Dug to Spring.

"So," continued Dug, "I'm going to set the dogs on him. I thought you'd want to see that, so I waited. They're hungry and there's nothing they like to eat more than chicken rustler. They raised the alarm so it's only fair that they should eat him."

"Thanks! That's kind of you all to wait. I'd love to see the dogs eat a criminal." Spring smiled at the man.

"Good, now first . . ." He spiked one of the cooking chickens with a pronged iron pole and sliced the breast from it, then picked up a black sack, which Spring took to be the robber's, put the chicken breast into it and walked up to his captive, who recoiled. Dug told him to stay still, pulled open the hem of his tight black trousers and stuffed the bag down the front.

"Pig Fucker, Sadist, come here," he called. They rushed to his side. Their shoulders were higher than Dug's waist. Spring was pretty sure they'd grown since she'd last seen them, and they'd been stupidly massive then. Dug pointed at the man. "Prepare to hunt!"

The dogs flattened themselves to the ground and bubbled out low growls that made Spring tingle all over, not in a good way. Dug winked at her. This was a new trick. Spring was not sure that she approved.

The thief squeaked unhappily and strained his bound wrists, which held firm behind him. Dug was good at knots.

"Off you go," said Dug.

"What?" said the thief.

"I'm letting you go. Don't worry, you won't be alone. The dogs love a chase almost as much as they love the taste of people who try to steal from me. So you've got twenty heartbeats."

"No, you can't! Wait! I've got gold! I can give—"

"Nineteen. Eighteen . . ."

The thief took off at a sprint. With his hands tied behind his back, he didn't look too different from the chickens he'd come to steal. When he'd gone round the corner, Spring let out the laugh she'd been holding in.

"Two, one, go!" Dug finished his count, Spring put her fingers in her ears. The dogs barked as loudly as she'd expected them to, then hared off after their quarry.

"Good, huh?" he said to Spring. "Did you see how they lay down and got menacing when I told them to? They really are becoming very good dogs."

"The man, they won't . . . ?"

"Oh, they won't hurt him, not at all. I can't say the same for his trousers though, because they're going to get that chicken." Dug's big shoulders rocked with one of his rare, genuine chuckles and Spring laughed along with him.

They heard happy barking and a man's scream from the road, and laughed all the more.

Chapter 3

Ragnall stared. It couldn't be. How could Felix be sharing Caesar's birthday entry?

Drustan pulled at his sleeve, but Ragnall couldn't turn. Felix's eyes found his, looked from him to Drustan and flashed with joyous recognition. Keeping his eyes on them, he turned to whisper something to Caesar.

"Come on!" Drustan said.

Pupil and tutor pushed through the smiling, clapping crowd. They were met with tuts, jostles and a few muttered comments along the lines of "fucking barbarians" and "find some manners, plebs".

Finally they emerged from the tighter throng, and weaved their way through the looser groups of guests to a door that Ragnall thought must surely lead from the garden to the street. Wherever it went, it was away from Felix. That was the important thing.

Ragnall grabbed the iron handle, twisted it and pushed. Nothing happened. He shook it. The door was locked.

"We're not the men you're looking for," Drustan said behind him.

Ragnall spun.

Four burly men had surrounded them. They were wearing the togas of partygoers but holding short, waisted legionaries' swords. They were looking confused.

"Oh, sorry," said one, "I was sure we was meant to be after you."

"No, not us," Drustan replied, "and you will help us open this door."

"Yeah, sure." The man took a step forward.

"Stop!" Felix's voice. The man stopped moving as if suddenly frozen. Partygoers parted and Caesar walked towards them, flanked by Felix.

"Caesar," said Felix, "these men are Gaulish agents, spying out weakness in Rome's defences."

The crowd gasped. As Drustan had explained to Ragnall, the Gauls had once sacked Rome. It had been over three centuries before, but the Romans still hated and feared the Gauls.

"We are not Gaulish," said Drustan. We come from—!" Drustan stopped talking as he realised that he was speaking in the British tongue, not Latin.

"We're from—" he tried. It was British again.

"He's trying to say . . ." Ragnall realised that he was speaking British, too. He tried again, thinking Latin, Latin, Latin: "Apples, pears, dogs, cheese, one, two, three—" he said, all in British.

Felix's lip curled with satisfaction.

"Does anyone know what they are saying? What are they after? Are there others Gauls here?" asked Caesar. His clipped accent was refined like Clodia's but sharper. He sounded more inquisitive than aggressive, more like a fascinated druid than an aggrieved general.

"They are druids. They are cursing you," said Felix. The crowd gasped. Gaulish druids' curses were the stuff of horror stories. One of the sailors on the way from Britain had told Ragnall about a rich Roman man who'd driven his chariot past a pregnant Gaulish witch collapsed in some desolate spot and ignored her cries for help. Her unborn child had died as a result. She cursed the man's family, saying that the first-born son of every generation to come would be torn apart by dogs between his fifth and sixth birthday. No matter what precautions they took, for more than ten generations now, dogs had found that family's eldest son.

"I see," said Caesar. "So these men have come to my party, taken my food and plan to repay me by invading the city I love?"

"Yes," said Felix.

The gathered Romans murmured disapproval and a couple shouted it. Ragnall sought a friendly face. Clodia was nowhere to be seen. He caught Cicero's eye, but the great orator and former consul looked down.

Caesar looked Drustan and then Ragnall in the eye. Both tried to speak again, but could stammer out only British words. Caesar made a *tsk* noise, shook his head and said: "How irritating. Felix, deal with them in some way that will amuse the guests. Let them pay for their interruption by entertaining us. Now I must be gone to another garden to see a new delivery. Those interested in wildlife should come with me. Felix will provide a marvellous spectacle for those who prefer his sort of diversion."

Caesar left. Half the crowd, including Cicero, followed in his wake. Felix remained, smiling like a happy wolf, surrounded by a few dozen Romans, mostly men, mostly regarding Drustan and Ragnall with the same hungry eyes as Felix. A rush of bowel-loosening fear almost made Ragnall collapse.

"So," said Felix, addressing his fellow Romans. He looked exactly as Ragnall remembered, although his hairline had perhaps retreated even further back on his egg-like head. "What would you like me do to with these Gaulish spies? Precedent would have me bury them, since Sibyl buried Gauls alive in the Forum, but it does seem unkind to deny the house gladiators some sport?" The little Roman druid opened his short arms to his audience. "The gladiators need practice. Shall we give them these men to fight?

Or shall we follow where Sibyl has led, and bury them alive?"

The clamour of mixed shouts soon organised itself into a united chant:

"Bury them! Bury them! Bury them!"

Chapter 4

Later, Dug and Spring sat outside in the clear, moonless night, spooning their way through big wooden bowls of chicken with parsnip, honey, goosefoot, watercress and garlic. The chicken was almost burnt and there was almost too much salt, just how Spring liked it. The dogs lay at their feet guzzling on carcasses. Spring had heard that animals shouldn't eat cooked chicken bones. She'd told Dug, but he'd said that Sadist and Pig Fucker didn't know that and given them all the chicken remains. They seemed to be enjoying them without too much trouble.

Dug had doused the fire so that they could see the stars properly. Countless bright little lights crammed every cranny of the sky right down to the dark land, and shimmered on the black sea. As well as the individual bright points, there were rashes and patches of light which Dug said were made up of even more stars, even further away. Spring asked him how he knew and he said he just did. That was good enough for her, she decided.

They spent a while spotting animals, faces and other patterns in the stars, then sat in happy silence broken only by the odd grumble or snort from the dogs or Dug. Their sounds had become more or less indistinguishable and Spring could picture Dug sitting here every night, looking up at the sky with the dogs, grunting away with them. Apart from cold nights, obviously, when he probably sat inside thinking through plans for his next farm innovation. The new chicken fortress that he'd shown her earlier was a formidable creation. A wolf, fox, stoat or any other attacker would have to face several ingenious certain-death challenges before it got near the impenetrable spiked iron door. Of course the whole design did nothing to prevent hen-napping during the day, when the birds were free to peck around wherever they chose. The chicken burglar had proved that very point. Spring had mentioned this to Dug, and he'd said that it was the chickens' own lookout where they went during the day, but he'd protect them while they slept. And besides, he reminded her, they were guarded by the dogs, whose efficiency had been proven by that day's rustler.

As they sat, Dug seemed to shed his contentedness and become uncharacteristically fidgety. Spring guessed that his thinking had led him round to a cause of consternation, a Lowa-shaped one no doubt, but she wasn't going to help him out. They'd talked about it too much already, and she couldn't understand why he didn't just stop moping and go and see her and tell her that he liked her.

"So," Dug said after a while, "what's the latest at Maidun? Did that boy try to bully you again?"

"He's my friend now. At least he pretends to be. He won't be bullying me again, anyway."

"Good."

"Yup."

"And, how's everyone else?"

"Do you mean Lowa?"

"She'll do. How is she? You still living with her? Has she mentioned me?"

"I'm sort of living with her. I've moved into my own little hut now, in the Eyrie right next to hers. But I don't see her much. She's gone a bit mad. She doesn't talk about anything apart from the Romans and Roman things. Do you know that their swords are made so that when they split your tummy open, your guts spill out and you die slowly? Well, they are. So Lowa's been with Elann Nancarrow and Atlas Agrippa a lot, trying to make a tummy protector that will stop the Roman's swords."

"With Atlas?"

"Did you know he was in the Roman army? Or something like the Roman army, anyway. He's round at Lowa's hut a lot. They talk for hours."

"I see."

"But they're not friends. One of the slingers told me that she would never forgive Atlas for his part in killing her sister and the rest of her women, even though everyone agrees now that it was Felix putting everyone under a glamour. I'm not sure that Lowa believes that it was Felix. I'm not sure that I do either. I think people do what they're told because life's easier that way, and after they've done something horrid people make up an excuse and call it the truth even though it's not . . . and besides Atlas doesn't like her much, the same slinger told me. She rammed a deer bone through his face, and it's hard to like anyone who's done that to you. I agree with that bit."

"Aye, but the two could cancel each other out. 'You killed my sister, I ruined your face, so we're even'."

Sadie whined. Spring leant forward stroke him, then straightened up and said: "I suppose so. But don't worry, they're not going to shag."

"Spring!" Dug sounded surprised. He shouldn't have been, Spring was ten now, or at least thereabouts, so she'd heard all about shagging from the older children. Or some things about it anyway. Enough to know that it was disgusting and she'd never do it.

"What? That's what you're worried about, isn't it?"

"No. Not at all. Lowa can do what she want."

"Oh good, because she'd been seeing a lot of Carden, and he is a very good-looking man. If I was Lowa, I'd shag him."

"Right."

"I'm joking, Dug!"

"I see."

She could see she'd gone too far. Dug was the best person in the world in every way, but she just didn't get this part of him. "Sorry, sorry," she said, "I was joking. Lowa doesn't look at anyone like that. I'm sure she still likes you. Why don't you come back with me to Maidun tomorrow and see her? You haven't seen her since you came here."

"You're going back tomorrow?"

"I have to. Lowa's got some big war game planned. I'm not meant to be missing any training at all as it is. That reminds me! Lowa asked me to ask you if you wanted to come and join in? She said you'd be useful. Come back with me! You can tell Lowa you love her. And I bet you will like the war game."

"She definitely asked you to ask me?"

"No, I made it up. Yes! Of course she did, why else would I say it? She wants you to come!"

"Well, I would, but I've got a couple of people coming tomorrow to talk to about my hot-water plans. I can't let them get here and find just the dogs."

"Yes, you can, come!"

"We'll see," said Dug.

"That always means no," Spring pouted.

"Aye, you're not wrong there." Dug leant over to ruffle her hair. She felt half a smile growing, but an image of Dug floating, underwater and dead, flooded her mind. She shuddered.

"What's wrong?" Dug asked, recoiling his hand, eyes wide.

"Just a bit cold," she said.

"Oh aye, sorry, I'll get the fire started again." Dug stood up and bent over the wood pile. Looking at his broad back, tears filled Spring's eyes.

Chapter 5

The soldiers marched Drustan and Ragnall to a square lawn perhaps fifteen paces across, surrounded by a colonnade and a balcony. Above it all the sky was the pale blue that would soon pink into a sunset. Chattering partygoers wafted a variety of perfumes as they poured into the garden around them and filed up steps on to the colonnade. More appeared on the balcony and soon that too filled with toga-wearing men and the odd fragrant-looking woman. A few were deep in conversation, a few barked out jokes and others laughed, but most just watched the goings-on below with happy anticipation.

On Felix's request, the Romans on the lawn parted for four large, oiled Iberian looking slaves, who walked solemnly through the human passage, spades on their shoulders as if they were spearmen on parade. Felix gave them brief instructions, and the slaves sliced their spades into the sod. They cut out neat squares of turf and piled it carefully. So it will look neat when they put it back over our soil-suffocated corpses, thought Ragnall. He looked about, searching for a friendly face or an exit, but found neither.

Too soon, the slaves had excavated a square hole two feet deeper than Ragnall was tall. The soil was in four even heaps on each side of the hole, with a slave standing by each heap. Four other slaves rolled forward barrels of wet sand and tipped them on to the piles of earth. The spade-holders set to work mixing the wet sand with the soil.

"What are they doing that for?" Ragnall asked Drustan.

"It will clamp us in place more effectively."

"Ah." Ragnall felt sick. "I shouldn't have asked."

"Yes. It is something of a shame that that seems likely to be the last piece of learning that I shall impart to you."

On Felix's word, the hefty men who'd first accosted them grabbed them and pushed them into the hole. Drustan landed heavily. Ragnall heard a snap. He helped the old man on to his feet. He was in agony.

"Save yourself!" he said through clenched teeth.

Ragnall looked up. One of the captors pointed his sword at him. It was clear what would happen if he did try to climb out.

Some Romans managed to squeeze between the slaves to get a good gawp at the condemned men, and a good deal more watched from the balcony above. Ragnall looked for a friendly face, but found Cato, the man who may have eavesdropped on his conversation with Clodia. His eyes showed all the compassion of a sheep eyeing another dead sheep. Or, in this case, thought Ragnall, a soon-to-be-dead Sheeplord. Funny how his mind was making jokes when he was about to die. The whole thing seemed surreal.

He tried to shout, to beg for mercy perhaps or to at least ask for it, but it came out in British again. He could think of the Roman words, but couldn't say them no matter how hard he tried. The crowd laughed and mimicked his brutish noises.

"Give the Gauls a knife!" cried a woman on the balcony. "So that the blade might lend them an easy exit. Gauls are not so stout as Romans. The horror of burial will surely be too much for them!"

Some people laughed, and possibly it was meant as a joke, but one onlooker, a mean-faced man with a short fuzz of red hair reached a knife from his ankle sheaf and tossed it into the hole.

"Pick it up and give it to me," said Drustan.

Ragnall did as he was bid. "What are you going to do?"

"A knife in the heart will be a better death than choking on earth." Drustan pressed the point of the knife into Ragnall's ribs. "I will finish you quickly, if it is necessary," he said.

"It's just a game. A tease, surely." Ragnall could not believe that the Romans, the same people who built such beautiful buildings, would bury them in public. "They're not going to—"

"Begin!" shouted Felix.

Four spadefuls of earth hit their legs. The spades were capacious. Already their feet were buried.

"One!" shouted the crowd.

Ragnall pulled Drustan into an embrace. Drustan looked up at him, fear and pain in his never-before flappable eyes.

Ragnall wanted to weep. "You have been the best tutor you could have been. I hope you will continue your instruction—"

"Two!" More soil whacked against their legs. It was heavy and stone-filled, and it hurt.

"—in the Otherworld."

Drustan looked up and smiled. "You are too good and too young, Ragnall."

"Three!"

"You would have had a good life, but it has been ruined by others. Several are to blame – Zadar, Lowa, me."

"Four!"

"Not you."

"I should have never brought you here. We did not need to do Lowa's bidding. It was my foolish sense of adven—"

"Five!"

The slaves were skilled, their spades were massive and the wet sand and earth mix was effective. Already Ragnall could not move his legs.

"But above all, you must blame Felix. He was at the heart—"

"Six!" The soil reached the top of Ragnall's legs.

"—of all of this. It is he who made Zadar what he was."

"Seven!"

"I can see now that he has always been working with Caesar."

"Eight!"

"I can't see how or why – somehow Felix is blocking me."

"Nine!"

"Or perhaps Caesar's working for him. But he made Zadar—"

"Ten!" The soil was over Ragnall's midriff, nearly at Drustan's neck.

"Difficult to talk. You must kill Felix. Have our venge—"

"Eleven!"

The soil felt unbearably tight about Ragnall now. Drustan was silent, the soil around his neck. Ragnall strained to lift him, but couldn't. He started to cry.

"Be . . . brave. Kill Felix," wheezed Drustan.

"Twelve!"

Clods of soil whacked Ragnall's head. Drustan's mouth was buried. Ragnall sobbed. He wasn't brave. He'd never been brave. The world of heroes and great deeds wasn't for him.

"Thirteen!"

It was up to Drustan's forehead, nearly at Ragnall's neck. This was it now, it wasn't a joke, there would be no reprieve. Drustan would be dead in a few heartbeats, Ragnall not long after that.

"Fourteen!"

The earth was over his chin. Breathing was almost impossible now. He looked up. Felix was staring with what looked like lust in his eyes. Cato was grinning like a bully watching a smaller kid taking a beating. What a shit, thought Ragnall.

That stopped his crying. Danu give him strength, he wasn't going to cry in front of that man. Not any more, anyway.

He was surprised to see Clodia push to the front of the balcony about them. She caught his eye. She shook her head and a tear ran down her haughty cheek.

"Fifteen!"

Soil cascaded on to his face. There were a few stones in it. He spat out soil. He closed his mouth tight.

"Sixteen!" His face was covered.

He felt Drustan move the dagger. He'd forgotten about the dagger. He held his breath. Would Drustan be able to . . .

He felt the knife point move away from his chest. There was a jerk. Even under the soil, he felt Drustan going limp. Drustan had killed himself. His tutor was dead. He was next, but there would be no knife to the heart for him.

"Seventeen!" came the muffled shout from the world above the ground. Ragnall felt oblivion spreading through his mind, sooner than he'd expected, then no more.

Chapter 6

The Monster bent down for another bite. Dug tried to lift his arms but they were held by an impossible strength. Teeth popped through flesh, pushed through fat and drove into muscle. The Monster clamped its jaws and pulled its head back, stretching ribbons of elastic, blood-dripping flesh. The ribbons twanged free and the Monster slurped them up through rubbery lips, splattering blood over its face. Then its hair disappeared, its muzzle retracted, its teeth shrunk and it was Lowa, looking down impassively, face smeared with blood. Her tongue poked from her lips and he thought she was going to lick them, but instead she said "Wake up, you shite," in a man's voice. "Wake up," she repeated.

Dug realised that he was dreaming. He pulled himself into wakefulness, increasingly unsettled by the flickering firelight that filled his eyes. He never lit a fire in his room, even on the coldest nights.

"That's right, wake up so you can see yourself die," said the same voice. Dug blinked a couple of times and saw that it was the chicken thief. He was holding a primed but laughably small bow and arrow and shivering with nervous energy. Next to him was a man that Dug didn't recognise, holding a torch. This latter fellow was around Dug's age. His wavy dark hair was swept back from a clean-shaven face that would have been heroically handsome, had it not been strangely narrow. He was well-dressed. He looked more like a king's advisor or a moderately successful merchant than your average burglar's mate. By the look on his face, he wasn't much happier with the situation than Dug was.

"You're going kill me because I caught you trying to steal my chickens and I let you go?" Dug said.

"Is that what happened?" said the torch-holder. "You said—"

"Shut up, Dad," said the chicken thief.

There you go, thought Dug. The failed chicken thief's told his dad a tale and dragged him along. If he was careful and sensitive, he'd be able to talk his way out of this.

"Is that a toy bow?" he said, realising as he said it that it was neither careful nor sensitive. He cursed silently.

"It's not a toy!" the chicken thief shouted. "It's a special bow for close-quarters work, and these are close quarters and it will kill you just as well as the biggest bow in the world. So get ready to meet the gods." The chicken thief pulled the string back further.

"Hang on." Dug raised a hand, thinking that it would probably stop the little arrow if necessary, and wondering why Sadist and Pig Fucker hadn't heard the man shouting and come running. "You can't kill me just because I caught you thieving from me. If anything, I owe you an arrow."

"He's right, you fool," said the torch-holder, slapping his son over the back of the head.

"Ow!" The chicken thief opened his hands in surprise. The arrow loosed and flew to where Dug's head had been an eyeblink before, but thwocked into wood because Dug was already leaning over the edge of the bed to grab and hurl his hammer. The heavy metal hammerhead hit the chicken thief full in the forehead with a soggy crack. His head snapped back and he toppled. The father squatted down next to his son, then stood, glanced at Dug, and ran from the room.

With the torch gone, it was dark. Dug threw the wool blanket back, swung off his bed, took a step and tripped over the clothes that he'd dumped there the night before. He fell and landed on a knee and two hands. He groped about and found lumpy wetness. He guessed that it was the chicken thief's brains. His throw had been quite a bit harder than he'd intended.

He found the hammer, clambered to his feet, and walked swiftly through his spacious hearth room, knowing his way in the dark. He strode out of the front door and stopped.

"Ah," he said to the four people who stood in his yard in a semi-circle. As well as the torch-holder, there was a useful-looking young woman bouncing from foot to foot and aiming an arrow at him, a nervous looking boy with a sword and a bare-armed man with a swinging sling. The latter had possibly left his arms bare to display his arm muscles, which were certainly large enough to shoot a slingstone with lethal velocity. This lot were the chicken thief's family, Dug supposed.

He stood. He'd been striding so purposefully that he'd come too far from his door to duck back in. That would teach him, he thought. Where were his dogs? On his own he didn't stand much of a chance against four of them, particularly when two of them had projectile weapons. He'd have to talk his way out of this. He was thinking what to say – just blurting out the first thing hadn't helped much before – when the woman piped up.

"Are you sure Wim's dead?" she said, looking at Dug, but presumably not directing the question at him. She had a firm intelligence and air of command about her. Dug guessed she was the chicken thief's sister and the torch-holder's daughter, but effectively the head of the family.

"Yeah, Ruthanna, sorry. This man knocked Wim's brains out," the torch-holder said matter-of-factly. It he was upset about his son's death, it didn't show.

"Look," said Dug, "this has gone further than it should have. Your man Wim stole my chickens, so I taught him a lesson. I didn't even hurt him."

"You punched him and your dogs humiliated him," said Ruthanna.

"Aye, but he deserved it. Like I said, he was trying to steal from me. And I only hit him because he tried to hit me. Then I got my dogs to chase him just to scare him a bit. I knew they wouldn't hurt him. It seemed a fair return for trying to nick my chickens and attacking me when I caught him."

"He's right," said the torch-holder. "That's a fair return. More than fair. That Wim . . ."

"Good!" said Dug. "Some sense finally on this difficult night! So if you want to all be on your ways, I'll—"

"Dad, we'll never know if this man's telling the truth. Frankly I'd believe any stranger over Wim but—"

"Exactly," Dug butted in. "I'm telling the truth. I did nothing wrong."

"But," continued Ruthanna, pulling her bowstring, "the truth about earlier on is neither here nor there. He's killed Wim, and for that he must die."

"My name's Dug," said Dug. He'd heard that people were less likely to kill you if they knew your name. "I don't have to die. Haven't we established that it was all Wim's fault?" He glanced at Spring's shutter. It was open, but hopefully she was sleeping through this. She'd be bound to try to intervene and he didn't want them killing her, too.

"I'm sorry, but we do have to kill you now," said the man. "I know it's Wim's fault, but that is the way. Ruthanna?" He nodded at the woman, who drew her bowstring further back and aimed at Dug's chest.

"Aye," said Dug, torn between dropping to the ground or charging. Where the big badgers' bollocks were those dogs? There was a buzzing sound. Was that death coming?

Spring was on the edge of a clearing in the woods. In the middle of the clearing were four big bears standing around a little bear, threatening it with their claws. That's no good, she thought. She looked about and saw that the trees' branches were packed with bright-feathered yellow and black birds, all looking on silently. She wondered whether they might help the little bear? As if in reply, the birds, thousands of them, leapt from the branches with a great whoosh and attacked the big bears. The bears disappeared in a cloud of birds. A few heartbeats later the birds flew back to their perches. The big bears had gone and the little bear was left, blinking in bewilderment.

Ruthanna yelled as if stung, the torch-holder bellowed, Ruthanna yelled again, loosening her bow and swinging it about over her head. The other two yelped, slapping at themselves. The buzzing became a roar. The attackers were enveloped in a throbbing, shifting shadow. They screamed and screamed. The torch fell. Dug stood, mouth open, unable to see anything other than the odd flailing limb briefly flapping free of the cloud. The screams stopped. Dug was about to dart back into the house and close the door, but the bees lifted with a buzz that made his bones shake and flew away.

Dug picked up the torch. They were all dead, tongues swollen and protruding, their faces red from countless stings, bloated beyond recognition. The muscular lad's arms looked like hammered, rotten meat.

He peered in through Spring's open window. She was snoring gently.

He found the dogs asleep by the chicken house. He nudged Sadist with a toe to check he was alive. The hound woke up, grumbled and went back to sleep. Pig Fucker responded the same way. He guessed that they must have been drugged by some druid-made potion. They seemed fine, just sleeping, but he resolved to check on them after his unpleasant chores were done.

He loaded the five corpses on to a cart and wheeled it

along the valley. As the powdery orange of dawn glowed through sea mist, he hurled the bodies from the cliff.

Back at the house he cleaned up the worst of Wim's brains and put a rug over the rest. He listened outside Spring's door and heard her snoring still.

He decided not to tell her or anyone else about the visitors in the night. Hopefully the sea would take the corpses off to become someone else's mystery, but if they were found at the bottom of his cliff and reported to Lowa, he'd claim ignorance.

Chapter 7

Ragnall woke. He was lying on his back, on a cool, hard surface. The stars were brilliant above him in the clear, moonless night. He remembered. Drustan was dead. He himself was dead. So where was he now? There was only one place he could be. The Otherworld. He gasped in fear, but at the same time felt a thrill of excitement. What would he find here?

He lay still, listening, and looking at the stars. The stars were very similar to, if not the same as, the stars in the living world, but here, if he wasn't mistaken, they were brighter. Chances were it was always night in the Otherworld. Or perhaps day and night here were geographical entities? Perhaps you arrived in the dark places and had to find your way to the lands of the light? Perhaps the better the life you had led, the more and brighter the stars to guide your path to the light? In which case he could pat himself on his ghostly back. He'd been awarded barrel-loads of stars.

All around was silence, but . . . there! A soft cough. Could it have been the snuffle of some great beast prowling on huge, soft paws, its wide head crammed with poison-drooling teeth? Ragnall thought it could. Was the Otherworld a wild land, where giant animals preyed on people? That seemed likely, at least in the Dark Places, before you fought your way to the Land of the Light. The idea didn't scare him. It galvanised him. He'd slay the evil beasts.

Slowly, so as not to alert any predators, he turned his head from side to side to get his bearings. Soil tumbled from his hair on to his stone bed. Nearby were towers and angular piles of rock, and single-branched trees with what looked like ropes . . . they looked more like hangmen's gibbets than trees. He shouldn't be surprised, he told himself. This was the Otherworld. There were going to be surprises. And adventures. And reunions.

Further away, he could see lights. Perhaps the lights of human settlements, built against the beasts, where people gathered before making the journey to the Land of the Light?

He would do better, he decided, in this world. He may have been a decent fellow in the previous one, but he had done nothing outstanding. Here, he was going to be a hero. The hero.

Carefully, quietly, he felt about at his side. If the Otherworld fit his fantasies, he'd have a mighty sword girded to his waist. He'd take this blade and adventure across the Dark Places. He'd need neither food nor water. He'd rescue others from the beasts and lead them into the Light, where he'd find his father, his mother, his brothers . . . Drustan perhaps he would meet on the way. With Drustan's cunning and his strength, they would prevail.

There was no sword. He was still wearing his toga. Far off, but unmistakeable, he heard the donkey-bray laugh of a young, upper-class Roman. He sat up. Soil from his hair tumbled down his back. He leant forwards and shook his head until there was no more earth to come.

The area immediately around him was in darkness, but nearby were hills and illuminated buildings that looked an awful lot like Rome. Closer, the piles of rock and angular trees came into focus and he realised he was on a building site. The tall strutures weren't trees or gibbets, they were cranes. The cough he'd heard was a guard. He could see him now, heading away, torch aloft.

By the position of the lights of Rome and the size of the unlit area, he even knew which building site he was on.

Pompey, scourge of pirates and recipient of three Triumphs for military victories, was using his immeasurable resources to build a colossal theatre on the Field of Mars. Ragnall had walked past it with Drustan a couple of days before. They'd commented on a particular block of stone, saying how massive it was. Drustan had marvelled at the ingenuity needed to cut it, and speculated on how they might have brought it to the site. They'd talked to one of the workers and found out that Drustan's speculations had been correct.

Ragnall was atop that very stone. He realised what Drustan must have done. He looked about, but there was no sign of the druid. Surely he would have transported both of them? Or had he given his life to make magic powerful enough . . . ? No, it wasn't worth considering. Drustan could not have sacrificed himself to save Ragnall. He couldn't have done. Drustan would be just as alive as he was, only elsewhere.

Wherever he was now, surely Drustan would head for the apartment they'd rented – their lofted hovel, as his old tutor had called it – on the top floor of a block in the Aventine? Ragnall would go there and meet him.

He climbed down his stone and out of Pompey's building site with ease. Its high wooden wall had been built to keep people out, not in.

He walked home, keeping to the side streets. Even at night they were full of men, women, rag-clad children, stray dogs, dusty pigs and easily flustered chickens. At one point he had to break cover and cross the Forum, where suddenly everything was cool and spacious – a stone pavement, elegant ladies and gentlemen gliding about in clean togas – then it was back into the pell-mell, slummy tangle of filthy alleyways that made up most of the great city.

He ran up the rickety flights of stairs and slammed open their door. Drustan wasn't there. No matter, he'd wait. There was nothing else he could do. Or was there? Was he being stupid, going back to their rented apartment? Nobody apart from them knew that they lived here, they'd given false names to the landlord, and if Felix could use magic to find him, then he'd find him wherever he went. No, the best thing would be to stay put and wait for Drustan.

Chapter 8

For the first time in her life Lowa knew relative peace. The Romans were coming, that was for sure, but there was no sign of an imminent invasion. There was no immediate, obvious enemy, no rival to fight. She'd never been so stressed.

She had three main problems, she mused as she strapped on the ungainly new iron armour that Elann Nancarrow had made for her. One, she had no idea how soon the Romans were coming, or where they might land. Spring still insisted that they'd be there "quite soon", but merchants and other travellers insisted that there was no sign of any Roman move towards Britain. So somehow the Romans were keeping their preparations secret. With any luck, Ragnall and Drustan would be back soon and they could tell her what they were up to. Until they did, she was in the dark, and preparing to meet a foe without knowing anything about the size or composition of its forces. She sometimes fantasised about knowing exactly where they were going to land and preparing a load of surprises to knock them straight back into the sea. She wished that she could make the whole coastline one big death zone – the salt flats pocked with hidden, spike-filled pits, beaches covered with caltrops and all the cliff paths blocked and guarded by archers who'd shoot anyone who tried to climb – but that was far too massive an undertaking and, besides, the fishermen and seafaring merchants wouldn't like it.

Problem two was Spring. Not the girl herself. Lowa like having her around. She lightened things up and Lowa enjoyed teaching her what she knew, especially about archery, which

Spring was taking to like a fish to water. The girl was such good company in fact that Lowa had nearly given up trying to work out if Spring had used her magic to make her go off Dug temporarily. No, the problem with Spring was that there was only one of her. Lowa had to rely on only one soothsaying druid's prediction, and that prediction was far from specific. With Drustan in Rome, Spring was the only druid whom Lowa believed in. There were plenty more around, all raving about Romans, but many of these were drunk and most were certainly charlatans. A few seemed sensible, but Lowa had no proof of their abilities and she mistrusted them. She'd felt Spring's power and knew that her magic was real. She'd seen evidence of Drustan's magical ability in the arena, when he'd found her hiding under the bridge, and possibly when he'd claimed to have changed the wind direction for the battle with the Dumnonians. But what if both he and Spring had been mistaken, or, more likely, what if things had changed and Spring didn't know? Drustan had told her that Roman invasion would have come sooner if it hadn't been for civil war in Rome and a slave revolt. Perhaps something else had happened? What if they weren't coming for a century? Or, more likely, what if a hundred thousand fiercely trained legionaries were climbing into boats in some secret cove that very day?

So Lowa desperately wanted another believable druid to consult, several preferably, but she couldn't find any. She'd sent Mal and Nita to the Island of Angels to see if there was any help there. They'd been well received, but Mal said that they'd seen no evidence of real magic, nor been able to find out anything more than a general sense that the Romans were coming. They had found out a good deal more about Rome, its history and its army from the island's scholars, which had already come in handy, but Lowa would have much preferred if they'd come back with a team of reliable druids who could have told them exactly what the Romans were up to.

Third problem was her army. First, it was small. By freeing the slaves and reducing the crushing taxes in the lands that Maidun had conquered, Lowa had massively reduced her income, making it near impossible to keep the twenty thousand men and women who were already in the army, and she wanted more. A lot more. The tribute she had secured from Dumnonia provided some funds, but more important were the contributions that she'd negotiated with the loose agglomeration of tribes that occupied the tracts of land east of Maidun's territory, bordered by the Channel to the south and east and by Murkan land to the north. Before Lowa's time, the eastern tribes had been terrified that Zadar was going to invade and enslave them, and, indeed, that had been his plan. So when Lowa usurped Zadar and displayed her military capabilities by immediately triumphing over the Dumnonians, the eastern tribe sent delegations pleading loyalty, and, more importantly, tribute. Lowa negotiated a tithe – one-tenth – of their agricultural output. Still it wasn't nearly enough. She would have liked an army five times the size.

Size wasn't the only problem with her forces. The army she did have kept fucking around and buggering off. Very few of them took anything seriously. It had been easy enough against the Dumnonians when she'd split the army into three, each with a clearly defined task, but they'd need much more advanced manoeuvrings against Rome's tactics and ferociously well-trained legionaries and, so far, she hadn't been able to make her men and women see the value of working in small groups. There was no honour, excitement or fun in learning how to move around the battlefield like interacting flocks of birds, only hard, boring work, which the average Briton did not have the stomach for. The one exception was her cavalry, her Two Hundred, but, in a way, their cohesion and skill just exacerbated the problem. People didn't see the point of acting like the Two Hundred if they didn't share the glory of being part of the Two Hundred. "Why should I dart around like a twatty Warrior when I'm just a bog-standard soldier?" she'd overheard someone say. She didn't sympathise and she wouldn't have been like that herself – she would have worked her tits off to prove she was better than anyone in the Two Hundred – but she could understand the point. It didn't help. She couldn't garrison the entire coast; she needed a superbly mobile army and for that she required dedication and discipline. Those two characteristics, it seemed, were impossible to teach.

The lack of dedication led to another problem: her soldiers kept deserting. Often the leavers were key people whom she'd thought she could rely on. No doubt they'd heard of trouble at home – flood, fire, bandits or something similar – and running to help was a reasonable response, but Lowa wished that they'd come to see her first so that she could have used her army to solve their problems. That would help them and, as a bonus, develop some camaraderie amongst the smaller army units she was attempting to form.

Hopefully the war game that she was going to try today would get people working together. Mal and Nita had learnt it on the Island of Angels, and it did sound like a good idea.

There was, potentially, a fourth problem, one that both Mal and Atlas warned her about often. Another possible arse-ache for Maidun Castle was the rest of Britain. Dumnonia still had a much bigger army and she'd humiliated them. To the north, possibly with a larger army still, were the Murkans. Lowa should be worrying more about these potential local enemies than the Romans, both men argued. She knew that they had a point, but she also knew that they were wrong. Rome was their enemy, Rome was the worry, and it was Rome that they had to focus on. She couldn't tell herself why, she just knew.

She buckled the final strap of her abdomen and chest armour, basically a fitted iron sheet that protected her from neck to privates. She wasn't convinced by it yet. Elann faced a balance between the armour being thin and light enough not to hamper movement, yet thick enough to deflect a thrust from Rome's sharpest, finest iron swords. This current model managed to block a sword, to a degree – Atlas, Carden and a few others could stab a sword through it, but most couldn't – but it was very heavy and hampered movement too much. Atlas was in favour of forgetting the heavy armour and teaching the soldiers to avoid or block sword blows instead and Lowa was coming round to his way of thinking.

She left her hut just as Spring walked through the gates of the complex that they shared on the Eyrie.

"Hello, Lowa!" she chirped. "What's up?"

"Hi. How was Dug?"

"He sends his regards."

"I thought he might come back for the war games. Did you ask him?"

"I did but he had something to build or something."

"Right. Well, you better get your kit together. Be quick and I'll wait for you."

"Sure thing!"

Spring ran to her hut. Already, Lowa noticed, her gait was more like an athletic adult's than a girl's. She was shooting up like a nettle and broadening out at the same time. Their running training was working well, and she was almost as good an archer as she was a runner. The idea of Spring's progress made her smile. There wasn't much else to smile about.

Chapter 9

There was a tap on the door. Ragnall got up from the uncomfortable bed and opened it, hoping it was Drustan. It wasn't. It was several large Romans. Ragnall opened his mouth to say something, but the foremost Roman shoved him in the chest two-handed, hard as a horse's kick. He felt his legs working in a backwards run to keep himself upright. He thumped into the wall, burst straight through the thin barrier and flew out into the Aventine Hill's fetid morning air in a shower of dried mud and splinters. The last thing he saw of the room was his attackers' surprised faces. You're surprised? he thought.

Time stopped. His mind zoomed six storeys down to the ground, then splayed out past Aventine's teetering immigrants' tower blocks, through glorious, stinking Rome, across the giant fields and labouring slave gangs of the denuded Italian countryside, across dark Gaul, all the way back to Britain and his home tribe of Boddingham. His thoughts bounced off Boddingham's broken ramparts and whooshed back, full of information on how far he had come, how much he had seen and more pertinent detail about the relatively short but still very much long enough distance from the top storey of a six-storey block of flats to the ground.

Drustan had talked about falling just a few days before, after they'd heard about people being thrown from the top of tower blocks by hoodlums. It wasn't the impact that would kill you, Drustan had mused, it was the bounce. The force of landing would break most of your bones, but that was fine, you could live with broken bones. When you bounced, however, your broken bones would slice through all your organs and that would kill you. So, Ragnall had suggested, the trick would be to grip on to the ground when you landed, so that you didn't bounce. Drustan had agreed, but pointed out that it would be tricky with ten broken fingers and toes.

But Ragnall didn't land on the road with a bone-smashing thump and organ-slicing bounce. He landed with a slapping splosh in the open cesspit shared by the surrounding tower blocks. He gasped, and sucked in a disgusting mouthful as the foul gloop closed slurpingly about his head and he was buried again.

His feet found solidity and he launched himself what he hoped was upwards, kicking like a madman and swimming his arms, grasping for air and life. He surfaced, sucked in sweet but horrible air and swam to the side. He crawled up and out of the pit's lip, choking as he went. On all fours, he vomited horrible vomit, then vomited some more. When there was nothing left, he leapt up and ran north to the River Tiber. He didn't think it through. He wasn't trying to escape his pursuers. He'd forgotten about them, and been overtaken by some deep, primeval urge to get the diseased shit of a thousand plebs out of his hair, clothes, mouth and every other orifice. Cleanliness, suddenly, was all. He ran through the streets with animal speed, leaving a wake of complaining, shit-flecked citizens.

A short time later, somewhat cleaner and more level headed, Ragnall arrived at the one place that might offer safety.

"Please tell Clodia Metelli that it's the British man with a Roman soul?" he said to the four door slaves. They did not look convinced. "That's all I ask," he continued. "If she doesn't want to see me, I'll go. But please do ask her. Surely she won't mind being asked? I've got nowhere else."

The slaves talked amongst themselves for an interminable

time and finally one went off to find Clodia. The rest stayed standing several paces away, hands on sword-hilts. It was fair enough, considering his toga was ripped from hem to nipple, and he stank. The Tiber had removed the lumpier muck, but its water hadn't been much sweeter than the cesspit's.

A good while later Clodia came to the door. To Ragnall's surprise, she didn't look surprised to see him.

"Come in," she said with a smile and no trace of her "street" accent. "You," she called to a hall slave. "Have him cleaned. Show him somewhere to rest then bring him to the blue salon an hour after sunset."

"Aren't you surprised to see me?" asked Ragnall.

"Should I be?"

"You saw me buried."

"It takes more than death to make a man spurn my invitation." She glided away, leaving a delicate floral-scented cloud that somehow penetrated Ragnall's reek.

He was taken to what he presumed to be a guest chamber, a room perhaps six times the size of the apartment that he and Drustan had rented. Four perfectly cut stone columns rose from an intricate blue, gold and white mosaic floor to a ceiling painted to resemble a bird-filled summer sky. Around the walls was a painting of a party at which topless women mingled with well-groomed farm animals. Despite the summer heat outside, a cooling breeze shivered the fine drapes in the doorways.

Bedroom slaves spread a sheet on the floor and undressed him on it, noses curling, then led him to an adjoining room where two washing slaves washed him, shaved him, cut his hair, perfumed him, then led him back into the chamber and the big, soft, clean bed. He climbed on to it and fell asleep immediately.

The first thing he saw on waking was a pretty young African girl sitting on a chair by his bed, watching him.

"I'm your waking slave," she said. "Tell me when you're ready and I'll take you to the blue salon. Will you need help with your ablutions?" He said that that would be nice. She clapped her hands and a new pair of washing slaves appeared.

The Metelli household's blue salon was longer, wider and higher that any longhouse Ragnall had seen in Britain. The floor was an epic mosaic of gladiators fighting a herd of lions and a handful of winged lizards that might or might not have been mythical. The walls were painted with scenes of mostly topless nymphs pursued by men sporting members the length, thickness and flexibility of conger eels. The crazy-donged men were representations of the Greek fertility god Priapus. Ragnall had seen a lot of him around Rome. The Romans had no qualms about adopting others' gods if it suited them. They didn't, as Drustan had said when they'd discussed it the other day, have qualms about many things.

Ragnall thought of his father's partially rotting, crudely decorated wooden longhouse, which had seemed so palatial as he was growing up. Looking at the astonishing opulence, he wondered if he had, in fact, died and come to the Otherworld. The candles lighting the room gave off no smoke, only a more intoxicating version of Clodia's floral perfume. There were tables of shiny fruit, a couple of sheaves of the most golden, perfectly proportioned corn, and black and orange vases taller than him, decorated with more naked men. These ones were racing or throwing discs and spears, rather than chasing women, and their private parts were dramatically under-sized. Ragnall suspected that the vase men had been averagely hung once, but had wilted under the disdainful gazes of the Priapuses on the walls.

He found Clodia at the far end of the room, reclining on a large bed of plump, plush cushions, with a jewelled goblet in one hand. Her hair was loose about her shoulders and she was wearing a short toga. Her legs looked wonderful.

Next to her, dressed in a red gown and sipping from a similar goblet, was either a beautiful woman or a very effeminate man – a man judging by the breadth of the shoulders – perhaps a little younger than Ragnall, with a mane of unnaturally blonde hair. He looked at Ragnall with narrow, drunk but predatory eyes.

Clodia nodded towards the young man. "Ragnall, meet Heracles; Heracles, this is Ragnall. Ragnall, have some wine."

She pointed at a nearby table, where a goblet sat waiting.

"Thank you. Do you know anything about Drustan?"

"Drustan?"

"Drustan Dantanner, the man I was buried with."

"They pulled his body out of the earth and burnt it. Crassus was arguing with Pompey about how long a human's body took to burn, when they remembered that they had two on hand. They had some digging slaves exhume your friend, but you'd disappeared. Everyone thought it was very odd, maybe even Gaulish magic – they all thought you were Gauls for some reason – but Caesar gave one of his knowing smiles, so we all knew it was one of his magician's tricks. Pompey lost the bet – he'd said the body would burn for three times as long as it did – but refused to pay. He flew into a rage. He said that you would have burnt for longer and somehow Caesar had known in advance that he and Crassus would be making the bet and that he'd arranged the whole thing to fox him. He left in a rage. There aren't many men as paranoid, solipsistic and downright stupid as Pompey. I was wrong to be worried about him uniting with Crassus and Caesar."

"He's dead?" Drustan couldn't be dead.

"Your friend? Yes. I saw his body, I saw them burn him. I should say he's dead. But I saw you buried and you're standing here, so who knows what's possible these days? I would not be surprised if Caesar's magician Felix was involved. Overly interested in the dead, that one."

"Felix is Caesar's magician?"

"Yes, the one I mentioned. He disappeared for a decade and has now returned. But I don't like to talk of such people when I'm at home. Please, do drink your wine."

Ragnall picked up the cup and downed it.

"Good!" She clapped her hands twice and called: "More wine!"

Ragnall had no idea how long he spent living with Clodia Metelli. He never left the house. There was no need. Its interior and courtyards ranged wider than a medium-sized hillfort. Even minor rooms – all the guest bathrooms, for example – were roomier that a king's hut. Each room had a team of slaves, who treated Ragnall as if he were their master. He never saw Metellus Celer, their real master. Clodia managed to keep him apart from all her live-in guests.

The talk from outside was mostly about the annual election for the following year's two consuls. Apparently Julius Caesar was certain to win, although Cato, the man who'd warned Ragnall off Clodia, was desperately trying to undermine him. At some point, Caesar, to nobody's surprise, won. He was to share the consulship with a man called Bibulus, however. Bibulus was Cato's son-in-law and reputedly his patsy. Everyone said that the next year would be a tumultuous one.

The news that Felix, Zadar's druid who'd killed Anwen, was also Caesar's magician, disturbed Ragnall greatly, but he couldn't find anybody who wanted to talk about it. In the end he gave up worrying, because he was too busy having a good time. At last, he was spending whole days doing whatever he wanted to do. He had had enough of people directing his every move. His parents, the druids on the Island of Angels, Lowa and even Drustan all saw him as someone to order about. He was sad that Drustan had been killed, of course, but this freedom he had found was wonderful, and Clodia's house was the most marvellous place in the world. He was so much happier here than he'd been anywhere, so how could it be wrong?

He drank, smoked and ate substances that helped to settle, develop and excite his mind. The house was full of people like him, young, attractive, intelligent men and women, from all over the world. Pleasure quickly overtook his hesitant innocence, and soon he was delighting in a wide range of drug and drink-fuelled sexual escapades. To begin with it was only Clodia, when she was always there, then he started hooking up with the others while she was out of the house. He became briefly obsessed with a slender Macedonian girl who had eyes like mountain pools whom Clodia had named Pydna, which Clodia found amusing for some reason. He became a little bored with her skinny frame, and a brawny German woman called Millinga with thighs like a horse's became his favourite. He surprised himself one day when Heracles beckoned him into a bedchamber and he followed. For the next moon, he didn't want to be with anyone but Heracles, although he still did his duty with Clodia, and many others during the regular orgies.

As much as the sex, he relished the conversations; hours on end spent talking to people his own age. Most were from very differing cultures, but they all had similar ideas about how the world would be better in their peaceful, free-loving hands. Ragnall developed several plans about how he'd take these ideas back to Britain, stop the wars and start a wonderful way of living for all.

But for now he was going to rest. He'd had a shitty time. He deserved a break from Britain's mud, blood and endless striving.

He knew that his parents and teachers would have disagreed with the morality of what he was doing. They would, in fact, have been disgusted. But see where their rules had got them! The same people who would have been horrified by Clodia's orgies were the ones who went to war and killed people. Which was worse? Lowa had convinced him he was a rapist even though she knew he wasn't, and she'd made out like it was the worst thing in the world, but she'd killed his family and lied about it, and she'd killed hundreds of other innocent people. That had to be worse. And they'd made her queen! Ragnall was going to change things when he got back. Rome was immeasurably better than Britain, and Britain could learn much from it. He'd bring Rome to Britain.

It was yet another lovely morning and he was relaxing on a big bed with a few others, when a messenger slave came looking for him. Clodia wanted to see him, alone. He smiled.

He arrived at the blue salon, and was surprised to see that there were several other men there, serious types with armour and swords. All men and Clodia was not his type of orgy, but these did not look like orgy types anyway. Then he recognised Caesar and, next to him, Felix. The swelling pool of happiness that had been growing inside him flowed from his every pore like water from a sieve.

Clodia was standing with them. She looked at him, huge eyes as sad as a cow's, shaking her head in apology.

He turned to run, but two guards were already blocking the door.

"Kill the Gaulish spy!" said Felix.

"Not in my house," said Clodia.

"It's not your house," sneered Felix, "it's Metellus Celer's house and you are an embarrassment, a Copper Coin—"

"That's enough, Felix," said Caesar. "What is your name, Gaul? What are you doing in Rome? What are your plans? Are there others?" As he had at his party, he sounded interested rather than belligerent.

"My name is Ragnall. I am British. I mean you no har—"
He stopped, realising that he was speaking British again, not

Latin. Felix winked at him. "I am . . ." he tried again, still British.

Clodia stamped a foot. "What sorcery is this, Caesar? This man is not Gaulish, he's British, and he speaks perfect Latin. What is your witch doing to him? I will not have it in my house."

Caesar raised an eyebrow at Felix, then turned to Clodia. "From Britain, you say?"

"This man is dangerous. He will bring you down. He must be killed, now." Felix spoke in a rush.

Caesar peered into Ragnall's eyes. It was hard to hold his gaze. It was as if the general, politician or whatever Caesar was could read his thoughts and see his memories. He thought of a few recent ones and blushed.

"No," said Caesar. "Clodia, may I buy your slave?"

"Yes," she answered with a sigh. Ragnall guessed that a request from Caesar wasn't really a request. "On the condition that you don't kill him."

"Thank you, Clodia. I have no intention of harming him, unless he causes me to. He is going to tell me about Britain. If he proves useful and interesting, he will lead me there."

Part Three

Britain, Gaul and Eroo

Chapter 1

Bruxon pulled the fur tighter about his neck and pressed his chin into his chest. By Toutatis, he thought, it was never this cold in Dumnonia. The snow was coming horizontally now, upwards even. In Dumnonia, snow had the decency to fall from the sky. On the godless island of Eroo it seemed to come out of the very earth. The journey northwest across the sea from Dumnonia was hardly a long one, but Eroo was a different world. Since they'd landed the snow had let up for about ten heartbeats, but only to become a freezing, soaking rain in the interim. They called Eroo the Green Island, but so far Bruxon had only seen black, white and grey.

The sled bumped down into a roadside ditch and lurched out again. Bruxon grabbed the edge.

"Careful, man!" he cried.

"You've got a careful man. Careful dogs is what you want," replied Maggot. "Man can ask the questions, but the dogs answer how they will."

Yet another annoying, don't-I-see-the-world-in-a-deeper-way comment from the druid. No surprise there. Maggot was full of sayings and advice, but Bruxon saw him for what he really was – a snob who thought he was wiser and better than everyone else. He dressed up his arrogance in woo-woo mysticism and a pretence that he cared for everyone, but Bruxon knew he was a conceited, self-interested charlatan.

Annoyingly, despite being a smarmy egotist with the dress sense of a teenage show-off, Maggot was an undeniably capable man, not just as a healer, but as an organiser, motivator and negotiator. That was why Bruxon had installed Mearhold's former druid as Dumnonia's new chief druid to replace the one that Samalur had killed, and insisted that he come on this mission to Eroo.

He'd already proved invaluable. When they'd landed on Eroo's craggy shore it was Maggot who'd persuaded the murderous locals to spare their lives. When they'd put their clubs and slings away, Maggot had spoken privately to them at some length. The snarling savages had become genial hosts who'd fed them well, plied them with mugs of their strange alcohol while drinking more of it themselves, then shown them their absurd all-legs-and-no-arms dancing. If Maggot had landed on his shore unannounced and full of patronising platitudes, Bruxon would have gouged his eyes out and sent him back to sea in a burning boat.

The hairy coast-dwellers had even lent them dogs and a sled, although they had insisted on keeping the rest of the delegation hostage as security on their loan. That wasn't a problem, since Bruxon didn't need anyone but Maggot for the embassy inland. If he were to fall ill or be injured, the druid would know what to do. If they met bandits, chances were Maggot would make friends with them, and Bruxon didn't know anyone else who'd be able to drive a dog sled competently though a blizzard without losing their way.

He glanced across at the druid. Infuriatingly, Maggot seemed impervious to cold. He was dressed only in tartan trousers, a tatty waistcoat and a ridiculous amount of jewellery. His eyes were half closed and the look of intense concentration on his face was clearly designed to suggest that he was directing the six Eroo wolfhounds with his mind. Bruxon shook his head. Infuriating.

The sled's skis creaked as the hounds strained up a hill. Up ahead the snow flurries parted for a moment, and Bruxon saw the craggy bulk of Manfrax's fort looming high on the cliff top. He shuddered. The mission to Eroo and his proposal for Manfrax had seemed like a magnificent idea when he'd planned it, but now he was regretting his decision. He tried to remember what had sparked the scheme, but couldn't. That was odd, given that he prided himself on his ordered mind. He put it down to the cold.

The road veered away from the cliff and along a flat river valley. "You think you're nearly there and the road swings away," said Maggot, presumably impyling some tiresome philosophical point. Bruxon ignored him.

The snow had let up a little, perhaps due to the lee of the cliff, so Bruxon pulled back his fur hood. The six horse-sized draft dogs shook their shaggy grey coats and picked up the pace.

Snow-blanketed, large wooden structures lined both sides of the road. They weren't huts and they were too big to be carts, although some of them had wheels. Could they be some kind of art, Bruxon wondered? Maggot would know, but he didn't want to ask him.

"War machines," said Maggot. "These fellows on your left are catapults."

"Why are they so big?" Bruxon asked, stifling the unwelcome idea that the druid might be able to read his mind.

"They must have some very big cats to pult," Maggot grinned at him. "These smaller ones on your right are giant bows. You could kebab five horses on each of their arrows. See those towers up ahead?"

Bruxon could see them.

"They roll those right up to your town walls, and over come Manfrax and his horde like ants into a dead fox's hole."

"There are so many . . ."

"Manfrax hasn't conquered all of Eroo with his charm now, has he?"

Bruxon looked at the hundreds of war machines and a

coldness that was nothing to do with the weather crept into his mind. "Maggot, stop the dogs." Maggot pulled the reins, the dogs slowed and the sled slid to a halt.

"Maggot, am I about to make a mistake?" he asked.

"By doing what?"

"By asking Manfrax to bring his army to Britain. What else could I mean?"

"I thought you might be wondering whether to kiss me."

"Maggot!" The man was intolerable.

"OK, let's look at your trouble," Maggot smiled. "Your shit king was beaten in a battle. You became king, but you immediately told Lowa that your army was hers to command, thereby making Dumnonia a vassal to Maidun and a slave to Lowa's whims. You hate this. You've got used to being a king now, so you want to fly like an eagle, spear mice with your beak and crap on the world from lonely but magnificent heights. To achieve that, you have to crush Maidun and destroy Lowa."

Bruxon nodded. Maggot might be a fool, but he wasn't stupid.

"Now, a day's sailing across the sea in Eroo, we have Manfrax, a nasty bastard who makes Zadar look like a puppy. He's conquered everyone there is to conquer on his island, and is looking for other tribes to slaughter. So you ask him across the sea, you feed his army, point it in the direction of Lowa and let go. He smashes her army and takes her land. Your one condition for helping him is that he leaves you alone. Sounds like a good plan."

"It sounds like a reasonable plan. But what—"

"If he attacks you? If he goes back on his word? You forget that the Romans, the only people who could beat Manfrax, are on their way. They'll kick Manfrax back to Eroo. Then they'll look about for someone strong to be client ruler of all of Britain, and who's their only choice? Hello, Bruxon, head of the mighty and intact Dumnonian army."

"And the Murkans?"

"We talk to them when we get back. Explain what's going to happen and how it's all roses for them. They join in. And if they don't like it? Then you point Manfrax at them, too. They smash the crap out of each other. Rome comes over and mops up. Same result. Dumnonia rules."

"So you are certain that we shouldn't turn back?"

"No," smiled Maggot. "Two reasons. One, right now, Dumnonians are the slaves of a smaller tribe. You can't allow that to continue."

"And the second reason?"

"Them." Maggot pointed up the road.

Emerging from the snow ahead of them were six horsemen, huge in their furs, faces invisible in dark hoods. Sticking out above each, silhouetted against the snow, were the unmistakable shapes of double-headed war axes.

Manfrax's longhouse was in fact a large cave, carved out by man or nature, or perhaps a mixture of the two, beneath his fort. To Bruxon, it looked like an Otherworld imagined by ignorant Warrior types who thought there was something noble about swilling back far too much beer, eating messily, shouting repetitive banalities at each other and playing games that often involved drinking each other's urine.

The rowdy crowd quickly quietened when Bruxon and Maggot walked in, followed by their escorts or captors. Bruxon was not sure which, since they had remained rudely silent on the way up from the valley.

Smokey, log-thick torches protruding from sconces all along the cavern's walls lit up two tables which ran the length of either side of the cave. From benches alongside each table, perhaps two hundred shaggy-haired, dirty fur-clad men and women stared at Bruxon and Maggot with aggressive insolence. The air was thick with the eye-watering stink of body odour, vomit and dog excrement.

Hate-filled eyes followed them as they walked to the end of the hall, picking their way through an obstacle course of dropped bones and sleeping Eroo wolfhounds. The dogshit was impossible to avoid. Its mephitic underfoot squelch made Bruxon nauseous, partly because he guessed that it wasn't just dogs' dung. The only sounds, other than their excrement-muffled steps, were the crackle of the torches, the odd whine from a hound and the clacking of Maggot's jewellery.

At the end of the hall, perched on a vast leather cushion, was Manfrax. He was a big man, unsurprisingly, since combat was how one became king in Eroo, and Manfrax was king of all the kings. He did, however, look unexpectedly refined. His eyes were clear, and his hair and beard cut short and neat. Bruxon guessed that he was about thirty, around five years younger than Bruxon himself.

Next to him on his cushion was a woman who must have been his queen, Reena. Her long black hair was tied back to reveal a face with skin so pale that Bruxon thought he could see the bone beneath it. Her thin lips were twisted in sourness and her thin, bumpy nose was topped with eyes so close together that she was practically a Cyclops. She was no beauty.

Either side of the cushion, chained, dirty and naked, were skinny young men and women. They glanced at the newcomers with terror-filled eyes. They all had wounds of some kind, some of which were fresh enough that they oozed glistening blood.

"King Manfrax," began Bruxon.

Manfrax held up a finger, bidding silence. With the other hand, he flicked a small dagger at one of the chained prisoners. It stuck in the man's shoulder. The man reached for the knife. He pulled it out without making a sound, and tossed it on to a pile of daggers in front of Manfrax's cushion. The drinkers gave a single, shouting cheer and were quiet again.

"You see," said Manfrax, in the sing-song accent of Eroo, "he knows what'll happen to him if he makes a peep. Those are all his friends who didn't manage to stay so quiet." The king gestured with his head to a large heap of gore beside the platform. The mound shone black and red in the torchlight, its slimy surface punctuated by the odd recognisably human protuberance – a foot here, a hand there, and a young man's face with open, staring eyes. "Now, what can I do you for you two?" Manfrax continued, sounding like a happy baker greeting the first customer of the day.

Bruxon told him about Lowa's victory over Samalur, and explained what he wanted Manfrax to do.

The king of Eroo listened politely, then said: "And what's to stop me killing you both slowly and invading Britain without your help?"

"There's nothing to stop you," said Bruxon. He'd expected this posturing. "If you kill us, you can still invade, but as well as Lowa's forces and her powerful druid, you'll be facing a hundred thousand-strong Dumnonian army, all in a strange land with no supplies. If you don't kill us, we will show you safe harbours. We will feed and shelter your troops and you will have to fight only the Maidun army."

"That doesn't sound too bad," said Manfrax, "but are you not worried that when I'm done with Lowa I'll turn and bite the hand that fed me?"

"That is a concern, but I think you are a man of your word and—"

He was cut off by a roar of laughter from Manfrax, which spread through the whole hall and lasted a good deal longer than Bruxon felt was necessary. When it finally petered out, he wasn't sure what to say next. Maggot spoke up instead: "We were thinking, that to guarantee Dumnonia's help on t'other side of the sea, that we might do one of your blood shakes?"

Manfrax, for the first time, looked impressed. "What do

you know about our blood shakes, you strange looking wee man?"

"It's an ancient Eroo tradition. Some might say that a people with such a disgusting, cruel tradition must be the most evil creatures that ever crawled from the belly of the earth and that they deserved to be wiped out like a plague of shit-covered rats in a grain store." Bruxon couldn't believe Maggot was talking to Manfrax like this, but the king of Eroo smiled through it as if he was hearing something else. "Me though, I reckon, it's useful, because it cannot be broken, even by a king. If you do break the blood-shake's oath, your own men and women would be obliged to kill you with the long-loved, time-honoured tradition of ramming a red-hot sword up your arse."

"You are more than you look," said Manfrax to Maggot.

"Yeah, and I look amazing." Maggot danced a quick Eroo legs-only jig, his jewellery and adornments clacking and jingling. He finished by spreading his arms wide. Manfrax let out a massive laugh, which was again taken up by the hall. Bruxon felt a little redundant.

"All right, all right, a blood shake it will be. I'll have . . . you." Manfrax pointed at one of his chained slaves. The skinny man's eyes flew wide. He fell to his knees, arched back and then slammed forward, smashing his head on the stone floor. A puddle spread, shining blackly in the torch-light. He quivered, then lay still.

"Oh, for Bel's sake, what a weed. It's not that bad," said Manfrax.

"It is that bad," Maggot whispered to Bruxon.

"Grab her!" Manfrax shouted to one of the hooded men who'd escorted them from the valley, pointing at one of the woozier captives.

The man gripped the skinny, naked girl by the arms and shuffled her over to Manfrax.

"Right, Bruxon. Get yourself up here, man, and we'll get

this blood shake shook. Then you just need to suck my nipple and we'll be done."

Bruxon turned to Maggot, his mouth falling open.

"Did I not mention the nipple-sucking?" whispered the druid with a grin. "It's an ancient Eroo custom, older than the blood shake. Quite unavoidable, I'm afraid."

"And the blood shake?"

"It'll be the nastiest thing you ever do. But it is binding."

"Come over here, my guest king, I'll show you the blood shake. Couldn't be simpler. Get yourself a knife off the pile there, yes that's it, one of the fatter, pointy ones. Now I'll hold the front of her neck, you hold the back. When I nod, stab her in the lower middle back, off to the side a little. Wiggle your knife about a bit, then put your hand in. Avoid her spine and you'll find my hand in there. Take a firm, firm grip, then we shake hands, hard as we can, until she'd dead. Got it?"

Bruxon almost gibbered, but he managed to control himself and simply nodded. He was glad the girl was facing away from him.

Chapter 2

Lowa spotted the messenger when she was still a good way off along the valley. By the way she sat on her horse as stiffly as a haughty virgin princess passing a tavern late on a summer feast day, it was Adler, one of her staff from Maidun. Adler must have ridden several hours to find her a good thirty miles east of Maidun Castle, so something interesting must have happened. Lowa shuddered with excitement at the idea that the Romans had landed. But they probably hadn't, if three years' experience was anything to go by. Much more likely, somebody had overreacted to some trifling event or was covering their arse or had just wanted to show off that they were able to send a messenger to the queen.

"Excuse me," she said to the knot of tribal leaders and farmers, and walked off to meet the rider. She was happy to leave their agrarian discussion. She'd managed to squeeze more tribute from the south-eastern farming tribes with flattery, generosity and gentle menace, and now her standing army numbered thirty thousand men and women, but, by Danu's tits, the careful negotiation was boring. There were days that she was seriously tempted to return to Zadar's more direct murder-and-enslavement methods of tax collection. That she didn't do so, that in fact she was doing her best to ensure everyone under her rule had the food, shelter and warmth that they needed, gave her a bit of a kick. She hoped it also went some way towards making up for the misery that she'd caused on Zadar's orders.

She walked along the track, high up on the valley side,

looking down over the fertile fields that fed her army. She wore leather iron-heeled riding boots, as always these days, with a pale cotton skirt and a light leather jerkin. She'd taken off her tartan woollen poncho and left it draped over her horse, since the day was unseasonably warm. Her bow and quiver were on her back, and one of Elann Nancarrow's finest thin swords scabbarded on her waist. Since she'd been beaten twice by Chamanca in mêlée fights, she'd taken to training with the sword most days, and now she was at least a match for the strongest and most skilled men, like Atlas and Carden. Annoyingly, Chamanca still whipped her every time with her unnatural speed.

Adler swung off the horse and stood, all sinews taut, a muscle twitching on her handsome face, as if awaiting inspection. A bit too formal this one, perhaps, but she'd lose that with age.

"What's up?" asked Lowa.

"The Romans have burst from their territory, massacred tens of thousands of Helvans and are moving north through Gaul."

So, thought Lowa, here they come. Finally.

"Have Ragnall and Drustan returned?"

"No. The news comes from the Helvans themselves. They've sent messengers, I presume in all directions."

Lowa nodded. It was more than two years since Ragnall and Drustan had left for Rome. She heard nothing from them since and suspected that they were dead.

"Any other details?"

"Sure." Adler nodded. "The Helvans have long planned a migration from their lands in the Alps to western Gaul. The Helvan king Ogotor had arranged it all with the Gaulish tribes. They were to have safe passage to a new territory on Gaul's west coast. A moon or so ago, a huge number of them – half a million, the messenger claims – set off, burning their towns behind them to prove their resolve."

"Yup." Lowa knew all this from merchants. "What went wrong?"

"One of the Roman consuls of last year, Gaius Julius Caesar, has command of the Roman province in southern Gaul. He also has north Italy – or toga-wearing Gaul as they call it – and Illyricum, but it's from southern Gaul that he's marched. He raised a large army, moved north out of Roman territory, and blocked the Helvans' passage. They asked him to move. He told them he'd think about it for three days. In those three days he cleared the farms and forest for miles around, and built a wall across the Helvan route. The wall is the height of three tall men, stretching further than the eye can see in both directions. The Helvans say that mere people couldn't have made such a wall so quickly and are convinced it was built by the gods, monsters or witchcraft. Some of the Helvans approached the wall, asking for passage, but the Romans have hired the best archers and slingers from Crete, Numidia and the Iberian islands. They cut the Helvans down in their hundreds. When their families tried to collect the bodies, the mercenaries shot them too."

"I see." The lovely spring day seemed colder.

"It gets worse. The Helvans tried to divert around the Roman wall. They headed north, then swung west to cross the Suconna River. They're disorganised, so their marching order is fastest first, slowest last and they became more strung out the further they went. Three-quarters or so had crossed the Suconna River, but still tens of thousands of elderly, infirm, families with children, farmers with herds and so on were trailing on the eastern side of the river. The Romans attacked this slower group at night and killed them. All of them. The messenger said that the Helvan dead were countless."

"They killed the children?"

"Everyone."

Lowa nodded. So it had begun. She'd been right to believe

Spring and prepare an army. The Romans would murder their way through Gaul, cross the Channel and attempt to take Britain. Anyone who didn't capitulate would be enslaved or killed. That would be their intention, anyway, but they hadn't factored Lowa and the Maidun army into their plans.

If they were in southern Gaul at the beginning of the year, it was unlikely that they'd be in Britain until the following year at the earliest, but that was still far too soon. There was too much to be done. But she'd been right. Still there were people who said that she should worry about internal foes – the Murkans and the Dumnonians, there were even rumours of a vast army that had taken all of Eroo and was looking for new land to conquer – but she'd been right: the only significant enemy were the Romans. Anybody else they could deal with afterwards.

"Thanks, Adler," she said. "Ride hard back to Maidun. Find Elann Nancarrow, Carden Nancarrow, Atlas Agrippa and Chamanca the Iberian and tell them to meet me at my hut at sunset."

Chapter 3

Chamanca and Atlas watched from the branch of an oak tree as Roman helmets bounced along below. Atlas, crouched on the broad bough in front of the Iberian, was in dark clothes, his skin was dark and he'd muddied the blades of his axe, so that Chamanca could hardly see him from half a pace away. Carden was well hidden in a ditch at the base of their tree. Provided none of them did anything stupid, like sneeze, the passing Romans would never see them. Which, thought Chamanca, was something of a shame. She needed a fight. The wet voyage and the long ride to the south of Gaul had been boringly blood free. What's more, Roman blood had been the first she'd ever tasted as a child in Iberia, and she was looking forward to trying it again it with warm nostalgia. It was her favourite, although that was possibly less to do with its flavour and more because the Romans had killed so many of her friends and family and taken her land. Also, she was aching to see how the beautiful little sword that Elann had given her combined in combat with her dainty but deadly ball-mace. She suppressed an urge to kick Atlas off his perch into the stream of quick-marching soldiers below and get the blood flowing.

The soldiers had been passing for some while now at a jog, silent in tight-arsed, dreary discipline. Their pace was irregular, but that wasn't, she knew, down to slackness. Their strides were deliberately uneven to prevent the sound of their beating feet travelling to the Helvan camp a couple of miles away. The Romans were boringly good at soldiering.

The Helvans, on the other hand, were fools. Their king of kings, Ogotor, had died, or been killed more likely, shortly before their migration across Gaul had begun and they were now led – if you could call it being led – by a gaggle of squabbling tribal leaders. That was why they'd given the Romans time to build the wall that had checked their exodus in the first place, it was why the Romans had slain a quarter of their number without the rest of them even knowing it was happening, and why they were now gathered in a sprawling camp and, although a vicious army was nearby and keen to kill them all, they had no patrols in the outlying countryside. Lowa would have posted a network of shouters like a spider's web for at least twenty miles around, but, even though Chamanca and Atlas had suggested it to every leader they could find, they hadn't even put watchmen on the fringes of the camp. Atlas said that none of them wanted to lose face in front of the others by seeming to be afraid of the Romans. Idiots. They were going to lose a lot more than their faces.

It was with pure luck, and some intelligence, that she, Atlas and Carden had found the marching Romans. The Helvans knew from a captured patrol that the Roman army was short of food, although none of them seemed to have worked out that this meant the Romans would launch an attack before they had to retreat south to their grain supplies, because it would be better to beat the Helvans quickly and take their food instead. Atlas had said that if they were to try anything that night, then the best thing would be to split their forces and come at the Helvans from two sides at dawn the next day. The main Roman army would lure the Helvans away from their camp, then a subsidiary force would sweep down, probably from the unpopulated, wooded hill behind the Helvan camp, and kill the young, old and sick who were left in the camp, and capture their stores. It was an evil, shitty, utterly dishonourable plan and exactly what

Chamanca would have done had she been in command of the Romans.

The final soldiers passed below and, very quickly, all was silent. She was glad. Her leather shorts and her narrow iron chest guard had been warm enough when they were moving around, but she had become cold sitting immobile in the tree.

"Was that all the Romans? What shall we do?" asked Carden, climbing out of the ditch with his stupidly long iron sword in one hand, looking about himself like a bear coming out of hibernation.

Chamanca, Lowa and Elann had tried to persuade Carden to replace his sword with one of Elann's excellent little blades, and to get Atlas to leave his axe behind and do the same. They were going to be doing a lot more travelling, sneaking and hiding than open-field fighting and their weighty weapons would be an encumbrance. Both men had refused. She understood. She would never have given up her usual tools, her ball-mace and her teeth, and it was easy for her, even useful, to add the little blade that Elann was so proud of. For the men with their two-handed weapons, it would have been pointless.

"It was two legions?" she asked Atlas.

"I counted two eagle standards and around eight thousand men," replied the Kushite, "so, yes, two legions. You also saw, I'm sure, that they were carrying only weapons and small rations. It's as we suspected. That was the force that will sweep into the back of the Helvan position tomorrow after their army is drawn out by the rest of the Romans."

"What's our plan?" Chamanca asked.

"Surely we check that the Romans have gone where you said they would, then tell the Helvans?" said Carden. "If it's only eight thousand Romans on the hill, the Helvans could march a convincingly big army out to the main Roman force, and leave forty thousand or so behind to surprise the surprisers."

"That would work," sighed Chamanca, "if the Helvans had any sort of command structure. As it is, if we tell them that there's a force of Romans hiding on that hill, they'll run up there in drabs and drips trying to prove how much braver they are than the others and they'll be killed. Then, when the main Roman army attacks, the Helvans will get excited, forget about the Roman pincer plan, and all turn to attack the new big shiny army with its waving banners. The forgotten force on the hill will sweep down and kill everybody from behind. So, if we tell them, the only effect will be to weaken the Helvans and put them in even more disarray before the Romans launch at them."

"Surely they're not that stupid?" said Carden.

"Have you seen children playing football?" asked Chamanca. "They all run around following the ball, all together in a big group. They all want to be right in on the action and have no patience or concept of strategic positioning. The Helvan army is like that. Basically, a bunch of fucking idiots."

"Indeed," said Atlas. "We need to prevent the Roman attack from taking place at all, and chivvy the Helvans along to their new territory. Once our Helvan friends are happily ensconced in a sensible network of hillforts, the Romans will find them a tougher target and their march to Britain might take long enough for Lowa to assemble an adequate defence."

"Oh," said Carden, "sorry, I should have realised that it's up to us to stop several thousand Romans. Silly me. Do you want to jog down to the Roman camp and tell Caesar not to attack or will I? Atlas, really, our best plan—"

"Shush, Carden, for Fenn's sake," snapped Chamanca, "let us think."

They stood in the night. The nocturnal animals, scared into silence by the passing Romans, returned to their chupping and chirruping and were soon making so much noise that it was almost too late when they heard the sound of sandalled feet running towards them.

"You two, hide now." Atlas sprinted down the road, away from the approaching footsteps. They were coming from the direction in which the Romans had gone. Chamanca and Carden jumped into the roadside ditch. Poking her head up carefully, Chamanca saw Atlas stop forty paces away, take his axe from his back and stand, legs spread, weapon ready. She ducked as the Romans swished by.

"Contubernium, halt! Three-line square!" The footsteps scuffed to a halt. Chamanca hadn't heard Latin spoken since she'd left Iberia. It was such a flat language, no song to it. By Makka, she wanted to kill a Roman.

There were nine of them, stopped on the road just up from her and Carden's hiding place. Iron helmets shone dully on eight of them. The leader wore a ridiculous black plume sprouting from a well-polished bronze helm. All sported metal-reinforced leather armour, a skirt made of thick leather flanges, bare legs, metal greaves and leather sandals with criss-cross straps. They were armed with medium-length broad swords. A nasty weapon, Chamanca remembered, used mostly for the gut-stab, to slice into the soft vitals, leaving the recipient screaming in incapable agony and dying slowly.

Almost before their commander's order was out, the Romans had sorted into a three-man-sided grid of nine, with enough space in between each to use their swords unhindered. Their elaborately helmeted leader took the centre spot. Not the bravest of men, then.

"Watch for ambush!" came the order, but it was unnecessary. Already the Romans were peering into the bushes and up and down the road. Atlas' plan had probably been for Chamanca and Carden to attack from behind while he distracted them. He'd underestimated their training. They'd have a procedure for exactly the situation they were in, perfected over centuries and drilled into them again and again on the parade ground. With the vagaries of individual decision-making removed, their response to the lone man in the road had been automatic, unified and perfect.

She'd seen people underestimate the Romans before. They were all dead now. Not that the Romans were invulnerable, far from it, but they took a bit more killing than the average fool. Chamanca's hands tightened around the handles of her sword and her mace. She made an effort to breathe calmly and slowly. There was going to be blood.

"Cut him down," came the calm order from the Roman leader.

Atlas roared like a charging aurochs. She and Carden leapt from the ditch. The back line of Romans hadn't been distracted by Atlas' shout. They spotted the new threat immediately and readied themselves.

"Two more sir, to the rea—" the leftmost of them managed before Chamanca's ball-mace smashed his jaw. Trained they might be, but they weren't ready for her speed.

"Down!" shouted Carden.

She dropped into a crouch, chopping her blade through the leg of the central Roman. Her attack was unnecessary, since Carden's swinging sword severed the heads from both remaining backmarkers. She was glad, however, to see how easily her new blade cleaved flesh and bone.

She dived backwards, avoiding the arterial spurt from the man's thigh, on to her hands. She flicked over, spun, and landed on her feet to face the Romans. All this gymnastic leaping was unnecessarily flamboyant, but she meant to surprise the remaining Romans into surrender. It worked.

Atlas had killed the three at the front. Two junior soldiers and their boss were staring at her like head-whacked fish. Atlas' axe flashed from behind them and split the leftmost soldier from neck to waist. A great wash of blood drenched the other two. Their swords dropped with thuds on to the hard-packed road and they whimpered. There was always a point at which people forgot their training.

"That one," said Atlas to Carden, nodding at the legionary. Carden lifted his sword.

"No! Please! Not him! Not him! Don't kill him! I'll do anything! Take me!" The leader was screeching in passable Gaulish, which was close enough to the British language that they understood him. He was a large man, but fat, not muscular. His voice was high-pitched and lispy, but that could have been from his terror. Chamanca smiled.

Carden took a step forward but Atlas held up a hand. Carden stood back. "Chamanca," Atlas said. "Why don't you have a drink?" Chamanca could have kissed him. He'd seen what she too had seen. There was something stronger than the chain of command between the captain and the soldier. Atlas grabbed the captain by the chest and pulled him away, axe blade at his throat.

Chamanca lashed out at the soldier with her blade and then her mace. The blade sliced through the leather chin-strap, the mace knocked his helmet flying. He stood, blinking at her in shock, tears pouring from big eyes. He was young, a boy really, with a pale, girlish face.

"Kneel!" she commanded.

He knelt. She walked round behind him, pinned his arms with her legs, grabbed his hair in her hands. He fell forwards. She went with him, twisted his head, and sank pointed teeth into his neck. Warm Roman blood flowed into her mouth. She swallowed. The taste was better than she remembered. She unclamped her teeth with a lovely sucking noise, looked up at the plume-headed man and smiled.

"Oh Diana," he said, "please stop. Please don't hurt him any more."

"Who are you, where were you going and why?" asked Atlas, his Latin fluent and without an accent.

"I'm Publius Considius. Tribune Publius Considius. I'm going to Caesar to report that Titus Labienus has taken the hill and is ready. There, that's all. Let him go!"

Atlas nodded at Chamanca. She bent down again and took a long suck of blood from the young man's neck. She hadn't pierced anything vital yet, but there was still plenty to drink.

"I've told you everything!" whined Considius.

"What is Labienus ready for?"

"He's to wait for Caesar's attack. Once the Helvetians are committed, he's to take the camp."

Chamanca almost asked what Helvetians were, but realised that it must be the Roman word for Helvans. They'd made up Romanised versions of perfectly good tribe names in her homeland too. It had pissed her off.

"Take the camp?" Atlas twisted his axe blade into the man's neck.

"All right! His orders are to kill everyone and everything, take all the supplies and burn anything that can't be plundered. Now I've told you everything. Please let him go."

Atlas released his hold on Considius, who held out a hand and backed away, staring with horror at Chamanca. She winked at him.

"We'll let your friend go," said Atlas, "tomorrow evening, after there have been no Roman attacks."

"But there will be!"

"There will not be. You will tell Caesar the Helvetians have guessed his plan. They ocuply the hill themselves, they have Labienus pinned down, and have set ambushes for any force that tries to rescue him. Luckily, Labienus had found a safe position. He can easily hold out until the Helvetians move on, but pleads with Caesar to hold. Tell him that Labienus said: "Certain death awaits the force that attempts to relieve us. Hold, we will reunite, and we will win this war on another day.""

Chamanca was pleased. That did sound like the sort of bullshit spouted by vainglorious Roman commanders.

"He won't believe me!"

"He will. You look like you've only just made it through

an ambush. And if he doesn't believe you, we'll kill this one. Slowly. Now go."

Considius looked one last time at his friend, then turned and ran.

"Chamanca, he's yours," said Atlas.

"Oh, come on Atlas," said Carden, "we said we'd let him go."

Atlas took a deep breath, then spoke quietly. "The Romans have murdered thousands of Helvans. Their plan tomorrow will be to kill, among others, all of the Helvan children. If this man escapes us somehow, that is certain to happen. We have no choice but to kill him. Chamanca?"

"Hold his legs, please," she said. Atlas did so. Carden stood back. The legionary bucked, squirmed and sent his heart pumping furiously, which suited Chamanca just fine.

Chapter 4

Chamanca could not stop yawning as they approached the Helvan camp in the first light. It was a long time since any of them had had more than a short nap. Carden was in the same state, but Atlas looked bright-eyed and alert as always.

It wasn't so much a camp as more people than she'd thought were in the whole world spread out across the wide, denuded plain. There had still been a few clusters of trees when they'd first found the Helvan camp, but these had been cut down overnight. The cook fires were so numerous that it looked as if the land had sucked down all the stars. Thousands of tiny smoke tendrils merged into a large, low cloud, pink in the sun's first rays. Atlas started talking about the need to leave some trees standing and generally manage the consumption of resources and Chamanca yawned all the more.

The wooded hill which hid Labienus' two legions of merciless killers rose out of the plain to the north like a formori's head out of a lake. There was no sign of the occupation. The Romans, Bel curse them, were far too disciplined to light cook fires or make any other giveaway signs.

Atlas was certain that the hidden soldiers wouldn't attack unless Caesar's force did, and that Caesar's attack wouldn't happen if Considius had done what he was told, and if Caesar had believed him. Carden, showing surprising insight, had said that Considius could have been faking his affection for the soldier, to trick Atlas into doing exactly what he'd done.

Atlas had insisted that that was nonsense, but Chamanca could see that the idea had rattled him a little. Chamanca also thought it likely that Caesar would send scouts to verify Considius' tale, but there was no point in mentioning it because there was nothing more that they could do. If the Romans did attack, the three Maidunites would have to try their best to arrange some sort of Helvan response to the force on the hill.

When they reached the tents, the Helvans were up and striking camp with hasty purpose, abuzz with the excitement of travel. It looked like their scheme had worked. The Romans should have attacked already if they were going to, since soon the Helvans would be on their way.

By the time they found the people they'd befriended the day before, next to the ancient circle of stones where they'd left them, Atlas was sure that it was too late for the Romans to attack. He asked if they could travel on one of their ox-carts. The Helvans insisted it would be an honour to have such fine Warriors aboard their humble conveyance. Despite their military shortcomings and their own hardships on the long march, the Helvans that they'd met had been generous and welcoming.

After telling the Helvans to wake them if the Romans did launch a late attack, they climbed up into the cart. Sleep was the only plan.

Chamanca woke briefly when the cart jerked to a start. Atlas and Carden were snoring. The sun was still low but already warm. Cart creaks, animal snorts and the children's laughter filled the air. The Helvans were streaming peacefully westwards. The Romans hadn't attacked. She put her head back down and was asleep within a few heartbeats.

She woke, by the position of the sun, in the middle of the afternoon. The cart had stopped. Atlas and Carden were still asleep. She stood. The cart was at the top of one side of a large, gently sloping valley.

"Fenn's piss," she said. Something had gone very wrong.

On the opposite slope were four Roman legions, twenty thousand men, arrayed in three rows. Iron helmets and gold eagle standards shone, banners flapped and rectangular shields rested on the ground in a faultless battle line. Near the top of the far side of the valley, two more Roman legions formed tidy squares.

The slope directly below them and the bottom of the valley was thick with Helvans charging towards the Romans. There were many, many more Helvans than Romans, but their attack was wholly chaotic. They were piling towards the enemy like a crowd of children let go by their parents on the edge of a fair. Some were walking, weighed down by heavy weapons, but most were running. The last part of their attack was uphill, so the younger and fitter and the few that were on horseback sped ahead of the others, futher thinning the attack.

The Romans waited for them.

An elderly, heavy-arsed Helvan woman came waddling past.

"What's going on?" asked Chamanca.

The woman started, looked about everywhere before finally spotting Chamanca up on the cart. She put her hands on her hips. "You gave me a fright! Why aren't you with them? You should be attacking! We're going to crush those bastard Romans. I'd be in the front line if it wasn't for my knees. Go on, hurry on down the hill or there won't be any left for you to kill! A fit young woman like you lazing about up here. It's a shame." She shook her head.

"What happened to the migration? Why aren't we heading west?"

"Where have you been all day? We changed direction first thing to follow the Romans. The cowards are retreating south.

We've caught them and we're going to have our revenge before they reach safety. We'll teach them a lesson for killing our children at Suconna River! My daughters have promised to bring me one alive. I'm going to cook him slowly. Now, stop your chin-wagging and get down there before the fight's over!" The woman waggled a finger at her then waddled away.

Chamanca woke Atlas and Carden. They stood and watched as the wailing Helvan charge reached the Roman front line. There was a rippling, crunching sound, then a few yells, then the dreadful harmony of hundreds of people screaming in pain. The Roman line didn't budge a footstep. The rush of the Helvan attack dissolved like water chucked at a red-hot forge. Their dead and wounded piled up. Chamanca couldn't see from her valley-side perch, but she pictured them lying in piles, immobile and dying, eviscerated by those wicked Roman swords.

"The fools," said Atlas.

"Should we get down there?" Carden asked.

"We should not. We'd be killed, too." Atlas stood, hands on hips. He was in his customary dark green tartan trousers and leather jerkin. Sworl-decorated iron bands encased each wide forearm, and his dung-brown skin was shiny on biceps wider than a slim woman's thighs. His matted hair draped lumpen and immobile despite the stiff breeze, and the edges of his axe shone in the high sun. He looked good. Chamanca could almost see the aura of heroism surrounding him, which she thought was pretty impressive for a man who'd just declined to join a battle.

The Roman line advanced. The masses of Helvans swirled. Some fled, some threw themselves at the enemy as individually and ineffectively as before. Where there were lulls in the Helvan attack, parts of the Roman front line swapped with the fresh second line. It looked like the third Roman line's role was to spectate.

Steadily, the Romans walked over the Helvan army like a line of scythers through a wheat field. On they came, a hundred paces forwards, two hundred paces. Fleeing Helvans, many with bloodied wounds, ran up the hill and passed the cart that Chamanca, Carden and Atlas were watching from. At first it was just a few, then it was a multitude, crying the laments of the defeated:

"Flee! Flee!"

"Save your lives!"

"The devils can't be killed!"

Atlas shook his head. "Come on, this is over. Let's go."

"Wait," said Chamanca. Along the valley to the east, not yet seen by the Romans, another mass of Helvans was approaching. They were jogging in an organised line. There were a lot of them, matching the Romans for numbers. If they were well commanded, and it looked by their good order like they were, then the battle was far from lost.

"All right, let's hold for a moment," said Atlas. The trumpets of the new force blared a rattling blast. All the hairs on Chamanca's body stood on end. As one, the entire battlefield looked up and saw the newcomers from the east. There was a pause that felt like a stone thrown straight upwards reaching its zenith, then everything changed.

The Helvan retreat held, coalesced, reversed and became a new, huge attack on the Roman line. It was by accident rather than design, but for the first time the attack was unified. For the first time, the Romans took a few paces back. In places the Helvans breached the wall of Roman shields. Not for long: the Romans quickly hacked them down and closed the gaps, but it was a start, and more and more gaps were opening in the Roman shield wall. Legionaries were dying in significant numbers.

"Let's join them," said Carden, reaching for his sword.

"Yes. Come on!" Chamanca tightened the thong on her leather shorts.

"Wait," said Atlas. "Hold a few heartbeats."

"No!" Carden protested, "the time is now. If we can rally a couple of hundred, we can punch through—"

"I see your point, but humour me and wait and watch for twenty heartbeats. If you still think we should join the attack after that, I will be at your side."

Carden looked like he was about to leap from the cart, then said, "All right then," and relaxed. Chamanca tilted her head to each shoulder, loosening her neck, and lifted her arms above her head. It was always good to stretch before a fight and she had twenty heartbeats to fill.

Below them, the third line of Romans was swinging round from its position behind the second line. Smoothly as liquid metal poured into a mould, it reformed on a perpendicular front in faultless ranks, ready to face the threat from the east. In perfect synchronicity, a volley of pilums whooshed up from the new Roman line.

The vanguard of the new Helvan attack faltered under the hail of spears, but still came on in reasonable order. The Romans waited behind their shields. The Helvans hit them. The Roman line held firm, then advanced, swords stabbing and chopping. The majority of the foremost Helvans turned to run, but they were hampered by their advancing siblings in arms and all was confusion. The Roman war machine rolled over them, dying Helvans and blood-soaked soil in its wake.

The newly enlivened attack on the original front had also fragmented from a united, punching fist into disparate, fleeing fingers. By the end of Atlas' twenty heartbeats both Helvan attacks had become retreats, perhaps a thousand Helvans had died, and the Romans were advancing again, now on two fronts.

"Fuck," said Carden.

"Yes," agreed Atlas, "let's head north and see if we can find stiffer resistance. Now I've seen them fight, I'm more convinced than ever that we must stop this army from reaching Britain."

"Britain is screwed," said Carden.

Atlas shook his head. "No. It will need a lot of work, but Lowa can beat that army."

"You really think so?" asked Chamanca.

Atlas looked less sure. "With a lot of work, and some luck. That is assuming that the Roman force doesn't grow and doesn't contain any powerful elements that we don't know about."

Chamanca took a last look at the rampaging but still ordered Romans. She could not imagine any scenario in which any British army would defeat them. Worse, though, she had a strange feeling that there was more to the Roman army than they'd seen so far.

Chapter 5

"Sell the attractive women, the strongest men and any appealing children to the slavers. Give the rest to Felix," said Caesar.

"Julius, is that wise?" While others would prevaricate and mince words with Caesar, his right-hand man Labienus spoke his mind. "Even if I ask the men to be loose with their definitions of attractive, strong and appealing, I'll still hand Felix more than ten thousand Helvetians. You gave him that many after Suconna River. None were left alive a week later."

"What he does with them is his decision."

"They may be barbarians, Julius, but so many—"

Labienus was halted by a look. "Felix is working for me," said Caesar, "for the benefit of all Romans and the Empire. He is to be afforded a free hand."

"Indeed, Julius, but the men are talking. There is much murmuring about Felix's mysterious activities, and the strange legionaries who do his bidding. A good many are claiming that Felix is using dark magic to create monsters."

"Oh, for the love of Jupiter, can't the centurions drum their bucolic superstition out of them?"

It was Labienus' turn to give Caesar a look. "Sir, we both know that their fears aren't entirely superstition, bucolic or otherwise. I'm certain that you allow Felix's activities because they benefit Rome, but perhaps we should keep his business and his people away from the men?"

"All right, all right," Caesar shook his head. "Give the

prisoners to Felix. I will tell him to keep his activities out of sight and out of mind. And you, Labienus, will find these agents who persuaded Publius Considius to lie to me."

Labienus coloured. "Of course."

"I cannot understand why you sent only one messenger from the hill. If it weren't for yesterday's victory I'd be taking a dimmer view of your failure. I might have become very *cross*, if you get my drift."

"I followed standard procedure. Crucifixion would hardly be—"

"No, no, you're right. But don't let standard procedure get in the way of common sense again. You may go. Ragnall?"

Labienus left and Ragnall Sheeplord, sitting at the scribes' bench where he'd been pretending not to listen to the conversation, looked up from his scroll. "Sir?"

"Follow me, with the usual." Caesar swept from the large tent without a backward glance. Ragnall grabbed the bag containing the bedroll and standard legionary's morning rations and ran outside after the general.

It was coming to the end of the fourth night watch, shortly before dawn. In the peaceful air he could hear the screams of Publius Considius from the far side of the camp. Ragnall had never seen Caesar more angry than when he'd found out that Titus Labienus had been in position above the Helvetians and that Considius had lied to him. They'd caught the hapless Considius trying to escape on a donkey, dressed as a woman. It wasn't a clever disguise in an army entirely comprised of men. The dissembling messenger had been keeping Caesar's torturers busy ever since.

Caesar paid the noise no heed, striding away so purposefully that Ragnall had to half run to keep up. Approaching his forty-second birthday, the general's hairline was in full retreat, but his wiry, fat-free frame quivered with apparently limitless energy. Ragnall wasn't sure whether the man's vivacity was the cause of his desire to be the greatest general in history, or caused by it. Whatever it was, Caesar was obsessed with military achievement. He was incensed that Alexander the Great had conquered the world by the age of thirty, yet his own significant martial successes to date had only numbered a few minor battles in Spain. He had much catching up to do.

Much, perhaps even most, of Caesar's energy was directed towards conquering Britain. The conquest of Gaul would be a stepping stone towards this. That was the initial reason he'd brought Ragnall on to his staff. Now, Ragnall liked to think that Caesar saw him as a son. That might have been pushing it a bit, but he was certainly one of the great man's favourites and privy to a good deal that the rest of the staff were not. This did not include why Caesar was obsessed with Britain; Ragnall guessed it was simply because it hadn't been conquered before, by Alexander, Darius or any of the greats. Then again, they hadn't conquered Gaul either. But Gaul was well known to the Romans. Although many Roman merchants sailed there regularly, and Rome contained plenty of British slaves, many Romans still thought of Britain as a romantic, semi-mythical place. Perhaps that was why Caesar wanted it so badly? There were plenty of resources in Britain, to be sure, and sometimes Ragnall thought Caesar must have been after these, but there were plenty of resources on the more convenient side of the Channel as well.

Ragnall also had no idea what Felix was up to, but he trusted Caesar, and if he said it would help Rome, that was good enough for Ragnall. He had long ago given up any idea of revenge against Felix, and his initial horror about the idea of Romans conquering Britain had been entirely reversed. Roman ways would make Britain so much better. And if Lowa, the woman who'd killed his family and lied to him, was destroyed in the process of introducing those ways, then so be it.

They arrived in the clearing. Ragnall laid out the bedroll next to Caesar's speaking platform and placed the rations next to it. The common factor in all successful Roman campaigns, Caesar had told Ragnall, was the support of Rome; not necessarily the consuls, Senate and Tribunate, but the people – the citizens at home and the legionaries in the field. Hence the charade that he slept outside like one of the soldiers and ate the same rations. While the Senate were raging that he'd hired new legions illegally, marched them from Transalpine Gaul in breach of rules that he himself had set down as consul the year before, then massacred an entire people, the Roman man on the street would be marvelling at the humble proconsul sleeping outside and eating like a pleb.

The citizen's image of Caesar would partly come from tales told by legionaries returning home, and partly from Caesar's diaries and letters, constantly written and copied by a team of scribes. Joining this writing team was Caesar's latest idea for Ragnall's development. "About time the barbarian learnt to write," he'd said. Ragnall was glad. Writing and reading was perhaps the most impressive facet of the Roman way of life he'd seen so far, better even than underfloor heating in marble bathrooms. To Ragnall, the concept of recording thoughts and being able to send messages so easily was both an incredibly advanced and forehead-slappingly simple idea. He could not believe they hadn't thought of it in Britain. Surely it was as obvious as the wheel? He was embarrassed to come from a place that couldn't write, and all the keener to be part of the Roman invasion that would change his homeland's benighted ways.

The moment the sun peeked over the horizon, the thirty top centurions, five from each of the six legions that comprised the invasion force, arrived in the clearing.

Caesar rose from his bedroll, nodded a greeting, bit into

a hard bread roll and climbed on to the platform. He liked
to address the centurions from an elevated position. If no
natural lumps in the land were available, he'd have a platform
built. Short of time, he'd sit on horseback.

They knew as well as Ragnall did that Caesar hadn't
spent the night there, but they understood what he was
trying to achieve. The more land and people they
conquered, the more riches for them, so they went along
with his image-boosting fabrications. They all agreed, for
example, that the Roman attack on the Helvetians at
Suconna had been in retaliation for atrocities against
captured Romans, rather than the straightforward criminal
attack that it actually was. They all agreed, too, that the
Gauls had pleaded with Caesar to prevent the Helvetian
migration, while the truth was that the Gauls had agreed
to it years before, and the last thing they wanted was a
Roman army in their lands.

These lies were so persuasive and pervasive that they'd
become the truth, even for people who'd been there and
seen the reality. It was all a massive self-delusion. In reflec-
tive moments, usually after a few mugs of wine, Ragnall
saw that the Romans, himself included, didn't question
their own despicable behaviour; they simply forgot about
it. Their actions were horrific and the justifications for
them the most appalling hypocrisy. But the next day
Ragnall would forget that he'd thought like that and get
on with the business of supporting Caesar in his amazing
adventures.

Journeying along in Caesar's charismatic wake, he was
happier than he'd ever been. When, every now and then,
Drustan's or perhaps his mother's voice whispered from the
Otherworld to ask him what in Danu's name he thought he
was doing, then he invited them to kindly bugger off. His
family and his tutor had done nothing more for him than

die and leave him alone. Caesar had given him fineries, comfort and a fascinating life. Ragnall owed him everything.

General and proconsul Caius Julius Caesar began the meeting with a description of the previous day's battle. He commended everyone's skill and bravery, but said that the main cause of the victory was he himself riding to the front line, dismounting and sending his horse galloping away so that he couldn't retreat, then fighting in the front line with the legionaries.

"Thus I proved," said Caesar, "my unshakeable faith in the Roman soldier. I had no concern for my safety because, with a stout legionary at each shoulder, I did not consider myself to be in danger. The men saw my courage, drew from it, and won a famous victory."

Like many of his lies, there was some truth in it. Caesar had in fact dismounted, sent his horse away and walked along the Roman front line, encouraging the legionaries and asking several of them about their families – he was preternaturally good at remembering his legionaries' names and personal details – but he'd done it while the Helvetians were still a good mile away. As the enemy had advanced, Caesar had walked back to a position several hundred paces beyond the range of any Helvetian projectile. Before that, in case the Helvetians had launched a rush of cavalry while Caesar was bolstering the troops, Ragnall had been nearby with a spare horse.

The centurions nodded and commended Caesar on his bravery.

"But the mighty Romans cannot yet rest," Caesar continued. "The Helvetian scourge is defeated, but our Gaulish allies have been plagued with yet another insidious invader, and have asked for our aid. So, my friends and countrymen, it is with sadness that I tell you that we must travel further from the bosom of our homeland to face a new threat! However, with ready joy I await to hear your resolve. We march immediately, to repulse an innumerable force of Germans under the tyrant king Ariovistus."

While the centurions cheered, Caesar leapt off the platform, rolled up his bedding, tucked it under an arm, took another bite of his bread roll and marched from the clearing. Behind him, the centurions all said what a marvellous, honest man he was.

Chapter 6

Atlas and Carden blocked the road, weapons ready. Chamanca stood on the verge, sling swinging. The Roman slowed his horse to a stop.

"Hello!" he said. "What can I do for you?" He was a wide-eyed, eager-faced young man with a malice-free smile. Straw-coloured hair grew from a centre spot and flowed regularly down into an even fringe, so that it looked like he was sporting a newly made, inverted wicker bowl on his head. He did not seem at all troubled to be halted by three heavily armed barbarians.

"Where is the Roman army going?" asked Atlas.

"North-east, to a town called Vesontio – that's what we're calling it. I think the locals call it Wesontius or something like that?" The scout nodded to himself.

"Why?"

"There's a German king, Ariovistus. He's crossed the Renus with thousands and thousands, and invaded a Gaulish tribe's land. The Sequani, those are the Gauls. They've asked us to remove the Germans, so that's what we're off to do!"

"Why Vesontio? Ariovistus is nowhere near Vesontio," said Atlas.

"Lots of supplies in Vesontio, it's said to be very easy to defend, and it's the Sequani capital. I guess Caesar wants to plan or debate or whatever it is they do with the Sequani leaders. Oh yes, and they say that Ariovistus is headed for Vesontio. We've got to get there before him. That's the point, that's why we're in a hurry."

"All right," said Atlas, stepping to one side and nodding to Carden to do the same, "on your way."

"Atlas . . ." said Chamanca, eyeing the young man's neck.

Atlas gave her a dark look.

"Fine," she said.

"Thanks! Bye!" said the scout. He kicked his horse and was gone.

"Sorry, Chamanca," said Atlas, "I think—"

"Don't worry, I know." Part of her wanted to be sucking at the surprisingly forthcoming scout's neck, but part of her was glad that Atlas had let him go. They'd seen so much death in the last few days that even her blood lust had been diluted.

"What's going on?" asked Carden, who still hadn't picked up a word of Latin.

"He said the Romans are riding for Vesontio to head off a large force of Germans led by Ariovistus." explained Atlas. "He must have meant Wesont, a big Gaulish town, and Ariovistus is the German king Hari the Fister. The Sequani that he mentioned are the Skawney, a Gaulish tribe, and the Renus is the River Renos. It is true that Hari the Fister's tribes have settled on large swathes of Skawney land, and that the Skawney are far from happy about it, so it is possible that the Skawney asked the Romans for help. But I doubt it. About a dozen years ago the Skawney asked for Fister's help against another tribe. He crossed the Renos and defeated the Skawney's enemies, then didn't go home. I am sure that the Skawney won't make exactly the same mistake with the Romans. More likely the Skawney don't know Caesar is coming, and the Romans intend to take the land that the Germans have conquered, and all the Gaulish land in between here and there. If they control the land west of the Renos, the river will be a barrier between them and the Germans, and the Gauls will provide all the resources they'll need to invade Britain."

"Why is he called the Fister?" Carden asked with a chuckle.

"It's a bastardisation of a family name from a German tribe," Atlas replied.

"It's not because he——" Carden beamed with puerile joy.

"No, it's not."

"So what do we do?" asked Chamanca.

"We go to Wesont. We talk to their leaders and help them to prepare a welcome for the Romans."

"What was it like, living in Rome for all those years?" Carden asked Atlas as they walked along the road.

"I don't want to talk about it."

"I'll tell you about the Romans in Iberia if you like," Chamanca said.

"Please do!" Carden ducked around Atlas so that he was walking next to the Iberian.

"I had an aunt who lived in Salduey. The town's leaders made a pact with the Romans and opened their gates to a legion. The Romans killed the leaders first, then all the men. Then they lined up the women——"

As they marched through the fine summer day, Chamanca told tales of Roman depravations in Iberia. She had plenty to tell.

They arrived at Wesont on foot, four days later. They'd exchanged the horses they'd travelled south on with the Helvans for food, and now every animal in Gaul capable of bearing a burden, it seemed, was being used to flee the advancing Roman army. There was not a one to be bought or stolen. So they'd had to walk, carrying their supplies. Atlas, by his surliness, was weary and footsore. Chamanca had enjoyed the exercise. The heat had been a little unpleasant for the first two days, but cool weather had rolled down from the north with drifts of thin, refreshing rain. Chamanca had thought it was refreshing, anyway, but the two men seemed even less happy than in the heat, and had almost come to blows when Carden had mocked Atlas about the way his locks of knotted, curly hair had shortened and fattened in the wet air.

The town of Wesont occupied a freakishly well-fortified position. A fifty-pace-wide river running north-east to south-west hit a hill, swung north then flowed in a wide loop, almost completing a circle before bouncing off the other side of the same hill and reverting to its south-westerly course. The result was a thousand-paces-diameter circle of land about nine-tenths encircled by low cliffs and the river, joined to the surrounding land only by the hill, which formed an isthmus about five hundred paces wide. Across this neck of land was a high, man-made earth bank, topped with a broad palisade. The only way in was a large gate, flanked by two stout towers. The gate stood open.

"Close that gate and, with a few hundred troops, you could defend this place against anything," said Carden.

"You could," said Chamanca, "but where are we going to find a few hundred troops?"

For the last two days the fields and villages they'd passed had been near-deserted. Approaching what should have been a busy market town, there were few people about. The gate was guarded only by a young woman, sitting on a chair by a gatepost, looking at them appraisingly and fearlessly.

She was pale-skinned with a small mouth, broad, pink-tinged cheeks and large, dark eyes, framed by a shoulder-length helm of healthily shiny hair, black as the underside of a black dog. She wore a fine green cotton dress, well-made sandals that criss-crossed up trim ankles and the curve of her calves, and she had a slender, intricate silver toque around her pale, graceful, biteable neck.

"What's the news, kiddo?" said Atlas as they approached.

It was unusually slangy language for the Kushite and when they'd spotted her, his steps had become so much springier that he'd almost pranced up to the gate. Clearly he found the woman attractive. That didn't surprise Chamanca. Despite his erudite demeanour, Atlas was an avid shagger of a variety of women. Chamanca had enjoyed more than one bout with him when neither of them had had anyone better to do. She'd been meaning to again on this trip, but Carden had a strange knack of getting in the way.

What surprised her was that he'd shown that he was keen on this woman. She had never before seen Atlas' reserve drop like that. Either something weird was going on as a result of their long march, or Branwin the goddess of love had whacked Atlas with her magic bone when he'd laid his eyes on Wesont's gate maiden.

"The news is that you should move on." Her voice was level and assured. "There's nothing here any more. The druids have shrieked that the Romans are coming and there's nothing we can do about it, and messengers have confirmed their wailings. Half the town have fled, half the town are preparing to fill their purses with the invader's coins and half the town are drunk."

"That's three halves," said Atlas.

"I'm in the drunk half so my calculations are probably off."

"You don't seem—"

"I'm not. It was a joke." The woman was deadpan.

Atlas laughed for the first time in a couple of days, far more than the jest required. Carden laughed along. Chamanca had noticed that he often laughed because other people were laughing. It made her impatient. "What else can you tell us about the town? Does anyone intend to defend it?" she asked.

The woman explained the situation further. She was Kapiana, daughter of Kaplax, who was one of the Skawney leaders. The Skawney, she said, were ruled by an ever-changing

committee, voted in and maintained by a system so complicated that it made love look simple. The only thing they
needed to know about the committee was that they were a
cluster of crooks, and every decision that they made was
great for them but disastrous for Wesont and the rest of the
Skawney.

For example, they'd asked Hari the Fister across the Rhine
for help that they didn't need against another tribe. He'd
crossed the river with more Germans than you could shake
a sausage at and stayed, taking half of their land. Refugees
from Skawney's eastern lands had fled the Germans and
clogged the once elegant town of Wesont. The committee,
having caused the refugees' plight, first took advantage of
them, then, when they'd stripped them of their treasure and
possessions, persecuted them. To create reasons to chuck
them out of the city, they'd made begging illegal and installed
a curfew that was impossible to keep for people who were
living on the streets. The current situation was that many
innocent people had been exiled, some had been killed, and
those who remained were living in the shittiest accommoda-
tion, knocked together with whatever materials came to hand.

Now the committee had asked the Romans to get rid of
Fister, which was indubitably going to prove an even worse
mistake for the people and an even more lucrative windfall
for the rulers.

"Why did they not learn from the German occupation?"
asked Atlas.

"Oh, they learnt plenty. They found out that the people
suffer under an invasion, but the committee grow rich. While
others starve, they can buy expensive trinkets for their
daughters." Kapiana tapped her silver toque.

"Will you show us to this committee, please? They can't
know what the Romans will do. We have to tell them. The
Germans occupy only the east of your land. The Romans will
take all of it. They will kill many of you and enslave the rest."

"I'll take you to the committee if you like, but, at best, it will be a waste of time. At worst, and most likely, it will be fatal. They do tend to kill strangers who bring them unwelcome advice. And you won't tell them anything new. They know exactly what the Romans will do. Do you think we don't know about Iberia? About toga-wearing Gaul? About Illyricum? About the massacre of the Helvans at Suconna River? You underestimate the selfishness of the Gauls if you think for a moment that our rulers give the tiniest of craps about any of that. They themselves will thrive, and that's all that matters. If the Romans torture and kill the little people, who cares?"

"You seem to," said Atlas.

"Do I? Well, there you go. But I can't do anything."

"I have a plan to slow the Romans down. Perhaps even to send them home. Will you help us?" The Kushite put a hand on her shoulder.

Kapiana looked uncertain.

"It will be fun," said Chamanca.

For the first time since they'd met her, Kapiana smiled. "All right then."

Chapter 7

Thirty-five thousand Romans marched one hundred and twenty miles north to Vesontio in five days. A hundred and twenty miles further from Rome, Ragnall told himself, and a hundred and twenty miles closer to Britain.

So confident was Caesar of the terror caused by his treatment of the Helvetians that they travelled in normal marching order, rather than a more ambush-ready formation. Ragnall rode in the senior staff retinue, happy to be on horseback. With the official position of Caesar's advisor, he was given a free rein, literally, so he amused himself on the journey by riding up and down the line and checking that everyone was in their correct places. Of course they were – they were Romans – but it still impressed him. Doing what you were told the whole time was a completely alien concept where he was from.

The marching order was the same for any large, multi-legion Roman army. Auxiliary cavalry scouted ahead and patrolled the flanks of the mass of marching men, led by the approximately four thousand eight hundred legionaries of one ready-armed, baggage-free legion. If tens of thousands of angry barbarians came screaming out of the trees, this lead legion was meant to bear the brunt, so it was chosen the night before by the drawing of straws. The soldiers saw luck and the gods as more reasonable arbiters than the taking of turns. Riding past, Ragnall thought the advance guard seemed much more relaxed than usual, as if Caesar's nonchalance had trickled down to the ranks. It was fascinating, he thought, to see how much the army was an extension of Caesar. Of course there was banter, bragging and jokes at the general's expense, but overall they were like trusting children. Which made sense – he was like a father, in that his whims could lead them to fortune and glory or misery and death.

Within the advance legion, as within every legion, the four thousand eight hundred soldiers were split into ever smaller command groups. Ten cohorts of four hundred and eighty were each segregated into three maniples of one hundred and sixty. Within each maniple were two centuries of eighty men, and within each century were ten contuberniums of eight. The titles were old. "Century" meant a hundred but it contained only eighty, and the leader of each contubernium was called a decanus, which meant leader of ten, although he only commanded eight. Reforms had changed the numbers, but not the names.

These variously sized units could be commanded and manoeuvred in a vast array of combinations, giving the Roman army impressive fluidity on a battlefield. Ragnall had also seen that these team divisions engendered fierce, sometimes violent but ultimately useful levels of competition. Most legionaries strove to be the best in their contubernium. Each contubernium sought to be the best in the century, but they were also proud of their century as whole, then their maniple, cohort and legion. In Britain, it had been all about the prowess of individual warriors, then the army as a whole. The Romans' multi-levelled teamwork was vastly more effective.

After the single legion advance guard came the surveyors. At the end of each day's travel the surveyors would find a flatish, well-watered spot and lay out markers for the legionaries to chop down trees, assemble tents and build a rectangular defence of ditch, bank and palisade with a gate on each of the four sides. In a perfect world, the camp would slope gently in the direction of the enemy, but simply finding an area of habitable land large enough was often as well as they could do.

So every night the army slept in a little walled town, bigger than most towns that Ragnall had seen in Britain, Italy or Gaul. In its centre, the general's tent would have a hundred feet cleared around it in every direction. Spread around the general's digs, in razor-sharp regularity, were zones for each rank, culminating in large leather tents for the eight legionaries of each contubernium, all arranged in rectangles with broad roads between them. Around the camp but inside the wall was a clear, two-hundred-feet wide swathe, intended to ease defensive movements, give safe grazing land for horses and provide storage space for siege equipment, food stocks, slaves, captives and all the other supplies.

At first, Ragnall had found the building of an identical new camp wherever they stopped to be a bewildering waste of time. Now that they were such a long way into potentially dangerous territory, he appreciated the mental and physical security that the camps provided. It was also a good way of keeping the soldiers busy when they finished marching. If they were digging and building, they couldn't be fighting, gambling, having sex with each other or doing anything else dangerous or detrimental to morale. Moreover, ditch digging was good physical exercise. The standard ditch depth was one pace, tripling to three paces when an enemy was nearby. Men who dug these each time the army moved – every legionary in other words, often every night – would build muscle and be all the more able to hurl a pilum into charging ranks or thrust through ringmail with their sword.

Following the camp-planning surveyors on the march were the pioneers and engineers, ready to nip to the front and clear fallen trees, build bridges, drain marshes and otherwise remove or overcome obstacles. Next came the general's baggage and the general himself, on horseback of course, shielded by his praetorian guard. In Caesar's case, these were men picked from his favourite legion, the tenth, some mounted, some on foot, clad in black versions of the standard legionary's leather and metal garb.

Behind the general came the rest of the cavalry, then the siege equipment – wheeled towers, catapults and the like, dismantled and loaded on horse- and ox-drawn carts – then the senior staff on horseback, then the remaining legions marching behind their eagle standards, followed by their baggage carried on around a thousand mules for each legion. At the end was a rearguard of more auxiliaries, spread like a trailing net to detect assaults from behind.

The whole thing was huge, equivalent to a city wrenching free from its foundations and relocating every day. It should have been impossible, or at least a chaotic mess, but it worked because everyone knew their place. The Roman organisational genius thrilled Ragnall. There was a hive mentality that benefited everyone, within which individuals could shine. Could there be a better way to live?

The rearguard was officially the end of the procession, but there was another, usually very large unofficial group: the hangers-on. Every Roman army was followed by a contingent of merchants, slave dealers, prostitutes and others who might profit from the needs, wants and plunder of soldiers, as well as those wives and children of legionaries who had no homes or means of supporting themselves away from their soldier husbands and fathers.

Some of the richer merchants had guards, and the richest had squads of keen-eyed mercenaries and thick-browed thugs. Otherwise, this mass of stragglers was given no protection by the army, so they tended to huddle close into its lee, mingling with the auxiliary rearguard. When there was a serious danger of attack, and the hangers-on would have most benefited from the army's protection, the army would drive them back and kill anyone who came within a few hundred paces. At these times the top merchants and prostitutes could usually buy or wheedle themselves a place in the convoy, but the lot of the camp straggler was not, for the majority, a happy one.

This march was particularly fast, since Caesar claimed that Ariovistus and the Germans were also headed for Vesontio. In fact, scouts reported that the Ariovistus' army was at least seven days' travel away, and showed no sign of moving. Ragnall guessed that the dramatically fast march was for exactly that reason – drama. "He went how far? In how many days? With how many men?" the citizens of Rome would ask each other, rather than the more pertinent question of "why did he go there?".

On the evening they arrived at Vesontio, Ragnall wandered along with many others past the digging legionaries, away from the camp on the plateau to the south and into town. With Ariovistus so far away and as a reward for the swift march, Caesar had sanctioned an evening of revelry for those ranked decanus or above.

Ragnall was alone in the crowd. He told himself he didn't care, but he was in fact painfully aware that everyone else was in groups, or at least strolling along in chatting pairs. He did not have many Roman friends, only Caesar really, if he could be called a friend. He had never had the chance to fraternise with the soldiery, and the rest of the staff seemed reluctant to become close to him. He guessed that it was because of his links to Felix. People knew about his miraculous survival of the burial at Caesar's party and suspected he'd been in league with the magician. It was probably that, he thought, mixed with the fact that the soldiers tended to flock in their prescribed groups, either military or ethnic. Since Ragnall wasn't part of any military division and was the only Briton, he had no simple social bonds like the others did.

He went to a tavern and failed to join in a few conversations, so left to have a look around. Vesontio was a strange place. It was like a Roman town occupied by the shabbiest of barbarians. What might have been pleasantly airy squares surrounded by stone buildings were crammed with a jumble of haphazard wooden shacks. Broad roads with proud houses either side were jammed with wooden shelters that looked like they'd been smashed to pieces and reassembled in a hurry. What might once have been a decent little park was reduced to a few hacked-up tree stumps. The whole place, the former park especially, stank of human excrement.

Peering out from the dilapidated dwellings were sorrow-eyed, filthy, malnourished people. The town was crying out for Roman leadership. In Rome, the poor, one of whom Ragnall had once been, were all shunted to the Aventine Hill, which they could ruin as much as they liked (although it was still a lot smarter than Vesontio's noisome shanty). The sort of human detritus that was so much in evidence in the centre of Vesontio was kept well away from the decent people of Rome. If they got their act together and made something of themselves, as Ragnall had, then they moved from the Aventine and left the shabbier people to their shabby ways. It was a fair, sensible system.

The richer-looking people who lived in Vesontio, those few who hadn't fled from the Romans, seemed to all be in or around the taverns, busy pleasing their visitors, flitting about obsequiously, filling Roman mugs with wine. Ragnall didn't like it. He knew that the Britons wouldn't give up so easily as these cowardly Gauls, and part of him was proud of that. He sort of wanted the Britons to put up a decent fight, but also he wanted them to capitulate like lambs before lions, so that Roman ways might come to Britain all the sooner and he'd have his revenge on Lowa. It was confusing.

By the time Ragnall arrived in his third tavern, there had been a massive shift in mood among the Romans. The usual soldiers' bawdy, competitive conversation, in which he who shouted loudest had the floor, had evaporated to leave a residue of subdued hubbub, as if everyone were sharing bad news.

Ragnall tapped the shoulder of a passing Gaulish serving girl whose black hair shone in the torchlight. She turned, met his gaze and raised an enquiring eyebrow. He introduced himself, asked her name, and if she knew what everyone was talking about.

"I'm Kapiana. They're all talking about the Germans. It seems that somebody's told them the truth. We were told not to," she said. Her heart-shaped face was set in an attitude of unimpressed, even defiant matter-of-factness which surprised Ragnall, given what he'd decided about the Gauls while walking around Vesontio.

"The truth?" Ragnall asked.

"We were asked not to tell you," she sighed and looked about herself, "but, since the secret's out, I don't suppose there's any harm. The Germans ruled by Hari the Fister are not people, not men and women like us. They are formoris, trolls and other such demons and beasts. It seems that they've been gathering for years in the German forests, growing stronger and more numerous. They've killed and eaten their way through all the villages in the woods and now they're spreading west. They take on human form most of the time, but change into huge, twisted, fanged beasts before you can say Cromm Cruach."

"Nonsense," said Ragnall. "Children's stories." He wasn't convinced by his own words. If she'd been some wide-eyed dimwit he wouldn't have believed her for a second, but this woman's straightforward delivery made her tale sound plausible.

"That is exactly what I said to begin with," she said. "I wish I still thought that way."

"What changed your mind?"

"People disappearing, livestock mutilated. A field of sheep not far from the city wall became a field of wool, bones and blood overnight. I said it was bears or wolves, forced from the mountains by harsh weather. But I knew it wasn't. I'd never heard of animals causing anywhere near that much damage, and the weather had been milder than usual. Then . . ." Kapiana shook her head and sucked in a long breath through gritted teeth.

"What?"

"About a moon ago, a thousand horses – maybe more – came galloping from the east, each one carrying the blood-dripping legs and lower torso of a rider. The riders' upper halves were missing."

"Missing?"

"The horses galloped to our wall, swerved west and disappeared, but we took some of them down with slings. We examined what was left of the riders. I'd seen similar wounds once before, on a rabbit that had been bitten in half by a dog. Someone suggested that they were fleeing when attacked by great winged beasts that swooped down, took their heads, arms and chests in their mouths and bit them in half. I can't believe that. I don't see why they wouldn't have ducked or leapt off their horses, or been knocked off when the beasts attacked, or fallen off afterwards – at least some of them! But I can't think of any other explanation. Can you tell me why the lower halves of a thousand people might come galloping from the east?"

Ragnall took a swig of wine and looked hard into her eyes. She met his gaze.

"Do you know who the riders were?" he asked.

"I don't. Plenty have guessed, but nobody knows. We know only that there's something terrible in the woods."

"There must be another explanation," he said.

"My thoughts exactly. But have you ever stood on a hill and looked across the Renos? The German forests on the other side stretch for as far as you can see on the clearest day. Nobody knows what's on the other side of the trees, or even if there is another side. Are we so arrogant to think that undiscovered creatures, even demons, cannot live in those endless woods because we never see them on the civilised fringes that we inhabit?"

"Well . . ."

"What I do know is that last year I would have laughed at me if I were you, so I respect your scepticism. But now I know differently." She shivered, though the evening was warm. "You seem like a good man, so I implore you to believe me and save yourself. You're not a Roman. Are you auxiliary cavalry?"

"Something like that."

"Then leave now and go home. It's the Romans' fate to be eaten by monsters, not yours. Leave."

Kapiana walked away. A few heartbeats later, she was deep in conversation with a table of centurions.

Chapter 8

"They want WHAT?!"

Ragnall and the other scribes all started at Caesar's shout, then returned to writing, more quietly than before so that they might hear the reply. The scribes were hidden from Caesar and whoever he was shouting at by screens decorated with pictures of Aquae Sextiae, the battle some forty years before in which Caesar's uncle Marius and his legionaries had killed a hundred thousand Germans.

"They want to go home." Ragnall recognised Labienus' voice. "Five of the six legions are demanding immediate return to Roman territory. The twelfth would have gone already if the tenth hadn't prevented them. There were fights. A couple of deaths. Several companies of the auxiliary cavalry galloped away at first light. Iberians, all of them."

"Thank Jupiter for the faithful tenth. Which legion guarded the camp overnight and stayed away from Vesontio?"

"The tenth."

"I see. Do we know what happened in Vesontio yesterday evening?"

"I do not, I have men finding out."

"Do that. Use the praetorians if you need. And gather the centurions—"

"Sir . . . ?" Ragnall poked his head around the screen.

"Ragnall?" Caesar asked. Labienus looked surprised and then irritated that an advisor had interrupted the general. Ragnall reddened, but Caesar gestured for him to continue.

"I know what happened in Vesontio."

Ragnall repeated the tales of monsters in the forests that had enthralled him and everyone else the night before.

Caesar banged his fist on a map table. "Jupiter's sandals! Roman officers taken in by barbarian fairy tales . . . there is more to this than we can see." After his initial flash of anger, he sounded more fascinated than annoyed. "The officers must have been so deeply affected that they repeated the stories to the men on their return. Ragnall, who is this Gaulish orator who can deceive an entire army?"

"There was no one orator. All the Gauls seemed to believe what they were saying. They were very convincing. And . . . is it not possible that creatures that we haven't previously encountered live in those endless dark forests? Perhaps they have migrated recently from the unknown east, where for years they've been mustering—"

Caesar held up his hand for silence. "Labienus, keep every man away from the town. In fact, pull them all back and lock down the camp. If any man steps outside the walls, his century will be decimated. Send Felix to me."

"What about foraging? We are short of firewood and—"

Labienus saw the look on Caesar's face, stopped talking, held up his palms, bowed, turned and walked briskly from the tent.

Chapter 9

"Morning, Atlas." Chamanca smiled up at the tiptoeing Kushite. Dawn sliced dusty bright lances through the shutters of the three-bed room that Kapiana had allotted them, but Chamanca would have recognised Atlas' heavy footsteps in total darkness, even over Carden's snores. Both he and Carden were big men, but Carden had mastered the art of stealthy movement while Atlas had never come close.

"Hmmph," said Atlas. He placed his axe carefully on the floor, dropped his woollen cape and climbed on to his creaking wooden bed.

"How was Kapiana?"

Atlas rolled over, facing away from her. A few moments later he rolled back, grabbed his woollen cape from the floor and rolled over again, pulling it around him. Heartbeats later, he was snoring.

Chamanca lay awake, listing to the men's snores. She had never before slept in a town's stone building and she didn't like it. She'd stayed in huts with stone walls, but you could step out of those easily enough. Here, you had to go through at least three other stone-walled rooms before you were in fresh air and that was too removed from the real world for her. It was like being buried alive. The window didn't help, high up as they were. It was like a display of unreachable food to a hungry man.

She tried her best to drop off. The way to sleep with a snorer, she knew, is to align your breathing with theirs and pretend to yourself that it is your breath making the snoring sounds. That might have worked with one, regular snorer, but Carden and Atlas were grunting like a whole sounder of confused wild boar. She lay, looking at the black ceiling. She tried to fantasise about Kapiana and her slender neck, but for some reason her thoughts kept coming back to Atlas sleeping with the Gaul. For some reason, it annoyed her.

She was woken a good while later by a hubbub outside. She sprang up silently and jinked open a shutter. They were a storey up, with a good view of the high street.

A group of black-clad Roman soldiers was moving slowly through the town, questioning people. At their head was a figure she recognised – Felix. Even from behind, at fifty paces, he was unmistakeable. She gasped. What the Fenn? What was Zadar's druid doing with the Romans in far-flung Gaul?

As if feeling her gaze, he turned and looked up at the window. She ducked, then felt foolish. It was a bright day, the room was dark and she had the shutter open only a finger's breadth. There was no way that he'd be able to see her. Slowly, she rose up and put her eye to the slit again. Felix was still looking straight at the shutter – at her, it seemed.

Fenn! she thought to herself, crouching down. Had he seen her? Did he know it was her? Did it matter if he did? As far as Felix knew, she, Carden and Atlas were professional soldiers, whom he'd last seen . . .

Who was she kidding? This was Felix. Chances were he'd seen her and read her mind. Chances were, if he was with the Romans now, that he knew all about them and their mission already. So what could they do?

"What's up, Chamanca?" asked Carden from his bed.

"We may have a problem," she said.

The Iberian argued for leaving immediately. There were boats all along the city walls, so they could have been across the river and away to the Roman-free north in moments. Atlas said that their mission was to hamper and, if possible, stop the Roman army from reaching Britain, or at least gain information, so they had to stay in Wesont until they knew what the Romans would do next. There was no point sacrificing their entire mission because a flighty Iberian thought that one man might have seen her, when there was no way he could have done. Chamanca said that Atlas wanted to stay only to protect Kapiana, which was noble, but stupid, suicidal and of no help to Lowa and Britain. Felix had seen her, and they should go. Atlas said that this was nonsense, they should stay. After far too long arguing with the Kushite, Chamanca asked Carden to have the casting vote.

"Whatever Atlas said," he replied.

So they stayed in their room, Atlas taking watch at the window since his dark face would be harder to spot from the street. Chamanca was nodding off to sleep again when Atlas gently closed the shutter.

"Sobek," he said.

"What's Sobek?" asked Carden.

Atlas ignored him. He looked to be deep in thought.

"He or she is a Kushite god, I think," said Chamanca. "Atlas says it as a curse the whole time. You must have—"

"They've got Kapiana." Atlas' voice was quiet.

"What?" Carden asked.

"The Romans are leading her down the street at pilum-point. Only her. How could they know that she—?"

"Felix," said Chamanca.

"How could he know?"

Chamanca had never seen Atlas this disturbed. It unnerved her. "Felix knows," she said. "He knows we're here, he knows why, he knows about you and Kapiana and he's trying to draw us out."

"If he knows we're here," said Carden, "why doesn't he come and get us?"

"I don't know? Because he's a shit? Maybe he wants to be able to say that the British attacked the Romans first? It's no coincidence that he paraded Kapiana under a window that Atlas was looking out of. He knows that Atlas will want to rescue her."

"In that, he is correct." Atlas picked up his axe.

Chamanca put a hand on her hip. "Atlas, what did you say about our mission here? I cannot remember. Are we acting for the good of Maidun and Britain as a whole, or is our goal to fall in love with a woman that we've spent one night with and jeopardise everything for her?"

Atlas narrowed his eyes and flared his nostrils and seemed to hold his breath. "You're right," he said eventually, deflating. "So what should we do? Because I don't see 'nothing' as an option."

"Stay here," said Chamanca, "I'll have a look around, see if I can find out what's happening."

Chapter 10

Elann Nancarrow's iron came from central Britain, several hundred miles north-west of Maidun Castle, where a fierce little tribe called the Kerbees controlled a rich source of the highest quality ore and used secret methods to produce the hardest, least brittle, most malleable metal. They defended their mines and their methods like a gang of vixens protecting cubs.

"Any idea how the Kerbee tribe make the iron?" Lowa had been walking up to Maidun's Eyrie, but drizzle had become a deluge, so she'd ducked into the cover of Elann's forge complex, along with one of Elann's cats, which shook itself like a dog then curled up next to the fire.

Lowa was happy to shelter there. She liked watching Elann heat, hammer and cool rough bars of iron into exquisite weaponry.

"I know exactly how they make it." Elann rarely said more than necessary. Lowa had never heard her ask anyone a question, or even seem to notice anything outside the direct parameters of weapons smithing. She'd accepted her change in boss from Zadar to Lowa without a murmur. Indeed, the day that Lowa had killed Zadar and walked up into Maidun, above the triumphant roars of the frenzied crowd, she'd heard Elann's hammer beating away on iron as if it was just another day. Lowa supposed Elann must have hated Zadar for the murder of her son Weylin, but it didn't show. Lowa had sent her other son, Carden, to Gaul. Elann had never asked after him.

"So if you know how to make this excellent iron . . . ?" Lowa asked.

Elann scowled down at her work for a moment, then carried on hammering. She was a short woman, with an incongruously large head, a jutting jaw that was never troubled by a smile, and the bulging biceps of someone who hammered metal all day, every day. It was a mystery how a woman as short as Elann Nancarrow had produced two such hulking sons as Weylin and Carden. It was another mystery that she'd taken enough time away from weapon smithing to conceive them.

"Then we could make iron like theirs here," elaborated Lowa, "in large quantities, and produce better weapons for the whole army."

Elann hammered on.

"Couldn't we smelt iron as fine as the Kerbees' and make hundreds of swords with it?"

"We couldn't'

"Why not?"

"Three reasons."

". . . Which are?" said Lowa eventually.

Elann hit the hot sword four more times, examined it, grunted with satisfaction and thrust it into a clay oven filled with hot charcoal. She pulled off her huge leather gloves, slapped her hands against themselves, swallowed a draught of water from a clay mug, then looked at Lowa.

"Reason one, the ore here is bad. The Kerbee tribe own and guard the best ore mines in the world."

"So we could buy more iron from them, or, if you know their methods, buy ore and make the iron ourselves?"

"Reason two, they never sell their ore. I am the only person outside the Kerbee tribe to whom they sell their iron ingots, and they limit the number that I am allowed. They will never increase that number."

"We could take it?"

"Reason three, to take their iron we'd have to kill all of them."

"How many are there?"

Elann lifted one eyebrow. It was the most extreme display of emotion Lowa had ever seen from her. "It is difficult to think of a cause that would justify the extermination of a tribe. Besides that, they are protected by their god Crendin. She's a mountain at the moment, but if the iron is threatened, she will become a giant and smite the Kerbees' enemies."

"And of course," added Lowa. "The Kerbees have excellent weapons, so killing them would be a costly business."

"Not far from impossible," said Elann. She put her gloves back on and reached for a lump of iron. It was clear that the conversation was over. Lowa hadn't been serious about killing all the Kerbees to get their metal. Or at least not totally serious . . . But where did one stop? If she could sacrifice one person to stop the Romans from taking Britain, she definitely would. A hundred? No bother. A thousand? Yup, probably. Ten thousand . . . ? Tricky. More?

It wasn't a simple question. Hopefully it would be made easier when Atlas, Chamanca and Carden returned with intelligence about the Roman army – if they returned. She was certain that the Romans needed to be stopped, even more since hearing what they were doing in Gaul. She knew that sending them back across the Channel would mean sending many, many troops to their deaths. So, if she could kill, say, a thousand Kerbees in order to gain weapons so good that ten thousand fewer of her own soldiers died, surely she should? No, she didn't think she should. But why not? Zadar, she remembered, had always said that all his killing and destruction was for the greater good. She was still collecting many of his taxes, if not the slave quotas. She'd sent several friends to Rome and Gaul, possibly to their deaths, and those were just the first few of the many lives she was going to throw away to defend Britain from the Romans. What was her justification? Who was she to decide who died? Was she just another Zadar, fucking up others' lives for her own ends?

Elann was hammering red-hot iron into the shape of a warhammer's head. That got her to thinking about Dug. He was never far from her mind, not least because Spring never stopped talking about him. Lowa had done many things that she felt terrible about if she let herself, including killing a whole village's worth of people under Zadar, maybe even a whole town's. However, the only thing she'd ever done that made her feel sick with shame was shagging Ragnall in front of Dug. What had she been thinking?

She resolved to go to Dug's farm, to apologise and throw herself on his mercy. Then she shook her head. It was a resolution she made often. She'd even started the journey once and got as far as Maidun's gate before making an excuse to herself to turn back. She'd spoiled her relationship with Dug beyond repair. Lowa knew that she would rather face the entire Roman army on her own than stand in front of Dug and tell him that she would give up everything she owned to turn back time to that evening in the woods, to change what had happened. To tell him, in fact, that she thought about him the whole time and she supposed that that meant she loved him.

Chapter 11

Ragnall stood on Vesontio's wall with most of the senior clerical staff and a few of the praetorian guard. Along the wall from him, on top of the short gate tower, were Caesar, Titus Labienus, Felix, six praetorians and a long-haired man in chains whom Ragnall didn't recognise. Held by two of the praetorians was Kapiana, the woman who'd told Ragnall about the German monsters. For a normal troop address, that entire space, wall top and tower would have been populated by senior centurions and just a few praetorians. Ragnall and the rest of the clerical staff would have had to watch from behind the soldiers, hearing second- or third-hand reports of what was being said at the front. However, with most of the centurions in disgrace for believing the Gaulish rumours, Ragnall and the others had been given the positions of privilege. It gave the young Briton a buzz to look down over so many people. Especially since he'd believed the Gauls' stories too, but seemed to have got away with it.

Gathered below, stretching from the town wall to the Roman camp, were the entire army and all the townspeople, the latter guarded by the remaining praetorians and the trustworthy tenth legion. The other five legions were arranged in their usual no-nonsense parade-ground squares. Beyond them, the hangers-on and auxiliary soldiers milled about in unruly flocks.

The tower was only three paces higher than the walkway, so Ragnall could easily see Felix's smirk, and that Kapiana,

despite her attempt at a haughtily insouciant pose, was terrified. Probably with good reason, knowing Caesar and Felix.

"Good soldiers of Rome and people of Vesontio!" Caesar's
clear shout rang out in the still summer's day. "We are further
north than any Roman army has ever ventured. We have
come to protect our Gaulish allies from the German barbarians. We are here to guarantee the safety of their women
and children. That is our primary cause but do not forget,
my fine legionaries, that we are also here for the glory of
ourselves and for Rome! To shine the light of our great race
into the darkness!"

A short, unified and manly cheer rang out from the Roman
ranks.

"We have defeated the Helvetians in two glorious battles,"
Caesar continued. He looked to the south and pointed there
with three fingers, his middle finger bent under his thumb.
This was an orator's trick that Ragnall had seen him use
before. He didn't understand what it did, but it seemed to
work. There was another shouted cheer. "These battles were
won by the bravery of the legionary, and the stalwart leadership of the centurion!" His gaze and his three-finger point
swept back to the men. Another cheer.

"But we are not gods! We are only men. We will make
mistakes. We have made one here." He paused, looking
around and nodding. Even though he didn't catch his eye,
Ragnall felt as if Caesar was talking specifically to him. It
was another oratory skill. "Exhaustion and sheer distance
from home have weakened our minds! Many of us have been
fooled by treacherous Gaulish tongues." Caesar pointed and
glared at the long-haired prisoner. He was a weedy fellow.
"This man is a German!" he shouted. "We captured him in
the forest, twenty miles west of here. He is one of the monsters
which has caused you all so much terror!"

The general waited for everyone to have a good look at
the pathetic captive, then commanded: "Guard! Remove his

chains." A praetorian did so. "Now give him your sword and make some space." The praetorian hesitated.

Caesar turned to his audience. "My guard is sworn to protect me and to obey me. You see his dilemma! I have ordered him to give the German his sword, yet he thinks that this will put me in danger. I say this. I am in no danger from any German with a sword! The Germans are not devils. Nor are they trolls, nor winged dragons. They are men. They are German men. And I have nothing to fear from a German man, because I AM A ROMAN!"

Three short cheers rang out this time. Ragnall knew it was pantomime, little more than a bard's act, but it worked. He himself was on tiptoes, excited to see what would happen.

Caesar unsheathed his sword and nodded. Felix and the others shuffled back. The praetorian gave the prisoner his own weapon. The German screamed, lifted the sword and launched at Caesar. Caesar parried high, then cracked the flat of his sword into the side of the prisoner's head. The prisoner reeled. Caesar lifted a leg, planted the sole of his foot on the prisoner's buttock, and propelled him off the tower. The man fell towards his spectators without a sound and landed face first on the packed earth. His neck broke with a snap and his body crumpled into a pile.

"The invincible German!" Caesar shouted.

Three more cheers resounded from the Romans. The people of Vesontio, encouraged by a few of the better dressed men and women, clapped unenthusiastically.

"But what of the stories?" Caesar continued. "Where did they come from? I could tell you, but why would I, when I have here the Jezebel from whom the lies flowed? Let her speak!"

Kapiana strode forward purposefully. "I am Kapiana of Vesontio!" she shouted. "I made up the stories about the Germans. I encouraged my people to spread them. My goal was to demoralise. I see now that I was wrong. I understand that we need the Romans. That they are a great people. I accept my punishment. I am no better than the conniving Carthaginian Jezebel. She was pushed from a tower to be devoured by dogs. I willingly deliver myself to the same fate." She walked towards the edge of the tower. Behind her, Felix smiled.

"Wait!" shouted Caesar. She paused. "We made a mistake in believing her lies. It will not be our last mistake. History will measure us not by the mistakes we make, but by how we respond to them.

"I will let this brave young woman kill herself. But that will be the end of it. Her sacrifice will be the Skawney tribe's sole punishment. Another general might burn this town and enslave the townspeople for their treachery. I will not! We will leave these people free and unmolested, and we will remove the scourge of the Germans from their lands. Thus we will show the decency and the power of Rome!"

This time, the cheers from Vesontio's ranks was as loud as the Romans'.

Caesar continued: "This woman, Kapiana, has accepted her errors, and has agreed to bear Vesontio's punishment. We despise her deceitfulness, but we salute her bravery. Kapiana, continue."

Kapiana stepped up onto the tower top's low wall.

Chapter 12

Chamanca, Carden and Atlas were lying on a flat roof at the edge of town, level with the top of the tower from which Caesar was addressing his troops. The three Warriors were concealed among large earthenware pots of herbs which supplied a communal eating house below them. They peered through herbal fronds to the tower, where a black-clad praetorian guard was removing chains from the bearded captive.

"By the way he's moving, he's drugged, or—"

"Felix. It's Felix's doing," said Carden.

They'd discussed Felix's powers earlier. Atlas and Carden had both claimed that there were times during Zadar's rule when Felix must have controlled their minds – when they'd killed Lowa's women and tried to kill Lowa herself, when Carden had watched passively as Chamanca had murdered his brother. Chamanca had nodded in agreement and stayed quiet. Her mind had never been controlled. She'd done everything Zadar had asked, including slaying Carden's brother Weylin, because she enjoyed killing people. She suspected that the other two hadn't found it too hard to carry out orders and the magical explanation was a convenient excuse, but she kept quiet.

They watched as Caesar kicked the little man off the tower and turned his attention to Kapiana. Atlas stiffened and reached for his sling. Chamanca put a hand on his arm. "No. Remember why we're here."

"I can't let them—"

"You cannot do anything against thousands; not here, not now. You and Carden must go to the German king – Hari the Fister. Explain Roman tactics, help him plan. If the Germans have half as many as these townspeople claim, and they're led by someone with half a brain, they'll stop Caesar before he gets anywhere near Britain. So go. Make sure they don't fuck up as badly as the Helvans did."

Atlas nodded. "That makes some sense. And you?"

"Me? I've never been good with orders so I'm going to make a little display here. I want to show the people of Wesont that the Romans are vulnerable. I want to show the Romans that the Romans are vulnerable."

Atlas poked his head up. He looked along the roofs to where they came closest to the wall. Chamanca followed his gaze. It was perhaps fifty paces from the tower where Caesar held Kapiana. Along that stretch of wall were maybe forty Romans, most of whom were heavily armed, and . . . "That's Ragnall," he said.

Chamanca nodded. "It is him, definitely. He must have joined the Romans. That's why we received no word from him and the old druid."

"Why would he do that?" Carden asked, poking his own head up.

"A young man sent to a city full of temptation," said Atlas, "with information to sell and a story that will get him into any party? We should have known he'd turn."

"Where's the old guy?" said Carden.

"Drustan," said Atlas, "Can't see him. Maybe he's back in Rome. Look at Ragnall smiling. He's certainly no prisoner. He'll have told Caesar everything he knows about Britain's army and defences."

"I'm going to spoil his day." Chamanca leapt into a crouch.

Atlas put a hand on her leg. "Chamanca, you may get as far as Ragnall. But no further. Those Romans have trained all their lives—"

"But I am the best."

"Yes, but there are many more of them, and, besides, Felix will stop you with his magic. You can't fight that. Only magic can fight magic."

"You think I have no magic? How then do you think I move so quickly? Why am I still alive when so many have tried to kill me?" Chamanca slapped his hand away, jumped over a plant pot and then onto the neighbouring roof.

She sprinted along the building tops and leapt between them, ball-mace in one hand, short sword in the other. By good fortune the last roof was thatch, so it provided the bounce she needed to clear the wide gap on to the town wall. By another stroke of luck, everyone on the wall was looking away from her, towards Caesar's show on the tower.

She used the momentum of her leap to drive her sharp blade though the neck of the first guard. Blood jetted and she heard a gasp from several spectators. Good, she thought. Her show had begun.

The praetorians on the wall turned to face her. She dropped into a slide, cracked open a kneecap with her ball-mace and severed an Achilles tendon with her sword. She leapt out of the skid, smashed a cheekbone with a back-handed mace flail and severed a windpipe with a forehand sword-slice. She dodged a downward strike, jabbed her slim blade into the sword-swinger's guts and withdrew, leapt another praetorian's side swipe and crowned him with her mace.

The trick with fighting, she thought, carving and whacking the life out of the next three praetorians before they could strike at her, was neither to think nor to stop. She didn't know that her ability to move so quickly and instinctively was magic, as she'd told Atlas. She didn't care. It worked and she liked it.

Two non-soldier types threw themselves off the wall. Probably a good thing. She had no qualms about killing unarmed people, but her display would work better if she killed only the armed ones.

The next two looked like the stiffest challenge so far. They pushed others away to give themselves space then flashed their swords about as she came at them, presumably hoping to dazzle and demoralise with their skill and teamwork. She dived at their feet, spun on to her back and drove her sword up one man's anus. The oh-so-clever Romans should have worked out a way of protecting their lower halves, she thought.

Then, as she crunched her ball-mace into the other praetorian's balls, the arse-spitted guard stabbed down with his blade. It pierced the bare skin between her ribs and pelvis and deep into muscle before she twisted away. Hypocrisy, she thought, the curse of all people. Just when she'd been thinking the Romans needed more lower armour, she'd been reminded that she was clad only in leather shorts and a light iron chestpiece. She always told people that she wore so little because she needed the movement, but really she dressed like that because she looked amazing. That sort of vanity, if the gods had any say in anything, was always going to lead to trouble.

So, her first wound of the day. Quite a serious one, by the blood pulsing out of it, but not enough to slow her down yet. She somersaulted her legs over her head and whirled. Four praetorians came at her and she spun through them, leaving them dying in her wake.

Her sliced side throbbed with potentially debilitating waves of pain. Her right leg was soaked in blood. Bel! But not far now. Ahead was one more praetorian, then a very surprised looking Ragnall, then a bunch of terrified toga-wearers who probably weren't going to be a bother, then the tower.

Kapiana was standing on the edge of the wall, facing the massed soldiers and townspeople. Caesar's guards were standing along the near side of the tower, swords ready to hack her down when she tried to climb up.

Felix appeared between two of the praetorians. He grabbed one and sliced his throat open while pointing at the guard between her and Ragnall. That was a surprise. The guard shuddered as if struck by lightning, then came at her faster than she'd ever seen a man move before. He stuck downwards with his sword. She parried with her mace, but he was stronger. His sword chopped into her shoulder and lodged in bone. She dropped her mace and tried to push his sword arm away. She couldn't. She cut into his thigh, but he grabbed her sword arm in a superhuman grip.

He smiled like a madman and sliced his blade deeper into her shoulder. She heard the squeak of iron cutting through bone. Not a nice noise. She punched his side. Ribs cracked under his leather armour. He didn't notice. She punched, harder, again and again. She felt his ribs splintering into soft organs, but he was unfazed. His eyes rolled back so only blood-flushed whites were showing, but still he sliced that sword into her shoulder.

She gave up punching, grabbed his sword arm again, craned her head forward and bit deep into his wrist. Arteries popped and she drank. Delicious blood. She felt power flow into her stomach and out along her limbs. She wrenched her sword arm free of his grip and stabbed her blade up into his armpit, severing tendons. His arm went limp. She pushed his sword out of her shoulder. He staggered back. She crouched, leapt and spun, walloping the side of her foot into his shoulder. He tumbled sideways, off the wall.

She walked towards the tower, blood-drenched. She'd dealt with the praetorians on the wall. The remaining toga-wearers gave up trying to open the heavy, locked door that led into the tower, climbed over the edge then leapt down from the battlements, leaving only her and Ragnall on the walkway. On the tower above Ragnall five praetorians waited, swords ready.

"Chamanca . . ." Ragnall said.

She winked at him and launched. She landed on his shoulders, crouched and sprang for the top of the wall and the waiting praetorians.

"Thank you Ragnall!" she shouted in Latin as she flew, loud enough for the furthest watching soldiers to hear.

One blade pierced her cheek, another cut into her calf, but she landed firm on the tower. She felt calm. The woman Kapiana was standing on the low parapet, looking outwards, unruffled by events behind her – clearly under some kind of glamour or heavily drugged. Caesar was in the far corner, brandishing a sword next to Felix. The five praetorian guards were behind her.

Felix thrust his hands at her, palms flat, as if pushing an invisible boulder. Suddenly she felt like she'd been wrapped in an impossibly heavy iron blanket. She shook her head and felt the foul force seep in through every pore of her skin. As it entered her veins, the cloying tendrils of magic changed from foul to fair, and the power that had rendered her motionless suddenly fizzed energy into her muscles. The guards were coming at her, but to her they seemed no faster than statues. A praetorian raised a sword. She whacked its sharp blade into the throat of the man next to him.

She was a flurry of limbs and iron, stabbing her blade into an eye, driving a knee into a groin, mace-smashing an elbow, crushing a Bel's apple with the sword hilt. The last guard she simply pushed off the wall.

After one, maybe two heartbeats, only her, Felix, Caesar and Kapiana remained. She leapt at Felix. He squeaked and fell. She was on him, teeth in his neck.

Then came the blow.

She managed to turn. Caesar was there, holding a sword

with blood on it. Her blood? Time returned to its normal pace, perhaps slower. She felt weak and beaten. Consciousness was flowing away fast.

"Assassins always forget the general's sword," said Caesar, raising his weapon again.

Chapter 13

"Fuck off, you Roman twat! Fuck off, you Roman twat!" the German children chanted, tripping along merrily next to Ragnall's horse. They were healthy looking mites, aged between five and ten, he reckoned. Some of them had circles of flowers in their hair. "Fuck off, you Roman twat! Fuck off, you Roman twat!" they sang as they skipped.

It wasn't the most sophisticated of insults, but after a while the young Briton could stand it no longer.

"Fuck off yourselves!" he shouted.

"Oi! You watch it! Don't you dare talk to our kids like that!" said a thick-armed, lank-haired man, waggling a meaty finger at him. The man was wearing nothing but sandals and a scrap of black, furry leather pouched around a weighty-looking cock-and-balls bundle. Dark pubic hair sprouted from the garment's hems. Ragnall couldn't tell which fur belonged to the man and which to the luckless animal that had lost its skin so that a German might have warmer bollocks.

"Sorry," said Ragnall. By Jupiter, he was unhappy.

"Fuck off, you Roman twat! Fuck off, you Roman twat! Fuck off, you Roman twat!" the children continued.

"I'm not Roman!" he shouted.

The children paused for a heartbeat, then resumed in joyous unison with: "Fuck off, you twat! Fuck off, you twat! Fuck off, you twat!"

Ragnall had met someone once at an orgy in Rome who followed a monotheistic eastern religion. She'd told him about one of their great druids, a fellow named Ezekiel, who'd been teased by a gang of children about his baldness. He'd complained about this to his solo god and the deity had sent a she-bear to slaughter forty-two of the children. Ragnall had drunkenly suggested, and by doing so massively offended the woman, that a more intelligent, less reactionary god might have sent Ezekiel a hat. Now, for the first time, he sympathised with Ezekiel and his brutish god. He called on Camulos, British god of animals, to send a bear to kill them, or at least a frightening dog to scare them, but no animals came and Ragnall rode on through the children's rude chorus until, mercifully, the path narrowed and rose into the trees, away from the tent town. The children ran off, presumably to find someone else to torment.

Away from the settlement, the path rose up the valley side, dipping and climbing sharply as it traversed tributary streams etched into the main valley's flank. Worn by heavy use and light maintenance, the track was a mess of ruts, holes, loose scree from landslips, fallen away sections and teetering overhangs that might collapse at any moment. This nigh impassable trail was the only route to the summer seat of Ariovistus – or Harry the Fister as the locals seemed to call him – king of the agglomeration of German tribes that was occupying half of Gaulish Skawney territory. Below the rough track, winding up the valley floor next to a frolicsome stream, were the traces of a decent road, smashed and blocked by boulders, tree trunks, mud and other debris from floods, rock falls and avalanches. When this became Roman land, thought Ragnall, roads like that would be cleared regularly, especially if they led to the seat of a leader. And the children wouldn't be quite so cheeky either. Even more, now that he was away from the distractions of Rome, Ragnall saw that things would be so much better under the Romans for Gauls, Britons and probably the rest of the world.

Unfortunately, his chances of seeing the day when a resplendent Roman army marched on to a conquered Maidun Castle were slim. Caesar had believed him when he'd said that he had done nothing to help Chamanca or anyone else against the Roman cause. The rest of the army hadn't. She'd shouted out her thanks to him after killing several praetorians, then killed a few more and tried to kill Caesar, so every Roman soldier was certain that Ragnall was in league with the enemy. She knew his name, so they must both be conspirators. They had no other argument or evidence than that, but it was enough for them. He'd tried to shake several people's convictions – Caesar and Cato knew each other's names, didn't they, but the two were hardly friends – but his logic had fallen on dumb ears. The Roman soldiers weren't ones to let sense get in the way of an interesting story. A furious Iberian woman had shouted out his name, so he was in league with the enemy. That was that.

Caesar had said that he was sorry, but Ragnall was irreversibly sullied in the six legions' eyes. Thousands had called for him to be beaten to death and hundreds had offered to do it. If Ragnall were ever to be accepted again, he needed to do something incredibly brave and indubitably beneficial to Rome.

Luckily, Caesar had said, he had just the mission. Ragnall was to report to Labienus, who would explain the terms he was to deliver as Rome's envoy to Ariovistus. Labienus had told him the message for Ariovistus, with seemingly genuine regret (Labienus really was, Ragnall thought, a decent fellow). The message was: "If you do not cross the Renus river back into Germany before the next full moon and stay away from Gaul for ever, Caesar will slaughter you and all your people."

Ragnall knew that the demand was a long way from realistic, especially when you remembered that the Roman army had no more right to that part of Gaul than Ariovistus did, arguably less, since they'd arrived more recently, and that the German army was more than twice the size of the Roman one. It was like a small man walking into a much larger man's house and telling the larger man to leave, it was his house now, because he said so. Oh, and he should leave his wife behind too.

So, if Ariovistus was anything like kings and queens that Ragnall had learnt about on the Island of Angels, he'd reply to Caesar's ridiculous demands by sending back a vital part of the messenger who'd brought them – invariably the messenger's head, usually with his private parts stuffed into his mouth. Ragnall gulped and almost pulled his horse to a halt.

He really could run away. He could ride north then west and back to Britain. It would be a dangerous journey to make alone, but a lot less dangerous than riding into the German headquarters and delivering terms which pretty much demanded that they made him chew on his own balls.

But he didn't want to go home. He'd found a new home with the Romans. The idea of returning to Britain, or at least British ways and people, made him shudder. And you never knew. Perhaps Ariovistus would turn out to be a marvellously compassionate man who'd send him back to Caesar with another suggestion? Ragnall's father, king of Boddingham, would never have harmed, let alone killed, a messenger. Perhaps Ariovistus would be like him? Perhaps he'd even agree to Caesar's terms?

A gap opened in the trees to the left. In the meadow across the valley a troop of marmots stood on their hind legs, front paws lolling on their chests, heads swivelling to watch him pass. He liked the fat, furry animals, but was surprised to see so many thriving near a gigantic German camp full of people who favoured furry groin warmers. Perhaps it was a good omen?

An hour later, he came to a gateway in a spiked barricade that stretched across the valley, guarded by men and women.

They were all dressed like the man who'd shouted at him, in nothing but thongs about their waists attached to furry pouches and sandals. One of the women reminded him of Lowa. He tried not to look at her tits as he told them who he was. They told him to dismount and let him through. The Lowa-alike took his horse, and a gruff man told him to wait at the edge of a large, newly built but already stinking German village.

He stood there, feeling awkward while people walked from the village to stare at him silently, then walked away, seemingly underwhelmed. Eventually the gruff man returned, showed him to one of several paths that led up the valley and told him to follow it until he found the king.

It was a pleasant walk, away from the pungent ming of the Germans' settlement, along the grassy, wooded edge of a steep valley. The gradient stretched his legs satisfyingly after the long ride. At one point a fat black squirrel with a tail like the most flamboyant centurion's plume sat on the path watching him and scampered off only when he was almost on it. He took this to be another good omen.

Presently the path opened out, and Ragnall found himself at the top of a sort-of cliff perhaps two hundred paces high. He couldn't have called it a proper cliff, but it was definitely more than a steep slope. It had plenty of sheer faces, but there was the odd big bush, and several grassy ledges of varying sizes grazed by small, scraggy-coated and apparently sure-footed sheep. A haphazard array of sharpened stakes had been hammered into the slope's face, their ends pointing diagonally upwards. Ragnall couldn't see what they might be for. Possibly, he thought, they were for hanging sheep's feed bags in winter, but that seemed unlikely, since they probably took the sheep down the mountain when the snows came.

He stopped wondering about the stakes when he spotted,

spaced along the edge of the cliff for two hundred paces, a line of naked people, a group of nearly naked people and a couple in clothes. The naked people were bound, blindfolded and tethered to metal pegs. The first fully clothed person was surely King Ariovistus, or "Hari the Fister", surrounded by a dozen large German men and women. The second was a tall, one-armed woman at the far end of the line of naked prisoners, standing alone on a rocky outcrop, blonde hair blowing in the wind.

Ariovistus was maybe sixty years old. He was the fattest person Ragnall had seen outside Rome, but he looked strong and solid, not flabby and easily exhausted like the wobble-breasted overeaters who lowered the aesthetic tone at Roman orgies. All his bodyguards, advisors, friends or whatever they were, were clad in the same thongs and fur triangles as the villagers. The women had bare breasts, some flat and floppy, some pert and interesting. Ragnall had heard that all Germans wore this skimpy garb year round and didn't feel the cold. Ariovistus clearly hadn't heard that rule, since he wore leather trousers and a red tartan wool cape, nor had the distant woman on the rock, who was wearing a long blue dress.

Ragnall was about to holler a greeting, when Ariovistus took three big bounding strides towards a prisoner. He was surprisingly nimble for such a large man. He sliced through tethering twine with his sword and pushed the blindfolded captive off the cliff. The man roared in horror and fell. Ariovistus, his entourage and Ragnall rushed to the cliff edge to watch.

The bound prisoner landed on his feet on a grassy shelf, missing a grazing sheep by a foot. The sheep carried on munching, apparently unaware. It looked for a moment as if the man's fall might end there. Perhaps, had his hands not been bound, he might have grabbed hold of grass or sheep, but slowly, slowly, he toppled forwards. He fell another twenty paces and was impaled through the lower torso on one of the stakes. He screamed, convulsed like a dying fish and was still. Ah-ha, thought Ragnall. That's what the stakes are for.

Ariovistus and his people looked to the woman in the blue dress on the outcrop.

"Dead!" she shouted.

The Germans whooped and shouted. Backs were slapped. Ariovistus turned his attention to Ragnall.

"Ah! Good! The Roman envoy! Welcome! I'm Arriervister. But everyone calls me King Hari the Fister – or just plain King Hari." The king had a richly mellifluous voice, cherry-red cheeks and watery blue eyes. The grey curly hair on his head showed traces of the ginger it had once been, but his shrub of a beard was bright white. He smiled broadly and his eyes creased into twinkling slits as he strode forward, took Ragnall's hand and gave it an energetic pumping.

"Hello. I'm Ragnall," Ragnall managed, wondering if he'd imagined this avuncular fellow pushing a man to his death.

"Ragnall! Ragnall. Not a Roman name."

"No, British."

"Ha! But you are now with the Romans?"

"Yes."

"How wonderful! You must tell me all about how that came to be. But not right now! You find us right at of the beginning of a game of Trial By Falling. The rules of the game are simple: they're all in the name! Ha! These good fellows and lovely ladies," he put one hand on Ragnall's shoulder and used the other to indicate the line of nude captives, "have been accused of a variety of crimes. Other tribes and other kings might go into that bothersome business of witnesses, arguments, evidence and all that guff. We prefer to speed things along and make it enjoyable for everyone. So today the mountain is deciding who's innocent and who's guilty. It's not always the mountain – we don't

always have a mountain – but today it is. You saw the fellow
fall just now?"

"I did . . ."

"We all wondered if he'd killed and eaten someone else's
duck, as someone or other had told us. Now we know he
did! The gods decided that he was guilty of whatever it was
he was accused of. I'm pretty sure it was duck theft, duck
cooking and duck eating. And now we know he did it! Ha!
And at exactly the same time we discover his guilt, he's
punished! You see? It's clever, uncomplicated, quick and
everyone's happy!"

Almost everyone, thought Ragnall, but he nodded.

"Now, I'd be – we'd all be – deeply honoured if you tried
the next one?"

Ragnall thought he must have misheard.

"Here," King Hari handed him his sword, hilt first. "You
saw me, it's easy! Cut the cord and push! Opposite to giving
birth. Ha ha!"

Ragnall took the sword. The thought that he might attack
King Hari and the Germans poked its nose out from one of
the braver recesses of his mind, but the much larger self-
preservation section shooed it back in. He walked towards
the nearest captive; a hairy, thickset man.

"No no no," said King Hari, shaking his head with a grin.
He walked along the line, beckoning Ragnall. The courtiers
or whatever they were followed. King Hari stopped and
nodded at a captive. It was a girl. She was slight, stooped
and shaking with silent sobs. She might have been fourteen
years old. "This one."

Ragnall's bravery nearly surfaced. It really nearly did. He
almost – almost! – did the heroic thing and attacked the
German king, but Hari the Fister stepped behind two big
women and a ferret-faced man and the moment was gone.

He walked to the edge and took a good look at the slope
and its various features, then returned to the girl, chopped

through her tether and shoved, angling leftwards. She fell. Somehow her arms came free as she tumbled. Ragnall realised how noble it would have been to cut her bonds before pushing her, and sort of regretted not doing so.

She bounced off a stake, missing its spike. She landed arms first on a ledge about halfway down. They heard the crack of a bone breaking. She yelled, but grabbed a shrub with her uninjured hand. It didn't hold, but it slowed her enough that she slid down the rest of the slope without suffering further injury. She lay on the grass at the bottom for a moment then sat up, held her wrist and rocked.

"Alive!" shouted the woman in the blue dress.

The Germans cheered.

"Well done, well done!" King Hari was beaming. He walked back from the cliff edge. "That was superb. A very nice angle. So, you have terms from indomitable Caesar, the noble slayer of innocent Helvans?"

"I do."

"Am I going to like them?"

"I shouldn't think so."

"He is a dreadful man." King Hari smiled and shook his head, as if amused by the antics of a charmingly mischievous child. "So, what does he say?"

Ragnall told him. Some of the nearly naked Germans cursed. King Hari's smile twitched, but remained.

"I see," he said, "and he's expecting you to return with a reply?"

". . . Yes." Ragnall held his breath.

"Well, you won't be doing that! Ha ha!" King Hari's mouth held the smile, but the look in his eyes made Ragnall want to follow the girl off the cliff. "The Romans have no business in a territory that's mine by right of conquest. Unless of course they want to conquer the conquerers, which they're welcome to try. Many have tried to destroy me before, but brought destruction only on themselves. Do you know, Ragnall, that I haven't slept under a roof for fourteen years?"

"Uh . . . no?"

"Well, I haven't. And why not? Because I've been campaigning! I am a seasoned campaigner, a general who has never lost a battle – as your leader will soon find out! Ha! Now, by Toutatis, to more immediate matters. How are we going to work out whether Ragnall the British Roman envoy lives or dies?" He looked around himself exaggeratedly. "If we only had a way of deciding guilt from innocence. Some sort of a trial, if you will . . ." He panned his narrow eyes around the valley, until they came to rest on his line of naked captives. "Oh! Look here! Ha! Just the thing! How lucky we all are!"

He turned to Ragnall, brimming with good cheer. "Now, will you undress yourself, or shall we do it for you?"

Chapter 14

A sea mist swirled in the bracken as Mal and Nita walked uphill through the wide clearing, ten paces behind Lowa and Spring. The woods were closely managed by the Aurochs tribe that populated the Forest of Branwin. They chopped down their fuel and building wood only in clearings like this one, which explained the well-used cart track that they were walking along. Mal was relieved to see some sign of civilisation after creeping through the eerie woods for so long. You never knew what was behind the next tree when you were in the woods, and then you never knew what was behind the tree after that. The suspense was relentless. Mal always ended up hoping that something, anything, would jump out from behind the next tree just to get it over and done with.

So he was glad to be out of the trees for now, even if it was going to be only a brief respite.

They'd been going for a while, but they'd had not a sniff of an aurochs. On the two occasions he'd been to the Forest of Branwin previously, when he hadn't been hunting, there had been aurochs everywhere. However, the giant wild cattle were famously canny. Usually the sacred beasts had no fear of humans, who fed them and rarely harmed them. However, the moment you picked up a spear and looked for something beefy to stick it in, the enormous animals vanished.

Generations before, aurochs had roamed the entire island of Britain, but since they were made of meat, covered in leather, connected with sinews that made excellent twine, veined with fat for candles and soap and much more, they had been hunted to extinction everywhere but in the Forest of Branwin. Here, the local tribe, who called themselves the Aurochs, maintained the forest and protected its bovine inhabitants. Every now and then, they hunted an aurochs, and, very rarely, they invited an outsider to do so. This latter honour they had bestowed on Lowa.

The Aurochs were effectively a client tribe of Maidun, but Lowa's rule benefited more than burdened them. She'd reduced their taxes from exorbitant to manageable. She'd sent Maidun's finest agriculturalists to teach them new farming methods. She'd introduced them to her idea of bards and druids teaching all children, not just the high-born ones. She'd liberated several of their enslaved loved ones and freed two Aurochs women from the Whorepits (although one returned a moon later, Mal had heard). She still demanded men and women for her army, but now she'd made soldiering a full-time, paid job, rather than something that farmers were forced to do instead of farming, positions in the Maidun army were sought after rather than feared.

In all, Lowa had improved the lives of the Aurochs tribe after the previous tyrant had made them miserable, so they had given her this great honour of hunting and killing one of their massive sacred animals.

Lowa, Mal knew, was far from thrilled by the prospect. She had any number of tasks that were more pressing than chasing a freakishly large cow through the woods. However, she'd already put it off to the verge of impoliteness, so here they were. She'd asked Mal and Nita along since they were her top generals with Atlas and Carden away and she wanted to show respect to the Aurochs tribe. Mal couldn't think of anything much worse than a day in the woods hunting a dangerous monster that had done them no harm. Nita was thrilled, however. She'd been in a good mood for the entire five days that they'd known they were going on the hunt, which was a good mood record by about four days.

Spring also seemed pleased about the aurochs hunt. Other than to sleep, she'd hardly stopped talking about the hunt from the moment they'd ridden out of Maidun the afternoon before until the hunt had begun. Now she was striding up ahead with Lowa at a cracking pace.

In the three years that Mal had known Spring, or Silver as she'd called herself when she'd wheedled her way into his chariot yard, she'd turned from a gawky child into an almost elegant woman. She must have grown a foot and her childish puppy fat had morphed into a lean, powerful frame, like a stretched, more graceful version of Lowa's well-muscled limbs.

If ever the gods had loved someone, thought Mal, it was Spring. She zinged with infectious, optimistic energy. It was hard to be with her and maintain a poor temper. Mal was sure that there was magic in her. It was more than just her cheering effect. He'd seen her calm when all went mad in the arena, and she was friends with Dug, and she had some great bond with Lowa, so he was sure that she'd had something to do with the extraordinary events on the day that Zadar died.

And if anyone had ever given a crap that Zadar was her father, they didn't any more. She was Lowa's child now as far as everyone was concerned. Indeed, walking along together, picking silent steps on the path, longbows swinging in unison, chins raised in pursuit of their prey, it was hard to think of a pair who looked more like mother and daughter.

Mal's thought train was broken by Nita's hand on his arm. Spring and Lowa had stopped on the edge of the wood. Spring motioned for them to approach quietly.

"There's an aurochs, a big male one," Spring whispered, pointing, eyes shining, "a hundred paces into these trees, directly that way."

"How do you know?" whispered Nita, gripping Mal's arm.

"Saw him," said Spring.

They crept around the edge of the trees to get downwind of the beast.

"I am a cat," said Spring to herself. She thought of Elann's cats up on Maidun stalking rats, bees, each other, people's shoes . . . They crept, low to the ground, slow, steady, definitely never stepping on a twig. Never on a twig! Spring's soft leather shoes made no sound and they were not going to. She paused, reached over her shoulder and slowly slid an arrow from its quiver. She felt Lowa do the same thing behind her. She reminded herself not to get too far ahead. Mal and Nita were going to take the beast with spears, as was traditional. Her and Lowa's role was to step in if things went wrong, which apparently happened a lot where aurochs were concerned.

She could smell the beast up ahead. Its aroma was beefy, old, strong – not massively dissimilar to Dug – and, in fact, could she sense sadness there? A sadness like Dug's of an old, loved life lost? It was funny, she thought, that she could sense the aurochs, that she'd known where it was without seeing it.

She paused, suddenly struck by sadness herself. No, it was fine to kill it. The Aurochs tribe had pretty much made them do it, and that meant that Branwin – goddess of the forest that they were in, and love, and, Spring had learnt recently, aurochs – thought it was a good idea. If Branwin wanted them to kill the animal, then she must have wanted it in the Otherworld with her and they were doing the animal a favour.

The track led to a clearing by a pond, and there it was.

Her breath caught in her throat. She'd heard descriptions, but never seen one before. He was better than a bear! Better and bigger. He looked so strong, so proud. He was standing there by the pond, as if waiting. Did he know he was about to die? She tried to look into his mind but she couldn't. But he did look as noble and melancholy as a brave man waiting for death.

The aurochs' shoulder, Spring reckoned, was about the same height as Dug's head, but his rear legs were lower, so his back sloped upwards and he looked like he was about to leap over the moon, like the cow in the rhyme. Now that she thought about it, hadn't Mal said something yesterday about that rhyme originally being about an aurochs?

His fur was blackest black, his head the size of man's torso. His horns launched outwards and upward from his head, then swept together, so their sharp-pointed ends aimed forwards, like two swords permanently poised to pierce. If he'd ducked his neck and thrust those horns into someone's stomach, then flung his head back, it would have been like a strong man tossing a mouldy turnip with a fork.

They said that Branwin had made this beast, but Spring seriously doubted that the goddess of love had designed him herself. Makka, god of war, must have been involved. Although, she conceded, he was beautiful, too, with his slender legs and grave, noble eyes.

Mal and Nita crouched down next to her, spears in hand. Suddenly their spears – the best, according to Elann, that she'd ever made – didn't look so effective. Surely you needed more that those pointy sticks to end the life of such a creature?

What was more, they couldn't kill him here. The only paths through the woods were the ones made by the aurochs themselves, so they'd have the colossal bother of butchering him and carrying him from the woods bit by bit, rather than loading him on to a cart and taking him to a village with superior animal-chopping facilities. It wasn't Spring's worry, though, Lowa would know what to do, so she crouched and waited to be told.

Spring had heard stories of great hunts, passed down for centuries. Wily teams of humans would take on some enormous beast. If they did triumph, it was only after a massive effort and the kind of teamwork that would leave your head spinning with its cleverness, and, of course, there was always a heartbreaking loss – the top hunter's true love being swallowed by a great fish maybe, or a hairy beast with horns impaling the chief's youngest son, just as the son managed to gouge its eye out with his stone knife . . .

Lowa briefed them on their roles. She and Spring shouted "Ya!" at the aurochs and he plodded out of the woods. When he was in the clear, he stood still, next to the cart track, breathing hard. Mal walked up, stuck his spear in his neck and the aurochs fell over. That was it. It was nothing like the hunts of old. They wouldn't be telling the story of it that evening, let alone in hundreds of generations' time.

Spring knelt next to him as he huffed out his last few breaths. His big eye looked into hers with aching sadness. Crying gently, she put her hand on his gigantic head. Images flowed up her arm and into her mind. She saw the slaughter of his kind by humans. She saw aurochs chased in their dozens over cliffs, fleeing burning forests to be met with spears, their orphaned, panicking calves caught and clubbed to death. Then, in a flash, she saw the future. She saw Romans, she knew that they were Romans, killing all the remaining aurochs, all of them, and piling their bodies into great carts.

Usually when she felt the coming Romans, it was a cloudy thing, impossible to touch, more a case of knowing something rather than seeing it. This was as real as if it had happened in front of her. The Romans were going to kill all the aurochs in Britain, she had no doubt of it. So now she knew. No matter what they did, the Romans would take Britain. She looked up at Lowa. The queen had been watching her with the dying aurochs, smiling with rare compassion. Spring resolved not to tell her that their defence against the Romans was doomed. She knew that Lowa was going to try to beat back the invader, no matter what.

Chapter 15

"You must let me kill her, Julius. You saw what she did on the wall," said the voice. It was Felix. Chamanca would know the clipped tones of that nasty little druid anywhere. She decided to keep her eyes closed a while longer.

"I saw what she did to the praetorian guard. I saw your magic fail. Then I saw her beaten. By me."

And that must be Julius Caesar.

"From behind, when she had several wounds, any of which on its own would have incapacitated the strongest gladiator." Quite right, thought Chamanca. "We must kill her now and we must be certain that she is dead." That she didn't like so much.

"Can she not join your legion, Felix? She seems a little too . . . wonderful to simply destroy. I want to keep her. I will keep her."

"If you must, so be it. But I cannot have her in my legion. And I cannot guarantee holding her, because my magic does not seem to affect her. I think she may have even absorbed it . . ."

I did absorb it, and I used it.

". . . but I've never seen any evidence in her of anything but the most brutish magic. I don't think she is able to bend others to her will, or break metal, so if she is kept very well chained, she shouldn't escape, but . . . I would rather kill her. We should case her in concrete and throw her in a lake."

"You're sure she'll survive her wounds?"

"Yes. She was wounded often fighting for Zadar and I never saw any infection, only miraculously quick recovery. Perhaps I should try rubbing her wounds with excrement—"

"No, Felix. I want her to be healthy. Caesar has decided. She will return to Rome with us."

"Because you want her as a gladiator! Of course. She'll be good. Very good. You will have to build an arena that also acts as her jail, so audiences will be small, but once word gets out you'll be able to charge what you want. I'd pay a lot to watch her tear apart two or three big, cocksure barbarians."

That doesn't sound so bad.

"Indeed. It is settled. There is one more question we need to answer. Why is Zadar's creature in Gaul, and why did she attack us on Vesontio's wall?"

That is a good question.

"I suspect that she's in Gaul because she follows violence," said Felix. "Blood is her food. You suspect that she may be spying for the new queen Lowa. She isn't. Chamanca has tried to kill Lowa twice, so Lowa would not use her. When I left Maidun, she was unconscious on the arena floor. She must have escaped. My guess is that they slit her throat and left her body in the open, as is their way, and she got up and walked away off."

You're wrong there, my clever druid.

"I see. Then take her and ensure she cannot escape. Is there anything else?"

"I am keen to try my legion in combat, perhaps against the Germans?"

"Yes . . . but they must remain hidden from the men. I don't want news of their abilities travelling in any direction – neither to our enemies nor to Rome. I will look for an opportunity to test them and you will be patient until I do."

"Thank you, O Caesar."

Chamanca heard the druid leave. So, Felix had his own legion? She did not like the sound of that.

Chapter 16

"If Caesar's army is a lion," said Atlas, "then your cavalry are like mice with swords that can slice his heels and bring him down."

"And what animal are the rest of my soldiers?" King Hari the Fister asked, happily.

"To Caesar's lion? They are sheep."

The overweight German bellowed with laughter. Atlas raised an eyebrow at him, then continued: "Move your people from this tight valley to the open land fifteen miles southwest of here. Build a fortification between Caesar and his supply line. He doesn't have enough soldiers to attack a manned wall. He has very few cavalry, so you will be able to torment him with yours. Destroy this small cavalry so he will have no reply to your own mounted men and women, then attack and retreat. Wear him down. Pick off foragers that stray from the guard. Slaughter any small groups that leave the camp. If you kill a hundred, two hundred Romans every day, the rest will crumble. You have time, numbers and food and he does not. He has only six legions and his supplies are limited. Chip away and you will win."

Ragnall was impressed. Without, as far as he knew, any detailed knowledge of the Romans, Atlas had laid out exactly what Ragnall himself would have suggested to Ariovistus for defeating Caesar's army, had he been of a mind to advise the jovial old murderer to do anything other than take a running fuck at a rolling hedgehog. Ragnall had been treated well, but apparently surviving the fall from the cliff wasn't enough.

Ariovistus wasn't convinced of Ragnall's innocence, so he'd be taking part in the next trial, too. And, if he survived that, the one after, and the one after and so on until the king knew whether he was good or bad – or, in plainer speaking, Ragnall realised, until he was dead.

"But, Atlas, my men and women want a glorious battle!" King Hari chuckled.

"Then attack him with your full force. It will be glorious, but for the Romans, not for you."

"Hmmmm." King Hari sat down on a log-hewn chair. "What do you think, Flotta?"

The one-armed woman in the blue dress from the outcrop, who Ragnall now knew to be Flotta the Left, King Hari's chief druid, said: "The gods have sent Carden and Atlas to us. These Britons have seen the Roman army fight and their reports tally with everything we have heard. Their plan is sound. We should follow it."

"And should I kill myself now, or wait until I am declared coward and stuck with spears by all my friends who'd rather that they ruled? Ha ha!" King Hari laughed as if this was the funniest joke ever told.

"All right," said Flotta. The druid had the lilting accent of the frozen north, very white teeth and blonde hair gathered loosely into two short ponytails. Her perky breasts pushed up at the light fabric of her blue smock like broad-nosed puppies under a sheet. Despite his predicament and his various pains, Ragnall's gaze kept returning to her. It was odd, he thought, that in a land full of bare-breasted women, the woman he found attractive was the one who covered her chest. Drustan would have had something to say about that. Ragnall suppressed an upwelling of sadness, and along with it, as usual, the unwelcome question of what exactly he'd thought he was doing, aiding the Romans. No, he told himself. The Roman way was still the best way, and it was Felix, not the Romans nor Caesar, who had killed

Drustan. Felix was the bad apple that spoiled the bumper harvest.

Flotta continued with a saucy smile. "Oh, my poor king, you would love to attack I'm sure, but we cannot, not while the auspices are so appalling." She shook her head in mock disappointment. "You see, just yesterday I sliced into a living deer with a golden sickle. A two-headed snake leapt from its stomach. The leftmost of the snake's heads devoured a large red beetle, but the right head twisted around and bit the left head again and again until the beetle was freed. The snake died, the beetle crawled on to it and drank its blood. So the gods have spoken. No way can we attack the Romans . . . until the full moon after this one?" She looked at Atlas.

The Kushite nodded. "That should suffice. If more time is needed, you will find another abomination?"

"I might."

Ragnall was sitting at the edge of the gathering. You'd think that everyone had forgotten that he was there, but when he'd stood up earlier with the idea of quietly wandering off, one of the guards had looked at him and waggled his sword in an unequivocal "I've got my eyes on you, don't do that again" message.

Earlier, he'd been amazed when Carden and Atlas had appeared in the clearing that functioned as King Hari's open-air longhouse. If they'd been surprised to see him, they didn't show it. What they did do was tell King Hari that he was Lowa's spy in Rome who'd turned traitor.

King Hari had laughed at that, almost as much as he'd laughed when Ragnall had survived his plummet down the cliff. Ragnall hadn't found the fall too funny. It had been even more frightening than being buried alive. When he'd been buried, it had all been so fast that he hadn't really believed it was happening. Here, King Hari had gleefully ensured that he knew exactly what was to come. Blindfolded, hands bound, he'd stood for an age, listening to others falling and Flotta's shouted results – all "dead!" apart from one "alive, but dead soon!" He'd begun to think it would be a relief to be pushed from the edge, but, when it finally came, it wasn't.

Because of the shock after the long suspense, he liked to tell himself, he screamed and voided his bowels – piss and turd at the same time. Then the world had rushed around him, he'd thumped and bumped for an age, and finally found himself lying on his back, mercifully still, apparently unbroken, his lower half soaked in his own urine and clagged by his own stinking excrement.

"Alive!" Flotta's cry had come from above, and Ragnall had wept with relief. He shuddered at the memory.

"That's decided then!" said King Hari, back in the present. "Tell everyone we move out at dawn tomorrow. Now," he looked up at the sun. "We have a backlog of criminals to judge and time for a trial before dinner. Come on everybody! Ragnall?"

Ragnall climbed to his feet slowly. Fear almost made him cry. What, he wondered, did good old King Hari the Fister have in store for him next?

They walked uphill into woods, over a shoulder of land, then tramped downhill through the trees, along a rocky path next to a tumbling stream. Ragnall thought about running again. The hero in a bard's tale would kick a captor and be away, hiding in mud pools to evade patrols, leaping down waterfalls, sprinting over pastureland and back in Caesar's tent reporting the Germans' plan by dawn the next day. But that was a story and you couldn't do that in real life. What could he do? Assuming he got away from this guards, which he wouldn't, he didn't know anything about the local geography, apart from that it was crawling with hostile men and women in furry pants, pretty much all of whom would best

him in a fight. He'd just have to hope he survived whatever
Ariovistus had planned for him next, and keep his eyes open
for an opportunity to escape.

Or maybe, maybe he could find help? He stooped to adjust
his sandal, then stood so he was walking next to Carden.
The British Warrior looked every part the hero. His leather-
clad torso rose in the shape of a Roman five symbol from a
narrow waist to great round shoulders. His shining mane of
black hair framed a brow and chin as strong and stony as
those on any of the statues of Hercules in Italy. Carden
Nancarrow would have escaped or died trying. Surely he'd
help a fellow Brit? Especially if Ragnall persuaded him that
he was still on their side, that he'd wangled his way into the
perfect position to supply Lowa with information to undermine the Romans.

"Carden," he whispered.

"Yup!" said the Warrior, without looking down.

"They're going kill me. Can you help? Say something,
or—"

"Did Chamanca live?"

"What? Uh – yes. She's injured, but she'll live. Caesar's
interested in her, so his own physician is treating her. But
can you help me? I could get back to the Romans, keep
gathering information for Lowa . . . and rescue Chamanca?
I'm sure if you had a word with King—"

"Nope. Sorry. You're on your own."

"But we're on the same side."

Carden looked down, his eyes dark. "We are?"

"Of course! I'm pretty much Caesar's right-hand man now.
If one of you lot learnt to read, I could send you messages
about all his movements? Or I could send a messenger? Or
maybe a pigeon . . . but then you'd still need to read. Point
is, I'm in the perfect position to help."

"All right," said Carden, "I'll have a word with the Fister."

"You will?"

"Yup."

"Oh, thank Jupiter." Ragnall wanted to hug him.

"Carden, there's no need to talk to King Hari," said Atlas' bass voice from behind them.

"But . . ." said Ragnall.

"He said he'd help," said Carden.

"I was listening. He was blathering about reading and messengers and pigeons. If he truly was our man in the Roman camp and always had been, he would have considered these things before and have a plan or two on how to do it."

"I . . ." Ragnall stammered.

"Now that," said Carden, "is a very good point. But should we not help him out anyway?"

"Why?"

"Because he's from Britain?"

"No, we leave him. It doesn't matter where he's from, now he's a Roman and he's King Hari's captive. It is not our place to interfere."

"All true," said Carden, "but we should still help a Brit in trouble."

"It matters who he is, not where he's from. I'm not from Britain but I'm not your enemy."

"You're British now."

"I'm not but . . . just don't help him, all right? He's King Hari's now. We will not interfere'

"Okay!"

"But I can help if you let me go!" Ragnall pleaded.

"But I know you wouldn't," said Atlas. "You'd go back to Caesar and you'd help him against us. Walk ahead and don't speak to us again."

Ragnall did what he was told, shaking his head at the injustice of it all.

They emerged from the woods into a flower-filled, grassy

meadow that shone warmly in the early evening sun. Butterflies fluttered delicately between bright blooms and bulbous bumblebees buzzed. A family of marmots stared with toothy surprise at the new arrivals for a moment, then ducked into their holes. The meadow was some forty paces across where they were, between wooded valley sides, widening for two hundred paces to where the grass became a strip of shingle beach, then a marble-smooth lake, stretching off along the valley floor and dotted with ducks and pelicans.

Ariovistus had made the trial seem spontaneous, but it clearly wasn't. At the meadow's near end were more near-naked Germans and twenty or so wholly naked captives gagged and lying face down on the ground, ankles trussed to wrists in front of them. Next to them was a large siege catapult. Ragnall's head dropped. It was no great feat of deduction to work out what was about to happen. King Hari winked at him.

Everyone stopped apart from Flotta the Left, who headed off for the lake, presumably, thought Ragnall, to take up her post as "alive" and "dead" caller.

King Hari boomed out happily: "More criminals to face justice. Gaulish horse thieves, this lot. Or are they whorish gorse thieves! Ha ha ha! Now. I'll go first to show our guests how it works. In a nutshell, if they get wet, they go free! Ha!"

With some help, King Hari cranked back the catapult's arm. On his word, two of the large attendants strode forward with giant iron-headed, three-pronged forks. King Hari pointed out a captive. The men pushed their forks though the thick twine binding the alleged horse thief's feet and hands together, interlocked their forks' tines and lifted. When he was dumped into the catapult's scoop, the captive's gag came loose and he unleashed a stream of the vilest invective.

"Oh dear, or dear," chuckled King Hari. "I don't like this one much. All that bad language. I do hope it doesn't affect my aim. It might, though! Ha ha!"

The catapult was on a turntable. King Hari pulled a lever, and shoved the catapult round until it was definitely no longer aimed at the lake. The Gaul cursed at him all the while.

"And let's try for a bit more height." With help from two guards and the pulling of two more levers, King Hari moved the large leather and wool-wrapped crosspiece back towards the scoop holding the curled-up Gaul.

"Right!" He pulled the shooting lever. The catapult arm shot upwards and cracked into the crosspiece. The captive zoomed into the sky, shouting ever quieter curses. His trajectory was not far off directly upwards, a little towards the woods at the meadow's edge. His flight slowed. Perhaps a hundred paces up, he hung in the air for a heartbeat, then fell, screaming. He landed with a thud twenty paces from the onlookers.

"Dead!" came Flotta's cry from the lake. King Hari laughed himself into a coughing fit, reddening so much that Ragnall thought he might burst into flame.

"Too much crossbar!" he said when he'd recovered. "You'll all learn, I hope, from my . . . mistake. Ha ha! Who's next? Atlas, would you like to try?"

"No thank you," said Atlas.

"I'll give it a go!" said Carden, rolling up his linen sleeves. Ragnall wasn't surprised. During the winter that Ragnall had spent at Maidun, Carden had been desperate to be involved in any game or competition. If none was happening, he'd start one. Ragnall had once played hit-the-molehill with him. He'd thought he was pretty good with a sling, but Carden had won with ease.

"Good, good!" King Hari slapped him on the back. "Pick a captive!"

Carden choose a medium-sized man with a long moustache, then walked around the siege engine, tongue between his teeth, like a man inspecting a horse from a famously dishonest dealer. With the help of the Germans, he cranked the firing arm, swung the catapult back towards the lake and moved the crossbeam forwards. As the captive was loaded, the Briton walked round the machine again. He sucked a finger and held it up to the wind. He shook his head and made a few more adjustments.

"Good luck!" he said to the panic-eyed captive, patting him on the head, "and try to keep your knees and elbows tucked into your stomach, like this." Carden crouched and pushed his elbows into his midriff. "Blink if you get it? You do? Good!"

The Briton waited for an eagle to pass by overhead, then loosed.

A screech of twine and wood, a whump as the beam hit the padded crossbar and the man was gone, heading down the valley through the air, spinning in a tight ball, at around the same height as the top of the trees that flanked the meadow.

"Ooooooh!" cooed the onlookers, other than Atlas and Ragnall.

He landed short of the lake, bounced once, and again, then hit the water with a great splash. Ducks and pelicans scattered. Flotta peeled off her dress and dived in after him. The onlookers waited in silence.

"Come on, come on, Danu help him . . ." Carden muttered to himself.

"Dead!" came Flotta's shout.

The Germans cheered.

"Bel's bollocks!" shouted Carden.

"Very, very good effort," King Hari said, grinning happily, "best I've ever seen on a first try. Go on, have another go. Oh, and I almost forgot – Ragnall, would you mind disrobing and joining the captives on the ground? You can choose him

if you like, Carden? The gods love this one. He's a marvellous looking young man, but a bit wet. And maybe about
to get a bit wetter! If he's lucky! Ha ha ha!"

Carden looked Ragnall up and down. He pinched the ring
of fat that had agglomerated around Ragnall's midriff in
Rome. "He might be a bit heavy, but maybe with a bit more
crossbar . . . yes, I'll give him a go. Can I move the catapult
nearer the lake?"

"Would that be fair?" King Hari seemed serious for once.

"I suppose not," Carden admitted.

"Indeed! And fairness is all! Ha ha! But don't worry, my
fine British visitor, I've seen bigger men fly further. Not too
high, that's the secret. Not too low, either – that's another
secret. None of them are really secrets! Ha!"

The catapult's cup stank of disease. Ragnall wondered if it
had been used to fling decaying animals – or humans,
knowing merry old King Hari – into a besieged fort.

"Now tuck your arms and legs like the last guy," Carden
said. "I don't want to blame him, it was partially my aiming,
but he did untuck halfway through. He would probably have
made the lake otherwise. But then again, you are heavier . . .
Cross your feet over. Can you link your fingers? Yes? Good.
That might help. Don't uncurl and you might make it."

Ragnall squeezed his body into a ball and prayed to Jupiter
and Danu.

"Ready?" yelled Carden. He didn't wait for a reply.

A lurch, a bang and a whoosh, and he was flying. It felt
like he'd left his guts on the ground. He tumbled, elbow and
knees tight, eyes screwed shut. He wondered if Carden had
asked him to tuck so that he'd fly further, or so that he'd
bounce further along the land. He felt the thongs around
his calves come loose and his sandals slip off, and he
wondered crazily if his footwear knew that he was about to
die so were fleeing like rats from a foundering ship.

Just when he was thinking he'd been in the air far too long, something slapped into his back, hard, knocking the air from him. He bounced, slapped down again and then he was underwater and sinking. He struggled to free his wrists from his ankles. He had no breath in his lungs. His back nestled into mud. Weeds waved up at the sun-dappled surface. The lake was not deep. He wrenched at his binding. He couldn't free himself. His head was swelling with the need to breath. How vexing, he thought, to have survived the flight only to drown. And how annoying to drown in calm, shallow water.

Then his hands and feet were free and something was pulling him upwards. He was on the surface, choking and gasping.

"Alive!" he heard Flotta shout, next to his ear.

There was a distant cheer.

He saw a chance. There weren't many swimmers faster than him, and the nearest captor with the standard number of arms was a good distance away. He pressed a foot into Flotta's midriff and pushed her away. He flipped, and took a powerful stroke. A hand grabbed his hair and pulled him around. Flotta's forehead crashed into his nose. Light whirled, then all was darkness.

Chapter 17

Chamanca's wounds healed in days. She'd always been a quick healer. The bed that she'd been chained to while she recovered was taken out of her tent and in its place, while she sat wound in heavy chain, two engineer types dug a deep, narrow hole and filled it with a yellow-grey, lumpy liquid. They held a thick, waist-high oval loop of iron in place while the liquid solidified into rock. Four of the black-clad legionaries guarded her with swords while the engineers passed chains though the loop and soldered them on to her wrist and ankle shackles.

So there she was, legs and arms attached to a wheel of iron set in stone. She was impressed by the neat job. Escape would be difficult.

Everyone left, bar one engineer who stayed behind to gloat. He told her that the liquid stone was a substance called concrete, one of the many inventions that showed how superior Romans were to barbarians like her. That was why it was the Roman duty to conquer, to enlighten benighted lives.

She told him that the Romans might be great, but he himself looked like an inadequate little freak, not fit to pick the nut husks from her turds. And besides, she'd seen concrete in Iberia and been equally unimpressed by it then.

Back in Iberia or Britain, the average man would have responded to a jibe like this by trying to outdo the insult, but Chamanca knew that most Romans were conceited, humourless and unable to accept mockery, especially from their social inferiors. Roman men were markedly shorter than barbarian men, many not much taller than her, and she suspected that it was something to do with that. What was it that Carden had said to her? Being small didn't turn men into pricks, but Danu knew which men were going to be pricks so she made them short as a punishment. She liked that.

The response of the Roman engineer supported her prejudice. His face stretched in surprise then screwed into a mask of rage. He charged, punches flailing. She dodged a couple of blows, took a couple more to draw him in, then clamped her teeth on to his wrist and sucked warm blood. His hits grew weaker until he passed out. She stopped drinking then, reluctant for some reason to finish him; she shouted for someone to take him away before she changed her mind.

The next day Felix came to the tent with a couple of burly legionaries, showed them how to feed her safely using a pan on a pole and told them that they'd be crucified if they spoke to her.

Chamanca had nothing to do but sit, think and rub her ankle and wrist chains against the iron loop. Her rubbing, which had to be quiet enough for the guards outside her tent not to hear, had no noticeable effect. She disliked the optimists' philosophy that no matter how hard something seems at the outset, if you try again and again you'll get there in the end. Try running through a stone wall, she thought. But she persevered. It was a project.

After two days attached to the loop with no human interaction other than furtive glances from the silent feeders, a shiny chest-plated centurion with a plumed helmet under one arm swept into her tent. He stood and looked her up and down, his thin, pink tongue protruding just a little from his lips. She squirmed under his glare. She was used to being ogled, encouraged and enjoyed it even, but this was like being licked all over by a toad. She was about to suggest that the centurion fuck off when he undid his leather skirt, took his erect penis in his fist, hunched over and began to masturbate furiously, eyeing her torso and legs all the while.

Chamanca watched as his elbow worked away, wondering how she might use him. He was a tall, fit looking fellow, with an off-centre patch of white at the front of his otherwise black hair, as if he'd been shat on by a bird. Penis in hand aside, he did not look like a pervert. She guessed that perverts probably never did.

Very soon after he'd begun, the centurion pumped out a couple of gluey jets of semen that, thank Fenn, fell well short of Chamanca. His open-mouthed smile twisted into an ogre's grimace as he milked the final few globs of pearlescent ooze from his detumescing cock, then tucked himself away and scurried from the tent.

It had been unpleasant and not flattering, but on the upside it had relieved the boredom. So she wasn't that upset when the onanist returned the next day, and the next. She tried to talk to him, but he was too excited beforehand to respond and too shameful afterwards.

"I will," she said to the centurion on his sixth visit, as he set to strumming, "say naughty things to you in exchange for news."

"What . . . sort . . . of naughty . . . things?" he managed, before ejaculating and running from the tent. Fenn's tits, she thought, and went back to rubbing her chains on the loop.

The next day, as he unbuckled himself, he whispered: "What news do you want? Answer quietly so the guards don't hear."

"Everything about the army – what it's doing, what the plans are."

He came closer, but not so close that she could bite him.

"All right. We're camped perhaps a mile from the Germans.

That's around fifteen hundred paces in Barbarian measurement." He sounded intelligently didactic, like a clever father explaining a difficult point to a daughter who was a little too young to understand it. "They're dug in well behind a high wall with a clean, steep face, and a well-angled, stout palisade. We could break through this wall, but we would lose half the army doing so. The only option is to goad them into coming out, which we're trying to do by marching past their camp and shouting insults. That usually works with barbarians – they're a prideful bunch – but this lot are holding back. Meanwhile, their cavalry is attacking anyone who leaves our camp – foragers mostly, and our own, smaller, less capable cavalry. Frankly, their tactics are good and, so far, we have no reply to them. If they carry on like this, we will have to retreat."

"How long before your supplies run out?"

The centurion glanced nervously over his shoulder. "I'll tell you more tomorrow. Now you tell me how much you'd like to take my cock in your mouth."

Chamanca laughed. "That is funny. I would love to have your cock in my mouth, but I don't think you would like it very much." She bared her pointed teeth.

The centurion looked disappointed. "Can you say that again, but in a more alluring matter? Perhaps say it in barbarian?"

Chamanca sighed.

Chapter 18

Sapphire should have been in a good mood. They'd all but wiped out the Roman cavalry, and the few that remained had fled into a dead-end valley. She and the rest of the German cavalry had only to follow them in and finish them off. She did feel sorry for the poor Romans. Their ignorance of the landscape had been as much of a log on their funeral pyre as their inferior headcount. Time and time again she and the others had chased foolish, outnumbered men into swamps, to cliff edges or impassably steep slopes. Some had even got themselves trapped in the loop of a river's meander where it had been a doddle to take them out with slings. That was the other thing. The Roman cavalry were armed with swords and spears, so it was easy to kill them with slingstones before they even got close. So she did feel sorry for them, but she was also glad that most of them were dead and that the rest would be soon. They said that when the cavalry was gone the Romans would leave and they'd be at peace again. Well, everyone else would be at peace. She wouldn't, not until she'd dealt with Kondar.

Sapphire had grown up in one of the many smaller tribes ruled over by King Hari the Fister. It hadn't been Hari the Fister when she was young, it had been someone else – a woman – whose name she couldn't remember. She wasn't interested in politics. In most German tribes, men and woman formed unions for life, or at least until they could no longer stand one another. In her tribe, however, they saw monogamy as stressful, miserable and unnecessary, so everyone lived communally with everyone. Childcare was shared, and sex was whenever, with whoever. Fornication was fun, like a game of capture the fort. Would anyone ever suggest that you only ever played capture the fort with one other person for the rest of your life?

So why oh why had Sapphire agreed to move into Kondar's hut permanently, and not to make love to anyone else? She did love Kondar, in a way, or at least she liked being loved by him. Or at least she had done. When it had begun, he'd pleaded so much and told her so many times how much he loved her that she'd agreed to step away from social mores and be faithful to him, to live as man and wife as they did in other tribes. It worked for a while, and they had a lovely little baby boy named Rontik. Sapphire had assumed that they'd look after him themselves, like they did in monogamous tribes, but Kondar did not seem to have any trouble with communal childcare aspect of their culture, so they handed young Rontik into the care of the tribe.

The valley was narrowing. Both sides were mostly bare rock cliffs, and wherever trees had managed to grow it was far too steep to climb. In two or three more turns they'd come to the unscalable waterfall at the head of the valley. The Romans would have to mount a last stand there, but there were so few of them left that she expected they'd kill them all without loss to their own side. She checked her sling and stone bag. All fine.

So they'd had their baby and gone on living together, but lately any fun that there'd ever been had evaporated and she'd felt so smothered by Kondar's constant presence, and his jealousy when she so much as spoke to anyone else, that she'd told him that their arrangement was over. She's said it wasn't the sex, because it really wasn't, or at least it wasn't just the sex. He'd wept like a toddler, wailing and coughing. He'd even been sick. In between the histrionics, he pleaded and pleaded and told her he'd change. He begged her to take a moon to think about it. And she, fool that she was, had agreed. She knew she'd feel exactly the same in a moon, and she knew that it would have been better for both of them if she'd stuck to her slingstones at the time. But she'd agreed. Possibly she was being kind to him, possibly she was trying to make things easier for herself. Whatever it was, after they'd finished off the Roman cavalry she'd have to go back to the tribe and go through it all again. She hoped he wouldn't be there. She'd hoped he'd run rather than face her rejection again. But she knew he wouldn't have, because he was desperate to clutch at any chance that they might stay together. She hoped, and she did feel bad for thinking this, that he'd get the message this next time and that he'd leave the tribe. It wasn't a charitable thought, but flirting with other men – even talking to other men! – was going to be ruined with Kondar looking on like an abandoned puppy.

Yes, the moment she got back she'd tell him that she'd shagged her fellow rider Grax a few days before, which was true, then she'd spend the next few nights in Grax's hut to prove the point. If Kondar went mad and attacked her or Grax, well, they'd kill him and that would be that. He was no fighter, Kondar, and it was hardly her fault that he was behaving so strangely.

She'd been a fool, she should have listened to the elders and walked away from him right at the start, but at least she knew now, and it was somewhat heartening to resolve to do something that would solve the problem.

Up ahead, riders were stopping. Well, this was odd.

Blocking the valley, hemmed in by cliffs on both sides, were what looked like twenty or so big metal carvings of men, but they weren't carvings, they were moving. She made a tight tube with her hand and peered through it – she could see more clearly that way for some reason – and saw that they were men, large men, dressed in crazily heavy iron armour with big blades on the shins and wrists. Each was

holding a huge sword that looked too heavy to lift in one
hand. In the other, each was holding a chain attached to a
skinny man or woman dressed in tatters. These small, rag-
clad people were moving slowly and strangely, as if drunk,
exhausted or both. Most odd. The only vaguely normal
looking one among them was a short, balding man in a
short-sleeved jerkin, sitting on a woolly pony smiling like a
demented imp at the approaching Germans.

What was going on? Had they happened upon a group of
bards who'd launched into an impromptu show? Everyone
else was as confused as she was, sitting on their horses and
staring.

As they watched, the little balding man gave a command.
The leftmost of the armoured warriors forced his captive to
the ground, put a metal-booted foot on his head, then all
his weight. Just the day before, Sapphire had watched a cow
gave birth. As she'd cooed at the sweetness of the calf, a
great sac of afterbirth had pulsed out of the mother's gaping
vagina, hit the ground and split with a great slapping smack.
The captive's head now made exactly the same noise as it
burst. Immediately afterewards, the iron-clad man leapt as
if he'd been stung by a wasp and ran with incredible speed
and clattering of metal towards the German line. Meanwhile,
the next iron man lopped the head off his captive with a
swing of his great sword and came running too.

Slingstones spanged harmlessly off the first armoured
warrior. At the German line he leapt, lashed out with a foot
and severed a horse's head with his ankle blade. He landed
with an almighty clang, swung his great sword in a wide
arc and chopped two riders in half. He picked up the horse's
head by the mane, tossed it up in the air, watched it fall,
then kicked it into the German ranks and sent another two
riders tumbling from their horses.

The second armoured warrior hit the line. A brave cavalry
man shattered his sword on the thick helmet and was

eviscerated by a backhand swipe from a wrist blade. More iron men were killing their captives and coming. A few Germans fought back, but none of them lasted more than the blink of an eye. Humans and horses fell as the armoured warriors advanced. She saw her recent lover Grax raise his sword to strike at one of the attackers. A moment later his head was spinning into the air.

Fuck this, thought Sapphire. Here was dark magic. Flight was the only option. She dragged her horse round by its reins. Most others had had the same idea, and soon she was part of a stampede, galloping back the way they'd come. She looked over a shoulder. She couldn't see any pursuit. She felt a rush of relief, tempered by the horror of what she'd seen and the worry of what might come next. Had the iron-clad soldiers been Romans? Demons? A new race of men who didn't like Germans? She didn't know. She had to get out of there, find baby Rontik and then get further away.

Then the bodies began to fall. Clad in the same rags as the iron infantry's captives, they fell silently down the cliffs on both sides and landed in tangled heaps. One of them hit a rider, who screamed, fell from his horse and lay still.

At first Sapphire thought that the dark figures that followed were more bodies, but, no, they were lithe young men with swords, half tumbling, half leaping down the cliffs, swifter than mountain deer. Several reached the valley floor. They were clad all in brown leather, including their heads, apart from a slit cut for the eyes. They moved so quickly and so weirdly that they couldn't possibly be human. She and some others shot slingstones, but almost all managed to dodge them. One of them jinked his head into the path of another stone, but the blow didn't even slow him. There was no escape. The leather-clad men jumped and spun and slashed and stabbed, chopping into both flanks of fleeing cavalry.

Sapphire gave up all idea of fighting, put her head down

and dug her heels into her horse. The good little animal set off at a gallop that would surely outrun anything on two legs. Shortly afterwards she looked over her shoulder. Two of the demons were running behind her, expressionless in their leather masks. They were catching up.

The terror was too much. She screamed and the world spun as she fell from her horse. She hit something hard and rolled to a stop. She opened her eyes just in time to see a sword flash towards her neck. She felt it hit, felt it chop, felt her eyes roll back so they could see only darkness. Was her head severed? Could she still think with her head severed, she thought? Then she thought no more.

Chapter 19

Before Chamanca could say anything, the centurion said: "The impasse is over. The German cavalry has been destroyed. We can now forage, supply lines have reopened and it will only be a matter of time before the Germans leave or we massacre them in a pitched battle."

"How did you destroy the cavalry?" asked Chamanca

"Officially," he said, "they were hit by a rockslide." He looked over his shoulder and came a little closer, but not close enough that she might grab him. "But I'm in Caesar's inner circle so I know what really happened. I could tell you, but I'd be risking my life – the information is top secret. I would expect a lot in return."

"Would you like to touch me?" she asked, flickering her eyelashes at him. She was hungry for blood and she'd had quite enough of this man perving at her. He could tell her about the cavalry while she drank his life away. He'd probably enjoy it.

"No, I don't like to touch. I like to look. Perhaps you would like to turn round and bend over, with your legs straight."

"And then?"

"That's it."

"Tell me how the Germans met their end first and I'll do it."

"You swear you will?"

"You have my word."

"Right. That vile, dark druid Felix has used some sort of

magic to create demon warriors. I would not believe it myself, had I not seen them train. I wasn't meant to. I rode away as soon as I realised what I was watching and thank Mars I wasn't seen. There aren't many of them, around fifty. But they're as powerful as an entire legion, possibly much more so. Some of them move like you did on the wall. Others are bizarrely big and strong. They are amazing and unnatural and it's an open secret in the upper ranks that they massacred the German cavalry with very little effort."

Was this a version of what Atlas had tried to do in Vesontio, Chamanca wondered? Was this a plan to feed her demoralising information then let her escape back to the Germans? Probably not. Spreading the rumour among merchants would be a more certain and safer way of feeding news to the enemy than freeing her. And she was hardly one to rule out the idea that magic could enhance fighting abilities. "How did he create them?" she asked.

"That I do not know. Nobody does. I've heard rumblings that the whole thing is somehow linked to Crassus's mass crucifixion of Spartacus's rebel gladiators."

"Mass crucifixion?"

"Six thousand, all on one day. They were rebels, but it was too much. Tasteless."

"Why do you think Felix was involved?"

"I don't know. I've told you all that I do. You already know much more than most of the centurions and all of the legionaries. Felix's legion is being kept well away from them to stop word of it getting back to Rome. A group of devils created by dark barbarian magic would not play well in the Senate. They will, however, be very pleased with the victories it will secure. Now please will you do what I asked?"

"Tell me one more thing."

"What?"

"What is the point? What is Caesar trying to achieve?"

"Conquest, simple enough."

"No, that's not it. There must be more."

The centurion looked over his shoulder again.

"All right. But if I tell you, when you bend over, I want to you to say over and over how much you'd like me to . . . to make love to you."

"OK."

"Caesar's goal is Britain. There is something there that he wants. That is all I know, I swear. Now, please do what I said."

Chamanca turned round, her mind racing. What could Caesar possibly want in Britain, other than conquest? Was it something Felix wanted? Out of nowhere, the beginnings of an idea as to what – or, more accurately, who – it might be came springing to mind.

Chapter 20

The Germans moved fifteen miles to more open ground. There was one trial on the way, in which Ragnall and other criminals were made to crawl along a stretch of stream converted by flagstones into an underwater tunnel. Ragnall had swum and dived a great deal on the Island of Angels, and he'd maintained some capacity for holding his breath. It was a long way from enjoyable, especially the part when he'd clawed past two newly dead who hadn't made it to the end, but finally he surfaced and heard Flotta's "Alive!"

Despite it all, he found that he was warming to King Hari. The man was psychopathic, sure, and had attempted to kill Ragnall three times, but he was perpetually cheerful and, apart from the murdering, a kind old soul.

He had had a short length of chain soldered on to Ragnall's ankles to hobble him, and there were always a couple of soldiers nearby who appeared to be guarding him, but other than that King Hari treated Ragnall as if he were part of his inner circle, which included Atlas, Carden and Flotta the Left as well as a dozen fur-panted men and women. Shuffling along with other captives, he didn't see the leaders often during the day, but every evening he'd eat with them next to their fire.

Nobody other than King Hari ever spoke to him, but he didn't mind. He didn't imagine that Atlas and Carden had anything friendly to say, anyway. He caught Flotta looking at him every now and then. Vanity said she might find him attractive, but the voice of reason – which always sounded a lot like Drustan – told him that she was gloating to herself about knocking him out with one blow.

One big problem with the evening gatherings was that there was no booze. The Germans, apparently, had seen how alcohol had weakened the Gauls and sworn off it. In his two years in Rome Ragnall had developed a healthy suspicion of people who didn't drink, plus, with the constant threat of another trial and a nasty death hanging over him, by Bel he could have done with some alcohol himself.

The German infantry, as Atlas had advised, dug in to block Caesar's supply lines, while the five thousand-strong cavalry remained nomadic, somewhere beyond the Roman position.

Every day, Caesar marched his army to the German wall, the legionaries taunted his soldiers, and King Hari held them back. Every day, reports came of the German cavalry slaying Roman foragers and winning skirmishes against the smaller and ever-dwindling Roman cavalry.

"The joys of small horse victories are beginning to pale. Should I ignore the Brits and use my army to smash these insolent Romans?" King Hari asked on the fifth evening as they ate around the campfire. It took Ragnall a moment to realise that the king was addressing him.

"No, I think everyone is right," said Ragnall. "You may have the numerical advantage, and some fine warriors, but the Roman army is the culmination of centuries of military analysis, theory and training. They move more like a flock of birds than a group of men."

"How do they manage this? Do they have larks under those helmets? Ha ha!"

"Each legion, each little army in other words, is split into groups. The smallest is made of eight men, called a contubernium. There a ten of these to a century . . ."

Ragnall found himself sitting next to a crackling campfire, explaining the structure and tactics of the Romans to a group of enthralled listeners. The vague niggle that he was betraying Julius Caesar was overridden in part by the fact that the general had sent him to his certain death as envoy to the Germans, and much more so by the joy of knowing more about a subject than other people and having them listen while he explained it. After a lifetime of being talked down to, it was great to be the one in the know for once.

So he told them everything he knew, from how the army's structure had been reformed into its current shape by Caesar's uncle Marius, to how one of the nails in the head of a pilum was a wooden dowel, designed to break on impact so that the enemy couldn't throw it back.

A few days later, Ragnall noticed that the atmosphere of warm, chuckling confidence that had been bubbling up merrily in the German camp had cooled a great deal. The daily report from their successfully rampaging cavalry had not come for three days. Meanwhile, increasingly plausible rumours were drifting in from the Roman camp that the German cavalry had been wiped out by a rockslide. Ariovistus sent spies who reported that, indeed, that was what all the legionaries were saying. The German cavalry had chased the Romans into a ravine where a rockslide had buried every last one of them. It was a sure sign that the Roman gods were more powerful that the German ones and that they were all doomed.

One woman, however, a beautiful prostitute who had hitherto reported on Roman manoeuvres with unfailing accuracy, told them that stories of demons and evil magic killing the German cavalry were rife among the upper echelons.

Over the next few days there was no sign of the cavalry, nor of a satisfactory explanation for what had happened to them. King Hari's avuncular smile morphed into a madman's grimace. He wanted to send all his force against the Romans immediately, but Atlas insisted that they must not leave the fortification. More cavalry was on its way from Germany and would be with them in two moons. The plan was still sound, only delayed. King Hari ranted that two moons was too long and that they must strike. Most of the Germans had favoured a full-scale attack from the off, and soon Atlas' few supporters swung their support to their increasingly bellicose king. Atlas remained unwavering in his advice to stand, but six days after they had last heard from the cavalry, the king announced that the German army would storm forth from behind their wall and destroy the Romans at dawn the next day.

Seeing that King Hari was adamant, Atlas offered to lead the right wing of the attack. He had, he said, a few scores to settle. Ragnall was overwhelmed by a swirl of admiration and contempt for the African. Atlas was the only one, other than Ragnall himself, who knew that the German attack was doomed, and he had advised against it all along. Yet here he was, offering to lead a section. What a hero, thought Ragnall, and what a fool!

Chapter 21

Dug reached the crest and a massive new view opened up. He liked a new view. He stretched out his arms and yawned in relaxed delight, despite the full blast of a stiff, Danu-loved south-westerly which whipped his hair and made his eyes water.

He enjoyed his walks with Spring. There was, however, also great pleasure in walking alone. Greater pleasure, possibly. After a few miles' striding, his thoughts and concerns always seemed to drift from his body, mingle with the plants, animals, air and sky, then return, bringing the world back with them, so that he was immersed in nature; less a human and more just another animal making his way across the land.

He was striding the great humpbacked white sea cliffs along the coast from his farm. To his right was an expanse of green grazing land dotted with a neighbouring farmer's brown sheep. Ahead, the cliff hurtled into the distance, rising and falling in precipitous chalk ridges until it disappeared, then reappeared as a hazy ridge of southwards-sweeping land. Further south was the great sea, much darker blue than the sky, whipped into lines of white foam by the wind. The fishing and merchant vessels that usually dotted its vastness would all be bobbing in bays today, their crews ashore, waiting for the wind to die down to safe sailing levels. Dug had spent a while working as a sailor. His favourite days had been those on which it was too windy to sail.

He'd reached a particularly high point of the rolling cliffs, perhaps the highest. He could see three more rises. The next was a small one, the following two each higher than the previous, but not so high as his vantage. Another human, the only other one he'd seen all day, came into view over the top of the farthest rise. From that distance she was a dot, running along the cliff path towards him, about two miles away. Soon after she appeared, she disappeared, behind the steep second rise.

Just a dot, two miles away, but he knew it was Lowa. But of course it wasn't, he told himself immediately. Even now, after three years, he was still seeing Lowa where she wasn't the whole time. This was just another one of those annoying, stomach-turning instances. But it really could be her. Few people went running on their own. Spring was the only other one he knew who did, and the distant figure wasn't Spring. He always knew when Spring was coming.

He realised he wasn't smiling any more. He felt nauseous. The hill-climbing sweat that had dried in the fresh wind burst anew from his pores. The fresh invigorating of the grass and sea vaporised, leaving only his own stale odour.

"Badgers' bollock blisters!" he said out loud. It pretty much definitely wasn't her. He strode resolutely down his slope, knees jarring, very much not part of nature any more. He tried to pretend to himself that he was interested in the fascinating rock formation here. It jutted out, away from the coast path, into a hammerhead-shaped peninsula. He knew when he got over the next rise that he'd see an archway running through the western hammerhead of rock. Now, that was definitely an intriguing bit of scenery, and he should probably have a good think about how and why the gods had made it, and if, indeed, there was any purpose? Perhaps there was no purpose in it and no need for a purpose? Perhaps the arch just was? Maybe there was no point to any of it? Perhaps—

It was Lowa. Her blonde head appeared over the next

summit then the rest of her, dressed in a light linen skirt and sleeveless shirt. If she was surprised to see him, it didn't show. She slowed her run and stopped when she got to him.

"Hello," she said.

Her angel-spun hair fluttered in the wind, her blue eyes shone steady and brighter than the white cliffs and all the sea and sky. Her smile was her smile, a little nervous, deeper down a little sad, but on the surface happy and lovely and full of life. She leant down, hands on knees and puffed out a breath that seemed to recover her completely, even though she must have been running at some lick to reach him so quickly, and for some distance to be all the way out here. She straightened up, pushing her hands against her hips.

"Hi," he said, "out for a run then?", regretting the words before he'd started to say them.

"Still as sharp as ever, then?" It was a deserved jibe.

"Well, you could be escaping from invisible ghosts, or just walking very quickly."

"I hadn't thought of that. You're right. But I am, in fact, out for a run."

"Aye. Spring not with you?" Badgers' tits, another Toutatis-cursed fool question.

Lowa looked left, along the gentle valley that led inland, then up the slope behind her, then out to sea, then back to Dug, her eyes glinting with amusement. "Apparently not," she said.

"No. How are you?"

"Right now, tired, and likely to be exhausted soon. I'm on a longer circuit than usual."

"Which is why I've never seen you out here before."

"Never been here before."

"That would explain it. So, all good?"

"Yes, you?"

"Aye. Just out for a walk."

"I'd guessed."

"I like it out here."

"It's great scenery."

"It is. Good cliffs." He could not think of a single thing to say.

She looked at him, a little confusion in her eye perhaps? Or was that sorrow? Regret, even?

"You'd better get on. Your legs'll seize up if you stop too long," he found himself saying. He wished that he could say something, anything, to make her walk with him for a while, to talk. To come back to his, to stay.

"You're right," she said, "I've already stopped too long. Have a good walk, come to Maidun some time!"

And she was off.

"Aye, I'll see you there soon!" he said to her disappearing back. His heart shouted for her to turn round. She didn't. He turned himself and strode on, doubling his place, ordering his mind to return to the discussion of rock formations.

Lowa blinked to stop herself from crying as she ran up the hill. She could not get to the top of it fast enough, and when she did she wanted to carry on up into the sky and never return.

She'd tried to be relaxed and funny – kind even – but she'd been utterly unable to come up with the words and, for some reason that Bel only knew, the words that had come out had been cutting and mean. At one point she'd just fucking stared at him like a loon! She wanted to die. And he'd been lovely and kind, and her aggressive sarcasm had been unpleasant, and he hadn't been able to see the back of her quick enough, telling her to run on, like you might tell a smart-arse child, but really you were saying "how about fucking off now, you annoying little turd?"

She crested the ridge and powered on downhill, faster than before, faster than she should be going on such a long run. Halfway down, she stopped. She'd go back and apologise. Not only for being a dick a moment before, but for everything. She'd tell him that she still thought of him all the time, that she'd been mad to shag Ragnall – she had been mad, consumed with grief for her sister and hatred for Zadar. She'd tell him that she missed him. *Tell him that you love him!* said a voice from somewhere. Well, let's not get ahead of ourselves, she thought. But I will be kind, I will see if he'll forgive me. *You've been on your own too long!* said the internal voice again. Oh bugger off, she thought at it, while conceding that it did have a point.

She turned and ran back up the hill.

He wasn't there when she reached the summit. He must have already cleared the next rise, which meant he'd sped up, which meant he wanted to get away . . . but she was resolved now and she wasn't going to think herself out of it. She sprinted down the hill.

Chapter 22

A few days later Chamanca was woken by the trumpets, howls and beating drums of a far-off battle. She bit the inside of her lip. No, not dreaming. The Germans were attacking. Her stomach ached to be out there, fighting with them. Or against them, it didn't matter. Hearing a battle that she couldn't join was the aural equivalent for her of a starving, freezing wanderer looking across an uncrossable chasm at a village celebrating its annual roast boar festival.

She continued working her wrist chains against the iron pole. Her perseverance was paying off to her surprise, and she'd worn more than halfway through. Given another day, she might have rubbed away enough to snap it with a shove. However, if the battle had started, she didn't have another day. If the Romans won, she'd be taken back to Rome and it would be a good deal harder to escape. If the Germans won, and blood-up, victorious soldiers found a gorgeous woman like her chained to a bar . . . well, she'd managed to persuade the Romans that she was still dangerous while chained to the loop, but if a few of them rushed her then she was in trouble.

She'd been working gently at the iron thus far, not wanting to alert her guards. Guessing that they'd joined the fighting, she started to rasp away with all her strength. Nobody came running in, so she guessed that she'd been right.

From the shouts outside, the Germans were almost on the camp.

"The gate is smashed! Run!" someone wailed. She wrenched

at the stupid fucking iron loop. The stupid fucking thing didn't shift.

The heavy door flap was flung aside and in swung the wanking centurion. He drew his sword, not metaphorically this time.

"Surely, you're not going to kill me after all the great times we've had together?" she asked.

"You made me betray my wife and my general." The centurion advanced, sweaty, white-faced and shaking. He stabbed his shining blade at Chamanca's bare midriff.

Chapter 23

Ragnall strained at his bonds, but it was hopeless. He was trussed to a post in the centre of the German camp by a long rope wound round and round legs, arms and torso, tied behind his back in a knot that he could neither see nor reach.

At around midday, King Hari came stumbling along the camp's muddy central track, alone, face bloodied but still smiling. "The battle is lost, Ragnall!" he said cheerily. "Atlas was right and I wish I could start the day again. No matter, I shall return to Germany a wiser man. Sorry to rush off so rudely, but, before I go, I have one more game of chance for you." He held up a blood-soaked hatchet in each hand. "Which of these would you like to be your agent of dispatch to the Otherworld?"

"Neither of them?" Ragnall tried.

"Ha ha ha! Very good. I shall miss your wit!" King Hari began the ancient choosing rhyme that Ragnall knew from childhood: "Eenah Meenha, Minha . . . Mo!" He looked from hatchet to hatchet with each syllable, finishing on the one in his right hand. "This hatchet then. Your luck holds! I'm right-handed, so less chance of a messy cock-up! Ha!" King Hari took a step forward, then looked over his shoulder. Ragnall followed his gaze, hoping to see Romans charging into the camp. No such luck. There was nobody there.

"Now, face or gut? Eenah Meenha . . ." King Hari stopped mid-chant, frozen in place, grin plastered on his bush-bearded face. His fingers opened and the hatchets tumbled to the ground, but otherwise he was motionless, frozen in place as if time had stopped. He fell back and his paralysed bulk whumped on to the earth.

Ragnall looked about as much as he could, straining on his ropes. The only movement was a few storks flying lazily overhead from the direction of the battle, utterly unperturbed by the scenes of slaughter that they must have just flown over.

He heard a brief sawing noise. The ropes loosened and fell away.

He spun to find who'd freed him. It was Flotta the Left. "Alive." She smiled.

She held out her dagger, hilt first, looked down at King Hari said, "Dead," then looked back at Ragnall and nodded.

Ragnall took the dagger. Flotta turned and walked away.

Ragnall had killed one man before, in the marshes when they'd escaped from Mearhold. It had been dark, he had no idea who he'd killed, and it certainly hadn't felt like taking someone's life. It had been more adventure than murder, part of their escape, impressing Lowa . . .

It had been easy, though. He'd just drawn the knife across the man's throat, hard, as Dug had told him to. He looked down at the blade in his hand. It looked sharp.

King Hari the Fister, called Ariovistus by the Romans, looked up at him. His eyes bulged with pleading. He couldn't move his mouth, but it was clear he was asking for mercy.

Ragnall had come to Hari as an unarmed messenger. He had never been a threat. Yet the German king had made him push a girl off a cliff. He'd put him through three horrific games of chance that he was lucky to have survived. Hari had executed helpless, bound and probably innocent captives in front of him. Then, if it wasn't clear enough what a horrible, horrible man he was, he'd broken off his escape – he'd risked everything – to come and murder Ragnall with a hatchet, while Ragnall was tied to a post. And Flotta had told her to kill him with her "dead" command, so she agreed that the old bastard should die.

Ragnall smiled. Tears burst out of the German king's eyes. Ragnall shook his head and raised Flotta's knife. It was way, way too late for tears.

Chapter 24

There, thought, Dug, there was the arch in the white chalk. He'd never seen the waves pound so high against it. How could the arch stand, he wondered? How did the cliffs hold out against the waves' relentless onslaught? He'd swum in waves like that − not on purpose and he never wanted to do it again − so he knew they weren't just water, they were aswirl with rocks, wicked-sharp shells and other marine debris. How did the cliffs stand? There, he wasn't thinking about Lowa any more. He was as tough as the cliffs.

He thought back to their conversation, winced, shook his head, and picked up his pace.

Lowa sprinted too fast down the steep slope, misjudged a step and slipped on a smooth flint. Her other foot jarred into a half-dug hole, her ankle cracked and she fell. She tucked her shoulder and rolled head over heels twice, using the second roll to fling herself back on to her feet. Her left foot hit the ground and she collapsed in a bolt of pain. This time she went down with no control, landing hard on her side, rolling until the slope evened out.

She lay, snorting into the chalky soil, feeling like an idiot, the pain throbbing up her leg so intense that she giggled. Slowly, she clambered on to her good foot and gingerly tested the other one.

"Ahhh!" she cried, the moment she leant any weight on to it. She looked about. Thankfully nobody had seen her fall over and hurt herself while chasing after a man. It wasn't a queenly look.

Fuck the pain, she decided; she'd catch Dug up and he could help her back to his place. It couldn't be far from here, and she'd be able to say everything she wanted to say while her ankle soaked in a bucket of hot water. Not quite the seduction scene from a bard's love story, but it would have to do.

Swearing and yelping, she half hopped, half ran up the slope. She reached the top. There was Dug, approaching the top of the next rise, walking as if Bel had set fire to his arse. She'd never catch him. Fuck dignity, she thought.

"Dug!" she shouted, into the gale.

He carried on walking.

"DUG!" she screamed.

He paused but didn't turn. He must have heard her. He'd stopped as if he'd heard her. But then he walked on and disappeared over the ridge.

She hopped for a couple of paces. She gave up. She'd never catch him. But there was no point, even if she could. Of course he didn't want to see her. She'd let him fall for her, acted totally as if she'd fallen for him, then shagged a boy two paces away from him, knowing that he'd see.

She lowered herself on to the grass by the path and sat back with a sigh. Her ankle was pulsing with pain, twice the size of the other one already and blooming angry purple and red. She looked about. Forget the embarrassment, she thought, a helpful passer-by would be very welcome right now.

Dug was trying and failing to consider what he might have to eat that evening when he heard her shout his name. One day, one day soon, he told himself, he'd be able to stop imagining that he saw and heard her everywhere.

"Dug!" It was screeched this time. Definitely her. He

stopped. Yes, he thought, definitely her, just like it had been all those times when it hadn't been her. It was a seagull's cry, no doubt, that his badger's arse of a brain turned into Lowa running after him and crying out his name. He wasn't even going to turn round. But he would pause long enough to hear it if she shouted again. Of course, he didn't hear a thing. Big badgers' ball-sacks, he was a fool. He walked on.

Chapter 25

Chamanca dodged, smashed a knee into the Roman wanker's balls, and heaved at her wrist chains. The iron loop snapped and she was free. Well, that was lucky timing, she thought. The centurion bent double and Chamanca crowned him with her metal cuffs. He went down, blood streaming. She fell on to her back, swung her feet up and through her wrist chain, then rolled back and over and sank her teeth into the collapsed centurion's neck. Sweet blood washed down her throat.

She wanted to drain him, for the joy of it and to kill him, but ever closer shouts and screams meant she had no time for indulgence. She jumped up. Her ankle chain was so short that two-footed leaping was more effective than a shuffling run. She bounced out of the tent, feeling like an idiot. She knew there was a blacksmith's nearby because she'd heard it. She just had to find it and take a hammer to her chains before any of the rampaging soldiers spotted a woman hopping through the camp like a tasty, disabled rabbit.

She blinked in the brightness and saw that she was on a road which, judging by the early sun, ran north to south through the camp. Uniform tents, identical to the one that she'd emerged from, lined both sides of it. None of them gave any sign of being a blacksmith.

She heard running and backed up against a tent, as if that might hide her. Legionaries burst through gaps in the eastern tent line, sprinted across the road and disappeared to the west. If they noticed the escaped captive, they had more pressing things on their minds.

She toddled along in small steps, looking into each tent. They all contained eight neat little camp beds, legionaries' travelling gear, and nothing else. No weapons, no chain-smashing anvil and hammer.

Germanic howls and the clash of iron on iron rang ever closer from the east of the camp. She reached a crossroads, looked to her right and there was a gang of German soldiers, six women and one man, blooded and brandishing weapons. They were wearing even less than she was.

They came at her.

"I'm on your side. I'm a Gaul," she said.

"We're not Gauls," said the foremost, stepping forward and raising a pace-long broadsword. It was one of many sorts of weapon you didn't want to face when your hands were chained and your movement was restricted to two-footed jumps.

"Chamanca!" came a shout. It was Carden's voice.

"Carden?" shouted Chamanca.

"You know Carden?" said the swordswoman.

"No, I just guessed that might be his name."

The woman looked confused, but she took a step back.

Carden and Atlas arrived at a run. Atlas swung Chamanca on to his shoulder without a word and they set off running again.

"Hello?" said Chamanca.

"We've got to get out of here," said Carden.

"But you breached the Roman camp? The Germans are winning the battle?"

"They're not. They're routed on the left and in the centre. We led the right as far as the camp, but right now the Roman reinforcements are swinging round and . . . never mind. Point is we've got to get out of here." They'd reached the cleared area between the wall and the tents, where the legions would usually keep their horses.

"No horses," said Atlas. "Didn't think there would be." They ran on, Chamanca bouncing on the big Kushite's shoulder.

Chapter 26

"Who the fuck are you and what the fuck are you doing?" shouted the praetorian, very close to his face.

"I am the envoy of Julius Caesar. The man I am sitting on is Ariovistus, king of all the Germans, who I have killed."

The praetorian leant back, eyed Ragnall beadily and stroked his wide chin, then walked on without a word.

He waited. The praetorian, he knew, would be one of an advance guard, checking that the camp was safe for Julius Caesar to ride in bravely at the head of the army, officially the first Roman into the German base. Sure enough, the general arrived a short time later, followed by his guard and a crowd of varied tribunes, top centurions and others.

The praetorian had clearly briefed him, because he walked his horse directly to Ragnall and dismounted. Ragnall stood and Caesar embraced him.

"Bravest of the British!" cried the general, indicating Ragnall with an outstretched hand, while addressing his retinue. None of them looked like they'd been in a battle, apart from Titus Labienus, who had a bloodied bandage around his neck. "Who now can doubt my envoy's loyalty? Ragnall the barbarian, taken captive by the Germans, has slain the tyrant King Ariovistus! No longer shall he be called Ragnall the barbarian. Caesar grants him the greatest honour. Hail Ragnall the Roman!"

"Hail Ragnall the Roman!" They all shouted back. "Hail Ragnall the Roman!"

Ragnall found himself smiling. So he was a Roman now in name as well as in spirit. It felt right.

Chapter 27

Manfrax stood up from from his grim throne, arms open, beaming with what Bruxon suspected to be false hospitality. A new but equally miserable gaggle of naked, injured and chained captives surrounded him. One was leaking blood and pus from a black-crusted eye socket into his own smashed up mouth, another had splinted spikes of bone instead of hands.

"I'd heard the British were cowards but that must be wrong!" His strange accent made it sound like he was singing. "Here you are, strolling in as if you were visiting your favourite aunty." Next to the king, the narrow-eyed Queen Reena looked even less friendly than before. Manfrax continued, his smile a little less bright: "Because only very brave men would dare suggest that I'm going to break that blood shake by coming to check up on me. Did you not understand what it meant? That is why you've come, isn't it? To make sure that I'm going to invade and that I'm not going to break my oath?"

Bruxon opened his mouth to speak, but could think of nothing to say. It could have been the cave that overwhelmed him, so huge and dark that its walls disappeared up into blackness, or the eye-stinging reek of excrement both human and dog, or the vilely abused wretches who girded Manfrax's throne, or the piercing glare of Queen Reena. Most disconcerting of all was the faux-charming brute himself. Manfrax's presence – his aura – filled Bruxon with an irrational, paralysing sensation. It was more than fear. The Irish king stirred, deep down in his guts, a strange thrill that wasn't altogether unpleasant. He told himself that the man was nothing but an Eroo braggart, not worthy even of his contempt. He'd seen his sort at home, men who drank every night until they were brave enough to start a fight. In civilised Dumnonia, these men were shunned, treated as unfortunate idiots by anyone with power or station. On barbarian Eroo they were the leaders and the worst of them all was king. The whole lot of them were peasants, not fit to clean the dogshit out of his horse's hooves. Yet something about the savage ruler made his heart race and his breath shorten.

Manfrax smiled at his discomfort. "Or even worse, perhaps, you've come to offer help? You know what we do to people in Eroo who offer help when we don't need it? We do something like this." Manfrax stood, long flint knife in hand. He grabbed the captive with no hands by the hair at the back of his head. The man didn't flinch as Manfrax jabbed the tip of his knife into his ear, then he actually smiled as the king pushed the blade slowly into his head.

Bruxon watched in horror as the man blinked rapidly, then began to spout words in an ugly, guttural language that he didn't know, then finally, mercifully died. He darted a look at Maggot.

The druid winked at him, then turned to Manfrax. "We've come, you great king of Eroo, you, for nothing of the sort. We are on a journey of leisure. Taking advantage of not having much to do, it being the end of autumn and all our supplies stowed, we have taken a boat across the sea to visit your island purely for the purpose of viewing it. We liked it so much last time that we simply had to come back and see more. Now, would it not have been terribly rude of us, had we been passing and not knocked on your door?"

Manfrax laughed. Bruxon didn't know if this was a good sign or not.

"I do like this one!" shouted the Irish king to his empty

hall. It was morning, and the revellers who'd filled the hall last time were off doing whatever they did during the day. The king's shouts echoed. "Go! Admire the cliff, see the villages nearby, and come back tonight and feast with me!"

"Thank you, majesty," Bruxon managed. He turned to go.

"But while we're here, and before you have all those other excellent conversationalists to enthral you late into the night," said Maggot, "how is your invasion army coming together? When should we expect you?"

Manfrax's eyes narrowed. He reddened with anger, then seemed to relax. "To be honest," he said, "I'm not totally sure." He sounded reasonable and calm. Reena was looking at him, mouth open, as surprised by the change in character as Bruxon. "It depends on a few factors," Manfrax continued, "none of which can be predicted with any accuracy. But, rest assured, I'm putting together the sort of army that will provide terrifying bedtime stories for hundreds of generations of children. And it will cross. The soonest? This coming year, late summer. The latest? Two years. It will definitely be on your shores within two years. It'll be worth the wait. I've got a wonderful surprise for you."

"You'll have to let us know a good few moons before you're coming, so that we can prepare," said Maggot.

"That seems reasonable." Manfrax stroked his chin.

"What have you done to him?" screeched Reena, standing up.

"Quiet, you." Maggot raised a hand at her. She fell back in her chair, mute.

Manfrax did not seem to notice, and said, "I'll send you a messenger three moons before we're coming, and another two moons before, in case the first one doesn't make it."

"Right, thanks. Come on Bruxon."

They turned and walked from the cave.

"What did you . . . ?" Bruxon asked.

"Me? Nothing," Maggot stumbled. Bruxon grabbed his

arm, and the druid slumped into his grasp. "Now get us out of here."

"But if you used magic on him . . ."

"He and she will forget that we were there. But he will remember what he agreed to do, and he will send a messenger. But we have to go. Now. I need to be on the cart before I pass out, or you'll have to carry—" Maggot passed out.

Bruxon slung him over his shoulder and was amazed by how little he weighed. He walked from Manfrax's hall, wondering for the thousandth time why he'd invited an invasion from Eroo in the first place.

Chapter 28

Now that Ragnall was a free citizen, Caesar told him to do what he wanted in the winter break from campaigning. So he returned to Rome with the general and most of the army, and strode across town to Clodia Metelli's palace. She welcomed him like a long lost pet and he spent the winter there, pirouetting between paroxysms of pleasure. The house was even more fun because Clodia's husband Metellus Celer's invisible but nevertheless looming presence was gone. He'd died shortly after Caesar had appropriated Ragnall.

Everyone said that Clodia had poisoned her husband, but nobody accused her directly. Her reputation for having detractors gang-raped in public was an effective buttoner of lips. Ragnall didn't think she'd done it anyway. She had no reason to. The massive beneficiary of Metellus Celer's death had in fact been Caesar, who'd inherited the governorship of Transalpine Gaul from the dead proconsul, to add to his other two provinces of Illyricum and toga-wearing Gaul to the south of the Alps. Caesar had launched his attack on the rest of Gaul from Transalpine Gaul, so none of his previous year's victories could have happened if Metellus hadn't conveniently carked it. But nobody was pointing the finger at Rome's latest and greatest hero.

If there were any whispered allegations, they were drowned out by bellicose and jubilant shouting in the Senate, at the Forum, in houses, shops, inns, restaurants and on the streets of the magnificent city. Julius Caesar had won two wars! In one year! Everyone was saying that Caesar had pissed all over the Helvetians, and kicked the Germans so hard up their arses that they'd flown across the Renus river and would never be heard of again. This, if anyone had doubted it before, was proof that the Romans were the greatest people who had ever lived. The Senate, Tribunate and other ambitious types saw advantage in agreeing with the citizens, and granted an unprecedented fifteen days of public holiday to celebrate Caesar and Rome's marvelousness.

Everybody, including Caesar, was claiming that Caesar had conquered all of Gaul. Ragnall knew that this was a massively premature declaration. Gaul was a rough square, bounded by the Alps and Pyrenees mountains to the south, the Renus river to the east and the ocean and the British Channel to the west and north. Thanks to Caesar, Rome now controlled more or less the south-east quarter. The south-west was already so loyal to Rome that it might as well have been a province – again more or less, you never knew where you really were with those two-faced barbarians.

The north of Gaul remained free and pissed off. Even as Caesar was marching on the Germans, the armies of northern Gaul and Belgium had begun to gather. Now, slowly assembling was a larger army that the Romans had ever faced before, the sort of eye-poppingly huge force that hadn't been seen since the days of Alexander and the Persians.

Caesar persuaded the Senate, consuls and Tribunate that this mass of ravage-minded barbarians, left unchallenged, would sweep south any day, destroying Roman interests in Iberia and Gaul, killing virtuous farmers and raping beautiful girls, before crossing the Alps like Hannibal, slaughtering Italians by the thousand and, most unthinkable of all, sacking Rome. Caesar said that even the wild, brutal British were sending legions of mercenaries into Gaul to fight the Romans, so the threat was more terrifying and severe than anyone in Rome could imagine. Moreover, Ariovistus, the conquered German king, was just one German king. There were plenty more who might cross the Renus any day and turn south to pillage their way through bountiful Italy and into Rome itself.

Caesar's doom-filled prophesies played perfectly on Rome's favourite fear of invading barbarian hordes. It was three hundred and thirty years since the Gauls had sacked Rome and a hundred and sixty since Hannibal had routed Roman armies on Italian soil, yet Ragnall was amazed at how often people mentioned those disasters, and argued that they were due for another one. At the battle of Cannae, Hannibal's Carthaginians had killed sixty thousand Roman legionaries in a day, yet there were statues of the general all over Rome. It was as if they enjoyed being reminded about it.

He remembered Drustan telling him that all people like to create a preventable doom to give importance and urgency to their existence. Drustan had been talking about a tribe who thought the sky was falling on their heads, but the same applied here. They were on the brink of catastrophe, everyone said, and something had to be done!

Luckily, Caesar knew exactly what that something was. They needed a buffer to defend their territories and soak up any invasion before it could pillage and rape decent people. For the sake of all those who relied upon Rome for protection, it was Rome's duty to bring northern Gaul under its control.

Ragnall knew this was disingenuous, Caesar knew it was disingenuous and everyone in Rome who wasn't a chest-thumping jingoist knew it was disingenuous. You might use the same "buffer" argument to occupy your neighbour's house. Moreover, where would and could it end? If northern Gaul became Roman territory, wouldn't they need to conquer a new buffer to protect the Roman soil of northern Gaul? And once that next buffer became Roman soil, a new buffer would be needed, and so on.

So the dupable populace were convinced by the threat of

barbarians to the north. Something needed to be done, and Caesar was the man to do it. Had not Alexander swept aside the impossibly numerous Persian armies? Had not Caesar already shown that he was Rome's Alexander? So Caesar was ordered to do what he would have done anyway, and march into northern Gaul to stamp out all threats to Rome.

If Ragnall knew that Caesar's' justifications were dodgy, it didn't stop him being swept up by the joyous fervour of the times. When Julius' summons came for him to accompany the army again, Ragnall bade Clodia goodbye and headed north with a spring in his step.

Chapter 29

Chamanca was pleased to return to Maidun, but she was far from happy with the weather. Iberia had been cold at this time of year, but she remembered childhood winters as dramatic and bracing, with brilliant-white snow piled paces high under dazzlingly blue skies. It had been a time to play, sleep and eat the supplies they'd amassed in warmer times. There was no snow in Britain, brilliant-white or not, and it was, as Carden had put it, cold enough to shrivel the bollocks off an iron aurochs. And so miserably wet! The trees, the bushes, the very hills were depressingly, soddenly, soaked through. The people were much the same. Chamanca was so cold that it hurt, even wrapped as she was in the double wolf-pelt cloak that she'd liberated from a Roman patrol when the weather had turned. None of the people they rode past had anything nearly as warm. People recognised them and greeted them on their way north to Maidun, but you could have counted the smiles on one hand with all its fingers eaten off by frostbite.

Finally they arrived at the Castle. Lowa met them in the main body of the fort and led them up to the Eyrie. She was limping, but said she'd almost recovered from a stupid running injury. It's why she'd walked out to meet them. She was going on it a little further every day. Even half hobbled and wrapped in so many furs that she looked like a small bipedal bear, she still strode along full of life and purpose. Her exposed face was clear-eyed, smoothly radiant and blemish-free. She had developed none of the eye bags, wrinkles, grey hair, spots and other atrophies that had afflicted all the other rulers that Chamanca had known.

Spring greeted them at Lowa's hut. The girl was now taller than both Chamanca and Lowa; she'd morphed into a grown woman over the year. She had almost fully changed from pretty into beautiful, but like Lowa's it was an odd beauty, a striking kind that would appeal only to some – very unlike Chamanca's beauty of course. Everybody fancied the leather shorts off her. Not that they could see them in this cursed weather.

"How much older are you now?" asked Carden, reaching to pinch Spring's cheek.

"Half as young as twice the age I was before, plus a year." Spring ducked his hand.

"What?" said Carden. Atlas chuckled.

The girl led them into the cavernous but cheerily warm queen's hut. As she brought them stew and bread and stoked up the two fires, Miller, Mal and Nita, Lowa's generals, welcomed them and quizzed them about their journey. Bruxon, king of the Dumnonians, was also there, but he greeted them with about as much warmth as the winter sun. That was his way, but Chamanca didn't trust him. He clearly didn't fancy her, which made him downright odd, bordering on insane and certainly untrustworthy.

Atlas told them all that had happened in Gaul, with interjections from Carden and Chamanca. The others asked questions throughout, particularly on Roman battle tactics, Felix, and his rumoured dark force. There would have been more questions on the latter, Chamanca was sure, if they'd known more. One thing she had been able to confirm was that the druids had been right – Britain was the Romans' target, or at least that's what someone very close to Caesar had told her when she was their captive. The conquest of Gaul was useful for amassing wealth and boosting Caesar's prestige, but its main function was as the launchpad for the British mission.

"Why Britain?" asked Bruxon.

"I don't know, but, given their interest in magic, I'd be surprised if it wasn't something to do with that. Perhaps some source of magic that will give them even greater powers?" Chamanca glanced at Spring. The girl got up to tend a fire.

"So," said Lowa, "when will they get here?"

"According to Chamanca's source," rumbled Atlas, "they intend to come this summer. But they need a fleet, and they need to defeat the army mustering in northern Gaul."

"They could make peace with Gauls, buy or steal a fleet and be here by Beltane."

"They could, but I don't think—"

"So, we'll continue to focus on mobile warfare, cavalry and chariots, we'll continue to drill our infantry and—"

"Should you not," said Atlas, "shift your focus from the Romans for a moment and have a look around?" He raised his dark eyes until they met Bruxon's. Bruxon held his gaze, but Chamanca saw an artery in his neck pulse unnaturally.

"At what?" asked Lowa.

"Three and a half years ago, Maidun was attacked by a very large Dumnonian army, much bigger than Maidun's. Well led, that army could still defeat Maidun, especially if Maidun—"

"That would not happen," interrupted Bruxon, "We have sworn—"

"Let him finish," said Lowa.

Atlas treated Bruxon to one of his looks that always made Chamanca feel about five years old, then continued. "So that army could defeat Maidun, especially if Maidun was fixated on looking in the other direction, towards a potential invasion across the Channel. Now, we also have the Murkans in the north, with whom we don't have a pact, and, potentially, have a larger, more powerful army than Dumnonia. As well as that, I've heard talk that King Manfrax of Eroo is looking for new victims."

"Bruxon has a pact with the Murkans and with Eroo. Britain and Eroo are united against the Romans," said Lowa.

"Are you certain? Caesar would not have beaten the Germans so easily, perhaps not at all, if the Skawney tribe hadn't aided him. That is how the Romans succeed. Spiteful tribes see a chance to defeat a hated neighbour, so they help the Romans. It is like a pig having his revenge on a fellow pig by opening the sty door to let the wolf in."

"My pacts are solid," said Bruxon, "and I can personally guaran—"

"Quiet, Bruxon," said Lowa. "You do have a point, Atlas. I trust Bruxon, but, now we know that we have some space before the legions land, I'll ensure the bonds are as strong as possible. As soon as the weather allows I'll lead a delegation to the Murkans."

"A delegation? I would take the army," said Atlas.

"No, they must train more. We've had three years learning how to wage war with teamwork and intelligence, the Romans have had centuries. I will take a delegation. Besides, if you're right about Eroo, and if the Dumnonians have been plotting behind Bruxon's back and either invade, then we'll need the army here."

"And us?" asked Carden.

"You three are going to go back and keep an eye on the Romans. If you can stick a spear in the cartwheel of their advance, so much the better."

The three of them nodded resignedly.

"There's one other thing," added Chamanca. "We found out what happened to Ragnall."

"Oh really?" said Lowa.

Chapter 30

Lowa rode at the head of the column, her recurve riding bow holstered, arrow-stuffed quiver on her back, slim sword scabbard slapping gently on her horse's flank. Miller was beside her, also dressed in battle leathers, longsword at his side. Behind them were sixty variously armed Warriors of the Two Hundred, Lowa's expanded and updated version of Zadar's Fifty.

Spring enjoyed the irony that if you didn't want to fight you had to display your arms as if you were Makka the god of war and his retinue. She was riding at the rear of the group, green woollen hood covering her head, quiver on her back and bow in one hand. After two days of uncomfortable riding through sweeping rain showers, the day was finally sunny with splodges of white cloud, but it wasn't warm yet. It was a good while since dawn, but if she breathed out from deep down she could still see her breath.

Bright plants had risen bravely from the winter soil and bloomed into flowers that speckled the roadside and forest floors with a crazy range of colours. They didn't impress Spring. Despite her name, she found spring the season too obviously lovely, with its show-off flowers and vomit-inducingly adorable baby animals. She preferred melancholy autumn, with hazy sunlight, pungent funguses and warm-smelling woodsmoke. As with music, sorrow was more beautiful than happiness in nature. She thought that if she was Spring, then Dug was probably Autumn. Did that mean she liked him more than she liked herself?

The bark of a dog brought her back to the present. For the last two days, perhaps eighty miles, they'd ridden through the open countryside of a land at peace. All the hillforts they passed were overgrown and unused. Instead of walled towns and fortified ranches, there was a smattering of farmhouses and little hamlets with no defences; no ditches nor a spiked palisade to be seen. One of the Two Hundred told her that this was what it had been like in the south before Zadar's time. People had moved away from the hillforts to undefended farms. When Zadar's ravages had started, the palisades had gone back up.

For the last dozen miles, nobody had run and hidden, as Spring would have done had she been a farmer or potter watching half a hundred heavily armed warriors ride towards her. The people had of course been wary, they weren't mad, but good old Miller had soon put them at ease with a few friendly quips.

That morning, the wide valley sides of the floodplain had narrowed in to a bouncing little stream, and they were following a track along its western bank. The barking dog was a sinuous, smooth-haired, happy little animal. It circled the horses a few times, then galloped up the road to a cluster of large huts next to a stone bridge. Smoke curls from the huts' roof holes created a morning haze. A larger cloud of smoke to the east proclaimed the position of Mallam's main settlement, but they weren't headed there. They were bound for Grummog, king of the Murkans, at his cliff-top fort.

They passed the huts without seeing a soul, wound uphill through some trees and the pale grey cliff of Mallam burst from the valley floor. Three hundred paces tall, the rock face filled the valley like an impossibly high and smooth wall. There were cliffs as high on the south coast near Dug's place, possibly higher, but Spring had never seen anything like it inland. Sea cliffs seemed to be on the defensive, cowering from the power of the waves and regularly succumbing to it in crumbling rockslides. The landlocked cliff at Mallam looked like it was on the attack, ready to rush down the valley like a great wave itself, to smash and crush everything before it. She looked away then quickly looked back. Had it moved forwards? Of course not. But it looked like it wanted to.

"You know what they say, don't you?" said Holloc, falling back to ride alongside her. He was one of Lowa's Two Hundred, a nice enough guy. Spring would have found him attractive if he'd been as clever as he thought he was.

"Depends who 'they' are and what they're talking about?"

Holloc looked surprised. He'd no doubt been expecting a standard "no, please do enlighten me oh clever older person" reply. Even though she was thirteen now and could fire a bow about as well as Lowa, people thought she was still a child. She couldn't remember ever thinking of herself as a child.

"Many, many generations ago," Holloc swept an arm to indicate the length of the rock face, "a great river ran over a mighty waterfall, right here. The river runs underground now. One day it will come back to the surface and the waterfall will start again."

"And what will that mean?"

"What do you mean, 'what will that mean'?"

"Oh, I don't know, there's usually something with these things, isn't there? Something like the dead coming back from the Otherworld on the day the waterfall starts flowing again? Or the gods coming to the earth and smiting the tribes who have slightly different beliefs to our tribe?"

"Not with this one, I don't think. That's it. They just say that the waterfall will come back."

"I see. Great story."

Holloc scowled at her and kicked his horse to rejoin the others. Spring shook her head at herself. That had been a bit mean. After so much time with Lowa, she'd become somewhat sarcastic herself. She liked it and thought it was funny, but sometimes it upset people. It was of course their fault for not getting she was joking, they should have been cleverer, but she still didn't like it that they were hurt. When she was queen, she decided, she'd make everyone who didn't get sarcasm or piss taking for fun to wear seagull feathers in their hats, so you knew not to joke with them.

Former waterfall or not, there was a gang of people peering down at them from the top of the cliff. On their left and her right was a giant, with short arms and an oversized head. Spring had never seen one before, but she knew it was a wicker woman. Wooden cages were nailed together in the shape of a woman and their bars interwoven with wicker. They'd fill the wicker woman with live animals, then set light to it. It was horrible idea, and Spring couldn't believe that it impressed the gods, but it was also kind of awe-inspiring. She couldn't take her eyes off it. A vision flashed into her mind of Lowa, bound and helpless, trapped in the burning—

She shook her head and the image cleared. It had been like a bad daydream, not a proper vision like she'd had with the aurochs. There was nothing to be afraid of here. They were a delegation, and nobody would ever break the ancient code and attack a delegation, especially a royal one. And, besides, she knew that this place wasn't as scary as it looked. Dug had told her all about Mallam before they'd left the south. From this direction, it looked like the most impenetrable fortress imaginable. However, come from any direction other than the south, according to Dug, and you could easily get around the cliff and the only defences were a few scrappy stone walls. The fort at Mallam, seat of Grummog, king of the Murkans, Dug had said, was all mouth and no trousers. The people from that part of Britain, Dug had added with a naughty look in his eye, were mostly the same.

"Come on, Spring!" yelled Holloc. Spring realised she'd stopped. She kicked on to catch them up.

Lowa and Miller had almost reached the track that led up the steep slope to the top of the cliff. The sixty soldiers from the Two Hundred were spread out behind them, riding in a more casual manner now they'd reached journey's end unmolested and could look forward to a feast and a rest. Some had ambled to the stream to let their horses drink, others were dotted about while their horses pulled toothily at the clumps of grass which sprouted all around the field below the cliff, between large bushes.

Spring looked about. On their long walks, she and Dug speculated often on how the land had come to look like it did; why specific plants lived in specific places and so on. Going by the washes of gravel all around, here was a place that flooded regularly. If it did flood, it meant that the only vegetation would be that year's growth – the grass – and no large bushes.

She opened her mouth to scream a warning exactly as the out-of-place vegetation burst apart. Four or five men and women jumped from each bush and stabbed spears into the Maidun riders. Spring watched, mouth open, as the few Maidun soldiers who'd survived the surprise attempted to rally, but were closed down and speared by the hundreds of Murkans who'd suddenly emerged.

By the cliff, Miller and Lowa were caught, pulled from their horses, spear points at their throats. As she watched, Lowa whacked away her guard's arm with her bow and fell back, stringing the bow as she fell, shooting an arrow into her captor, then almost immediately stringing and shooting another. Another Murkan fell and Spring realised with a jolt that she was in a battle, and so far all she'd done was watch like a dumb-struck dimwit. She reached for her bow, but something thumped into her and knocked her from her horse. She hit the ground. She shook her head. A man with a moustache trimmed into a straight-edged square was sitting on her, his legs pinning her arms. She opened her mouth to tell him how stupid he looked but he punched her in the side of the head. His moustache swung around and around, filled her vision, then shrunk, taking everything with it and she saw no more.

Spring came to. She was on a horse, her hands were bound and somebody was holding her from behind. Up ahead were Miller and Lowa, both riding on their own horses with their hands chained, spears at their backs.

The path – the track to the top of the cliff, Spring deduced – curled on to a broad expanse of flat, bare rock, criss-crossed with cracks and mini crevices. There were a couple of dozen more spearmen dotted about, but no buildings other than a black longhouse in the centre of the pavement, with the wicker woman looming behind it. Three sides of the field of rock were overlooked by craggy bluffs, dotted with tartan and leather-dressed Murkans, come to gawp at the captives from a safe distance.

The longest side of the rock-floored expanse was the top of the cliff. The view was vast. Spring fancied that she could see Maidun Castle, three hundred miles south, and, just beyond that, Dug's hut by the sea. She wished she was there. Here, a semi-circle of Murkans with long spears demanded that Lowa and Miller dismount. Spring looked behind her. The Murkans held six more Maidun people at spear point, including Holloc, whom she'd been rude to just a few heartbeats before, when things had been very different. Each of them had their wrists chained like Lowa and Miller. Presumably the rest been slaughtered at the base of the cliff. She'd liked a lot of them, but she didn't feel upset by their deaths, which seemed odd. She guessed that she would later. This must be what war was like. You had to get on with it and grieve when you had time. The man behind her dismounted and pulled her from the horse.

"Come on you," he said, pushing her in the back, "over

this way and no fucking funny business. Start acting the squirrel and I'll stick you with my fucking spear." He had an unpleasantly sharp, nasal voice.

"What do you mean, acting the squirrel?" she said.

"You know – larking about, causing trouble."

"Oh, I see. I thought you might be worried I was going to bite your moustache off. Why is it that strange shape? Did you lose a bet?"

She ducked his punch, said "OK, OK, sorry," and went where she was pushed, over towards the longhouse. The network of cracks on the cliff top, mostly about a hand-span wide, made it look like a giant version of a dried mud puddle. They picked their way over the gaps.

The longhouse was a heavily constructed, black wooden building, with curved iron blades splaying out from each corner of its roof and no obvious door. Spring followed Lowa and Miller and their captors round to the long side facing the cliff edge, which was open, without a wall. The six captured riders filed along behind them. All the Maidun people had their hands tied, but Murkan soldiers still followed them closely, spears ready.

King Grummog and his retinue were waiting, looking out over the edge of the cliff. The Murkan king was a wee man, sitting in a big wooden chair that made him look all the smaller. He was perhaps a little older than Dug, but it was hard to tell because his little body and limbs were all twisted. His shoeless feet and his hands were curled into claws and his round head jutted forward on a scrawny neck, forced there by the large hump of his upper back. He had the blinking eyes of a bird that expected to be thrown a crumb, but a straight, expression-free mouth.

Towering behind Grummog was a giant of a woman with puffy, piscine eyes and fat, shiny-wet lips which were the same pale yellow-pink as the rest of her face. The expression in those fishy eyes, Spring reckoned, said that she would watch you drown in a puddle rather than bend to help you. She wore a thick, dark wool waistcoat with a faded, smudged swirl decoration and a stupidly short leather-flanged skirt. Her legs were like bark-stripped oak trunks, each of them surely heavier that two of Spring put together. Her arms were heavy with fat-coated muscle, thicker at the biceps than Spring's thighs. Her broad, smooth shoulders were rounded with bovine strength and extra bits of muscle grew from midway along them almost up to her head, like scaffolding to help her neck support her thick skull. Sprouting from her meaty right hip was the large coil of a thick leather whip. On her left hand she'd grown and somehow thickened her nails, so it looked like she had bear's claws. Spring thought that she might be a Fassite – a giant from the island of Fassent. Everyone agreed that Fassent existed, just south of Eroo, but nobody set foot on the island for fear of the mythical giants that were said to live there. Spring had met a man once who said that he'd sailed past Fassent and giants had hurled rocks at his boat from the shore. She'd assumed he was lying, but this woman looked like proof that the myth of the giants was a reality.

Arranged in a fan shape, left and right of the strange ruling pair, were an array of tough-looking men and women, twenty or so armed with swords and spears. They watched in silence as the guard attached six Maidun riders and Miller to a longer chain which ran between an iron ring hammered into the rock ground and another set in a boulder the height of Spring. The boulder perched on the cliff edge. Spring did not like the look of it and neither, given the looks on their faces, did any of the others, but with hands bound and spears everywhere, there was nothing they could do.

"Queen Lowa," spat Grummog, "I wondered when you'd grace us with your magnificent presence." His voice was even sharper than Spring's square-mustachioed captor's, managing to sound offended and aggressive at the same time, like a bandit you've caught in the act of murdering a traveller who's claiming that it's all your fault while planning to attack you. It made Spring wince.

"I'm Grummog, king of all the Murkans," he continued. "And this beauty," he indicated the woman next to him, "is my queen, Pomax." If Pomax was flattered by the lie about her looks, it didn't warm her cold scowl.

"You are a fool, Grummog," said Lowa. Spring swelled with pride at how commanding she sounded.

"Am I? Well, aren't I lucky to have you to come up here and tell me? Would you like to explain why?"

Lowa told him about the Romans' progress in Gaul, and the news that they were set on conquering Britain. She told him about the power of Caesar's army, leaving out Chamanca's report on Felix's dark legion.

"You have made a terrible mistake in attacking my people, Grummog," she finished, "but, if you free us now and we draw up a pact to unite against the Romans, I will forgive you and instruct my soldiers' families not to retaliate."

"Ooh, thanks so much for giving me the chance!" Grummog was sarcastic and Spring hated him all the more. Sarcasm was not always appropriate. "I'm so lucky, me. But tell me, just for interest's sake, what will happen if I throw you and all your people off the cliff now?"

"The Maidun army will march here within the moon and slaughter you all. Then the Romans will come and take Britain, but that won't matter to you because you'll be long dead and forgotten."

"Oh, well, I suppose we'll just have to take that risk," said Grummog, sounding like a fatalistic traveller warned that there might be rain on the way.

"Grummog," said Lowa, "Caesar has pillaged, murdered and raped through southern Gaul. Northern Gaul is likely to capitulate within the moon, then he will come to Britain and take our freedom. However, if all the tribes of Britain can unite, then his army can be beaten. For the benefit of everyone, the first thing for us to do is to make an agreement to—"

"Stop, stop, stop!" Grummog waved his gnarled hands. "Stop your bleating, woman! You know, don't you, who benefits when someone says that something is for the benefit of everyone? The person saying it, that's who! Always! You've got a weak little position in the south and the Romans are going to piss all over you. I don't see why I should stop that. You know what I say? I say that it's," he attempted to copy Lowa's accent, "for the benefit of everyone for me to help the Romans against you, then live at peace with them. I say 'you' but I mean Maidun. You'll be well dead before they come. Dead and curled into a little ball of black meat and charred bones." He looked to his left, over at the wicker woman, then back to Lowa. He winked.

"The Romans will massacre you." Lowa's jaw was clenched.

"Your arrogance makes a fool of you." Grummog narrowed his eyes. "You think I don't have people with the Romans? You think you're the only one who heard the druid's warnings and decided to have a look what was happening? You come up here, thinking you're doing some sort of favour for the stupid Murkans? Talking to me like I'm a child? Shall I tell you what I know about the Romans in Gaul?"

"Go for it," said Lowa, sounding unimpressed.

"I will go for it!" screamed Grummog. "The Romans are unbeatable by anyone in Britain because they've been training for hundreds of fucking years, and we haven't and we don't have time—"

"My army can beat them."

"Shut up! And listen, for once in your fucking life! I know who you are, Lowa Flynn. I know what you did for Zadar. And I know that you're the last one to start preaching about fucking murder. You were at Cowton. Don't deny it, I know you were."

Lowa stayed quiet. She had, Spring knew, not just been present when Zadar's army killed every man, woman, child and animal in Cowton. She'd led the attack.

"My sister was at Cowton," Grummog continued. "On the wrong fucking side. She was a peaceful person. She left here because she didn't like me putting people in the wicker woman, but I loved her anyway. And she was killed for being in the wrong place. So don't you try and tell me that you're better than Caesar, me or anyone. And I'll tell you another thing I know. The Romans have killed a lot of people, but do you know the one thing that links everyone they've killed? The common factor, if you like?"

"I do," said Lowa, her voice like solid iron after Grummog's whining.

"You do, do you?"

"Yes. All of them were brave men and women who stood up to Caesar, not honourless turds who capitulated."

"Brave men and women who all died! The common factor is that they opposed the Romans. Lowa, you fight the Romans and you'll kill everyone who calls you queen. You fight the Romans, and you give your land to the Romans. That's what happens. I'm going to keep my land, I'm going to save my people, by helping the Romans take yours. And I'll tell you another thing you don't know, clever clever Lowa. It's not the Romans you should be worried about. You won't live to see the fucking Romans. Manfrax is sailing from Eroo any day with an army that'll smash yours. The Dumnonians, too. They aren't your puppies like you think. Bruxon, who you made king, went over to Eroo and asked Manfrax to invade. The Dumnonians will supply the Eroo army. They're going to tell him about your cavalry and your chariots and all your other secrets. You think the Romans are bad? You think they rape and murder? Wait until you meet the Eroo army. The Romans at least pretend to be civilised."

Lowa reddened. The twisted king grinned. "You didn't

know, did you? You only sent your spies over one sea. I sent mine both ways, because I'm cleverer than you. Manfrax has conquered Eroo and now he's going to use his army on Maidun. But he won't worry the Murkans, because guess what? The Dumnonians are going to ask me to join them and Eroo and I'll say yes – not immediately, obviously, because I know how to negotiate and get the best for my tribe, unlike you, you stupid woman.

"While you've been building your army to face the Romans, Maidun's destruction's been planned behind you. But don't worry, you're not going to see. I'm going keep you until Beltane. Then you're going in the head of the wicker woman, where you can think about how fucking brave and clever you are as you burn. And I tell you what. The rest of your life, before you burn, is going to be really, really shit. Pomax here is going look after you." Grummog nodded at the gigantic woman. For the first time, she smiled.

Lowa looked about warily. Spring did the same. With twenty spears at their backs, twenty swords in front and their hands bound, they were short on options. It was exactly the sort of situation that could do with some magic. Spring strained to pull power from within. She stared at Lowa, willing her to become a super-warrior. Nothing. She closed her eyes. She saw a vision of Dug that first time she'd seen him, when he'd killed Ulpius and unwittingly saved her. She felt a shift, as if a weight was being lifted out of her body. She opened her eyes.

Nothing had happened. Lowa stood facing Grummog, no more powerful than she'd been a heartbeat before.

"Right!" said Grummog. "I'm bored of these other southern bastards. Pomax?"

The big queen smiled and walked from the open-sided longhouse towards the boulder.

"No!" shouted Lowa, straining at her wrist bonds. Three

spear points pressed into her neck. Spring tried to run at Pomax, but strong arms encircled her from behind.

"You'll want to watch this," said square-moustache man in her ear, heaving her around to face the cliff top.

Spring couldn't see what Pomax was going to do. She had no lever, and there was no way that one person could move the boulder, even if she wasn't far off the size of an aurochs.

Pomax was going to give it a go, though. She squatted, placed her hands and a shoulder on the rock, then drove up into it, her thighs doubling in girth as bovine muscle bulged. The boulder shifted, leant and toppled off the cliff. The seven soldiers of Lowa's Two Hundred hardly had time to scream before the chain attaching them to the falling rock snapped tight and they flew, hands first, over the edge. Miller was the last to go, staring hate at Grummog.

While everyone listened to the cries of the falling, Lowa dropped away from the spears at her neck. She dived, rolled and bounced on to her feet, elbowed a Murkan in the neck and whacked her chained wrists into another's face. She spun to avoid a sling salvo and caught one of the slingstones. She continued her spin and hurled the stone at Grummog. He squeaked and half-raised his arms.

Somehow Pomax had sprinted back from the cliff edge. One of her hands flashed out and caught the stone, the other cracked her whip. Lowa tried to dodge, but the whipcord struck home, flicked around her torso and pinned her arms. She tried to pull away, but Pomax was a pace taller and three times her weight. She needed only one hand to hold the queen of Maidun. Lowa's only option was to run head first at Pomax, which she did. Pomax met her charge with a lazy backhanded slap across the face. Lowa's head snapped back, and she slumped. Pomax flicked the whip, Lowa pirouetted a grotesquely floppy dance and collapsed on to the bare rock, out cold.

Grummog turned to Spring, still in the clutches of square-moustache man, and smiled.

"Right, now. Spring." He said. Spring was confused. She hadn't said her name. How did he know her name?

"Or should I say Sabina?" Oh badger's balls, thought Spring. Sabina was the name her father, King Zadar, had given her. If Grummog knew that . . .

"Yes, that's right, I know who you are. My people saw you in the arena with your dad. I even know the stupid name you gave when you came back after running away. Well, I don't really – it's too stupid to remember – Ing-bo, Ong-bo something something? My point is, Spring, I know things. That's why I rule."

"Well done you. Your mum must be proud." Spring nodded.

"You southern cunt!" Grummog's face had become purple in the blink of an eye. "Just a child, but already so smug and so fucking superior. I was going to keep you, maybe whore you out to my men and then the Romans, but I've got a good mind to have you thrown off the cliff now."

"Why don't you, you pig-faced badger's cock?"

"How dare you, in front of my men and women call me—?"

"I'm sorry," said Spring, "I've insulted pig-faced badgers' cocks. You're actually much uglier than that. And smellier."

"That's it!" squeaked the king. "Pomax!"

Pomax looked at Spring, a hint of a smile on fleshy, glistening lips. She approached, coiling the whip with her clawed left hand. Spring almost fainted as her cockiness drained to be replaced by what she guessed must be fear. There was more to Pomax than size. Spring could feel magic radiating from the woman. That was how she'd been quick enough to best Lowa. Spring bet Pomax's magic wasn't as powerful as hers. If only she could find her magic again, she'd show the fish-faced giant. Surely it was meant to come at times like this? She strained. Nothing.

Square moustache held her tight while Pomax grabbed her neck and her thigh, encircling both easily with long, thick fingers. Her needle-sharp fingernails cut into Spring's. Square moustache released his grip.

The world swung as Pomax held Spring aloft. The Murkan queen walked towards the cliff edge, Spring thrashing above her head. She tried to whack the big woman's face, but couldn't reach. She clawed at her arms, but it was like trying to grip polished wood.

Pomax threw her upwards. She flew into the air, spun and fell. The giantess caught her again, one hand holding the back of her skirt, the other circling her neck from behind. She turned slowly, pivoting Spring so that she could see Grummog and the Murkans smiling at her. The girl writhed uselessly. She willed magic to bring Lowa back to life to save her, but the queen of Maidun lay motionless in a broken-looking pile.

"I'm going to kill you all," Spring said. They laughed.

Pomax turned. Spring could see the vast view and the road that she'd ridden along so happily, snaking away to the south. Funny how things can change so quickly, she thought, as Pomax hurled her off the cliff.

Chapter 31

"That," said Carden, "is the sweetest little position I ever saw. Are we sure we don't want these people conquering us? I'd love to be with an outfit that could set up something like that in a day. And, is it just me, or has it grown since we saw it last?"

"Caesar has hired two more legions, another ten thousand men," said Atlas, "and don't be wowed by their pretty camp. The Maidun army would never have given them the space or time to build it."

It was a lovely position, Chamanca thought, so different from the sprawl of Gaulish camps that faced it. She, Carden and Atlas were on horseback on a hillside that was thronged with an army larger than Chamanca had imagined possible. An agglomeration of tribes united under Queen Galba to prevent Rome's advance, the new Gaulish army was said to number half a million infantry, plus cavalry. Chamanca didn't believe that, but they had been riding along the hillside for an hour, and they'd been passing throngs of warriors all the way. The variety had been fascinating.

Trying to describe the typical Gaulish fighter, thought Chamanca, would be like trying to describe the plumage of the average bird. There was a large troop of survivors from Hari the Fister's tribe wearing nothing but their furry groin-cloths. Here was a small army of men and women with long, lime-lightened hair, all carrying spears with twisted points. Over there, looking down their neat noses at the lime-haired lot, was a knot of stiff-necked archers on sleek horses, their shining silk clothes interlaced with gold thread.

Even among this coalition of contrasting clans, Atlas, Carden and Chamanca attracted attention as they rode by. The Germans had spread word of the attack that Atlas and Carden had led into the Roman's base. The sacking of the Roman camp had been the only part of their battle that had been a success, so the German storytellers focused on it. Meanwhile, Gaulish bards had written several songs about Chamanca's stirring attempt to free Kapiana at Wesont.

Since they were easy to pick out – Atlas being one of very few massive African men and Chamanca the only Iberian woman wearing just a little more than the Germans themselves – everyone knew the British heroes by sight. Chamanca winked and waved at her admirers. Carden rode along looking at his hands, his ears burning red. The only acknowledgement that Atlas gave to the whoopers, cheers and invitations to join them for a drink or six, was to mutter that notoriety was not exactly what they needed.

On the other side of the valley, Caesar's army, which Atlas had proclaimed as a tenth the size of the Gauls' but more than ten times as useful, was enthroned in an untouchable camp. It was on a gentle slope, facing the enemy. Its flanks were protected by deep, staked ditches. At the near end of each ditch was a small fort, each bristling with scorpions – giant bows which shot arrows the size of palisade posts. At the base of the valley, in easy scorpion range, was a boggy marsh which would be impossible to cross at anything faster than a half-crushed snail's pace. Bisecting the marsh was a river, too deep to wade and no bridge in sight.

The Gaulish army, massive though it was, could not even consider an attack. They could have done a few days before, as Atlas had pointed out then and more than a few times since. However, the Gaulish chiefs had been mired in an irresolvable argument, each of them saying that they wanted to lead the attack while none of them actually did. Meanwhile, Caesar had manoeuvred his army to their near-perfect position.

The only non-suicidal way of attacking the Romans would have been to circle round behind them, which they couldn't do because the river was in the way and the Romans had smashed all the bridges. The nearest feasible ford was a few miles downriver. While the Gauls had been arguing over who might cross it first – again all pretending that they wanted it to be them – Caesar had built fortifications there, too. When, finally, one of the tribes had become bored with waiting and attacked the ford off their own bat, they'd found that the Romans had deepened it and used their magical liquid rock to fix metal pikes into its bed. The attackers had charged into the water, been stopped by the subsurface spikes as quickly as a riled guard dog reaching the end of its chain, and been minced, skewered and knocked senseless by Roman scorpions, mercenary Cretan archers and Balearic slingers. The river was easier to cross now in the vicinity of the ford because it was clogged by a dam of swollen Gaulish bodies, but the Roman fortifications and their potent array of projectile defences remained.

So the Gauls could not use their whopping army. Nor could they feed it. Several clans had already peeled off and headed home. First it was a rumour, then as they rode further and heard it more and more, it became the official plan. The Gauls were to return to their own tribal lands and wait until Caesar attacked one of them. Then they were going to reunite and counter-attack.

"That," said Atlas "is a very bad idea."

"Do you have a better one?" asked Carden.

"A much better one. Let us talk to Queen Galba." Atlas reined his horse around and headed for the top of the hill.

Chapter 32

Spring fell.

She caught a glimpse of the huts nestling in the valley under their innocent coils of cook smoke. She thought of the happy little dog that she'd seen that morning and was sad that she wouldn't see any more dogs. And thinking of dogs, what about Dug?

The moment Dug appeared in her mind, she paused in midair. Everything shook. Her body twisted in on itself and she felt as if she were a damp rag being wrung out by strong, determined hands. Pomax's hands? Then she was crouching on the ground.

She was perched on a stone wall at the head of the valley that opened up on to the limestone pavement above Mallam Cliff. She was maybe a hundred paces from where Pomax had thrown her, higher up the slope and further north.

So finally she'd found some magic, but too late to save anyone but herself. And she was far from saved. She hadn't fallen to her death, but she did seem to have landed on the wrong side of the enemy, in full sight of the Murkans.

"What the Bel! It's the Maidun girl!" a shout from the cliff top rang out, as if to confirm just how useless her self-deliverance had been.

She leapt off the wall and ran up the valley. It was flat-floored, perhaps thirty paces wide. Its grassy verges were strewn with grey boulders, collected around rocky outcrops. Small, solitary brown sheep munched at the grass, spaced out regularly along the valley sides as if they hated each other. As Spring ran past, each sheep looked up dolefully then returned to its friendless grazing. She had never seen such desolate looking animals.

In the centre of the valley, where there would normally have been some sort of watercourse, there was a well-used path, firm and dry despite the recent rain. This, thought Spring, is what they call a dry valley. It suited her. She'd spent the last four years regularly running long distances with Lowa and more recently on her own, so, with a hundred paces headstart, she was confident she could outrun anyone on this benevolently flat and unimpeded surface. So she'd get away, assuming that there were no adversaries in front of her, that she didn't come to a high wall or any other obstacle, that the Murkans didn't have any horses nearby, that she didn't trip and hurt herself . . . Her escape did slightly depend on several unknown variables working out in her favour, she admitted to herself, and wasn't perhaps as certain as she might have first thought.

She looked over a shoulder. Pomax was sprinting up the valley, Grummog's guards following. Spring ran on, not quite at a full sprint, fast enough to get away and slow enough to conserve energy for the long slog ahead.

The valley narrowed then ended in a steep upward slope. She had never seen a landscape like it. It was a lot more craggy and severe than the undulating south. The path continued, up steps dug into the left side of the valley head. Spring was confident that she could keep ahead of her attackers, even if she had to climb, but if she slowed down too much she'd come within sling range. She cursed the loss of her bow. She could have put three arrows in each of her pursuers before they were anywhere near sling range.

Spring was breathing hard by the top of the slope, but still full of energy. Here the path split. Ahead was another dry valley. To the right, the path curled round a scarp edge. She chose the right-hand path. It looked the most used, and therefore, she reckoned, the least likely to be a dead end.

Around the scarp was another dry valley. She glanced back and down. Pomax had pulled ahead of the rest and reached the end of the first valley. She paused, looked up at Spring, grinned, put her head down and thundered up the slope. Spring didn't like the look of that grin. It was the grin of somebody who knew something that she didn't.

She ran on.

Big badgers' cocks! The path led to a busy little village.

"Stop her!" squeaked what she assumed to be Pomax's voice from much closer behind her than she should have been.

Spring hoped for an instant that the villagers might be too surprised or stupid to work out what Pomax wanted before she was past, but no, the three nearest villagers were annoyingly ept. They spread into a line. Two of them, young men, were unarmed. The woman had a wooden pole with an iron hook on the end.

Spring unsheathed her sword. The villagers didn't flinch. Annoyingly, they didn't know that Spring had been training hard and could have gutted all three of them and hardly broken stride. The thing was, she wasn't going to kill them. The guards, yes, she would have offed them without another thought because the chances were that they were death-dealing meanies who deserved it. But these villagers? They were probably perfectly nice people working hard to feed their families. She had no right to end their lives to save hers.

She slowed. Pomax yelled "Ha!" behind her. The valley opened into the village, but there were fences and huts and no way around the three villagers. On her right was a strangely active little pond. A bouncing stream came rushing out of the village and into the pond, and went no further.

The stream went into the pond but didn't come out. The surface of the pond roiled and rolled and Spring knew what was happening, and what she had to do. She took a deep breath, held her sword above her head and dived into the dark, churning water.

Chapter 33

Galba, queen of the Soyzonix, had been elected overall
chief of the agglomeration of northern tribes. They were
keen on elections in Gaul, Chamanca had noticed. She didn't
like them – far too Roman.

Galba must have been nearly forty years old, but she was
tall and graceful with a youthful vim, dancing blue eyes and
the largest white-polished teeth that Chamanca had seen
outside a horse's mouth.

Carden's and Atlas' status as the only people to lead a
successful charge against Caesar's forces gained them an audience, but they had to dismount a good distance away. Galba,
apparently, believed that horses were devils, and didn't allow
them anywhere near her. Quite an irony, thought Chamanca,
for a woman who looked so much like one. Or maybe not?
Maybe you despised the thing you resembled? But that
couldn't be right, Chamanca thought with a smile, because
she liked beautiful women.

They walked alongside Galba as she headed between
tribes. Atlas explained his plan. He told Galba to have each
tribe select its best warriors, comprising more than a quarter
but less than a third of their number. The remainder should
return home, shore up fortifications and gather food into
storage.

The chosen warriors should be spilt into two forces, each
of which would still be more numerous than Caesar's army.
One force should march east and south to get behind the
Romans. The Romans would no doubt move rather than allow

the Gauls to encircle them. At this point, the other force, which should comprise mostly cavalry, could cross the river and harry their retreat. If the Romans kept going south, they'd be under such harassment that they'd have to fight, in which case the two Gaulish armies would launch a synchronised pincer attack before they'd dug in, and smash them. If the Romans somehow evaded them and headed north, they'd be trapped between the small fortified towns of northern Gaul – none of which they could hope to take without a few days' siege – and a Gaulish army which would destroy them soon after they stopped.

"What a fantastic plan. Marvellous," said Galba, smiling broadly and touching Atlas lightly on a hefty bicep.

"So you'll carry it out?"

"Yes. We will follow every word. It's such a good idea. I'll start right now with the next tribe. 'More than a quarter, less than a third.' Marvellous. What an excellent plan. Simple, easy for all and it answers all my questions about supply and attack. I cannot believe I didn't come up with it myself. You may return to Britain knowing that a great victory is taking place behind you."

"We'll stay and help if you like. If each of us took command of a cavalry section—"

"No, no. No need for that. I'm very grateful for the plan, which we will definitely use, but I'd like Gauls commanding every section. They think the Romans are unbeatable. I'd like to show them that they're not. You head home, we'll be fine."

"But—" One of Galba's guards put a hand on Atlas' shoulder. Their audience with the queen was over.

Chapter 34

She tumbled, water roaring. Her back whacked something hard, she paused, then zoomed along again, spinning. She dropped her sword. She was part of the rushing water now. Hands scraped stone. Feet, back and head bumped rock.

She'd hoped that the pond might lead swiftly and smoothly to a waterfall that spilled into an underground lake in a chamber lit by a million luminous mushrooms. She'd swim to the side, where she'd find a glowing fungi-lined path leading to the surface. And perhaps a bundle of food – why not?

But no, she was in a tunnel. It wasn't going to surface anytime soon. Chances were it did go into some cavern, but the cavern was full of water with no way out. She'd been a fool. She was going to drown. She began to panic for breath. She tried to calm herself. Perhaps, she thought, this was why she'd been having all those nightmares about Dug being dead under the sea. It was her who was set for a watery death. Well, good, she thought. She was glad it wasn't Dug.

Dug . . . Dug . . .

Then she knew, and it was as if she'd always known.

Her magic didn't come from the earth or the air or the gods. It came from Dug. Yes, she felt it when he wasn't there, and had even used it a little before they'd met, but it only surged and charged when she was with him, from that time she'd stopped Ulpius from killing her to when she'd beaten Felix.

But he hadn't been there in the arena, when she'd given Lowa the power to defeat the chariot and Chamanca . . . but he had been nearby, and they'd shared a purpose. Having the same goal, she reasoned, must be their link as much as a physical one. Maybe more so? Who knew? What she was suddenly certain of was that her magic came from Dug.

What a shame, she thought, that she should realise that now, as she died, as the water swirled and she ran out of breath. She felt at peace, though. They said that this happened when you drowned. Although how the badger's bum beard "they" knew what drowning was like, she did not know.

She bumped along. The current slowed. She felt herself rising. She opened her eyes. Blackness. Her shoulder bumped rock. It seemed to be above her. She kicked to turn herself, then pressed face and hands against it, searching for an air pocket. There wasn't one. It was as she'd dreaded. The underground stream hadn't led to some open, underground cave. Instead it had widened and the current had slackened. So this was it. Get ready Otherworld, she thought, here I . . .

Except . . . Except it was an awfully long time since she'd taken a breath, but she felt fine. Totally fine. Was she dead, then? No. She felt magic surge. Shadows swam and solidified and she could see. She was underwater, in a rock chamber with pale yellow walls. The current was half-arsed eddies where she was at the top of the cave, but a few paces below it surged along enthusiastically, carrying specks of rock on its eternal task of moving the land grain by grain into the sea.

She tucked then kicked off the rocky roof and shot through the water like a fisherman's spear to rejoin the stream.

Chapter 35

"That's it? They're going?" said Ragnall, to nobody in particular. A few hard-jawed men around him nodded. Standing in between the scorpions on one of the neat little forts that the Romans had built overnight, Ragnall, Caesar and an assembly of tribunes and centurions watched as the Gauls swarmed up the opposite side of the valley and away, leaving a wrecked, mud-churned landscape and the odd tendril of smoke from an unextinguished fire.

"Caesar has outmanoeuvred them," said Caesar. "They cannot attack and they cannot remain. They must retreat, then they must divide into smaller forces. When they return to their towns and villages, they must bow to Caesar or face destruction."

A few of the centurions exchanged glances. Whether it was the result of bathing in a whole winter's worth of hero worship, or he genuinely considered himself too superior to use the standard "I"s and "we"s of other men, Caesar now almost always referred to himself in the third person. He'd been chucking in the odd third-person remark for a while, but now it was pretty much constant. So, instead of "I would like you to bring me ten captives" he would now say "Caesar wants you to bring him ten captives". Ragnall had heard murmurings of surprise at his theatricism, and he'd heard a few legionaries take the piss when were certain that they were out of any praetorian's earshot, but generally people accepted it. The previous year's plunder and slave receipts had made every man at the head of the army wealthy, even the most junior legionary was substantially better off than he'd imagined possible, and they all owed it entirely to Julius Caesar. One man had changed the course of history and made them all rich. So, as long as the gold was flowing, if he wanted to speak like a pompous arse he was more than welcome to do so.

Here again, right at the start of his second year of campaigning in Gaul, he'd shown tactical brilliance. He'd worked the army as hard as any general could, but they'd done what he told them because he'd always been right before. The forced march, the short rations, the gruelling night of chopping and digging and building had put the Romans in a perfect position. They could not be attacked and the Gauls had to retreat. By understanding his enemy and demanding more from his men than most generals would dare, Julius Caesar had defeated by far the largest force that any modern Roman army had faced without a fight.

"What will we do now?" someone asked.

"Caesar will follow them," said Caesar.

Chapter 36

Atlas, Carden and Chamanca rode west, depressed. It was bad enough that the Gauls had fucked up so inanely and dishearteningly, but the night before they'd heard what Caesar had done to the German captives after the battle with King Hari the Fister. He hadn't killed them, as he'd done with so many Helvans. Instead, the Romans had blinded nineteen out of every twenty men, women and children. The twentieth had been blinded in only one eye. Then he'd set them free to walk home, led by the "lucky" half-blind ones. Chamanca could not stop thinking about tens of thousands of Germans, in agony, hungry, thirsty, stumbling along in darkness. She wondered how many of them would have died before reaching safety. Almost all? All? It did not bode well for the rest of Gaul, nor Britain.

"But Galba said—" Carden said.

"Galba is a dissembler and a fool," interrupted Atlas. "I should have known."

"But why is she sending all the Gauls home? Why did she say she was going to—"

"Because it was easier to say yes to me and avoid an argument than to disagree, even though she didn't consider my plan for a heartbeat. She lies as easily as she smiles. Sobek take her soul."

"So what will happen?"

"The tribes that comprised the Gaulish army will capitulate or be conquered. I suspect that Galba has done a deal so that her tribe will be free. That woman is a selfish fool who has doomed her tribe and all those that trusted her. That she could have done this after what Caesar did to the Germans . . ." Atlas shook his head, heeled his horse and sped up. Chamanca thought she'd seen the glint of a tear in his eye.

"Galba will do what she was planning to do before Atlas told her his plan," she told Carden.

"Which is?" he asked.

Chamanca looked at his strong, happy face, dappled with the morning sunlight that shone through the track's overarching leaf canopy. Were handsome men born dumb, she wondered, or had their looks always got them everything they needed, so they just didn't bother to be clever? "The plan that everyone was talking about. The one that made Atlas so angry?" she said.

"Uh . . . nope?"

"Do you pay any attention to your surroundings?"

"Depends what they look like." He eyed her up and down and winked.

Chamanca smiled. For such a stupid man, Carden was easy to like.

"Galba hoped," she said, "that the Romans would see the size of her army and run home. That hasn't happened. Her next plan is for every tribe to return to its villages, towns or whatever and wait for the Romans to attack. When one tribe is hit, all the rest will come to its aid and crush the Romans. But it won't work. They are fucked."

"Why won't it work?"

"Because," said Atlas, who'd calmed down and rejoined them, "she has no experience of the Romans and she doesn't understand her own people."

"What do you mean?" Carden asked.

Atlas sighed. "Most Gaulish tribes, like tribes everywhere, are selfish and cowardly. If another is besieged, they will not rush to help."

"But why not? There are so many of them!"

"It will not feel that way now that the great army is split. Say a tribe is attacked. Let us call it tribe one. Tribe two will vacillate about going to its aid, worrying whether tribes three, four and five are going to help. While they hesitate, they'll realise that all the others are dithering for the same reason. They'll send messengers and deputations to each other, spurring each other into action. They will eventually agree on a plan, maybe even a good one. But by then it will be far too late. Caesar will have defeated tribe one and visited some terrible punishment on any of them unlucky enough to survive the legionaries."

"I get it!" Carden said with relish, "then tribe two are attacked, and the same thing will happen. Tribe two and three will hesitate and—"

"No."

"No?" Carden was like a child denied a honey apple.

"Tribe two saw what happened to tribe one, so they surrender immediately for fear of suffering the same fate, and offer to help the Romans against tribes three and four. The Romans won't need any help, of course, because tribes three and four will surrender too. It is a lesson for Britain – present a united front in the first instance, or your chance is gone and the Romans are your new masters."

"But won't Galba recall the army once she sees what's happening?" Carden asked.

"Possibly. That's why Caesar will attack her tribe first, even if Galba does have an agreement with them. Unlike everyone else in this land, the Romans are not stupid. Evil, yes. Stupid, no."

"Well, I suppose that's that then. Back to Britain?" asked Carden.

"Not yet," said Atlas. "There are Gaulish tribes further west who might yet hold the Romans."

"OK then, who's next to let us down?"

"The most numerous are the Nervee. I spent some time with them a few years back. I knew their current king, Bodnog, before he was king. He was a good man. Hopefully rule hasn't ruined him."

Two days later they rode into the lands of the Nervee. It was strange countryside. The Nervee had no cavalry or chariot-based soldiers. To defend itself against tribes that did, they had criss-crossed their territory with high, thick hedges, and interwoven the branches of trees. These were linked together to create a huge, leafy labyrinth, like a massively larger version of the gates into Maidun Castle. Somehow Atlas knew the way through. Chamanca felt like a blinded German as he led her and Carden a twisting route into Nervee lands.

All this foliage harboured a multitude of wildlife. As they rode along between high walls of vegetation, birds swooped from side to side, squirrels chittered, wild boar groinked and deer pranced away then stopped to watch them in wide-eyed wonder before bucking and skipping off. Chamanca, to her surprise, found herself thinking that it was all rather lovely.

Chapter 37

Lowa woke on the hard earth floor of a hut with no orna-
ment or furniture, other than two stools bearing two
half-asleep guards. She was on her side, facing them. Slowly
she moved her limbs to test her situation. Those guards
looked pretty sleepy, and if she could just . . .

No. She was trussed like a paranoid farmer's best sow on
market day. She probed with her fingers. Her wrists and
ankles were shackled and attached by thin but strong chains
to an iron ring at her back. The ring was woven into a thick
leather girdle that seemed to have been sewn around her
waist. She strained against the bonds, but felt no give in any
part of them.

Perhaps the guards might be persuaded to let her go in
exchange for gold, sex or something else? She eyed them up,
trying to assess their proclivities. They were short, spiky-
haired men with matching, oversize moustaches. They were
certainly brothers, and could have been twins. They were a
fey looking pair, but that didn't necessarily mean they
wouldn't find her attractive. One of them noticed her looking
at him and almost fell off his stool. He gathered himself,
jumped up, ran to the open door and shouted, "Pomax! Lowa
Flynn has woken up!"

The other leapt up to join his brother in the doorway:
"Lowa Flynn is awake! Come and get her, Pomax!"

The first shouter hit the second on the arm. "I saw she
was awake first!"

"So what? We were both asked to shout."

"That's not the point and you—"

"Shut up." Pomax stooped her head under the lintel and pushed past them into the hut.

"Sorry."

"Sorry."

Pomax ignored them, grabbed Lowa by the ankle and dragged her on her stomach across the hut and out of the door. She blinked in the light. Before she could make much sense of her surroundings, she was picked up by, she guessed, the iron loop on the back of her leather waistband.

Pomax carried her one-handed through the village, swinging her as if she were a shopper heading home from Bladonfort Market and Lowa was her brimming basket. Lowa noticed that the nails on the Murkan queen's free left hand were strangely thick, each the length of half a finger and honed into points like a falcon's talons. How did she make them so thick? Lowa wondered.

Villagers gawped. They were scrawnier than their southern counterparts, but they looked handy enough and there were a lot of them. If she could somehow break her bonds and best her big-boned bearer, escape would still be near impossible.

Pomax shouted as she walked: "See the warrior queen of the Maidun! No more powerful than a bound lamb! Grummog's cunning and the might of Pomax beat her famous bow with ease!" Her voice was high-pitched and whining, as if borrowed from a much slighter woman who'd been repeatedly wronged.

They arrived at a sinkhole where the flooding stream disappeared underground. Pomax put her down, facing the turbulent pond. "This is where your girl jumped yesterday," she said. "We had her cornered here. She cried and pissed herself with fear. Then we came at her and she fell in. It must have been horrible, drowning down there in the dark."

Lowa knew that Spring wasn't dead. The last time she'd

seen her she'd been surrounded by spears, facing a king who would happily murder her in a moment, but somehow she knew.

"Have you got her body?" she asked.

"No one'll ever find it," said Pomax, "those tunnels lead down into the very bowels—"

"You'll never find it because you're lying. That girl is a great druid and she escaped you. And she'll be coming back for rev—"

Pomax cuffed Lowa on the side of the head, then picked her up. Lowa strained to take in her surroundings as she was carried around a mile down a path to the longhouse on the top of Mallam Cliff. Lowa's weight was no strain for Pomax – she didn't even swap hands on the journey.

Seven poles had been erected at the end of the cliff by the longhouse. Impaled on them were the six men and women of the Two Hundred, and Miller. Bones jutted from fall-broken limbs and their backs had been sliced open on either side of their spines, so that their ribs sprung out like pathetic little wings and, with some stretch of the imagination, it looked like they were launching to fly away south.

Pomax held her up so she could have a good look, and said: "Have you got something clever to say about that?" Lowa hadn't. "No? I thought not." She turned Lowa to face the wicker woman. "That's where you'll be going. But not for a while yet."

The big woman carried her over to the longhouse and unpinned her wrists. Lowa tried to wrench free of Pomax's grip, but she might as well have tried to pick up a menhir. The Murkan queen's strength was astonishing. She pressed Lowa against a low wooden frame, reattached her ankles behind her and her wrists to the front, so that she was kneeling, facing Grummog's empty throne. Pomax tested Lowa's bonds, then took a chair from the dais and sat behind her.

"What a—" said Lowa, before she felt a finger and thumb

grip her shoulder and squeeze. Sharp nails punctured skin and drove deeper, until she could feel them touching her collarbone, scraping against it. The pain filled her like nothing she'd ever known or imagined. Pomax let go and Lowa shook with sobs as agony throbbed up into her head and blood ran down her chest.

"I—" she said.

She felt a poke, then a claw pierce the muscle between her shoulder blades. It pushed in deep.

"I can feel your spine," Pomax whispered in her ear. "If I push just a little deeper and wiggle it, you will never move your arms or legs again. Nod if you understand. Carefully, mind. It's very delicate in there."

Lowa nodded, slowly. The spike in her back was so agonising that she couldn't let her breath out. Just as consciousness was slipping away, Pomax withdrew.

Lowa breathed out, sucked in air, then wept. She could not help herself.

"They say you're clever, so you might have worked it out already. You say anything, you get my nails. Nod if you understand."

Lowa wasn't going to give her the satisfaction. She stared stonily ahead. Pomax bounded around, squatted in front of her kneeling frame and gripped one of her hands in her own claw-free right hand. "Nod if you understand," she said. Her face was so close that Lowa could smell that she'd had honey for breakfast.

Lowa sucked in saliva to spit at her. Pomax leant back with whip-crack speed and pinched into Lowa's arm below her left elbow. Lowa gasped.

"My nails," said Pomax, "are touching between the two bones of your forearm. Now, let's push a bit deeper. Oh, look, they're sticking out either side. I said look!"

Lowa looked. Pomax shifted her arm around so that she could see both sides.

"See?"

Lowa saw the blood-soaked points of Pomax's claws poking out of her arm. She nodded, her mind so pain- and horror-filled that she couldn't do anything else.

"Now, what would happen if I pulled my nails towards your hand, splitting these bones apart?"

Lowa had never been tortured before. She'd previously believed that she'd be able to withstand anything by somehow channelling the pain or shutting her mind off to it. Now she knew otherwise. The torture had only just begun and already she'd have done or given anything to make it stop.

"No," she managed.

"What?" asked Pomax.

"Please."

"You don't want me to split your bones apart?"

"Please don't."

Pomax looked down at Lowa's held arm, then up at her eyes.

"Are you going to spit at me?"

Lowa shook her head.

"Are you going to speak?"

"No,"

"That was speaking." Pomax pulled her claws through flesh towards Lowa's hand, just a finger's breath. Lowa heard an animalistic scream and realised it was her own. "So, are you going to speak?"

Lowa shook her head.

"Are you going to kneel here like a good girl?"

Lowa nodded.

"Oh, Lowa, the mighty warrior queen from the south. I'm going to enjoy my days with you." The massive woman stood and walked round behind Lowa. Lowa knelt in silence for what seemed like an age, knowing that the northern warrior queen was just behind her. Her shoulder and her back felt like they had red-hot bolts hammered through them, but the pain in her wrist was worse. She suspected that the damage there was permanent.

I really should have brought my army, she thought.

After what seemed like an age, a quiet voice made her jump.

"Stay here," said Pomax. "Do not move and do not speak. I'll know if you have and I'll hurt you again. We've done shoulder, back and arm. What's next? Something . . . private? Or something vital. Oh, I do hope you talk so we can find out."

The queen of Maidun stayed quiet as the queen of the Murkans walked away.

Movement was returning to the fingers of Lowa's left hand when Pomax returned carrying Grummog in a padded shoulder harness, followed by his retinue. Pomax took the king from her back and placed him carefully on the throne. None of them acknowledged Lowa or even looked at her. She stayed quiet. They sat and chatted as if Lowa wasn't there until their first visitor arrived. She was a minor tribal chief whom Grummog had summoned. He demanded troops for his southward marching army.

"Have you not heard about Lowa's Two Hundred?" said the chief. "And the rest of her army? Amazingly well trained, they say. Oh no, I don't want to send my people to fight her, it would be sending them to their very deaths! She annihilated the poor Dumnonians less than half a moon after she killed Zadar. And Lowa's got a magic bow! If she shoots it and says your name, that arrow will find your heart no matter where you hide. How can we fight that?"

Lowa was desperate to say something along the lines of "quite right, keep your people at home or they'll all die", but even though Pomax hadn't so much as glanced at her, she could feel that she was coiled, ready to run over and inflict some new, appalling damage.

"Do you mean this Lowa?" asked Grummog, pointing at his captive.

"Is that her?" The chief was wide-eyed.

"It is."

"How did you capture her?"

"My people will kill . . ." was as far as she got before Pomax was on her, all five of her claws through her shirt and into her left breast. Pomax was saying something but Lowa couldn't hear it. She closed her eyes and screamed.

When she could see again, she looked up and saw Pomax back in her seat next to Grummog. Both were smiling happily at her. By the appalled look on everybody else's faces, particularly the chief's, her agony had not been a pretty thing. Waves of pain still throbbed through her. She was certain she was going to vomit for a long nauseous moment, but she managed to hold it.

"I'm sorry, Lowa," asked Grummog, "did you have something to say?"

Lowa stayed quiet.

"You may answer," said Pomax.

"You heard her," said Grummog. "Can you give me any reason why this chief shouldn't send her tribe south to take on your weakened little army?"

"No," she said, "I have nothing to say."

"Oh good," said Grummog. "It's nicer that way."

More chiefs came throughout the day to hear Grummog's demands for troops. All were reluctant until their attention was drawn to the captive Lowa, then each agreed to supply the number Grummog wanted. For the rest of the day, Lowa only spoke when Grummog asked her to and Pomax gave her permission, and every time she said what she knew they'd want to hear. Pomax didn't hurt her again and Lowa found herself feeling gratitude towards the woman. That's how madness begins, she thought.

Chapter 38

"All right, let's go," said Dug, swinging his hammer over his shoulder and heading for the paddock where his horse had lived a hitherto idle life. He had a horse because he could afford one and people who could afford a horse were meant to have a horse, but Spring had never seen him ride it.

She hadn't expected it to be that easy. All she'd said was that Lowa was captured. She'd prepared a speech about why he should rescue her. She was even planning to tell him about their magic link to each other if she needed to. As it was, she hadn't even got off her horse and he was already persuaded.

"Don't you need to pack up anything? Or do you need to—" she leant down from her horse, looked about to check no bandits were eavesdropping and whispered "—hide your riches?"

"They're already hidden, and I've got my hammer, so . . ."

"OK. Just try this, though. Take my hand." Dug did so. She closed her eyes. *Take us to Maidun Castle*, she said in her mind. She opened her eyes. They were still by the paddock, the only difference was that Dug was looking at her as if he thought she was even odder than usual. She closed her eyes again. *Come on, Danu, Bel, Branwin, Sobek or whoever it is, take us to Maidun.* She tried picturing the exact spot on the Eyrie where she wanted them to be. Nothing happened. *Bring Lowa to us here. Make her appear right here, in this paddock, oh wonderful and powerful gods,*

use the magic that lives in Dug and me to bring her here from
Mallam.

She looked up, into the paddock. Dug's horse looked back
at her, with a similar expression to Dug's.

"Oh well. Come on, let's ride," she said.

"What were you doing?" Dug asked.

"Praying," she said. He looked surprised, but didn't question
her further. She was frustrated. She was convinced that her
magic was linked to Dug. So she'd assumed that now she was
with him and she knew about the link, she'd be able to draw
on and control powerful magic. Apparently not. So perhaps it
wasn't linked to Dug? She felt silly for thinking it was, and
decided not to tell him her theory until she was certain.

She did tell him as they rode about the death of Miller and
the others, about Lowa's captivity and how they were going
to burn her in the wicker woman, and about the army invited
from Eroo by the perfidious Dumnonians. She told him about
her escape and how magic had transported her from the cliff,
how she'd been able to live underwater without breathing,
and about how she'd finally surfaced in a woodland pool.

To her surprise, Dug didn't question her story, just insisted
that they should get the entire army from Maidun and free
Lowa from the Murkans by force. She told him that Lowa
hadn't taken the army north in the first place because it was
needed in Maidun. Lowa didn't trust the Dumnonians – and
had been right not to, they'd found out – so the army had
to stay in case the Dumnonians flooded into Maidun the
moment they saw that its defences were down. If they took
the army north now, they'd probably come back to find
Bruxon laughing at them from the walls of a captured Maidun
Castle. Besides, she said, they had a better chance of rescuing
Lowa by stealth and, what's more, Grummog would stick
her in the wicker woman the moment he saw the Maidun
army coming over the hill.

Finally he was convinced, but then he insisted that they

go straight to the Murkan base at Mallam. So Spring had to persuade him, no, first they had to go to Maidun, to warn Mal and Nita, who'd been left holding the hillfort, about the army from Eroo and the Dumnonian treachery.

Eventually he saw sense. They trotted along in silence for a while. Spring would have liked to have gone faster, but Dug's horse was neighing and bubbling and making all manner of bizarre sounds, complaining about this unwelcome, weighty call on its services. If they went any faster, Spring was sure the animal would either lie down or die.

Despite the circumstances, she was happy to be back with Dug. Although they hadn't been on horseback at the time, Spring was reminded of that first day they'd met, and walked through the woods, holding hands. They'd spotted animal shapes in the clouds. She felt a surge of affection for the big man. The most important thing, she realised, more important than stopping the Romans, more important than protecting the land from the army of Eroo, was that Dug came through it all unscathed, because he was the best person who had ever lived and she loved him.

So why, she wondered, had she just persuaded him into the incredibly dangerous task of rescuing Lowa from Mallam? Because, she realised with a little jolt, Lowa was nearly as important to her as Dug. Besides, now she knew her magic was linked to him, surely she'd be able to protect him and surely, between them, they had a better chance of rescuing Lowa than anybody else?

"Will you tell me the story of the war against the halfmen, please?" she asked as they crested a hill and a new view opened up, huge and green. They were still a good way from Maidun.

"You're too old for stories now," Dug said. "And, anyway, I've told you that one before."

"How about the story of the flood then?" Spring smiled her most winning smile. "Please?"

"Well, it is a good one."

"Especially your version."

"My version is the true version."

"That's why it's so good."

"Hmm. All right then. Many years ago, when the last halfman was not long dead, the gods disagreed over some long-forgotten bollocks and went to war . . ."

Spring smiled and relaxed. Dug's voice was like a warm blanket and a bowl of stew at the end of a cold day.

Chapter 39

Caesar sent his cavalry to harry the disorderly retreat of the Gauls, ordering its commanders to kill as many of the enemy as possible without putting themselves in any danger. If, for example, there was a group of Gaulish children and a group of warriors, they were to draw the warriors away, circle back and slaughter the children.

Ragnall watched the horses trot out of the camp. When he'd heard their orders, he'd been surprised and disappointed. Surely orders to kill children could not be honourable? But he thought it through and was consoled. Caesar's goal to bring the enlightenment of Roman culture to the poor ignoramuses of the world was noble, and if more tribes were terrified of him and his army's cruelties, more would capitulate without a fight, and in total, fewer people, including children, would die. So his apparently inhuman orders were actually saving Gaulish lives. Issuing commands that could be used against him by his enemies back home, and seen by historians as unnecessarily ruthless, showed a commitment to the cause that went way beyond personal glory. Ragnall's disappointment morphed in to fierce pride.

He returned to the capacious leather headquarters tent and found Caesar dictating his diary. He was describing Galba as a proud warrior king, brave and intelligent, who had nevertheless been outmanoeuvred by his superior Roman mind.

Ragnall raised his eyebrows at the dissembling, but realised immediately there must be a good reason for it. However, Caesar had spotted his expression.

"What troubles you, brave new Roman?" said the general.

"Nothing," said Ragnall.

"No, there is something, I can see. Tell Caesar what it is. Quickly now."

Ragnall hesitated. What did Caesar want? The man was complicated. He could be inviting the challenge and keen to explain, or he could be in a bad mood and looking for someone to punish.

"Come on, come on."

Ragnall took a breath. "You never met Galba," he said. "And she's a woman – a queen – not a king."

Caesar smiled. Ragnall sighed in relief as the general lifted a hand in an oration pose and began to lecture: "There are two things that you must understand if you are to be a successful Roman, young Ragnall. The first is something that I have told you before. A general must have the constant, regularly refreshed support of the Senate, the Tribunate, and, most importantly, the citizens. Where are these people? In Rome. Where do I intend to spend the majority of the foreseeable future? Not in Rome. So what can I do? How might I achieve the always accreting admiration that I need for my goals in the field when I am not there myself to flatter and display? I will tell you. With mechanisms that operate in my absence. Some of these mechanisms are previous generosities and favours, some are people. Another is the steady flow of wealth back to the city. One, possibly the single greatest mechanism, is my campaign journal. This true account of our manoeuvres tells Rome's citizens, and the citizens of her Empire, that each decision Caesar makes is justified, that his means never outweigh his ends, and that he treats the enemy, if we should call him that, with respect and honour. The savage demands our help, we show the savage the benefits of Roman life. At no point do we infringe the dignity of the savage."

Ragnall thought of the order to kill children, the blinded Germans, the slaughtered Helvetians. He knew all these were done for good reason, but arguably it was somewhat dignity infringing to gouge someone's eyes out or kill his kids.

"I can see your uncertainty and I understand it, but the first lesson of a successful military campaign is to protect one's own civilians from knowing one's methods. Rome is built on cruelty, treachery and slaughter, but these are not subjects you'll find on the lips of its partygoers, unless they're decrying the methods of our enemies, of course. My army's end justifies its means, but it is better to keep the means hidden, like shit in a rose garden. Do you understand?"

"I do . . ." said Ragnall. It was reassuring to have Caesar explain his methods, even if Ragnall had worked them out for himself, however . . . "But why say that Galba is a man?"

"That you will come to understand. All that is important for now is that you accept that Caesar is always right. Do you?" Caesar's eyes sparkled for an instant, like a flash of fire reflected on water.

"I do," said Ragnall.

"So you will agree. We have seen no female soldiers or leaders among the Helvetian, German or Gaulish people. Women are not suited for fighting, let alone command. There are no female warriors or leaders in Britain, are there?"

Ragnall thought of Chamanca and Lowa. "No," he said. "I don't think there are."

The next day, units of cavalry returned from their chase with competitively gruesome tales of massacre, and the Romans struck camp. They marched into Soyzonix territory, where Galba was queen. Actually king, Ragnall reminded himself.

The first stronghold they came to was an old walled town hunkered on the shallow banks of a narrow river. Caesar rode to the gates, demanded surrender and received a display of bare arses in return. He ordered his engineers and carpenters to construct siege engines.

The townspeople refused to yield until the heads of siege towers reared up in the Roman camp, at which point they capitulated immediately. Two of Galba's sons, one of whom ruled the town, were marched out at spear point. The town's elders threw themselves down at Caesar's feet and begged his mercy. Caesar announced that the town would be spared and allowed to carry on as before, under the protection of Rome. However, to show the townspeople what would happen if they displeased Caesar again, Galba's sons were to be crucified on the town's wall, either side of the main gate.

Ragnall had heard of crucifixion but not yet seen one. People spoke about it in hushed, sometimes disgusted but generally reverent tones. He couldn't see the big deal. How bad could it be, being nailed to a piece of wood? Ragnall had been buried alive, pushed off a cliff blindfolded, fired from a catapult and near drowned. Could crucifixion be as bad as any of those? He didn't think so.

He found a spot to watch among legionaries and townspeople, who mingled happily. It was something that Ragnall had seen in Vesontio, and it had amazed him there, too. One word from Caesar, and the legionaries would have eviscerated every man, woman, child, dog and cat in the town. Everyone knew this, Romans and Gauls. Yet here they were chatting away, being introduced to children, buying each other drinks and being imposed upon to sample the local bread. People, thought Ragnall, were odd.

The first cross wouldn't fit through the wall's interior staircase because, as a few Romans around him told the Gauls and each other in knowing tones, some lackwit had nailed the crosspiece to the upright in advance, rather than waiting until it was in place. The cross had to be hauled up the wall on ropes. Badly made, hairy Gaulish ropes, Ragnall noticed, not the smooth, well-made Roman twine. Roman life was better, and these Gauls were lucky to see it.

The crowd was jostling but friendly, especially as Ragnall was now the heroic envoy who'd survived Ariovistus' tortures, but he realised he wouldn't see the nails go in from ground level, so he used his new status to gain access to the top of the wall.

Galba's younger son, the first to be crucified, was perhaps half Ragnall's age. He had a chubby face, protruding jaw, folded eyelids, small nose, and a fat tongue clamped between thick lips. He was alternately giggling, blowing raspberries and gawping amazed at the crowd, all the while pawing at the back of his own head. Ragnall had seen people like him before. In Britain he would have been called a Danu's Child. Ragnall hadn't seen any Danu's Children in Rome, but back home they were considered holy. They were more susceptible to disease than others, and, in their simplicity and trustfulness, more vulnerable to accident and attack, so it was a mark of success for a tribe to contain a happy, healthy Danu's Child or two. There had been two his age on the Island of Angels where he'd been educated by the druids. Ragnall, his peers and the druids would all sooner have hurt themselves than harmed a Danu's Child. It was the same all over Britain. Even the Murkans, famously mean and selfish, would share the last of their winter supplies with a Danu's Child. Yet the Romans were about to crucify one of them.

The Gaulish Danu's Child was smiling and playing with the legionaries as they walked him along the top of the wall to his cross. He poked at their thick leather armour with plump fingers and laughed throatily. One of them cuffed the back of his head and he looked shocked, then upset for heartbeat, then he started laughing again.

Ragnall considered leaving, but hadn't Drustan always

advocated seeing as much of the extraordinary as possible? Romans crucifying a Danu's Child on the walls of a Gaulish town was not an everyday spectacle for a young man from a small tribe in central Britain.

Galba's son blew bubbles of saliva and looked about with wide-eyed wonder as he was laid on the cross. Four legionaries took a limb each and another gripped his head. He was still giggling and chuckling. He'd clearly had the same indulgence as Danu's Children in Britain, Ragnall realised, so couldn't consider this attention from these strange men as anything other than a game. He looked down at the people in the town. Yes, now he looked for it, there was some resentment and fear in a few startled-horse eyes and too-loud laughs among the Gauls. The Romans were killing their cherished Danu's Child. If they tried to rescue him, they'd be killed, and Galba's son would be crucified anyway, so they could do nothing apart from hate themselves for their inaction.

A balding, sharp-featured man stood forward, a blacksmith's hammer in one hand and a heavy bag in the other. A surfeit of chest hair garnished the upper edge of his leather apron and short, thick arms sprouted from his wide torso. Below, on both sides of the walls, onlookers Gaulish and Roman strained to see the action. Ragnall's view was unimpeded.

The aproned man took a square-cut, foot-long iron nail from his bag. He felt Galba's son's wrist, looking for the right spot presumably, placed the tip of the nail, and raised his hammer. Galba's son, finally realising that something bad was happening, wrenched his arm away with an animal squeak of fear. He looked at his arm. The nail's tip had scored a red mark. Beads of blood bloomed all along the scratch. The Danu's Child looked at his wounded arm, eyes wide, chewing his jaw like a cow on the cud. Ragnall had seen the Danu's Children on the Island of Angels chewing like that when they didn't understand what was happening.

The aproned man cursed the soldier, who gripped the arm again.

A heavy sickness grew from Ragnall's stomach into his throat as the aproned man hammered the nail though Galba's son's wrist. Phlegmy roars from the child tore right into his heart. He almost rushed forward to free the boy. Almost.

The aproned man nipped round to the other wrist and repeated the action, barking orders at the legionaries to leave some slack in the arms. The boy's roars had become sobbing chokes. The aproned man secured the second wrist with two well-practised hammer strikes, then instructed the legionaries to lay the boy's feet one over the other, so that he might hammer one nail through both arches.

The cross was lifted and fixed into place. Galba's son was alternately screaming in fear and pain and sobbing in sorrow. Blood dripped from his fingers and toes on to the stone of the wall. Ragnall looked at the crowd. Most of them, Roman and Gaulish, looked horror-struck but fascinated. Some watched with unconcealed glee. Others, both Romans and Gauls, walked away.

"Do you want to hear something funny?" said a voice behind him. A voice that he knew. He turned. His hair was a little more receded than when Ragnall had last seen him, but his small-toothed grin was the same. So, Felix had caught up with them again.

"Guess how he's going to die, the – um – Danu's Child?" He grinned, as if impressed with himself for remembering the British term.

"From crucifixion?" Ragnall replied.

"More specifically," said Felix. "Is he going to bleed to death perhaps? Or die of thirst?"

"I don't know. I hope it's quick."

"Quick? Oh no, no, we don't want quick. Had you a hundredth of the understanding of magic that your pathetic old mentor mistakenly saw in you, you'd understand that quick is no good. Which reminds me – you!" he called to a legionary, who nodded. "Make sure I get this body. You'll be up there next if I don't." The legionary paled and nodded.

"No," Felix continued, "crucifixion is nastier than it looks." Ragnall raised an eyebrow. How could it be nastier? "Our boy here will drown."

Ragnall looked up at the nearly cloudless sky. Despite himself, he was interested. "Are we in for some rain?"

Felix laughed. "Drowning is when your lungs fill with fluid and you can no longer breathe. That's going to happen here, with no help from rain. But not for a long time, and therein lies the magic of crucifixion. Soon, the muscles in his chest will twist and cramp and become so agonised and weakened that he won't be able to breathe. With no breath entering the lungs, the body's fluids seep into them. Every single person you crucify will do the same thing next. The need to breathe will override all, and, despite the agony, he will push upwards on his feet – scraping those little foot bones against the iron nail – to try and lift himself and catch a breath. With no power in his arms and very little in his legs, he will be able to gasp only the smallest morsels of air, but it will be enough keep him alive."

Ragnall wanted to get away. He turned to go.

Felix took his arm. "Here's the clever bit. That little gulp of air will bring on a transformation. I must confess I'm not sure how it happens, but strength will return to his arms and chest. He will be able to lift himself and breathe again, as easily as you and I stand here breathing. As he breathes, his lungs will clear and the pain will return.

"That sequence," continued Felix, raising his voice above the Danu's Child's wails, "will repeat again and again. Each time the strength returns it will return a little less, until, perhaps a couple of days later if he's strong, he will no longer be able to fill his lungs with air. The fluids of the body will fill them and he will drown for a final, fatal time. Throughout it all, the panic and the pain will grow and grow. They tell you that being stabbed in the gut is the most gruesome death. They're wrong. Crucifixion is immeasurably more . . . excruciating."

"I'm going."

Felix stiffened the grip on his arm. "After smashing Spartacus's slave revolt a dozen years ago, Crassus, Caesar's friend whom you will know from Rome, crucified six thousand slaves, one every forty paces from coast to coast across Italy. Can you imagine this," he raised a palm at the boy, "multiplied six thousand times?"

Ragnall shook his head.

"The exercise was very . . . useful to me. But that's not why he did it. Do you know what made him visit agonising, fatal horror on six thousand people?"

"I don't."

"Pride. Nothing more than personal rivalry and the need for fame. Marcus Licinius Crassus defeated the slaves and killed Spartacus, but Caesar's other good friend, Gnaeus Pompeius Maximus – Pompey – tried to steal Crassus's glory. He arrived late in the day, chased down some fleeing rebel slaves and put five thousand of them to the sword. The shock of the massacre rang through Rome, thrilling the citizens, and everyone began to say it was Pompey, not Crassus, who had beaten Spartacus. So Crassus, purely so that he and not Pompey would be remembered as the hero who'd vanquished the slaves, crucified six thousand of his captives. He did this," Felix nodded up at the screaming boy, "to six thousand men and women simply to bolster his own reputation."

Felix's eyes hardened. "Understand this, Ragnall. Those two men, Crassus and Pompey, who will torture and kill thousands as easily as you might swat a fly, are now in league with Caesar – a man who has already slaughtered tens of thousands and not considered it too many. The three of them share power in Rome, with no challengers worth mentioning."

"So?"

"So, if Britain resists Roman rule, it's going to go very badly for the British. There are some in Rome who see such large-scale slaughter as distasteful, which is why Caesar tempers it here. In Britain, Caesar will be far from sensitive Roman eyes. He will be free to indulge his desires, one of which is to outdo Pompey and Crassus's cruelties and be more celebrated than them in the histories of generations to come. Britain is a great deal wider than Italy, Ragnall, and forty paces may seem too large a gap between crucifixions. I can see the entire Maidun army and all its people – the old and the very young – hanging on crosses stretching the breadth of the island, with only ten paces between each one. Can you picture it?"

Ragnall could. He swallowed.

"That is why Britain must not resist. You, pathetic as you are, might still hold some sway there. Look at the Danu's Child."

Ragnall tore himself from Felix's grip. He left the wall and headed back to the Roman camp. He wanted to run, but he kept himself to a walk, speeding up when he heard the bang of the hammer and the cries of Galba's second son.

On the way to his tent he came upon Caesar, walking briskly to some new business in the camp and dictating to his scurrying scribes on the hoof.

"Caesar showed mercy to the town," he said as Ragnall passed, "taking two of Galba's sons hostage to ensure peace. Caesar took the boys into his tent and treated them as if they were his own."

Chapter 40

"Dug! Spring!" said Mal, as they approached. He was sitting in the command area of the Eyrie with Nita, alongside few other high-up Maidun men and women and, Dug was surprised to see, Queen Ula of Kanawan.

"Ula!" said Dug. She was as beautiful as when they'd met her in Kanawan before Dug's battle with the Monster, but her eyes were harder now, as if she'd had a difficult few years. "What are you . . . actually we better tell you our news first. It's not good. The deputation north has been slaughtered. Lowa and Spring were the only survivors. They have Lowa captive and intend to burn her in their wicker woman. I don't know when, possibly the next full moon."

"Miller . . . ?" asked Mal. He and Miller had been good friends for a long time. Dug did not know what to say.

"He took a good number of them with him," said Spring, "and he died well and quickly. Neither Lowa nor I would be alive if it weren't for him."

"Damn," said Mal, putting his head into his hands.

"We have other bad news," said Spring. Dug was surprised. She was talking like a well-informed, intelligent, diplomatic ruler. Was this the same girl who'd just pleaded with him for the story of the war with the halfmen? "Dumnonia has turned traitor and invited Manfrax of Eroo to bring his armies across the sea from the west to Britain. Grummog of the Murkans is gathering an army to attack us, too. So, Dumnonians included, Maidun is about to face three armies, each one substantially larger than its own."

"But not so well trained!" said Nita.

"Manfrax's army is ferocious," said Ula. "That's why I'm here," she added, turning to Dug and Spring. "After I left you at Mearhold, I travelled with the Kanawans through Dumnonia. We found no welcome and no free land, so we went to Eroo. Everywhere we went on that beautiful but terribly sad island we saw destitute people and heard of Manfrax's evil deeds. His army torture for fun. We were lucky to escape back across the sea to Kimruk, where we've been living not far from the Island of Angels. A few days ago fishermen from Eroo told us that Manfrax's army is on the move again, this time bound for southern Britain. It's tens of thousands strong. There can be no holding against it."

"There can," said Nita. "Zadar's army was formidable. Lowa has enlarged it and improved it beyond measure. It's meant for fighting the Romans but it will serve well enough against Manfrax."

"And Grummog's Murkans, and Bruxon's Dumnonians?" asked Mal.

"Yes," said Nita, "but we will need Lowa leading it. The question is, how much of the army do we take north to retrieve her from the Murkans? There's always the risk that the Dumnonians will attack the instant they know we're gone."

"Which is why . . ." said Spring, then outlined her plan for her and Dug to rescue Lowa while the army stayed put.

Her listeners were sceptical initially, but Spring won them round with arguments that Dug couldn't follow. Shortly afterwards, after stopping only to provision on their way through Maidun, he found himself riding north with Spring and no one else, her leading one spare horse, him leading three.

Chapter 41

Over the next few days, Grummog and Pomax paraded Lowa around the Murkan lands. Grummog and others were on horseback. Pomax followed behind on foot, then it was Lowa, naked save for bandages over her injuries, wrist and ankle shackles and an iron hoop around her neck, attached to a chain held by Pomax. The Murkan queen hadn't hurt her since the tit grab and, thank Danu, none of her wounds had become infected. The twins who guarded her in the evening had applied poultices – they'd actually been gentle and kind – and the poultices had worked. Her puncture wounds were sore, very sore, but movement had fully returned to the fingers on her left hand and the pain was not nearly as severe as it would have been had the cuts become infected. So there were a couple of positives, thought Lowa.

The Murkans – teenagers, toddlers, Warriors, weaklings, the sick, the old and afraid, the young and confident, even a few Danu's Children – all left whatever business they were going about to run up and mock the Maidun queen. Some of them hit her before Pomax stopped them, but most of them spat on her, which Pomax allowed. Some of them flung pots of urine at her. One young man splashed Pomax's legs with his piss and Pomax dropped Lowa's chain, chased him, caught him with a whip around the neck, stabbed her nails into his lower back and pulled out a chunk of bone – a vertebra, Lowa guessed, but it was hard to tell with all the blood. Lowa, to her shame, stood and watched this, waiting for Pomax to come back and pick up her chain. She could have tried to escape, but the slim chance of getting away was massively outweighed by the terror of what Pomax might do to her next.

All along their route, Grummog and his cronies would crow to the people about how he'd bested the queen of the south, and how they could join him to do the same to her army. Walking behind, Pomax would shout that they should all come to Mallam for sunset on the next full moon, so that they might see Lowa burnt to death in the wicker woman.

Chapter 42

For the first time since they'd returned to Gaul, Atlas was in a good mood. Finally, in the Nervee and their allies, he'd found a relatively coordinated and obedient army. Finally, in the Nervee's king Bodnog, he'd found what he called an intelligent ruler – in other words, a ruler who listened to Atlas and accepted every suggestion that he made. King Hari the Fister had been like that for a while, but had always seemed flighty and it had not been a massive surprise when he'd gone against Atlas' advice and got all his people killed. Bodnog appeared to be a much more solid ally.

Atlas told Chamanca that the thing that really pissed him off about the embarrassingly easy Roman conquest was that the Gauls had so much information about Roman movements. The key to winning any war, and, to an extent, any battle, was information. The Romans were invaders in a strange land, so just about anybody in Gaul could ride up to the Roman army, take a look, talk to the cooks, most legionaries and even some of the centurions, then ride away. Thanks to scouts, and as much to travelling merchants, prostitutes and bards, the Gauls always knew exactly where the Romans were and where they were going. Yet they had done nothing with this knowledge. So many times the Romans were vulnerable. So many times the Gauls could have annihilated them. So many opportunities had been pissed away, Atlas had ranted, by this dunderheaded shower of morons more interested in settling local rivalries than staying alive.

Hopefully, things would be different with Bodnog and the Nervee.

As they helped prepare the Nervee army, they heard tales of more and more Gaulish tribes surrendering without a fight, as Atlas had predicted. They heard that the Romans had arrived at Galba's Soyzonix capital, a well-fortified citadel, the largest town in Gaul, surely capable of repelling any attack and lasting through any siege. The next day they heard that Galba had opened the gates without a struggle and ushered the enemy in.

Finally, they heard that Caesar's army was about to march west, into Nervee land. From around a hundred sources they heard the Romans' route and marching order. Atlas, Chamanca and Carden had already scouted the area, and the plan was clear and easy. An hour's walk from the Nervee capital was the perfect valley. One side was densely wooded. The other side was steep grazing land. The flattish bottom of the valley contained a broad road, along which the Roman army would march. The neck of the valley that the enemy would reach first was narrow, broadening out towards the Nervee capital. It was the perfect location for a very large ambush.

Bodnog, on Atlas' advice, set his people to clearing the undergrowth from the forest, so that the Nervee might move through it freely. They piled the removed scrub and debris on the edge of the woods facing the Roman advance, so that it would be impenetrable to their scouts.

Two days before the estimated Roman arrival, the Nervee prepared food, sharpened swords, axes and spearheads and carried bag loads of slingstones, buckets of drinking water and other supplies into the forest. The evening before, they all moved into the trees and found places to try to sleep. There were no fires.

*   *   *

Atlas, Carden and Chamanca sat in the darkness. They were near Bodnog, at the east end of the valley. The Romans would come from that direction in standard marching order – cavalry, an advance guard of one legion, then the surveyors and engineers, then Caesar and his retinue, then each legion followed by its baggage. The plan was to wait for the advance guard, Caesar and the first legion to pass. When the baggage of the first legion behind Caesar passed Bodnog's position, the entire Nervee army was to surge from the trees and attack. On the other side of the valley, high up and hidden by hedgerows, were people waiting to push huge boulders and burning logs down into the valley at the moment of attack. This might kill a good number of Romans, but more importantly it would obstruct the valley's narrow neck and hamper the following legions' advance, hopefully for long enough to enable the slaughter of the two advance legions and Caesar himself. After that, it didn't matter what the remaining two legions did. They could flee, in which case they'd be harried all the way back to Rome and destroyed, or they could attack a strong Nervee position in the valley and be cut down.

"Of course something can go wrong," said Atlas, "but I can't see what. Even if certain elements go awry, the Nervee will still win easily. The Romans will be spread out along the road. The Nervee coming from the woods will have ten fighters to every one of theirs. Surely we will win victory tomorrow? It can't be that simple, though. What have I missed?"

"You've missed two things," Chamanca said. "One, the Romans might find out that we're here and halt before they get to the valley."

"Yes, but then we still a have a large, ready army and we think again. What's the second thing?"

"The unknown. The unknown will always nip round behind you when you least expect it and fuck you in the arse."

Chapter 43

Dug and Spring rode hard, eating in the saddle and stopping neither to sleep nor rest. The only times they dismounted were to swap horses, so that each of Dug's horses spent only one hour in four carrying him.

Spring thought about her magic a great deal. She tried to make her horse's ears turn blue, trees burst into flame and giant hares fly overhead. Surely, she reasoned, now that she was with Dug magic should be hers to command? Apparently not. Her horse's ears remained stubbornly horse-coloured, the trees waved their unburnt leaves cheekily as she rode by and only the standard set of birds passed overhead. It frustrated her almost to the point of fury.

Perhaps, then, her magic wasn't connected to Dug? Perhaps she could use it only at time of massive peril? But that didn't work. She'd used it to make Lowa go off Dug and that had been only an annoying situation, not a dangerous one, then she'd been unable to save Miller and the rest at a time which was definitely majorly perilous. And besides, she just knew it was tied to Dug. So why were the badger-bumming horse's ears still brown?

Maybe magic can only work when the right god is looking at you, or bothering with you, she thought? Maybe each god had a whole gang of people to whom they gave their magic and couldn't be everywhere at once? After all, they were only gods. Or maybe magic had only worked before puberty? Plenty of idiots had told her that all sorts of changes happened inside to accompany the annoying body hair and pointless tits. But then again Felix and Drustan had magic. But they were men and maybe that made a difference? But she'd used magic to survive the water tunnels without breathing, well past puberty. Maybe puberty just altered one's abilities . . . ?

Whatever it was, unless something changed, they were going to have to get to Mallam and rescue Lowa using conventional means, which was a massive bugger, since she'd assumed that her magic would just kind of come back and they'd use that. It wasn't, admittedly, a great plan. As it was, they didn't really have any strategy worked out for sneaking past the whole Murkan army, rescuing a no doubt well-guarded Lowa and then escaping through enemy territory.

In two days and nights of riding, the only plan they came up with was to skirt the cliff and approach from the east, which Dug reckoned would offer the easiest access to the wicker woman.

Chapter 44

The head scribe had decided that Ragnall had not been pulling his weight recently, which was true, so he'd told Ragnall to work late on his own on the scribes' bench in the command tent, copying the day's accounts from another scribe's work. Ragnall could have refused probably – he wasn't really under the head scribe's jurisdiction any more – but he'd been troubled almost constantly by images of the crucified Danu's Child of late, so it was a relief to have the taxing and immersive chore of writing to smother his imagination.

He heard someone come in, but couldn't see them from behind the writers' screen. By the way he was moving about, he guessed it was Caesar. He was about to make himself known with a forced cough – he didn't want Caesar thinking he was alone in the tent and doing something embarrassing like farting or, worse, singing – when he heard someone else come in and Felix's voice say: "The Nervee are planning an ambush."

"When, where, how do you know? In that order," Caesar replied.

"Tomorrow. In a valley which has one wooded slope and one grassy slope. They plan to wait until the van, including your retinue, are in the valley, then attack from the trees. I know because I performed a ritual which allowed me to transport myself into the mind of Bodnog, king of the Gauls. He has an easy mind to enter."

"Is this ritual the reason for the blood on your toga?"

"It is."

"I see. Bring me maps of Nervee territory!" Caesar spoke just a little more loudly, calling to the clerks who sat outside the tent, day and night, ready to do his bidding.

"We don't need to change our plan or our route," said Felix, after the clerks had rushed in and rushed out again. There was the sound of a large scroll being unrolled. "We can use the attack against them. Here is the valley. There is space for manoeuvres here and here and fortifications here. All we need is time."

There was a pause, in which Ragnall guessed that Caesar was looking quizzically at Felix.

"I can control Bodnog," said the druid. "He has the plan fixed in his mind that he will not attack until he sees the baggage train of the first legion come into view after you and your guard. I'm certain that I can make him hold the attack until he sees the baggage train. He is that straightforward a man. So we hold back the baggage train, pile as many troops as we like into the valley and dig them in. As long as we don't show him a baggage train, he will not attack."

"How certain are you?"

"I know. His stubbornness provides the means. Nobody will be able to make him change his mind."

There was a pause.

"All right. You have never let Caesar down before. The plan is clear. Every legionary will enter the valley and form up before Bodnog sees any baggage. Thank you, Felix."

"There is one more thing. High up on the clear side of the valley, they are preparing some sort of rockslide."

"Do you have any more detail?"

"I do not."

"Right. Thank you."

"And one more thing . . ."

"Yes?"

"I'd like to use my legion. If I take them here, at the top

of the map, and come into the trees here, the legionaries won't see them."

"But the Nervee will."

"It will be the last thing they see. If any do escape, all they will have is stories of monsters in the forest. Moreover, my legion will kill a great many of them. They could mean the diference between victory and defeat and they will certainly save the lives of many legionaries."

". . . All right, but take care that they are not seen by our men. You may go."

Ragnall sat, wondering what to do. He probably shouldn't have heard that part about Felix's legions. He might be able, he thought, to sneak back and under the tent flap . . .

"Ragnall!" called Caesar, interrupting his planning.

Ragnall went around the screen into the body of the tent.

"I'm sorry I didn't make myself known. I was working late—"

"Never mind that. Caesar assumes you knew that Felix is up to something mysterious, you're bright enough to have worked it out. Just never mention it to anyone or Caesar will have you crucified. Now, I have heard that you are interested in joining the cavalry. You were on horseback in a battle in Britain, were you not?"

"I was, but—"

"Good. Look at this map. We are now off the edge of it somewhere here, almost exactly at the centre of this chair. You will liaise with the praetorian Rufus and show him this. Take him and his horsemen to this point here." Caesar jabbed the map by a series of green splodges. "There you will find the enemy preparing the rockslide that you heard Felix talking about. Find them, disarm the trap."

"What are these green lines?" asked Ragnall, pointing at the map.

"Hedges. Thick ones, built by the Nervee to hamper cavalry. You will need the map that links to this one, ask the clerks for it. The hedges are easy to navigate when you know where they are. You may go."

"But Caesar, I haven't fought—"

"Rufus will show you what to do. It will not be difficult. Go."

Ragnall went.

Chapter 45

"You two, out."

Pomax bent through the door, torch in one hand. The moustached guards fell over each other scrambling from the hut. Pomax closed the door behind them. Lowa was sitting on the floor, naked save for her neck iron, chained hands resting on her chained legs. She flinched as Pomax squatted down in front of her and lifted her clawed hand. The big woman smiled, took Lowa's chin in her taloned fingers and studied her face in the torchlight. Lowa didn't resist.

"You look terrified," said Pomax in her girly northern voice. "I almost feel sorry for you, because today you really have a reason to be. Not because I'm going to hurt you – although I am going to hurt you, a lot – but because it's wicker woman day."

So Lowa had nothing to lose. She shot both arms up, fists bunched, towards Pomax's chin. The northern queen's head shot back like a snake striking in reverse. She let go of Lowa's chin and caught her wrist chain.

"I don't blame you for trying," Pomax carried on conversationally as she pulled Lowa's hands back down to rest on her legs. "I would, too, if I was going to be tortured then die screaming in agony." She put the torch on the ground and gripped Lowa's chin. "Shall I tell you a story?"

"Do I have a choice?"

"Last year, I broke one of my fingers in a battle. Badly. Not one of those 'oh I think I might have broken my finger' things when you haven't actually broken your finger. This one was a proper big snap and my finger was all dangly and useless. See, it was this one, it's still swollen." Pomax took her hand from Lowa's chin and held up the index finger. It was, indeed, quite badly swollen at the base.

Lowa did not like where this was going. Pomax continued: "It was so painful, I had to leave the battle. I was dead surprised. I've broken my leg and stayed in a battle. The finger hurt more. I couldn't do a thing with that hand for weeks and it was so sore that I became quite morose. And do you know, I thought at the time, what would it be like if you broke all ten fingers? You would not be able to do a thing and you'd be so miserable that you wouldn't want to. I think you'd just want to die. Especially if you were something like an archer and used to using your fingers."

Lowa felt something very like fear creeping into her chest.

"So you've probably worked out what's going to happen now," said Pomax. Lowa, mustering all her strength from years of bending the bow, tried to pull away, but Pomax didn't even seem to notice as she took Lowa's little finger between two of her own and snapped it at the base.

She managed not to scream. She tried to wrench her arms free again, but her captor was too strong.

"Oh, very brave," said Pomax. "I reckon you might manage to stay quiet for the second one, too. You'll scream on the third."

"I will not," Lowa spat.

"We'll see!" said Pomax.

It turned out that Pomax was right, but Lowa was in too much pain by then to be angry about it.

Chapter 46

Ragnall and Rufus rode at the head of a dozen black-clad praetorian guards along the crest of the hill through a damp, first-light mist. As the horses clopped gently along, hooves muffled by cloths and the wet air, they talked in whispers about Rome. Rufus knew some fascinating stories about Crassus, and was enthralled by Ragnall's tales of Clodia Metelli's house.

Some people, thought Ragnall, were lucky to have the sort of happy, sparkly eyes that made others warm to them immediately. Or perhaps their friendly characters gave them sparkling eyes? Whatever it was, Rufus was one of these sparkle-eyed affection-magnets. Ragnall had liked him instantly; the more he liked him, the more they spoke.

As they approached their target, Ragnall suggested that the two of them might meet after the battle and see how much headway they could make into an amphora of wine. Rufus agreed with much enthusiastic nodding. He knew where they could get some great stuff.

They'd left camp with the vague goal of preventing something being rolled from the valley side on to the Roman army marching below, then learnt from the heavy-handed questioning of an unlucky but knowledgeable farmer that their exact goal was a collection of logs and boulders next to a copse, guarded by a handful of Nervee warriors.

As they rode, Rufus marvelled at Caesar's abilities. How could he possibly know about the trap, both the large-scale one in the valley and this little part of it? Ragnall didn't say anything, but felt a little smug that he knew Caesar's information source. At the same time he admitted to himself that he was sure to tell Rufus everything he knew before they'd got to the end of that amphora.

The farmer had said that they'd find the collection of ready-to-roll projectiles on the north side of the copse, and, indeed, up ahead was a stand of trees exactly as he had described. They hobbled their horses and advanced on foot from the south across short grass, swords drawn. Sheep skittered away from the line of soldiers, but there was no sign that the Nervee had seen them coming, or, indeed, that there were any Nervee in the copse. That didn't mean that there weren't. For all Ragnall knew, twenty arrows might have been aimed at them right then, ready to fly in a heartbeat. Without fully admitting to himself that he was doing it, he slowed his pace to let the others get ahead of him.

They arrived at the copse without being perforated. They crept over a low bank and through the trees. Ragnall could hear voices ahead, speaking a version of his language.

"Oh, she's lovely. And did you hear what she did at Wesont?" said a male voice.

A female one countered, "You believe anything. Did you know that she drinks blood? She's horrible."

"I spoke to her a couple of days ago," said another voice. "She was surprisingly approachable, and she had plenty of time for me. I find a lot of these top Warriors are like that. They like it if you just go up and chat to them because most people don't have the balls. I said we might get together for a drink some time and she didn't say no."

"Yeah? Well, she didn't say yes, did she? Don't think you've got a chance. Iberian women's legs are about as easy to open as a stone clam. Even if you did get near her, she'd rip your tackle off with those pointed teeth. Anyway, she prefers women. I was talking to Serenax and—"

Ragnall realised that they must be talking about Chamanca.

The story in the Roman camp was that she'd died of her wounds after attacking Caesar at Vesontio (although he'd also heard that she'd recovered, drained a centurion's blood, turned into a bat and flown away). She'd been the cause of his nightmare days with Ariovistus, yet he was still glad to hear that she was alive. Weird, he thought.

They reached the other side of the copse. A few paces clear of the trees were several huge boulders and four large oak tree trunks covered in pitch. There was a fire burning ready to light the trunks, and each boulder and trunk had long iron levers primed under it. It would have taken only a few moment's effort to fire up the logs and send the massive weight of wood and stone crashing down the steep valley side.

On the near side of the trunks and boulders were five Nervee, two men and three women, all dressed in tartan and leather, and, seemingly, unarmed. They were all looking eastward along the valley, waiting for the Roman army.

"OK you lot, hands above your heads." Rufus strode from cover, sword raised, followed by the praetorians. Ragnall realised that he should probably come too and he hurried from the trees. "There's no need for you to die unless you want to," Rufus continued, "keep your hands in the air and we'll tie you up one by one."

Ragnall was just marvelling at Rufus' clemency when a Nervee woman shot a hand down, plucked a dagger from her belt and flicked it into Rufus' neck. Rufus dropped his sword and reached for his throat. His sparkly eyes goggled and blood sprayed between his fingers. The praetorians launched forwards, knocked the Gauls to the ground and put swords to their necks. Ragnall ran to Rufus. Rufus raised a hand, as if to say "no, I'm fine, really", then fell back. Ragnall crouched next to him and felt for a pulse. It was weak, then it was gone.

"What will we do with these?" asked a praetorian. He

was talking to Ragnall. They were all looking at him and he realised that he was in charge now. He stood and looked at the kneeling Gauls. They glared hatred back at him. At his feet, Rufus' eyes were already staring into the Underworld, their spark gone. His mouth was still curled in half a smile.

"Find out their plans from the woman who threw the dagger," he said. "Kill the rest."

Chapter 47

Lowa stumbled down the dry valley to the cliff top, along-side Pomax. Here and there, lone sheep stared at them. She was, on the face of it, free. Pomax had removed her neck iron and her wrist and ankle chains. There was no need for them any more.

"Are we going slowly enough for you, dear?" Pomax asked.

"Yes," said Lowa.

They weren't. It would have been impossible to go slowly enough. Her useless hands were hanging by her side. Every step, no matter how careful, sent bolts of pain up her arms. She tried cradling her hands in each other, but the relief it gave one set of fingers was outweighed by the pain it caused the other.

Pomax had been right. All ideas of flight had flown. Before Pomax had broken her fingers, Lowa had not actually believed for a moment that she would burn in the wicker woman. She'd been in stickier situations and escaped. But now she could do what Pomax told her to and nothing else. She'd given up all ideas of flight and accepted that she was going to die.

"I must say, you're doing very well, considering," said Pomax.

"Thank you," said Lowa.

Chapter 48

Carden, Chamanca, Atlas, Bodnog and a few of the Nervee commanders were crouched on the springy woodland floor, watching the Romans march along the road on the far side of the valley. The multitudinous Nervee army was hidden in the woods behind them. Few of them were well-trained, full-time soldiers like the Romans, but they outnumbered the invader hugely, they seemed disciplined enough, and if they were half as fearsome as they looked, Chamanca reckoned that the battle was all but won. She pictured Lowa's face when she told her that the Romans had been stopped. She wondered if the queen would be able to hide the disappointment that she hadn't got to defeat them herself?

The Roman cavalry passed, then the one legion advance guard. Atlas identified it as the tenth, Caesar's favourite and most successful of his legions. The engineers and surveyors should have appeared after the advance but instead Caesar and his black-clad praetorian guard followed immediately, followed tightly by another legion. The engineers would have been busy that morning chopping a path through the Nervee hedges, but that was no reason for them to be out of place. The Romans walked silently, eyes everywhere, pilums ready.

"They seem very wary," said Chamanca.

"If they have any idea what we've got planned, then there's no way they would have taken this route. They're in enemy territory and aware that ambush is a possibility, that's all," said Atlas. But he looked worried.

After the legion should have come that legion's baggage
wagons and pack animals – the marker for the Nervee attack
– but instead the soldiers of another legion followed directly.
It was easy to tell where one legion ended and another began,
because each legion was proceeded by a standard-bearer, or
signifer, holding aloft a golden standard in the shape of an
eagle. They'd seen three now, plus Caesar's. They should
have seen only two before attacking.

"They've changed their marching order," said Atlas. "No
matter, the plan is still sound, but we must attack now."

"We attack when we see the baggage of the first legion
after Caesar. Not before. As agreed," Bodnog replied.

"That was the plan, yes," Atlas spoke carefully, "but
they've changed their order. They're already past the point
where the baggage would normally be. We must attack now."

"We attack when we see the baggage of the first legion
after Caesar," Bodnog repeated. He was not his usual ebul-
lient self. A nasty notion prickled Chamanca's mind. She
sniffed magic.

"But we're at exactly the point, in fact a little past," Atlas
tried again, "where the baggage of the first legion would
normally come in standard marching order. Now they've
changed that order. It doesn't matter that the baggage isn't
there. The baggage is not the reason that we planned to
attack at this point, it was only a marker. We should attack
now because we can use our whole force against only two
legions and Caesar's guard. Wait much longer and there'll be
so many Romans in the valley that we'd be fools to attack."

"We attack when we see the baggage of the first legion
after Caesar," repeated Bodnog.

"There is a glamour on him," said Chamanca. Atlas nodded.
The others looked confused. "The Romans have a powerful
druid," she explained, "he has used magic to take control
of Bodnog's mind. That is why he is being so strange."

"Nobody is controlling my mind," Bodnog snarled. "I've

never seen more clearly. We will hold until we see the first baggage train, as planned. It is what I said we will do and it is what we will do. I am king."

There were now two and half legions, some twelve thousand legionaries in the valley, plus Caesar's guard and the cavalry.

"But Bodnog," said Bodnog's second in command, a handsome and competent fellow named Persux. "Atlas has a point. The baggage was only a marker. The point was to—"

"Do you challenge me, Persux?" Bodnog's voice was low and threatening. He stood, as did Persux. Bodnog was half a head smaller than Persux, but a good deal heavier, built like a barrel with logs for arms and legs. He had no neck to speak of and a round, shaved head. "Because you know what needs to happen if you do."

"I do not challenge you, Bodnog," tears caught in Persux's throat, "I'd never challenge you, you know that. But surely you can see that we must attack now?"

"I see nothing of the sort. Do not try me further, Persux."

"Persux, you must take command," said Atlas, "this is not Bodnog speaking, it is the vilest of the Romans."

"Seize the Britons!" shouted Bodnog. "They are agents of Rome! They have planned all of this, all of this, to sink the Nervee!"

"There's no need to seize us," said Atlas calmly. "We lay down our weapons." He put his axe on the ground. Carden placed his sword down gently. Both men looked at Chamanca. "Don't we, Chamanca?" Atlas added.

"All right," she said, dropping her ball-mace and her blade.

"Good," said Atlas, "now, let us talk sensibly—"

"I told you to seize them!" spat Bodnog.

Persux and the other Nervee looked from Bodnog to the Britons. Here, thought Chamanca, was a nasty little situation. She looked at Atlas. He needed only to have given the sign and Bodnog would lose his throat. He splayed his fingers in a "calm" gesture. Meanwhile, the Romans continued to fill the valley.

On the hill above, Ragnall and the praetorians couldn't see any Nervee in the trees, but, before they'd killed her, their captive had confirmed that they were there, in their thousands.

"Why haven't they attacked yet?" asked a praetorian.

"'Cos all Gauls are cowardly cun . . . oh sorry, you're a Gaul, aren't you, Ragnall?" said another.

Ragnall didn't answer. He'd watched them murder the Nervee, then torture Rufus' killer for information. It had been unpleasant. The Romans must advance, he told himself, and, as Caesar had said correctly, the means justified the end. But he did not like killing. He thought that from now on he'd try to stick to an administrative role.

The idea of Felix controlling the mind of the Nervee king didn't make him feel any easier, but it did seem to be working. The Nervee were losing the advantage. Already the advance guard, the tenth legion, were digging fortifications further along the valley, where it widened and flattened out a good deal. More and more Romans were flowing into the valley. The cavalry had turned and was patrolling the trees' edge, perhaps looking for the Nervee who should have been hiding there.

It was not a bright move, Ragnall thought. The cavalry were offering a long, vulnerable flank to the Nervee in the trees. Either someone had made a mistake, or Caesar was surely too confident of Felix's control.

Chamanca was as frustrated as she'd ever been. They should have been fighting by now. She'd been promised a fight, and based on that promise she hadn't drunk anyone's blood the entire time they'd been with the Nervee. She'd even been polite to all the goggle-eyed farmers who kept on coming up and talking to her as if she was a friend. Fenn, they pissed her off.

Another thing that really pissed her off was when people changed plans. Now, because plans had been changed, she was thirsty and they were still standing in the fucking woods, arguing.

There were four legions in the valley. The Roman cavalry had even doubled back and was riding between the Roman infantry on the road and the Nervee in the woods. The horsemen were so exposed to the hidden Nervee forces that it made Chamanca salivate, yet the impasse in the trees continued.

"I'm tired of arguing with you, Britons. Surrender your arms or die."

"We have surrendered our arms. Look." Atlas nodded at his axe, gleaming on the woodland loam.

Bodnog looked confused. Atlas took a step. Nervee swords came up.

Fuck this, thought Chamanca. She streaked forwards, scooped up her sword, looped under Bodnog's broad arm and came up behind him with one hand on his throat. She'd planned to pin her sword point into his neck, but as soon as she touched him, all in a heartbeat, she felt a shock, then a bowel-loosening terror like she'd never known, then an aggressive calm. It was the same as she'd felt on the tower at Wesont and she realised that Felix's magic had flowed from Bodnog into her, then away.

Bodnog sprang from her. For such a rotund fellow, he was nimble.

"What the fuck is happening!?" he bellowed.

He looked round at them all, then into the valley.

"Why haven't we attacked?"

"You said not to . . ." started Persux.

"I said no such thing." Bodnog raised his sword, ran for the edge of the trees and shouted: "Chaaaaarge!!!"

* * *

"Here they come," said Ragnall to nobody in particular. All along the edge of the trees, there was a ripple, then a gush of warriors running downhill. By the time the Nervee's battle roar travelled up to their lofted position, the Gauls had smashed into the Roman cavalry.

The former Briton felt his mouth opening in wonder. The Roman cavalry disappeared under a wave of barbarians which hardly faltered as it surged over horses and men and rushed uphill towards the legions. At the west end of the valley, the tenth legion and the praetorians had dug in and looked secure, but the others strung out along the valley floor were exposed all along one flank and in all sorts of trouble.

The legionaries farthest into the valley ran to join the dug-in tenth. The rest turned and shifted quickly into ranks. Viewed from above, it looked ordered and rational, and showed the preternatural discipline of Roman troops. But their lines looked very thin compared to the masses of screaming Nervee storming towards them.

Chamanca leapt on to the back of the horse, pinned the rider's arms, wrapped her legs over his and plunged her teeth into his neck. She gulped warm blood. Oh, it was good. It had been so long. He struggled, but she grew stronger as he grew weaker. She supped long and deep, then looked around. She and her meal were about the only people in the valley still on horseback, other than one large Roman, hacking his sword at – no, he was down. The Roman cavalry, destroyed the year before by the Germans, had been destroyed again.

All around her Nervee were sprinting towards the legionaries, roaring with battle joy. Others were almost there. Atlas reached the Roman line first. He dodged, slapped away thrusting spears with his axe head, then swung his heavy weapon back, around and down. It split a shield lengthways and sent its holder flying back in an arc of blood. The Kushite threshed the axe from side to side like a man clearing a path through reeds and created a gap in the shield wall. He charged through it. Carden and Bodnog followed.

Chamanca yelped with glee, leapt off the horse and ran up the hill with the Nervee, blade in one hand, ball-mace swinging in the other.

The Roman front line was in tatters when she got there, but the legionaries were a tougher prospect than the cavalry. They were retreating in good order, spaced regularly, so that each might wield his sword and shield unimpeded. She saw three in a row fighting beautifully in unison – shield blows to stagger their attackers, sword thrusts to disembowel them, step back, repeat. She'd take them first. She felt fire in her legs. Moments later the three in a row were dying and Chamanca was looking for another target. She saw Carden a good fifty paces into the Roman ranks, hewing down men with his broadsword like a Makka-possessed harvester. She ran to join him.

"Fuck me," said a praetorian. Ragnall could not have put it better. The new cavalry was gone. Totally gone. Then the Nervee hit the Roman line. The Roman left, where Caesar and the tenth had had some time to prepare, held. The right, below them, crumpled, then crumbled as crowds of Nervee ran over them. More Gauls were pouring from the woods. From their eagle eye's view, the exodus from the trees looked like a barrelful of ants being poured out on to the valley floor.

"Here, take this, I'll get it off you later." Carden handed the Roman eagle standard to a less effective looking Nervee warrior.

"Sure!" she said, already heading away, looking glad of an excuse to leave the front line.

The standard was Chamanca's and Atlas' as much as it was Carden's. Capturing it had been far from easy, but it had been enjoyable. Piles of dead and dying legionaries and Gauls lay about them. A couple of legionaries came running out of nowhere, headed for the Gaulish woman with the standard, but Atlas darted in, bisected one with his axe and crushed the other's nose with a punch.

"What next?" said Carden. There was fighting all around, but the immediate battlefield was calm.

"There are three fronts," said Atlas. "The Romans have repulsed our right and are countering along the edge of the woods. They are beating the Nervee back. Behind us, more legions are coming into the valley, but it's a narrow front and we're holding nicely." How did he know all this, Chamanca wondered? "Up ahead," he continued, "are Caesar and his elite soldiers. There, the line is static. That is where we're headed."

"Everyone take a pole and prepare to heave," said Ragnall.

"What?" said a praetorian.

"We're going to send these trunks and boulders down the hillside. Now. Come on, everyone grab a pole."

The praetorian lifted his sword and came at Ragnall: "There are Romans down there. We send these heavy fuckers down and we'll kill our own. You're a Gaul. By Jupiter's balls, I don't know why you're in charge of us."

"Look." Ragnall nodded down the slope. "We might hit a couple of Romans, but we'll hit a lot more Gauls and we'll stem the flood of them that are heading for Caesar."

The praetorian looked. The others watched him.

"Bollocks, Gaul," he said, pointing down the hill. "There are too many legionaries. You can't tell us what to do." The praetorian lifted his sword. He was a great deal larger than Ragnall and his knuckles were hairy.

"Three points," said Ragnall, hoping that his voice wasn't

shaking too much. "One, I can and I will tell you what to do. Caesar himself made me second in command and Rufus is dead. Disobey me and you disobey Caesar. Two, you . . . fool, you're looking in the wrong place. The way the slope goes, our landslide will go there." He pointed much closer to the opening of the valley than where the praetorian had been looking, hoping he was right. "We'll hit Gauls, not Romans. Three, I'm not a fucking Gaul. I am British and we are a very different people. We smell better for a start, and we stand our ground. Do what I say, or I'll have you crucified. Call me a Gaul again, and I'll have you boiled alive in honey at Clodia Metelli's next party." Ragnall held the Roman's eye.

The Roman faltered.

"All of you, get on those levers and push this shit downhill, now!" Ragnall shouted.

He was a little surprised and much relieved when they did as he commanded.

It was funny how battles went. Winning the standard, they'd been in the thick of things. Everywhere she'd turned there'd been someone else to kill. Now it was like the battle had seeped into the ground all around them, leaving dead Romans and exhausted Nervee looking about, wondering what to do next.

"You lot!" shouted Atlas at a gang of them. "Head back up the valley, and you lot . . . oh, fuck."

Chamanca saw it at the same time as Atlas. They were both far too late. A burning landslide was roaring down the valley side, directly at them. She'd forgotten that the Nervee intended to block the valley. Seems they'd let it go a little late.

She turned to face it. The world slowed down for her. She pushed Atlas out of a flying rock's path, but a moment later an apple-sized stone bounced and struck him square in the middle of his broad forehead. He tottered, stupefied. She dodged a flying stone, leapt and kicked him on the shoulder, sending him stumbling towards a ditch.

She looked about for Carden as she sidestepped a tumbling boulder the size of a hut, but couldn't see him. The boulder landed, crushed two Gauls, and bounced on while the Iberian dived sideways to avoid a spinning, burning tree trunk which had already squashed several Nervee and set others ablaze. She landed on her feet, looking for the next projectile to dodge, but it was over.

And there she'd been, marvelling how quickly things had changed. Now they'd changed again and she was the only person standing for a hundred paces around.

"Carden!" she shouted.

"Over here!" A smouldering branch tipped up and Carden appeared. "Found a hole," he explained. "Where's Atlas?"

Atlas was out cold in the ditch where she'd kicked him, a trickle of blood leaking from a half-egg-sized bruise on his forehead. Carden pulled him out while Chamanca appraised the situation. The landslide had been devastating, but only for a relatively small section of the Nervee army. Behind them, it looked like the Nervee were holding in the neck of the valley and there were still many, many more to come from the trees. Below them, the Roman counter-attack had been checked, and Nervee were advancing there as well. Up ahead, Bodnog and more Nervee were pressing Caesar's position. The landslide had simply dented the Gaulish army. They were still very much in control of the battle.

"Wake up, Atlas!" Carden shook him.

Chamanca pushed him off, sat on Atlas and pulled open one of his eyelids. "He's not waking up for a while. Come on, let's get him out of here."

"But the battle?" Carden looked up the valley, towards the thickest fighting.

"We have played our part. It looks like the Romans will be finished soon."

"I don't get it. You don't want to see the battle out? There's a lot of Roman blood that isn't going to drink itself."

"I know," Chamanca sighed, "but if we leave him here unconscious, someone will probably come along and kill him to get his armour. We won't make a difference to the end of the battle, so we take Atlas to safety."

"OK!" said Carden, smiling. "I'll put him on my shoulder. You take his axe."

Chamanca led the way as they retraced their steps back to the trees. She had Atlas' massive axe over one shoulder, her ball-mace in the other hand and her sword scabbarded. They were in a no-man's-land scattered with dead and dying between two outward pressing fronts and it looked safe, but you could never be too careful in a battle. She told Carden to keep his distance from the bodies where possible – she'd seen plenty of people badly wounded and even killed by the final, spiteful sword flails of the dying.

As they neared the treeline, Atlas said, "Put me down."

"Oh, hello," said Carden, dropping the Kushite on to his feet. "Nice nap?"

The bruise on Atlas' head had grown to something resembling a young deer's horn. Carden laughed.

The African ignored him. "With the numbers still left to come from the trees, the Nervee—" He was interrupted by screams from the treeline. The Nervee were still running from it, but while before they had been brandishing weapons and singing battle cries, now they were unarmed, several were injured and bloodied, and all were fleeing in terror, screaming: "Demons! Monsters! Run! Run for your lives!"

Chapter 49

Spring and Dug rode north through the fine morning. Dug was just reaching a state of oneness with the swish of the winds, the chatter of the birds and the very language of the landscape when Spring announced that, up here, many more of the roadside huts were made of stone than you'd generally find further south.

"It's because the people have a stonier character up north," said Dug.

"They're more like stones? They sit around all day doing nothing? They can't speak? Can you skim the flatter ones across lakes?"

"They're tougher."

"Tougher?"

"Aye," said Dug.

"Remember that time you killed a duckling by mistake with your sling?"

"Aye."

"And you cried?"

"I did not. My eyes were already watering because the wind was cold."

"I wish I came from somewhere so tough that they cry when they kill baby birds."

"Come up north, you'll see."

"I'd like to. Can we go?"

"Maybe when you're a big bigger and can look after yourself around all those tough people. The animals are even tougher. Their favourite food is soft southern girls."

"I can look after myself."

"What would you do if a pack of wolves attacked? And we're not talking your spineless southern wolves. These are mean, big buggers that'd eat you up in one swallow."

"I'd put an arrow in your leg and run away."

"Aye, well that would work, but it doesn't make me any keener to travel up north with you."

"I wouldn't really shoot you, I'd shoot the wolves."

"All of them?"

"All of them."

Dug looked at the girl. She was staring ahead, mouth set, no doubt fantasising about shooting a whole pack of wolves. Well, if anyone could do it, he thought, it would, in fact, be Lowa. But going by the way she'd spent much of the journey skewering game from horseback at several dozen paces, Spring wasn't far behind.

Shortly after lunchtime they passed two men who said they were walking to Mallam for the burning of the wicker woman.

"Yes," said the smarter and elder looking of the two. "There're burning a full house of criminals at sunset, and that fabulous queen of Maidun in the head. Not that we have any chance of getting there on time. Someone had to make a pair of shoes before we left the farm!" He glowered reproachfully but affectionately at the younger-looking one, who had a complicated beard and woad patterns painted on his thick neck and brawny arms.

"Yeah, but look at my Branwin-kissed new boots!" said the youngest, but Spring and Dug were already away, speeding up to an uncomfortable canter.

"I thought we had plenty of time?" said Dug once he'd worked out again how to sit on the stupid animal without feeling like he was going to tumble off with every stride.

"She must have annoyed them," said Spring.

"I guess it was a bit much to expect meek compliance from that one."

They passed more and more people, but didn't stop to chat. Spring said they'd make it in time but only if they didn't fuck about. Dug marvelled at how her language had changed after living with Lowa, then returned to concentrating on not falling off. It wouldn't help their cause a great deal if he came from his horse and staved his head in.

They had to dismount at Mallam town and push through a throng of carnival-spirited revellers. It seemed that the imminent burning of a couple of dozen men and women in a huge person-shaped wicker cage put the Murkans in fine fooling. Nobody paid any heed to Spring and Dug, no doubt thinking that they were daughter and father come to see the fun. If anybody thought that their long, straight but gnarled walking canes were a little odd, they didn't mention it.

Chapter 50

A few injured Nervee staggered from the trees then there were no more. One of the last stumbled up to them, bleeding life-endingly from a neck wound, eyes wide. Atlas grabbed him as he fell.

"What happened? Where are the rest?"

"Monsters faster than hares . . . Giants in iron . . . killed everyone." The man's eyes closed.

Atlas hefted his axe on to his shoulder, said, "Come on!" and headed for the woods.

"Wait!" said Chamanca. Atlas carried on. "Look." This time he did stop.

"Bel's big bruised bollocks," said Carden.

Looming in the shadows at the edges of the trees were a dozen huge figures, motionless, watching. They were surely too tall and too broad to be men, clad in thick iron armour that looked impossibly heavy. Their helmets were like great inverted metal buckets with no adornment but slots for mouth and eyes. One of them lifted a sword longer than Carden was tall and swished the air.

Chamanca felt herself taking a step back, then another. It was more than just their size; she could feel some foul power surging from them. Was it evil?

"What are they?" asked Carden. "I thought Fassites were a children's tale?"

"Fassites?" asked Chamanca

"Mythical giants from an island near Britain," said Atlas. "These aren't Fassites. They are Felix's dark legion. Some of them anyway. Shall we see how powerful they are?" The big man hefted his axe.

"No, let's go," said Chamanca.

"Perhaps you're right," said Atlas, "I think we—"

"They've gone!" said Carden.

Chamanca looked to the trees. All was darkness.

Chapter 51

The wicker woman was a collection of cages, two for each leg, a two-storey cage for the body, then one for each arm and one for the head. Lowa was glad that they'd put her alone in the head cage. Below her, maybe fifty people were crammed and chained into tight spaces. A fight had broken out at one point in one of the arm cages, but the whole structure had rocked precariously and they'd stopped. They didn't want it to topple because it might have fallen off the cliff. Instead they were all waiting to burn to death.

The agony from her broken fingers had subsided somewhat, but they looked bad – a mess of twisted red and purple digits protruding from two hands swollen up like blue-black inflated bladders. Even if she were going to live a full life, rather than just until sunset, she wouldn't be using her fingers again. She sat still, holding her hands in front of her like a squirrel, looking forward to dying.

She'd been so stupid to come to the Murkans with such a small force. And to bring Spring! She was certain that Spring was alive, but she'd been certain that Grummog would accept her offer of allegiance against the Romans. She'd been an arrogant fool. They'd all warned her about enemies at her back, but she'd been obsessed with beating the Romans. And now she was going to die. And Spring probably was dead. And there were three armies that were going to crush the people she'd tried to save before the Romans even reached the Channel. They would have been better off under Zadar, they really would have been.

And Dug. She did not want think about Dug.

Lowa closed her eyes and tried not to listen to the moans and pleas to the gods coming from below. She wished they'd hurry up and light the fucking thing because even in her agony she couldn't think of anything but Dug and it was driving her mad.

Chapter 52

Dug and Spring finally escaped the crowds of Murkan town, remounted and rode west along a wide road. They were against the tide of pedestrians heading for the bottom of Mallam Cliff, but the people were perplexingly polite about moving to one side as they approached so they made swift progress. They turned north off the road and galloped up a valley with a bouncing stream and messily rock-strewn sides. The valley narrowed into a gorge, wound round a couple of corners and ended in two waterfalls, one above the other, each one about ten Dugs high. They hobbled the horses and left them at the edge of the stream.

Dug tied a length of rope around both of their waists – "So you can hold me if I fall," he said – and they headed up the waterfall.

"It's much easier when it's dryer," shouted Dug as he helped Spring across a section with slippery rock underfoot and the entire force of the cascade on her.

"Glad to hear it!" she would have said, if there hadn't been a waterfall in her face.

They reached the top, stripped, wrung out their clothes, re-dressed, packed up the rope, then headed along the widening gorge.

"Wait!" Spring whispered. She took a bow twine from an inside pocket, unwrapped it from its greased leather holder, used all her weight to bend her bow staff and strung it. Dug had insisted that this route wouldn't be guarded, but she wanted to be careful.

"Oi, you!" came a Murkan-voiced shout at exactly that moment, as if to prove just how much Dug knew about the ways of the Murkans. Above them was a lone spearman.

"We looost a sheep doon eeeer . . ." cried Dug in what Spring guessed was an attempt at a Murkan accent.

"What was that meant to be? Who the fuck are you?" said the spearman, "Wait there, I'm going to—"

Spring's arrow hit him in the mouth. Dug nodded his thanks and congratulations. She was shaking a little. Finally she'd killed someone. She'd known she was going to have to at some point. What a strange feeling it was though.

As she pressed her palm against the dead man's forehead to pull the arrow from his mouth, she saw a flash of his life. He lived – had lived – in a stone hut in the town with his wife and two children, but the person who had been on his mind the most recently was a friend's eldest daughter, with whom he was obsessed. Before he'd spotted the two strangers coming up from the waterfall, he'd been planning what excuse he might use next to visit his friend's hut. He had no plans to hurt or molest the girl, or even to seduce her, he just wanted to see her and hear her voice, and he hoped against hope that his infatuation might one day be reciprocated. He dreamed that she'd come to him in the night and that they'd leave together and find a peaceful, beautiful land, where the two of them would live out their days. He'd been glad that he'd been sent to guard the top of the waterfall, because it had given him time to be alone and think about her. It was the next best thing to being with her.

Beneath his pathetic longing, Spring saw that he wasn't a bad man. And she'd killed him because he'd been in her way. She'd decided that Lowa's life was more important than this man's, that her desire to rescue Lowa was more important than his life, and killed him without a moment's thought.

In tribal courts, rapists and murderers got more consideration than that.

As they crossed the moor, Spring was very near to tears. She resolved to be stonier, like a northerner, and tramped on behind Dug.

Her qualms at killing the Murkan dissolved a good deal when they saw the wicker woman that he'd been guarding.

"Badger's bollock bristles," whispered Dug.

They were lying on their stomachs at the top of a slope, looking down from the east on to the rock pavement and its giant man-made figure. It looked bigger than she remembered, but maybe that was because it was stuffed with people. All up and down the wicker structure human feet and hands were poking out and waggling around. Only the head was free of sprouting arms.

Around the wicker giant's base were sheaves of kindling. On the far side of the figure, but massing towards it, were maybe two hundred people – Murkan soldiers, men and women dressed in various takes on finery, and a shower of people in wicker hats who had to be druids. Had the situation been less serious, she would have laughed at them.

In the centre of them all was the towering bulk of Pomax. She'd made no effort for the festival, still wearing the same dirty tartan jerkin and leather flange skirt. Spring felt a tingle of admiration. There was something impressive about a queen who didn't feel the need for shiny clothes and the other regalia of rule. Lowa was like that, too. In different circumstances, Spring imagined that Pomax and Lowa would probably have been friends. She wondered if they'd been getting on during Lowa's incarceration.

Beyond the Murkan guard and rulers, the sun was nearly at the horizon, shining in her and Dug's eyes and lighting up their position annoyingly. If they tried to get any closer, they'd be spotted immediately.

"Which bit is she in?" whispered Dug.

"She's in the head."

"How do you know? Is your magic coming in?"

"No, the guy on the road told us she was in the head, remember?"

"Oh, aye."

But her magic was coming in. Suddenly she knew that magic was with her. It was the same calm confidence she'd had in the arena. The plan was clear.

Short of running at the wicker woman and bashing it down with his hammer, Dug did not have the first clue what they should do. The sun was nearly at the horizon.

"Any ideas?" he asked.

"Yes." Spring's voice was odd. Suddenly grown up. She said nothing more, just smiled at the wicker woman.

"Going to tell me?"

"Wait."

"OK . . ." The sun was very low now. "I hope you're sure . . . Do you know whether they light the fire when the sun touches the horizon, or when it disappears?"

Spring didn't answer. The sun touched the horizon, and two druids in wicker hats strode forwards with torches and lit the firewood around the bottom of the wicker woman. Soaked in pitch, it whooshed into flame.

Blood-chilling screams came from the burning figure. There weren't many good screams, but Dug reckoned screams of people burning to death were about the worst. Cheers rang out from Grummog and his crew, and an echoing roar rose up from the crowds that they couldn't see below the cliffs. He looked at Spring. She was smiling like someone playing liar dice who knew they'd thrown a winner. Whatever it was she had planned, he thought, looking at the flames licking up the wicker figure, they'd better get on with it.

*   *   *

The screams startled Lowa. Despite it all, she'd fallen asleep. She jerked her hands as the pain returned, which hurt them all the more. She clenched her jaw. Tears filled her eyes then ran down her face. She laid her ruined hands in her lap and waited.

The screams took on a higher, more urgent pitch. Changing from fear to pain, Lowa guessed, as the flames enveloped the people in the legs. She could feel the heat herself now. It wasn't unpleasant. Perhaps, she thought, she could go to sleep again, quickly burn to death without noticing, and wake up in the Otherworld. Of course, there wasn't an Otherworld, it was just a story for children and other fools. But she'd seen Spring's magic, and if there was magic maybe there were gods and an Otherworld? She'd been wrong about everything else recently. Maybe she'd be drinking with her sister, Aithne, again? Maybe her mother would be there? She'd been about Lowa's age when she'd been killed. How old would she be in the Otherworld? Maybe there were no ages there? Maybe people didn't look like people, and you became thoughts and emotions without the hindrance of a physical shell? She smiled. She'd find out soon enough.

She closed her eyes. The screams and the crackle and pop of the burning wood crescendoed.

"I'm going in." Dug stood.

"Wait." Spring got up next to him and touched his arm. "Give me your rope."

"But they're dying . . ." The screams grew ever louder.

"We're here to rescue Lowa. Rope, please."

Dug pulled off his pack, pulled the rope out and handed it to Spring. She tied one end to an arrow, ran closer to the wicker woman, stood on the untied end of rope, drew the longbow full – something that very few grown men could do – and shot her arrow into its head.

"Here." She handed Dug the end of the rope. "In thirty

heartbeats, pull the wicker woman over. Take this as well."
She handed him her bow. "And string Lowa's bow, too, while
I'm gone." Then she went.

Dug looked all around. Spring had vanished, not just
buggered off quickly or nipped behind something, but actually disappeared into the air. He looked behind himself again.
Nope, she really wasn't there.

He strung Lowa's bow, picked up the rope and saw that
the cliff-top spectators had spotted him. A large, bare-armed
woman was sprinting towards him, shouting at others to
follow her. She had something coiled in one hand.

How many heartbeats had it been? He had no idea. Maybe
twenty? Possibly thirty? The Murkans were closing fast. He
took the rope in both hands and pulled.

"Hi."

Lowa opened her eyes. Spring was squatting in front of
her, there in the head of the wicker woman. The girl glowed
with pure beauty, as she had when her magic had saved
Lowa from Chamanca. Had she been drowned as Pomax had
said? Was Spring here to guide Lowa into the next life?

"Otherworld or rescue?" Lowa asked.

"Rescue."

"Good. But my hands?"

Lowa lifted her useless fingers. Spring took them in her
own hands and blew on them. With a rolling rattle of snaps
and cracks, her fingers lengthened, shortened, straightened
and clicked back into place. She wiggled them. They felt
tender still, but healed. She felt for the wound in her wrist.
It had gone, as had the injuries to her shoulder, back and
chest. She smiled. She felt tired, drugged even, but, more
than that, she felt healed.

There was a lurch, and the wicker woman jerked a pace
off vertical.

"He's gone early!" said Spring.

"Who?"

"Dug."

"Dug's here?" Lowa heard herself asking, like a girl who's just found out that her main crush has arrived unexpectedly at a dance.

Spring unsheathed her sword, stood up and cut into the cage's bars. The wicker woman lurched again.

Dug heaved. He'd thought it would be impossible to pull the wicker woman over and it wasn't far off that, but it was coming. He'd hoped that Spring might have given him the sort of strength she'd given him against Tadman; she had just disappeared, after all, so was clearly full of magic, but he didn't seem to be any stronger than usual. It was going to be a close-run thing whether the Murkans got to him first. The big woman was coming fast as a charging hunting dog, and many more were close behind.

The wicker woman dropped a pace and a cloud of sparks exploded from its base, but it was still upright. The real woman was almost on him, sword raised. She really was a big one. It must be Pomax, the queen of the Murkans, he thought – Spring had told him about the woman besting Lowa and throwing her off a cliff. Anyone who beat Lowa was probably a better fighter than him. Standing with a rope in two hands wasn't the cleverest way to meet her attack.

Badgershit! Did he give up pulling on the rope and save himself? But Lowa was in the wicker woman, in the head, and the flames were licking up the torso. Probably, on the inside, they were already in the head.

Pomax was a pace away. Badger's tits, he thought. He heaved. Pomax's sword came down. He jinked to one side and tucked his chin into his chest. The sword clanged hard on the top of his helmet. He heaved and the rope came another half a pace. Pomax swung her sword round in a decapitation arc. Dug closed his eyes and hauled.

The rope went slack and he stumbled backwards. Pomax's
sword swing cut hairs from his beard. Had Spring's arrow
pinged free or had he pulled the wicker woman over? He
regained his footing. She was coming at him again, swinging
down at his shoulder. Behind her, the wicker woman was
falling.

He launched himself backwards to dodge the blow, picking
up his hammer as he hit the ground, and rolled. He came up
on his feet as the wicker woman crashed to the ground ten
paces away in an eruption of sparks. Burning figures ran and
crawled from it. Was one of them Lowa? And where was Spring?

He looked about for them frantically but realised that he'd
forgotten about Pomax when there was a loud snap and his
arms were pinned to his sides. Pomax's whip. He strained,
but it was no good. He was trapped. His hammer was still
in his hand, but the only things he could do with it were
hit himself on the shins or drop it on his own foot.

Pomax walked towards him, gathering in her whip as she
came. What could he do? He tried falling to the ground, but
she held him up. Badger's bollocks, she was strong.

She lifted the sword to chop at his neck.

There was a blur to his left. A nude blonde woman flew
past his shoulder, feet first, and whacked into Pomax's chest.

The kick would have killed most people. It knocked Pomax
two paces back. She smiled, seemingly uninjured, dropped
the whip and pointed her sword at her new adversary. "I've
got to beat you again, have I?"

Lowa was unarmed, maybe a third of Pomax's weight, and
naked.

Dug strained at the whip, but it held fast. He looked
around. The burning wicker woman had fallen on the
Murkans immediately behind Pomax, and the rest were
having to skirt round it. For now they only had to beat
Pomax. But she was enough, and Dug couldn't help.

The Murkan queen danced forwards, light-footed and

speedy, sword flashing everywhere. Lowa dodged, ducked, flashed out her left fist and punched Pomax hard on the nose. The much bigger woman swung blindly with the sword. Lowa dropped under it easily and slammed in one, two, three, four stomach punches, then drove her arm like a spear into Pomax's windpipe, crushing it.

Pomax clutched at her neck and tottered on the spot. Lowa leapt, spun and whacked the sole of her foot into the side of her adversary's head. Pomax eyes flew wide and she fell back.

Dug felt someone behind him. It was Spring, freeing him from the whip.

"My bow?" asked Lowa.

Dug was so happy to see her that he just stood, smiling, until a slingstone whacked into his arm and brought him back into the real world. He ran over to where he'd left her bow. Another slingstone whizzed past his head and he heard the thrumming twang of Spring's longbow. He handed Lowa her own bow. Spring was already slotting another arrow, one slingman down.

As Spring carried on, Lowa plucked an arrow from her quiver, nocked, drew and shot. Two more Murkans went down. Dug looked from one to the other and beamed.

"Did you bring a quiver for me?" Lowa asked.

"We hadn't planned on a battle," Dug said, gathering his rope. "Come on." So far she'd asked for her bow and her arrows. He wondered when she was going to remember to ask for clothes. He was in no hurry to remind her.

They headed east, back to the waterfall, Spring and a naked Lowa keeping the Murkan pursuers at bay with well-placed shots.

As they crested the hill, Dug looked over his shoulder. The Murkans were following hesitantly, nobody keen to be the next to take an arrow. Among them, he saw the large figure of Pomax climb to her feet and shake her head. Tough girl that, he thought.

Chapter 53

They rode south, hard, swapping horses regularly. After a few miles they turned west and employed the old walk-along-a-stream evasion trick.

The gentle rising sun sharpened the edges of the soft night, and Dug could see by Lowa's lolling head that she was in danger of falling asleep and tumbling from her mount. Spring had said something about Lowa taking a little time to recover from her injuries. Dug hadn't seen any wounds on her, but she certainly hadn't been her usual self. He wasn't much more awake himself.

"We'll stop up ahead," he said, his voice loud in the damp morning.

"Why?" Lowa sounded as tired as she looked. But she still looked amazing, thought Dug, despite being dressed in clothes far too large for her, stripped from the guard that Spring had mouth-shot at the top of the waterfall.

"Because you look worn out. If you fall off your horse and knock your brains out on a tree stump, nobody will ever believe that we rescued you."

"Hmmmm," she replied.

He was pretty sure they'd shaken any pursuit, but they did the stream trick again once more before finding a deserted forester's hut deep in the trees.

"It's used in autumn only," said Spring, "for chestnut gathering, by the spikey husks around it."

"Right," said Dug, yawning. "You two get some rest. I'll take first watch."

"No you won't," said Spring. "I feel like I've just woken after a thousand sleeps. Must be the magic. You two sleep, I'll guard. I'll sing if anybody comes."

Dug ducked into the hut after Lowa. Once his eyes adjusted to the darkness, he saw the only furniture in the hut was one broad wooden bed with neither bedding nor blanket. Lowa lay on the bed. Dug crouched on the floor to sweep clean a man-sized area with his hand.

"Come on, Dug," said Lowa, "the bed's more than big enough."

He lay next to her. She turned away from him. He turned in the same direction and put his hand on her arm. She didn't flinch, but her breathing quickened and deepened. He let his hand fall so his arm was around her. Her scent was flowers, musk and dried earth, exactly as it had been that day they'd met and slept in the clearing. Here they were again, in the same situation, fleeing from pursuers and sleeping while Spring kept watch. Surely that was a sign that they could start anew?

"Lowa?" he whispered, gently pulling her into him.

She gave a little gasp, shifted backwards towards his embrace, breathed in a long, rasping breath, and began to snore.

Dug chuckled, then lay awake for a long while.

Chapter 54

Ten days after Caesar had wiped out the Nervee, Atlas, Carden and Chamanca were by the rocky Gaulish coast. They'd escaped the battleground by heading up through the trees, in the path of Felix's mysterious warriors. They'd found no trace of a dark legion, only hundreds of dead Nervee, some killed cleanly, some chopped into pieces, some ripped apart and some crushed.

Late one morning, they walked past more ancient standing stones than Chamanca had ever seen in one place and into the coastal town of Karnac, in the land of the Fenn-Nodens tribe. The Fenn-Nodens, Atlas told them, were a collection of clans and tribes, part of a larger agglomeration called the Armoricans. They occupied a broad peninsula which did much trade with the Dumnonians, a short sail across the Channel in Britain. The Armorican tribes' territory stretched further north, along the coast opposite Maidun's lands and south-east Britain.

Atlas had insisted that the famously indomitable Armoricans were their best hope for preventing an invasion of Britain. They were also, Chamanca had pointed out, the last. Annoyingly, though, the Armoricans had rolled over in front of the Romans like a puppy snarled at by a war dog. They hadn't capitulated officially, but Caesar had insisted that a couple of the offspring of each tribal leader should visit him and stay for a while, and the children had been sent. So the Romans had hostages.

Worse, as if he were an imperious guest taking the elder

of the house's seat nearest the hearth while the householders watched in meek acquiescence, they'd let Caesar commandeer every boatyard and dock along the entire Armorican coast, and more on the broad river that led inland from Fenn-Nodens territory. The general had set them all to building the ships that would carry his forces across the Channel.

As they walked along Karnac's industrious wharf, all around was the busy sawing, banging and shouting of people who were being paid more than they'd ever been paid before, assembling ships at an unprecedented rate.

"Nobody would ever work this hard in Britain," said Carden.

"Indeed," said Atlas.

Atlas had insisted that they come to Karnac to find the leader of the Fenn-Nodens, but, seeing that the leader was already kissing the hem of the Roman toga, he'd decided not to rush straight in and start advising on war tactics. So right now they were, according to Atlas, on reconnaissance, judging what their next move should be. Chamanca reckoned they were wandering about like clueless idiots.

They came to the end of the dock. Here was an area that had once sprouted with well-placed trees, for fishers and workers to relax in the shade. Now it was a grassy area of freshly cut tree stumps, the wood taken for boat building. A couple of entrepreneurs had inevitably spotted a market, and were selling mugs of beer. The Fenn-Nodens who were too old, infirm or laid back to work on the boats were here, sprawled about on the grass, drinking in the sun.

"Might as well have a beer," said Atlas.

"Best plan yet," Carden nodded.

A short while later, a musician came wandering along, lyre in hand. He was an unlikely looking bard. He was old, perhaps fifty, but still with a full head of grey-black, curly hair. He wore the tight leather trousers and figure-gripping jerkin of a younger man, which seemed an odd choice to Chamanca, given that he was skinny to the point of feebleness, but with a belly like an eight-moons' pregnant women. If she'd had his figure, she'd have worn an ankle-length frock smock.

Despite his appearance, Chamanca saw that he was respected. As people noticed him they stopped their own conversations to watch him pass. When he arrived at the beer table, two men squabbled over who would buy him a drink until he magnanimously agreed to accept one from each of them.

He stood, surveying his potential audience.

"What's the news, Cathbad?" someone shouted.

"Tell us what's happening!" cried another.

Cathbad looked over his listeners. He had a long, pudgy face and an irreverent glint in his eye.

"I've ridden all night, from the seat of the Haddatookey tribe. Or, what was once the Haddatookey tribe. Because the Haddatookey tribe are no more. I have just witnessed . . ." He paused. His audience were silent. ". . . the biggest disaster in the world."

"What happened? Were there survivors? Are the Romans coming here?" people shouted.

Cathbad waited until they were quiet. "Julius Caesar is not a man to cross," he said in a low voice to draw his audience in; then, louder: "as the Haddatookey found out, to a dreadful, dreadful cost."

He took a long draught of beer and burped. "King Thaldor agreed to help the Romans against the Nervee. But Thaldor is a man who's always had trouble differentiating his arse from his elbow." Cathbad waited for the laugher and calls of "Too right!" to subside. "So he didn't manage to send his army in time, and he missed the battle. Caesar won anyway and this terrified simple Thaldor. He was convinced the Romans would think that he'd planned to help the Nervee and be out to get him. But what could he do?"

Cathbad rolled his eyes bardishly. Everyone was gripped by the story.

"I'll tell you what he did. He made a terrible mistake. The Haddatookey capital is the most impenetrable town in the world. Cliffs guard three sides and a high double wall protects the other. Thaldor and the Haddatookey must have felt safe there, because when Caesar and his army arrived they stood on the walls, showed the Romans their arses, and mocked them for . . ." – Cathbad looked around as if checking for something – ". . . being such ugly dwarfs!" Chamanca realised he'd been making sure there were no legionaries about.

This got more cheers. The Romans were generally shorter than the Gauls, and the Gauls loved to tease them about it, although rarely to their faces.

"The Romans, efficient people that they are, ignored the gibes, walked back to their camp and started to assemble siege engines. Now, can anybody guess how many they'd built before Thaldor crapped in his red woollen trousers and surrendered?"

"Ten?"

"A hundred?"

"A thousand?"

Cathbad smiled and shook his head. "One. One siege engine went up, and Thaldor crawled from the town like a worm. Now, as your rulers have had the sense to see, Julius Caesar is a reasonable man. I've met him and he's a good chap, some interesting views. But you don't want to cross him.

"Caesar ordered the Haddatookey to surrender all their weapons, and that was all. Such a decent guy. He even told them to lock their gates again, so that his own soldiers couldn't come in and trouble their young women or silversmiths.

"That should have been the end of it. But Thaldor, a man who makes seagulls look bright, kept some of his weapons. That night, he guessed that the Romans would throw a party then sleep the sleep of the drunk, because that's what he and the Haddatookey would have done after another tribe's surrender. So he armed as many as he could and led an attack from the gates."

Chamanca knew what was coming next. She looked at Atlas, who shook his head in disappointment.

"The Romans, being Romans, were waiting for them. They let Thaldor and his force walk into their apparently sleeping camp, poured from their tents, slaughtered the lot, then marched through the unarmed town's open gates."

Cathbad set down his beer mug and looked serious.

"Any children might want to block their ears. This is where it gets nasty."

Chamanca looked about. The few children there were bouncing with excitement. One man tried to put his hands over a young girl's ears, but she squirmed from his grasp.

Cathbad shook his head. "All the remaining weapons had gone out with the assault, so there was no resistance. The Romans got to raping. They're not a particular lot and they raped everyone in the town. Everyone."

The drinkers were quiet. Cathbad nodded and continued: "When they'd finished, they slapped all of them in chains. The next afternoon I spoke to a slave trader. She reckoned that Caesar had taken seventy thousand Haddatookey captive. I think it was more."

Cathbad smiled, ruefully. "And that, my dear Fenn-Nodens people, is why you do not fight Rome. And you never, ever tease them about their height. The little men don't like it!"

There was a hubbub of agreement.

"Come on," said Atlas, "there's no point staying here. Let's go."

"Home?" asked Carden.

"Not yet. First we'll tour the Armorican chiefs and see if we can find anyone with the courage to face the Romans."

Chapter 55

Dug woke on the bed in the hut to find Lowa's snores had been replaced by Spring's.

They waited for night to move, then kept to woodland tracks. They were certain that Grummog would have sent patrols looking for them, but they saw nobody. Initially Dug was awkward talking to Lowa and she didn't seem overly happy talking to him either. After trying and failing to convince himself that their silence was comfortable he fell back to ride alongside Spring. The girl, however, insisted that he and Lowa should ride ahead to bear the brunt of an ambush, and that she should ride behind, listening with her better ears for followers.

Slowly, a few observations here and a joke there turned into a conversation. By dawn, they were talking like old friends after the third drink. It was mostly about Lowa's rule of Maidun, preparing for the Romans, and this new threat from Eroo. Dug was surprised to hear Lowa asking for his council and listening intently while he gave it. He was more surprised to hear himself coming up with sensible sounding plans and logical solutions for logistical problems. When they finally got on to the subject of Dug's farm, Lowa seemed genuinely interested, and had some great ideas for what to do with all his surplus honey.

When he rode next to her, his jarringly bony mount became a bouncing cushion of air. Despite Dug looking for one, they didn't find a handily abandoned one-bed hut again, so when they rested behind thickets and banks, Dug couldn't find an excuse to repeat the curled-up sleeping arrangement. However, Spring kept herself busy making camp, foraging and scouting while Dug spent all his time with Lowa, feeling as happy as a drowning sailor who's been hoicked from the sea, lain on a warm feather mattress and is being massaged dry by the breasts of beautiful, busty mermaids. Nothing physical happened between them – nothing sexual anyway – but every time they touched – passing a waterskin or just brushing along – that part of Dug fizzed as if tickled by tiny bolts of lightning.

So he was sad when the journey ended and he was faced by the prospect of returning to his farm, alone.-This depite the retinue of farmworkers and merchants cheering the return of Queen Lowa, jogging and hollering alongside them even before they crested the final hill and Maidun Castle burst into view. By the time they reached the hillfort, it seemed that all of Maidun had flocked to greet them and they rode along buffeted by cheers and joyous shouting.

At the foot of the castle hill, Lowa climbed on to a wall and addressed the people, thanking them for their kind reception and, in advance, for the massive effort and sacrifices they'd have to make to meet the coming threats.

Dug was going to head off when she'd finished, but he loitered for a while then tried not to look too pleased when she beckoned for him to follow her through the gates and into the castle. He looked about for Spring, but she'd disappeared. He caught up with Lowa.

The wide body of Maidun Castle was more sparsely populated than its environs, but there were still plenty of people pressing up to express their joy at her return. Even Elann Nancarrow left her forge briefly to nod approval at the returning queen.

They walked up to the Eyrie and there were more people to greet them. Mal whooped with joy, and even surly Nita cracked a big smile and hugged Lowa, Dug and then Lowa again.

Finally, the gates of Lowa's compound closed behind them and they were alone.

Dug had been to Zadar's old compound only briefly before, but little had changed. At the far end, protected by a sunshade suspended by ropes from the wall, were chairs for the summer court. On the left was the palisade between the Eyrie and the body of the fort. To the right were three big huts. The only difference he spotted was a circle of bright flowers surrounding one of them.

"Not very queenly, I know," said Lowa, seeing him notice it, "but I like flowers."

"Aye, no, they're very nice. I've done a similar thing back at mine, although more blues. I find that . . . well, it's not really interesting. Listen, I ought to be getting back there. I've got some sheep which . . . I ought to go."

Lowa smiled at him, head tilted, eyes bright. "I was hoping," she said, "that you'd stay."

"Ba . . ." said Dug. "Urb?" he managed.

"Here, in Maidun. I'd like you to help me with the army's training."

"Oh, right, yeah, I could do that. I'll need to go home first and sort some things, but yeah. Would I get a hut in the fort?"

"You can have a hut in the fort if that's what you'd like." She looked strangely vulnerable. "But, if you'd like to, you could stay here. With me. In my hut. Our hut."

She raised her eyes to his. Tears welled.

The earth burst open, the sky collapsed and he strode forwards, took her in his arms and kissed her.

Part Four

Gaul and Britain

Chapter 1

Julius Caesar marched south followed by his loot. So numerous were the slaves from all over Gaul and the wagon-loads of plunder that they said the vanguard of the booty parade made camp every evening before the tail had set off from the previous one. "They" were exaggerating as usual, Ragnall reckoned but it was true that the Romans headed home that autumn with an obscene quantity of pillaged and reluctantly donated treasures, and a multitude of enslaved men, women and children.

When the conquering general arrived in Rome, he gave away spectacular quantities of iron weapons and tools, stone, bone and glass carvings, gold and silver jewellery, leather and metal armour and myriad other Gaulish curiosities. The citizenry let out a collective whoop of greedy joy to see their hero home. The Senate granted another fifteen-day triumph. Rome was aswirl with parties. New records were set in all aspects of party-related depravity, mostly at Clodia Metelli's palace. Society had decided that she probably wasn't an evil husband-poisoner after all and invitations to her orgies became the seal of social approval that winter. Stories of the excesses behind Clodia's closed doors flew around Rome and bolstered the babbling of bards all the way to the outer reaches of the Empire, more flamboyant with every telling.

The stories were as close as Ragnall came to the most debauched winter party season imaginable, because Ragnall was in northern Gaul. He wasn't even in toga-wearing Gaul, the Romanised southern bit. He was in fur- and shit-stinking leather-wearing Gaul, very much barbarian-side, a thousand miles from the nearest gang of well-washed girls kissing honey off each others' breasts in an underfloor-heated, perfumed marble palace, strewn with giant silk cushions and staffed by attractive slaves ready to bring you weird food, refill your cup or lick you clean as you required.

"It'll be good for you," Caesar had said. "You'll learn real soldiering and the legionaries will come to respect you." Well, great, Ragnall thought. The respect of five thousand sweaty men is so much better than four moons of the greatest parties the world has ever known. On the bright side, Caesar had left him a small sack of coins that wasn't much for a Roman but made him far richer than his chieftain father had ever been. Shame there was nothing to spend them on.

As had become his habit, Ragnall was complaining about all this to Publius Licinius Crassus, son of Marcus Licinius Crassus. Crassus senior was famous for several adventures, such as becoming the richest man in Rome largely through the villainous actions of his private fire brigade and, as Felix had gleefully elucidated to Ragnall, crushing Spartacus' Servile Rebellion and crucifying six thousand slaves on the Appian Way. These days, Publius's father was only third richest man in Rome after Pompey and the newly affluent Caesar, but he was still very much in the thick of politics. Crassus senior, Pompey and Caesar had formed a union that controlled all that went on in Rome. People called their association the "triumvirate". The word spread through the bards, as apt new words do, and now everyone was talking about the triumvirate as if they'd been saying it all their lives.

Ragnall had assumed that his father's fame was why Publius, Crassus junior, had been given the command of the legion left to shiver on the wind-pummelled coast of Armorica. However, if nepotism had bought him the position, then it was a lucky coincidence that Publius was an effortlessly competent leader. All but the most bone-headed of the well-fed, warmly housed legionaries knew that the off-season maintenance and control of a five thousand-strong garrison used to killing and taking what they wanted was a bastard of a job and that Publius was doing it well.

Publius was the same age as Ragnall, but already he'd commanded troops in Iberia under Caesar. It was him who'd turned the German assault that had destroyed the Roman camp in the battle against Ariovistus and before that he'd led the cavalry against the Germans. Ragnall had asked him about the latter, specifically the massacre of German cavalry by Felix's legion, but Publius would only ever say that it had been an atrocity, not a victory. The young commander loathed Felix with gusto, which was another reason for Ragnall to like him.

They were walking along the beach, something they'd taken to doing on the odd afternoons that Publius's duties allowed. Publius walked with a springy pace, his short but athletic frame somehow suited to walking on sand. He had an eagle-beak nose and a sharp, almost upward curving chin. He wasn't ugly – far from it – but his face reminded Ragnall of the goblin-like figureheads favoured by the more jocular maritime tribes. His closely cropped blond hair and grey eyes reminded everyone else that here was a no-nonsense Roman who'd have you boiled in oil if you crossed him.

The sky was white and bright, the wind a salty, ear-numbing lash whipping off the waves. On the beach, a few hundred paces ahead, seagulls and foxes were ripping strips from the washed-up corpse of a whale.

"It's not all orgies and wine for Caesar at the moment," Publius said loudly above the wind, once Ragnall's customary party-missing whinge was done. "I had a missive from a friend yesterday. A chap called Titus Domitius Ahenobarbus is running for consul. If elected, he will recall Caesar from Gaul and take the province for himself after his own consulship. If Caesar isn't a proconsul any more – which he won't be if he loses his command – he'll no longer be immune to prosecution, and there are dozens, possibly hundreds of people waiting to prosecute him. Caesar will buy top lawyers and bribe the jury, of course, but so will his opponents, so eventually he'll be found guilty of something that carries the death sentence. In practice that means exile, but that's pretty much the same thing for a man like him."

"What can they prosecute him for?"

"Oh there's an awful lot. Hiring entire legions illegally, invading territories illegally and then everything he's done with those legions in those territories – murdering Helvetians, murdering Germans, murdering a huge variety of Gauls, and raping and plundering the whole lot, of course. Any of those would sink him, and he's guilty of the lot. The legionaries are loyal, but dangle enough money and witnesses will poke their noses out of the woodwork."

"I thought the Romans were all mad for his adventures in Gaul?"

"Most are. Some aren't. Some are outraged that he's broken quite so many laws quite so blatantly – particularly because he enacted some of those laws when he was consul so the hypocrisy is amazing, even by Roman standards. Others really are upset by all the barbarian slaughter. Possibly they have a point. And, of course, if someone brings a successful prosecution, he assumes Caesar's titles and a good amount of his wealth, so it's tempting for your man on the make. Cicero started off by successfully prosecuting a governor of Sicily who all deemed to be untouchable, and he had nothing like the funds available to Caesar's enemies. But mainly I think . . ." Publius paused and watched a seagull glide sideways overhead, whale blood dripping from its beak. "Mainly I think he's in trouble because Romans are a paradoxical lot. They love a hero, but they hate a man who does too well. So perhaps Julius will be brought down simply because he's climbed too high. Caesar has become like Icarus, flying too close to the sun."

"That's very nicely put."

"Isn't it?"

"But hang on, with Pompey and your father's support . . . ?"

Publius looked around. The beach was still deserted. Up ahead three foxes were snarling at each other over a ragged chunk of whale meat, apparently unaware that they were right next to a gigantic carcass entirely comprised of the stuff.

"Well, that's the thing. It may be that my father and Pompey are behind Ahenobarbus and Caesar's other detractors."

"What about the triumvirate?"

"Like I said, Caesar has been doing too well. My father is no longer second richest man in Rome. How long before Pompey is no longer the richest? Nobody likes new money."

"So Caesar is doomed?"

"Probably. One thing that may save him is that Ahenobarbus is an absolute tit. Total arsehole. I've met him a couple of times, only briefly, but he still managed to convince me that he was impressively stupid and entirely charmless. People say he's so arrogant that to know him is to hate him, and, in my case, they're right. So that might work in Caesar's favour, but, then again, arrogance and stupidity have never been obstacles to high office. The opposite, as far as I can work out."

"But what will happen to us if Caesar doesn't come back from Rome?"

Publius smiled. "If Caesar doesn't come back, we go home."

Ragnall kicked a worm cast. Home. What an idea. For some reason, it made him think of Drustan, even though Rome was his home now.

Chapter 2

Bruxon, Grummog, Pomax, Manfrax and Maggot were on the tower at the top of Gutrin Tor, high above Maggot's old home, the once floating island of Mearhold, now trashed and mostly sunken after the Maidun army's heavy-handed attempt to capture Lowa. It was a blue-skied, still winter's day that made one forget just how unpleasantly cold winters could be. It was the weather for an honourable, vigorous pursuit like hunting boar on horseback, thought Bruxon. Instead, three kings were meeting to plot the destruction of a queen.

Bruxon had been unusually disquieted of late, tortured by the notion that he had made a grave misjudgement. Dumnonian pride demanded that Lowa be obliterated, but was there any dignity in others doing the work? Maggot insisted that there was. This way, Dumnonia had its revenge and remained unscathed, in the best shape to negotiate a peace with the Romans. They'd fooled Manfrax into thinking the Romans would let the Eroo army occupy Maidun land, and now Maggot was persuading Grummog and his humungous wife Pomax that the Murkans should join the Eroo attack on Maidun. It was all going, he said, to work out very well for Dumnonia. So now Maggot the druid was making all the decisions, not just for him, but for Manfrax and now Grummog as well.

Bruxon didn't like it, but he had ways of reminding the druid that he was king. That morning, he'd ordered that his guard clear the bones from the roof of the tower. They were the bones of Maggot's tribe at Mearhold, so moving them displayed a massive degree of contempt and disrespect. Maggot, in typically vexatious fashion, had responded by helping to clear the bones while singing some made-up bone-clearing chant. But Bruxon saw past his Bel-may-care exterior. He could tell that it wasn't only his frightful jewellery that had been rattled by the defilement of the remains. Once this was over and Maggot had served his purpose, Bruxon would enjoy killing him slowly.

"What's in it for me?" spat Grummog, king of the Murkans. It wasn't the most dignified look for a king, Bruxon thought, strapped to your queen's freakishly broad back with your twisted little limbs waving about, but Grummog didn't seem to worry about dignity. Since being king, Bruxon had tried to enhance his already measured, intelligent way of speaking. Grummog's voice, however, was a horrible mixture of whining and snarling.

"What's in it for me?" he repeated.

Bruxon was about to reply, but Maggot interposed: "Destruction of Maidun, security of your southern border so you can trot your army north and expand Murkan territory, improved position for negotiating with the Romans, enhanced esteem with your own men and women, a place in the tales of bards now and for ever . . . It would be easier," Maggot put a finger to his chin, lifted his leg and placed the sole of his foot against the side of his knee in an annoying mock-philosophical pose, "to say what isn't in it for you."

"My army is not used to fighting alongside another," said Manfrax. "It would be like two men sharing one woman. One of us could go the wrong way and end up in the shit." Clad in heavy furs, he loomed over Bruxon and Maggot, but was about the same height as Grummog's statuesque queen, so his head was level with Grummog's.

"You won't need to fuck them together," said Maggot, "you'll just need to fuck them at the same time."

"What if the Maidun forces split?" raged Grummog. "Haven't thought of that, have you?"

"The Maidun army is small," said Bruxon in measured tones, showing Grummog how negotiations needn't take the tone of a slanging match in a brothel. "If it splits, it will be all the easier to defeat."

"Oh yes, and where the fuck is Dumnonia in all of this? Why the fuck can't you do this on your own? I'll tell you why. It's because you're weak. Maidun already beat your shit army and you're scared they will crap all over you again. Queen Lowa will bend you over and stick her fist up your arse. Like she did before."

Bruxon was too enraged to speak, but, to his surprise, Manfrax spoke up, his sonorous tones a joyful salve after Grummog's spite-filled snarling: "The Dumnonian army is shite, to be sure, but that's not Bruxon's fault. He's a new king following a long line of shite kings. Sure, the Dumnonians could fight with us, but they'd get in the way. Good that Bruxon here knows that. They're better placed to support us, to guard our supply lines, to be our supply lines, to make the camps, to keep the roads clear. Maidun might be a small army, but a small wolf will kill any number of sheep, so we need to keep the sheep out of the way, and let the lions do the work." Manfrax stretched, showing powerful muscles beneath the flesh of those heavy arms, then continued. "So, my wee king Grummog, Eroo will do the fighting and so will the Murkans, but you'll keep out of our way and we'll keep out of yours. Once one of us joins battle, the other will take Maidun's rear. With Maidun rolled over and dead, Eroo will take her land, and you will have two allies to your south."

Grummog's small eyes shone: "I'm not convinced. Give me the Maidun territory as far south as Forkton and you might change my mind."

Bruxon looked at Manfrax. Manfrax shrugged assent.

"You may have the land as far south as Forkton, but not Forkton itself," said Bruxon.

"All right," said Grummog, "but how do I know I can trust you?"

Manfrax laughed. "It's time for a blood shake! Now, did you bring anybody with you that you don't like? We'll need three of them."

They selected one unlucky person from each delegation to die with kings' hands shaking in their guts. Bruxon thought of choosing Maggot, but he knew that the druid would wriggle out of it somehow, so he selected a serving girl whom he suspected of having an impertinent attitude. She'd thought she'd been chosen to do something useful because she was pretty, so he enjoyed watching her expression change as he stabbed her and thrust a hand into her stomach.

Shakes made and hands wiped, the three kings agreed that Manfrax's army would sail from Eroo as soon as it was able. The Murkans would head south at the same time. Soon, thought Bruxon, Maidun and Lowa would exist no more.

Chapter 3

"Dug?"

"Uh . . . Aye?"

"What do you think?"

Dug had been admiring the pulley and rope system that opened and closed his newly installed roof vents on Maidun's longhouse. They were open only a little as the day was cold, but luckily the beeswax candles from his farm and his re-arrangement of their sconces provided strong, even light and his repositioning of the hearth kept the cavernous room warm but relatively smoke-free. He'd been sort of listening, so he could sort of rerun the last bit of conversation through his mind. Had Bruxon been saying that he'd send a shout the moment the Eroo ships were spotted?

"I think it's a great plan," he hazarded.

Everyone nodded sagely apart from Lowa, who shot a "don't think you fooled me" look at him, and Spring, who was staring intently at Maggot, which was fair enough. Maggot was an odd-looking fellow. Dug hadn't seen him since Mearhold, when the druid had saved his life by cleaning his Monster bites with maggots. He was pleased to see him again, even if it reminded him of thousands of little beasts writhing around in his chest.

There was possibly a flash of annoyance in Lowa's glance, and that was fair enough, too. This was important stuff, and if he was going to sit on her council along with Spring, Mal, Nita and Queen Ula of the now itinerant Kanawan tribe, he should have been listening more attentively. He'd caught most of it, though. Bruxon's informants from Eroo had confirmed Ula's report and Grummog's claim that Eroo was planning an invasion of Britain. The spies had added that the invasion was all but certain to come in the summer.

"And the Dumnonians have in no way colluded with Eroo?" asked Lowa.

Bruxon smiled. "No. As I said, Grummog lied to you, in an attempt to divide us, then conquer. Both you and Ula know and trust Maggot, I believe?" They nodded. "He's been with us at Dumnonia for several years now, almost always at my side. If I can't convince you of Dumnonia's fidelity, then perhaps he can."

Maggot stood and bowed to all of them, flapping his wrists and jangling his bangles. "Your Dumnonian," he said, "is like everyone else. He or she is not good, and he or she not bad. He or she is both. But he or she, he, in Bruxon's case, has no plans to attack Maidun. He, as in me, Maggot, has seen Bruxon every day since shortly after you took Dumnonia's arse on the battlefield, slapped it about a bit and handed it back all black and blue." Dug looked at Bruxon. That was a forced smile on his face if ever Dug had seen one. Maggot continued: "And Eroo has not come to Dumnonia. I can't say for sure, because anyone who's sure about anything is a fool, but I'm sure as I could possibly be that Dumnonia is no friend of Eroo and Eroo is no friend of Dumnonia."

Lowa nodded, looking semi-convinced. "OK, Bruxon. Return home and prepare your army."

Bruxon and Maggot left, the latter jingling like a parade of decorated horses.

"Well?" said Lowa.

"I don't trust Bruxon," said Nita.

"No," agreed Lowa.

"But that doesn't mean he's lying," Mal offered.

"That's true," said Lowa, "and I do trust Maggot."

"I don't think," Dug said, "that Maggot is to be trusted." They all looked at him.

"Oh, he's a great guy and all and he saved my life and I like him. But he sees the world differently. He's a bit like a god. I don't mean that to blow smoke up his arse, I'm just saying he's aloof from us normal people. If the whim took him, I think he could lie to anyone."

"He's not lying," said Spring. Dug looked at her. "I don't know how I know," she continued, "but I'm sure everything he said was true."

"Bruxon could be operating behind his back," said Mal, "and presenting him to us as the perfect proof that he's innocent, because he knows that you lot know him."

"Also true," Lowa sighed, "but we're going to have to assume that the Dumnonians are on our side, because the alternative doesn't bear thinking about. The Murkans, Romans and Eroo are enough armies for us to deal with. Ula, you knew Maggot and must have seen a lot of the Dumnonians when you were queen at Kanawan. Do you have anything to add?"

"I can't add anything. I like Maggot too, but, like Dug said, he is odd. The only thing I can say is that the Eroo army is huge and brutal. I have no idea how you'll stop it, but stop it you must – or flee. I've seen what Manfrax does to the tribes he defeats. His depravity has no boundaries. If we're to stay here we must defeat him. But, honestly, I don't see how we can."

"We will," said Lowa. "Nita and Dug. I want you to continue with the army's training. Mal, I won't rely on Dumnonian shouts. I need someone I can trust on the coast, watching for the Eroo fleet. There's a hillfort by the sea, about ten miles north-west of Gutrin Tor, called Frogshold. It's an island in the marsh, but well connected by raised roads. Take two hundred cavalry and base yourself there. It overlooks the Haffen Estuary, which is the most likely place for an invasion. If they land to the north of you you'll see them pass along the Haffen, but also send patrols south along the coast constantly, and send a shout at dawn and dusk every day saying that all is well. Unless it's not, obviously. We'll work out a code so that I know it's you – Dug, can you do that?" Dug nodded. He already had a couple of ideas.

"What if the people of Frogshold object?" Nita asked.

"They won't. I cleared the plan with them a moon ago. They will feed and shelter Mal and the cavalry. However, they are strange, independent people with no love for outsiders. That is why I'm sending you, Mal. You'll need tact to maintain their support."

Mal nodded, looking far from happy.

"Can't someone else . . ." said Nita.

"I'm sorry, Nita, but Mal is the best person for the task. And you need to stay here to help train the army. If we didn't have at least three armies threatening us, any one of which could annihilate us, I'd worry more about your domestic bliss."

Nita nodded sadly.

Dug looked at his feet. Lowa could have sent him instead of Mal, but possibly she didn't want to disturb her own domestic bliss. Or possibly she thought Mal was more tactful, which he was, if Dug was honest with himself. He looked at Spring. She nodded sagely back. Her gaze had a strange effect. He felt faint for a moment, as if a wave of sadness from the future had just washed over him. It was probably nothing, he thought – most likely it was all that salted pork he'd had at breakfast having its revenge.

"What do you think the Murkans will do when Manfrax lands? Can we get them to fight each other somehow?" Nita asked.

"With any luck, Grummog will shore up his borders and stay put," Mal answered.

"Yeah, luck," said Lowa, "That's not something we can count on, going by the recent record."

Two days later, Carden, Atlas and Chamanca returned from Gaul on a British merchant boat whose captain was keen to avoid being pressed into the service of the Romans.

"Fuck, fuck, fuck," said Lowa when she heard their news. Dug thought that was a pretty accurate assessment. Caesar's new ships would be ready to sail in a couple of moons, so the Roman invasion should coincide neatly with Eroo's. What's more, they didn't have any useful information about Felix's dark legion, other than that it looked formidable from a distance, appeared to be immensely powerful and had done for a lot of Nervee's soldiers.

"We've been to every chief in Armorica," said Atlas to the hastily convened council. "There is resentment that could possibly be tipped into violence. However, the overarching atmosphere is one of resigned defeat. They've seen every other tribe that stood up to Caesar destroyed. Meanwhile, every tribe that has capitulated has not only been spared, but has also been given their less recalcitrant neighbours' land, and had no taxes levied."

"As soon as Caesar has the land secure, he'll start taxing the badger's arse out of them," said Dug.

"They know that," Atlas replied. "They are not stupid people. They've chosen the likely burden of paying tribute tomorrow over being raped, crucified or sold into slavery today. The rumours that Caesar has demons on his side are not helping them be any braver."

"You can sort of see their point."

"Indeed."

Lowa sat back to think. The council knew to be quiet. Dug looked at the returned Warriors. Atlas and Carden had been aged by their two years' campaigning in Gaul – in a good way, at least on the surface. They looked about as tough as it was possible for Warriors to look. Dug wondered if he'd ever looked that formidable in his youth. You don't realise that you're at the peak, he mused, until you're halfway down the other side and looking back up at it.

Chamanca looked healthier, fitter and, if anything, younger than when Dug had seen her last. She was wearing the same leather shorts and metalled chestpiece as when Dug had first seen her, unconscious on the arena floor. He realised he was staring, but she really did have the sort of figure that made you forget to breathe. As did Lowa, he reminded himself, looking away.

"We'll have to spark another war in Gaul," said Lowa finally, "and when I say 'we' I mean 'you'."

"Oh no," said Carden, "I've already seen more of Gaul than any honest British man should have to."

"It does seem the only answer," said Atlas. "The question is how."

"You said that the Romans have taken hostages?" Lowa asked.

"They're not calling it that," said Chamanca, "but, yes, they have the chief's children and other valuable captives from every Armorican tribe. The Gauls gave them up as soon as they were asked."

"And yet the Armoricans have no Roman hostages?" Lowa said.

"Surely they must?" said Dug. A swap of hostages was exactly that – a swap – each tribe sent valued members to the other, guaranteeing mutual non-aggression and good treatment of each other's captives. It was a whole different thing when hostages were taken in battle and ransomed, but that wasn't the case here.

"Nope," Chamanca shook her head. "That's how shit they are. They just handed them over, not a sword drawn."

"Be fair," said Carden, "the Gauls have seen everyone who stood up to the Romans tortured, killed or enslaved. You can understand—"

"They're still shit," Chamanca interrupted.

"They have been idiots not to take Roman hostages," Lowa said.

"Yes, we know that, but under the circ—" said Atlas.

"And that's what I'd like you to persuade them. Convince as many Armorican tribes as possible that they need Roman hostages to guarantee the safety of their own and to give them a negotiating position."

"You don't know the Romans, Lowa," said Carden, "they don't see others as equals. They can take hostages, but they won't give them."

"So we get the Armoricans to take them."

"As in capture Romans? Capture one Roman, the rest of them will go totally fucking bear shit."

"I think, dear Carden," said Atlas, "that that is rather her point. And it isn't a bad one. When should we leave? Today?"

"You're not leaving, I want Carden and Chamanca to go. You'll stay here and help with the army's training."

"We'll need Atlas, he speaks Roman the best," said Carden, looking like a child explaining why his favourite toy shouldn't be donated to a younger sibling.

"She's right," said Chamanca. "Atlas should stay. He has led troops in one battle against the Romans and planned another that the Nervee would have won if it hadn't been for Felix's tricks and monsters. He understands the way the Roman army works better than we do. We, on the other hand, have charm and looks and will better persuade the Armorican chiefs that they need to risk their very existence and take Roman hostages."

Lowa nodded. "Carden and Chamanca will go to ferment the rebellion and see if they can find out more about Felix's legion. Atlas will stay and show us how we're going to beat the Romans. If you could tell us how to defeat the Murkans and Eroo at the same time, that would be handy."

Chapter 4

Ragnall and Publius marched along the avenue of standing rocks near Karnac. Ragnall would have liked to stroll, but Publius didn't do strolling. There were thousands of the stones, ranging in size from not-quite-liftable boulders to menhirs the height of a man and taller, all arranged in long, irregularly spaced lines. Local legend said the stones were an invading army that their druids had petrified shortly after the War of the Gods. The explanation did not convince Publius, who was a rational man, despite whatever it was he'd seen Felix do in eastern Gaul. He was nevertheless both fascinated and irritated by the stones.

"If you're going to go to all the bother of moving these rocks here from Pluto knows where, and heave them into a pattern, why make it such a shoddy pattern?" he asked Ragnall. "It would have taken nothing, just string, pegs and a modicum of organisation, and they'd have nice neat lines instead of this mess. I mean if you're going to all this effort, why not do it properly?" He was almost pleading.

"Barbarians aren't like Romans. They're not so obsessed with straight lines and uniformity. They like irregularity."

"No. Can't be. An irregular pattern is not a pattern. It's unnatural. Humans like conformity. Nobody with any sense could have built it."

"Maybe it really was an invading army and the druids really did turn them to stone?"

"You don't believe that, do you?"

He didn't, but neither did he completely discount the

idea. "I've seen some strange things, and they say that magic was more powerful in the old days. Who's to say it wasn't? Who's to say they couldn't turn an army to stone? Maybe they could."

"If these stones are an ancient marching army, then why are they such different shapes and sizes?"

"Because it was an army of talking animals?" Ragnall laughed. "That's one's a fat wolf. That one's a rabbit riding on another rabbit's back."

Publius punched his arm. "Nice one, Ragnall! But, joking aside, what's really amazing to me about these stones is that they're like a frozen moment in the time of people thousands of years ago." He stopped and pointed at a rock the size of a sheep. "Look at this one. To bring it here must have taken many people's effort, and while those people were levering it into place, all around them other people were rolling other stones into their slots. Perhaps a boy rolling this rock was in love with a girl rolling that one over there," Publius pointed to a distant stone, "but in between them, working on that stone there, was her father, staring with hatred and planning to murder the boy. Then perhaps he did murder the boy, sparking generations of vendetta which were ended when another boy and girl fell in love. The whole saga lasted hundreds of years, yet still it happened ages ago and is long forgotten."

Publius looked at Ragnall as if expecting a reply.

"And . . . ?" tried Ragnall.

Publius sighed "Aren't you interested? Ragnall, aren't you amazed that thousands of generations have lived on the same lands as us, all with lives and desires at least as complex as ours?"

Ragnall looked around at the stones and he felt it; the overwhelming weight, the overwhelming sadness of all those thousands of men and women stretching back in time, every single one of them just as important to themselves as he was to himself. Every single one of them now dead.

Publius continued: "Isn't it simply stunning that right here, where we're walking, people have walked for centuries, for millennia, all with their own problems, loves, hopes, hates . . . and yet we know nothing. They came, they lived for decades, then they disappeared, leaving no trace."

"Apart from these massive stones?"

"That's the point! These people were the exception! Most people are happy just to die and disappear into the long night. That's why I really understand Caesar, even if I disagree with some of his methods. He doesn't just want to achieve amazing things, he wants to ensure that everybody knows about him for ever after. Don't you want that, too? I know I do. And I want to leave more behind than a mysteriously placed stone. Think, Ragnall. How important is your life? How much have you seen? How many emotions have coursed through your body and how many thoughts have tortured your mind? Do you want all that to be forgotten? Or do you want all your doings, everything you are, to be summed up in a thousand years' time by someone looking at a big stone that you put somewhere and thinking, "Hmm, I wonder who put that there", then going about their day? No, I'm going to be like Caesar. I'm going to become a general and I'll win wars, and I'll get a team of guys to follow me around and write what I tell them to write about me. In millennia to come, everyone will know my name, like we know Ramses, Romulus, Alexander, Ulysses . . ."

"How about Cran Madoc?" asked Ragnall.

"Who?"

"A British hero, as celebrated there as Alexander is in Rome."

"Never heard of him."

And that, thought Ragnall, is a problem. He was still keen to see Romans take over Britain and use whatever means were needed to achieve that, but it would be a terrible shame if the memories of men and women like Cran Madoc disappeared under the Roman sandal. He'd have to try to persuade Caesar to preserve the British culture and stories at the same time as introducing the Roman way of life. Thinking of Caesar . . .

"Shouldn't Caesar be back with the other legions by now?" he asked Publius.

"They are delayed."

"Delayed?"

"Caesar has gone to Lucensis or Ravenna – my reports differ – to meet Pompey and my father. Consensus is that he's trying to save himself, prolong his campaigning and revitalise the triumvirate."

"I see. And when is he coming back here?"

"I don't know. It's a big problem, though."

"Because you don't know what to do with the men?"

"That, and because we're nearly out of food."

"Just ask for more from the Veneti, surely?"

"The Fenn-Nodens. Veneti is a name the Romans have given them. We should have the respect to call them by the name that they call themselves. That's the sort of thing I'll sort out when I'm a general."

Ragnall thought it was a bit odd to worry about calling people the right thing while occupying their land, taking their food and generally treating them badly, but he didn't want a row. "Fine, sorry, general-to-be. Take food from the Fenn-Nodens then."

"We've taken all we can from nearby. Some of the Fenn-Nodens have already starved, and more will. Luckily it's only a few poor and weak so far. But if we took any more it would start to seriously impinge on people who matter and we'd have a revolt."

"So what are we going to do?" said Ragnall, wondering if the chief concern of the people who'd starved had been whether the Romans had got their tribe's name right.

"Other Fenn-Nodens towns and the rest of the Armorican tribes will give us food."

"You reckon they'll help? I've heard they're not overly supplicant."

"I reckon they'll do whatever I tell them to do. Or, more to the point, what you tell them."

"What I tell them?"

"Who better to send to demand food from the Gauls than Ragnall the super envoy? Half British, half Roman, all hero?"

Nauseous fear flooded in and washed away all happiness as he remembered his previous jaunt as an envoy. "Publius, please don't send me. I didn't achieve anything last time apart from very nearly being killed several times. I only survived because a German druid took pity on me."

"So you're lucky."

"I'm a bad envoy. I was sent to make peace and it ended in battle and slaughter."

"Which was exactly what Caesar wanted. You're a brilliant envoy."

Ragnall sighed. "Do I have to do it?"

"I'm sorry, Ragnall, but you're our best chance at persuading the locals to give us food. This time will not be nearly so dangerous. You'll be one of three envoys, and I'll give you my second best century to protect you."

"What's the best one doing?"

"Protecting me."

"OK." Ragnall sighed and gently kicked a menhir. Thousands of generations may well have walked this very field, but he doubted if any of them had had as tough a life as he had.

Chapter 5

Chamanca spat as they rode from the town.

The Romans had sent envoys to demand food from every town and village in Fenn-Nodens territory. She and Carden were staying ahead of the envoys, pointing out that it was the perfect opportunity for the tribes to take high-level Roman hostages, a reasonable move to counter the high-level Armorican hostages that the Romans already held. The Romans, they said, expected their envoys to be taken hostage and would respect the Armoricans all the more for doing so.

So far their pragmatic reasoning had met only short-sighted cowardice. It didn't surprise Chamanca, it was the same lily-liveredness that had led to the hostages being given up for nothing in the first place, but she was still disgusted. Most of the leaders whined about the invincibility of the Romans and the protection of their people being their foremost concern. A couple promised to think about taking the envoys hostage, but Chamanca could tell that these were the same as the promises that Galba of the Soyzonix had made to Atlas. By Fenn, there were few people she hated more than those who said "yes" because it was easier than arguing. One tribe tried to capture them to hand over the Romans. That hadn't ended well for the tribe, and Chamanca had got to drink some blood. That had been pleasing, but not helpful.

Her mood perked up as they approached the next town, a place called Sea View. Like all the towns they'd been to so far, it was a semi-independent part of the Fenn-Nodens tribe, under the wider union that comprised the Armoricans.

They rode on firm sand round a sweep of beach, the only way to reach the town and impassable at high tide. At its far end the sands rose up into the peninsula that held Sea View. The town was protected on its land side by a deep ditch and a wall topped by a doughty palisade. The isthmus it occupied was a cliff-fringed finger of land, with a scoop cut out halfway along on the side they were approaching from. Within the scoop was a small, walled harbour, defended by stone towers above its entrance. Surely, thought Chamanca, such an excellently placed and neatly defended settlement was proud enough to stand up to the Romans? It would be nigh-on impossible for any army to break the town's defences. The defenders would only need to hold the wall until the tide came up and drowned the attackers. If the town wall was breached in the brief window when the tide was low enough to allow an army to approach, the entire population could escape by boat.

"I can see why they called it Sea View," said Carden.

"I think it's dumb," said Chamanca. "You call this one Sea View, surely every town with view of the sea should be called the same? It's like calling a person 'Has Head'."

"So you can't deny it's accurate."

They rode on.

It took her a while to persuade Sea View's guards to open the robust looking, newly renovated gates and let them in. That pleased her. These Sea View Armoricans didn't seem quite as wet as the rest of them.

Inside the gates, a road led along the spine of the peninsula. Either side of it were large, well-maintained huts, stout storage sheds and busy workshops. The gate guard escorted them to a clear circular area in the centre of which was a towering, excellently carved stone statue of a beautiful woman with large breasts and a fish's tail, whom Chamanca took to be Leeban, goddess of the sea. Standing on short plinths all around her were various marine oddities.

"Wow!" said Carden, stroking a polished whale skull that was taller than him. "How big was this fish?"

"Biggest I've ever seen!" called a hearty voice. "I'd like to say that we caught the cove, but, sadly, he swam on to our beach and died there, despite the children singing at him to return to the brine. He must have been driven to take his own life by some terrible, terrible woe, to withstand the children's noise. Their caterwauling would have sent me as deep as I could dive within a heartbeat, no matter what watery misery was waiting for me!"

The owner of the voice strode up. He was an overweight man, perhaps fifty years old, with red facial hair, a very large nose and a small helmet perched on a tapering head. Escorting the man, judging by their boar necklaces, were two Warriors and an elderly man with a long grey hair and beard in an off-white robe, who had to be the druid.

"What makes you think the whale was a 'he'?" Chamanca asked.

The tiny-helmeted man leant back with a hearty laugh, wiped his eyes and said: "We males have a mystical instinct for these things, I think. And there was the tiny giveaway of his penis, longer than a fishing boat!"

"Ah."

"Ah, indeed! Now, I'm Chief Vastivias. You are Carden and Chamanca, from Britain. You've come to persuade me to fight the Romans." Chamanca was pleased. It took no great intelligence network to know who they were or what they'd been doing, but it was still more than any other chief had managed. "Before you begin, allow me to introduce my Warriors and our druid."

The Warriors were Modaball, a man even fatter than Vastivias, with long red hair in pigtails, bare-chested above bizarrely high-waisted blue and white striped trousers, and

Bran, a short man with a wily eye and a big blond moustache. The druid was Walfdan. He nodded formally to Carden, then took Chamanca's hand and kissed it. Chamanca took Walfdan's hand and kissed it back, which caused a good deal of amusement.

"Now, tell me why I should risk my village," boomed the chief.

Vastivias listened intently to Chamanca's arguments, stroking his russet moustache. For the first time since their mission had began, she felt that her points were being heard and considered, rather than pre-emptively dismissed.

When she was done, he sent them away and consulted his Warriors and druid, before calling them back that afternoon to say that he agreed. He conceded that they had been foolish to give up hostages so readily in the first place. They would capture the Roman envoys and keep them until their own people were returned. Vastivias had already sent riders to other chiefs to suggest they did the same. His own men, said Vastivias, would have a better chance of persuading them than a pair of odd-looking foreigners.

That made sense, so, with little else to do, Chamanca and Carden settled in at Sea View to wait for the Romans and help with the hostage taking. As usual, Carden made friends easily. He spent the days with Bran and Modaball, hunting boar, eating boar and drinking. Chamanca envied his effortless sociability, but only to a degree. She didn't need or want to make friends all over the place. She had a self-imposed rule about not drinking friends' blood, so the fewer friends the better. She spent the time assessing the town's constructions, evaluating its defences and talking to its people to try to understand their military capabilities.

Every evening there was a feast on long tables in the central clearing. There wasn't room for all the townspeople, so they took it in turns to come, but, as Vastivias' guests, the Britons were invited every night. Carden tucked into the food like a man who'd been told that he wouldn't eat again for a year, and even Chamanca had to admit that the Sea View's chef's roast boar was almost as good as blood.

Chapter 6

Publius sent three delegations of three envoys, each accompanied by a century of legionaries. Ragnall did not take to his two fellow envoys, Titus Sillius and Quintus Velanius, or, more accurately, they did not take to him. Officially, he was in charge, but Titus and Quintus didn't accept that a former Briton could be in change of a man born Roman, so they did their best to undermine him at every turn, disobeying his orders even if it put them out to do so. If he ordered a stop, for example, they'd carry on and halt in a less favourable place a mile up the road. He tried to talk to them about it, about anything, but they ignored him.

He tried talking to the legionaries but that was almost as difficult. Eventually, their centurion took him aside and quietly explained that someone as high ranking as an envoy was not meant to converse with the common soldiery.

So it was a drudgeful trip and he missed Publius's company, but this envoy duty was still at least a thousand times better than riding along that valley into Hari the Fister's camp on his own.

The Armorican leaders, thank Makka and Mars, were nothing like Hari the Fister either. All of them capitulated immediately to all demands, and already food wagons were rolling towards the Roman camp at Karnac. Sure, there were surly faces among the peasantry, and a shouted insult here and there when the odd brave shouter was absolutely certain that he or she couldn't be identified, but, for the most part, the tribal leaders greeted them like deeply indebted Roman restaurant owners welcoming a pissed party of purple toga-wearing diners.

There was something he didn't like about this next town, though. Its name, Sea View, was unimaginative at best. There were no roads leading to it, apparently because the inhabitants went everywhere by boat and didn't see the need for one, so for the last few miles they had to march single file along a path, which felt exposed; he expected a Gaul to pop out of the scrub and stick a spear in his midriff at any moment. When they arrived at the town, they had to wait for the tide to go out so they could cross the sand causeway that led to it.

All these difficulties added together to produce something that felt a lot like defiance; exactly the sort of defiance that might make them refuse an envoy's demands and cook him alive in whale blubber.

Hundreds of Armoricans gathered on Sea View's wall as the Romans approached. Ragnall told the century to hold and rode to the gate with the two envoys. He scanned the impudent Gaulish faces poking up behind the palisade. And saw Carden Nancarrow. Carden ducked as soon as Ragnall spotted him, which made Ragnall all the more certain that it had been him. He was about to tell Titus and Quintus what he'd seen when an inner voice bade him remain silent, at least for now.

He explained to the gatekeeper what they wanted and promised that the soldiers would remain a hundred paces away. The gatekeeper disappeared. They sat on their horses, Ragnall squirming slightly under the hate-filled glare of the several hundred Gauls. He had no idea what to do. He was certain that it had been Carden. Carden and Atlas had advised the Germans how to fight the Romans, so the chances were that they were both here, doing the same again, and Sea View was preparing to attack his delegation, or at least capture it.

So all sense said that he should warn Titus and Quintus. They could all have ridden on and sent a legion to destroy the town. But for some reason he stayed quiet. It wasn't because Carden had saved his life by choosing him to catapult into the lake – he was pretty sure that Carden's competitiveness had been the sole reason he'd tried so hard to ensure Ragnall survived his flight – and it wasn't because he wanted to undermine the Roman mission. He wholeheartedly and unreservedly believed that Roman conquest would benefit Britain immeasurably. It was, he decided, purely because Titus and Quintus had been such pricks to him. He was going to get his own back.

When the gatekeeper returned and said that Chief Vastivias would grant them an audience, Ragnall said: "Jupiter's bollocks!"

"What is it now?" asked Quintus, voice dripping with contempt. That resolved him.

"I've left my purse where we were waiting for the tide to go out," he said. "I remember where I put it. I went into the bushes to . . . well . . . I had to stash my purse somewhere safe and I forgot to pick it up."

"You can get it when we've finished here," Titus snapped.

"Sorry, I must go back now. That purse contains coins given to me by Caesar himself. I'll catch up with you in the town. Surely you're capable of beginning negotiations without me? You know how close I am to the general. He'd be upset if I lost his gift."

Quintus and Titus looked at Ragnall then at each other. He could tell they were unconvinced, but what could they do? He'd called their competence into question and he'd rolled the unbeatable friend-of-Caesar dice.

"All right," said Quintus. "But Publius will hear of this."

"I will tell him myself," said Ragnall, pulling his horse around.

The two envoys rode through the gate. The heavy wooden

doors closed behind them. Ragnall rode back to the legionaries. They parted to let him through and he rode away along the beach.

What had he done, he thought? He felt both thrilled and ashamed that he had betrayed Rome. Not Rome, he corrected himself, just those two cocks who deserved everything they got. *Being boiled alive in whale blubber? They deserve that for being a tad uncivil?* asked yet another little internal voice. *Oh piss off,* he replied.

Chapter 7

Dug lay on the wonderfully wet, cold ground, eyes closed, panting like a dying dog.

"Come on, Dug," Atlas' voice said from somewhere above him.

"I'm dead. Leave me alone."

"Up, Dug. It was your idea that I train—"

"I know, I know." Atlas was right. If they could whip every soldier to the peak of physical fitness, their chances of beating any army would increase massively. And leaders, annoyingly, had to lead by example. He clambered to his feet.

"Come on! Next time I won't be so gentle. Do you want to let your badgers down?" Atlas had split the army into companies, each comprising a hundred men and women. Every company had been given a name and a capable or well-known leader. Dug hoped he filled both of those categories, but he hadn't been impressing himself much recently with his capabilities. Everything was more tiring than he remembered it being last time he'd trained for war, a decade and a lifetime before. He'd been given the command of the badger company, which amused everybody for some reason.

Dug didn't give the tiniest crap if he came last in a long-distance running race, but he knew that his company would be upset if it lost, so he clambered to his feet.

Atlas set off at a run, following the hundreds of men and women who were already halfway up the hill. At the top, ahead of everyone else, was an unmistakeable blonde figure, jumping on the spot and shouting at the rest of them to catch up.

"Should have stayed on my farm," panted Dug as he lumbered up the slope.

Chapter 8

"They have done what?" shouted Publius.

"Sea View has taken Quintus and Titus as hostages."

"How dare they!"

"They're saying that we have some of them hostage, so it's only fair that they take some of ours as collateral."

Publius looked like he might hit Ragnall, but instead he shook his head.

"And why didn't they take you?"

"I had to go back along the beach. I'd forgotten something."

"Forgotten what?"

"A purse of coins. We had to wait for ages for the tide to go out before we could get to the town. I'd had to . . . visit the bushes, so I stashed the purse, forgot it, then remembered it as the gates of the town opened."

"Convenient. Can you show me this purse?"

"Here you go." Ragnall reached into his toga pocket and took out his purse. It hadn't been left behind in a bush but nobody knew that, and he had visited the bushes while they waited, and was sure that witnesses could be found to say that. He surprised himself with his skill at deception. Giving Publius a hurt look. "I'm sad that you needed to see it."

Publius seemed to deflate. "I'm sorry, old man. You're right. It's just that six more envoys have been taken by two other towns and we don't have nearly enough food yet."

Ragnall gripped his shoulder. "That's all right, I understand. What are you going to do?"

"There is only one thing to do. That's what's put me in such a bad mood, I suppose. I'm going to have to kill some of our hostages."

"Might that not cause more problems than it solves? I don't know how much I'd welcome an invasion that killed members of my family." Ragnall thought of Lowa killing his family, which made him think of Carden on the wall. He felt very guilty. He really should have told the other two about him and now it was too late. If he told Publius he'd seen the Briton, he'd be signing his own execution warrant. And now he was defending the hostages? What had got into him?

"I know, I don't like it either. There's no joy in killing women and children, and it could snowball into a full-scale rebellion, but it's standard practice. If I don't kill at least one hostage for every one of ours that they've taken, Caesar will want to know why."

"Is he on his way?"

"No. They're saying in Rome that his political machinations are as difficult and dangerous – and as brazen – as anything he's ever done on the battlefield. I'll send a messenger about the envoys, but I don't expect him to rush back."

Chapter 9

Two shouts echoed over the hills that day. The morning one came from Mal from his lookout on the mound of Frogshold to say that there was no sign of the Eroo invasion. The second one, from the north, said that the Murkan army had left Mallam and was marching south.

More shouts came over the next two days. The Murkan army was fifty thousand strong, which made it nearly twice the size of the Maidun army. It was mostly infantry, with about five thousand cavalry and no chariots.

"The problem," said Lowa, "is not knowing what Eroo is doing, how big its force is, where its force is . . . If Grummog is headed for Maidun, then we should ride out to meet him nearby."

"On Sarum Plain," Dug replied. They were in Lowa's hut, eating a breakfast of eggs and bread. Sarum Plain, where she'd defeated the Dumnonians, was the obvious spot: wide and flat, favouring their chariot-heavy army.

"If he's stupid enough to go that way," she said. "He's a canny fucker."

"But if he heads for the Haffen Estuary and links with the Eroo army when they land . . ."

"Then we're in trouble, even if we can persuade them to a battleground that suits our chariots."

"So the answer is . . ."

"To take the army north," said Lowa. "Defeat the Murkans before Eroo lands."

"And if Manfrax does come in the next couple of days?"

"Then we'll be in the right place. We can use Gutrin Tor or Frogshold as our fort and supply via Forkton if necessary."

"Which one do you favour?"

"They're both similar mounds protruding from the marshes, but Frogshold is better fortified and nearer the coast, so probably Frogshold. But the main thing, do you agree with me that we should mobilise and march now?"

"Yup," he nodded.

She'd known that was the answer, but it was good to have Dug to agree.

"So that's that," she said. "We go to war today."

Chapter 10

Bran appeared at Chamanca and Carden's open hut door at dawn and asked them to come to the central clearing. They walked through the misty morning and muted sounds of a village waking up and found Chief Vastivias, Walfdan the druid and Modaball the Warrior debating hotly. Vastivias was stabbing the air with a finger, Modaball was windmilling his arms and Walfdan was stroking his beard.

"Caesar has killed my son and my daughter," said Vastivias when he saw them. "In fact, he didn't even have the balls to do it himself. A deputy gave the order. Caesar is in Italy."

"Ah," said Carden.

"I am sorry," Chamanca added.

Vastivias nodded. "I could say that it was your fault and that we should boil you in whale blubber right now, but you were right. I made a mistake when I gave them as hostages without taking any in return. Their blood is on my hands, not yours. And on Caesar's."

"What are you going to do?" asked Chamanca.

"I'm going to destroy the Roman army and kill Caesar. I'm on the brink of sending out riders to gather forces. There's only one Roman legion in Armorica – five thousand men. We will take them without too much bother. Then Caesar will come with more men, and we'll kill all of them, too."

"It won't be easy defeating even the one legion," said Carden. "They don't fight like decent people. They link shields so they're like a giant crab with a thousand claws."

"We will smash them!" said Modaball, jumping on the spot, the fat on his chest and arms rippling.

"I'm sorry, but you won't," said Chamanca, "no matter how brave and skilled your warriors are. The Roman battle tactics are difficult to beat, impossible if your army is not coordinated. You Armorican tribes tolerate each other and coexist peacefully enough, but there are too many chiefs for you to work together on the battlefield. No matter your total numbers nor your passion, you will have many small groups attacking the Romans, rather than one coordinated army. And that, I am sorry to say, is exactly how to get wiped out by the Romans."

"What a load of boarshit!" Modaball puffed out his chest. "I could take the whole lot on myself. I could—"

Vastivias put a hand on Modaball's arm. "Quiet," he said. "It does not make us shy to listen to an independent, prudent voice, especially when our blood is boiling. Are we cowards if we circle a lion and wait for an opportunity with the spear rather than putting our head in her mouth? What do you suggest, Chamanca?"

"Last year, King Hari the German used attrition, the piece-by-piece destruction of their forces. Had he carried the strategy through, we wouldn't be having this conversation because the Romans would have been defeated last year. However, he became frustrated, committed all his forces into one battle – a much larger force than the Armoricans might muster – and he was destroyed by a smaller number of legions than you will face when Caesar returns. I suggest you learn from his fatal mistakes. Watch the Romans in Karnac. Any Roman leaves the base, he does not go back. You have an advantage over King Hari in that your Romans are already short of food. It won't be long before they're starving. Their morale will dissolve and they will have to retreat."

"And when Caesar's other legions return?" Bran asked.

"Fenn-Nodens towns have been built well, in good

locations, and are almost all defendable. So you hold out. You have wells, your food comes from the sea. You are perfectly placed to resist, much more so than any of the other Gaulish tribes that Caesar has defeated. And if the Romans do breach your walls, you have boats, so you sail to an ally. You could go to Britain even. You will be welcome in Maidun's lands." Chamanca hoped this was true. It probably was. She continued: "The Romans do not have the numbers to garrison your towns, so when they leave, you return."

Vastivias shook his head. "And rebuild our smashed buildings? Not to mention our smashed pride."

"Buildings and pride will be a great deal easier to restore than the lives of your people should you attack the Romans head-on. Stone, wood and swagger are disposable. Your riches, your lives and your children you can take with you on your boats and save for another day."

"Your aim," said Walfdan the long-bearded druid, "is to prevent the Romans invading Britain. You intend to use Sea View to this end, as a desperate forest tribe might cut down trees to prevent a fire reaching their huts. Your plan will kill us all, but that is unimportant to you as long as the Romans are slowed."

The old man held her gaze.

"You're right," she said, "when you say that we mean to stop the Romans from invading Britain. But why do we want to hold the Romans back? I'll tell you. When the Romans take a land, they keep it. They will kill anyone that they see as the slightest threat, like a farmer killing one animal to prevent its disease spreading to another. They will lie. They will break treaties like they break kindling to fit a forge. Under the Romans, as a people, you will cease to exist. You may live, but it will be a living death. I have seen it in Iberia. The men and women became no more than miserable sheep. Thousands were put to work in mines so poisonous that birds flying overhead dropped dead from the sky, and so brutalised were they that they went to this work with no complaint. So that is why I want to stop the Romans from invading Britain, and it is why you should want to stop them from taking Armorica. If you do not panic, if you plan intelligently, if you understand the Romans, then you have every chance of beating them."

"You make a good argument," said Vastivias. "And I have no desire to become a sheep. Bran, Modaball, send messengers at once to all the other towns and tribes. Tell them that Armorica's men and women may be divided by geography, but we are one people. Together, we will defeat Caesar. Meanwhile, where are those Roman hostages? Let's get them out and have some fun. Modaball, find our largest cauldron and fill it with whale blubber, there's a good chap."

Chapter 11

Caesar's legions arrived back in Armorica but Caesar did not. Publius was sent south to quell an uprising against the invader and replaced with someone who was apparently a naval expert. Ragnall, keen to assuage his guilt for allowing Titus and Quintus to be taken hostage, headed to the command tent to introduce himself to the new legate and find out how he could be useful.

To his surprise and annoyance the guards refused to let him in at first, relenting only when Ragnall said that people had been boiled in olive oil for less than barring Caesar's chief envoy from entry.

The tent was busy with smartly dressed Romans whom Ragnall had never seen before. They parted to allow him through. A dough-faced, black-eyed man looked up from Publius's map table, saw Ragnall, and looked back to the maps.

Ragnall knew that face. It was Decimus Junius Brutus Albinus. Ragnall had met him several times at Clodia's in Rome, where Brutus had used connections to wheedle a place in the party house. Unfortunately he was blessed with neither looks nor wit, so almost everyone had shunned him. Ragnall, remembering what it was like to be an outsider, hadn't. He'd tried his best to have Brutus included in the fun. Brutus proved too self-centred and dim for party games, so Ragnall had dragged himself from the revelry and chatted to the awkward Roman, or, more accurately, listened to Brutus' self-promoting stories and boorish opinions. Time rarely went as slowly, Ragnall realised, as when your friends were having fun within earshot and you weren't. The more he heard from Brutus, the more he disliked him, but he'd also felt increasingly sorry for a man with such an unpleasant disposition and such unfortunate looks, so he'd kept up an amicable pretence and invested a good few hours in him that could have been spent with vastly more entertaining, interesting people. Brutus owed him for that.

"Hello, Brutus," said Ragnall, holding out an arm to shake. "Welcome to the far side of the world."

". . . And who might you be?" Brutus ignored Ragnall's outstretched arm. Instead he looked to each of his gathered advisors, smiling like an obnoxious man who's just proved a point.

Ragnall was speechless.

"I swear I've never seen him before in my life!" Brutus added. "Run along, will you? There's a good fellow. We've work to do here."

"Brutus, I'm Ragnall. Ragnall Sheeplord. We met several times in Rome. I spent hours talking to you at Clodia's. You told me a lot about sailing."

"Really? You can't have made much of an impression. But then again, Clodia doesn't pick her party companions for their brains, does she?" He rolled his eyes at his cronies. A couple of them chuckled. "Now will you go or should I have you removed? We have work to do."

"I'm Caesar's chief envoy. I know the land around here. I've visited almost every tribe that's rebelling and can give you invaluable intelligence. I understand the—"

"Guards?" interrupted Brutus mildly, nodding at two hefty legionaries. They stood forward.

"I'm going!" said Ragnall, holding up his hands.

Ragnall walked away in a funk, oblivious to the noises and smells of the Roman camp. Why, by Makka, had Caesar sacked Publius and sent Brutus to command? Actually, it was pretty obvious. Publius's war against the Armoricans had not been going well. Foraging party after foraging party had been killed. Every time Publius approached a town with his army, the Armoricans took to the water in their boats like ducks fleeing from leopards. The tactics were cowardly but successful and however much Ragnall liked Publius, he had to admit that he had failed as a general. The Armorican problem needed a naval solution, so Caesar had sent a man with a maritime background.

He looked back across the bay. Yup, there were many more ships bobbing about than usual. Brutus must have called them all in from the various harbours and shipyards. They had been built for carrying troops to Britain, but first, Ragnall guessed, they'd serve well enough to block the Fenn-Nodens' escape routes. It was what Publius should have done. Amazing how easy answers were when they were placed in front of you, and annoying that Brutus had thought of this one.

Chapter 12

Vastivias' ship crashed through the waves. Up ahead four whales surfaced, low sun glaring off their fat wet backs as they spumed spray into the immense morning sky. Following the flagship, rolling before the stiff wind, were hundreds of ships, leather sails full. Above, a multitude of seagulls kept pace, no doubt mistaking the armada for an oversized fishing expedition. As far they were concerned it was no different; there would be plenty of fresh meat bobbing on the bay before the day was out.

Chamanca stood on the plunging prow, shivering with pleasure after every blast of brine. A captured legionary had told them the Romans' naval plans. The answer, as Vastivias had grasped straight away, thank Fenn, was to amass the Fenn-Nodens' ships and destroy the Roman fleet before it could attack individual tribes. Chamanca was content. Thus far, her and Vastivias' plans had worked. The Fenn-Nodens had killed a good number of the enemy with few losses by attacking vulnerable Romans then immediately fleeing in their boats when retribution threatened. It had been far from heroic, but it had worked.

Now the Romans had a navy, but it was doomed. The Fenn-Nodens simply could not lose a naval battle. Their salt-crusted men and women had been sailing for countless generations, while the Romans' ships were new and their crews inexperienced. They hadn't seen the Roman fleet yet, but reliable reports said it was half the size of the Fenn-Nodens'. The Roman boats were smaller and more lightly built, designed for one fair-weather crossing to Britain rather than years of pounding through storm waves. The enemy's boats were lower-sided too, so it would be nigh on impossible for them to board the Fenn-Nodens'. All that would point to victory, but, on top of all of it, there was the clincher that all the Roman ships were oar-powered. The Fenn-Nodens had sailing ships. That made them reliant on the winds, yes, but all the old salts had said that this particular breeze came every year, and would blow for several more days. With this wind the sailing boats were faster and more manoeuvrable than the rowing ships. Once the Fenn-Nodens had taken out enough rowers with the sling men and broken enough oars by ramming them with their heavier boats, the Romans would be dead in the water, vulnerable as injured lambs separated from the herd.

Who needed Atlas? Chamanca's plan was nicely whittling away Caesar's invasion force, and now they were about to destroy its only means of reaching Britain.

She looked back along the boat. Vastivias was at the stern, pointing at the coast and talking to the helmsman. Nearer, Carden had arranged a competition among the slingers to see who could hit a seagull. She almost shouted at him to stop wasting ammunition, but there were so many bags of sling-stones hanging from the edge of the boat that it didn't matter, and it was no bad idea for them to practise shooting from a rolling platform.

Up ahead to their right was a craggy island. To the left was the headland that marked the western extreme of Karnac Bay, where, if their information was correct, the Roman fleet was waiting.

The first Roman boat came into sight. Its hundred or so oars were all awry, sprouting from the sides like straw from a badly packed bale. The Roman ship must have spotted them a moment later, because the oars all suddenly moved, but in different directions. A few snapped. The wrenching crack of splintering wood reached Chamanca across the water a good heartbeat after it happened, followed by shouted Roman curses. Chamanca patted her sword and her mace, and smiled. Brilliant sun sparkled off the sea and the prow's white spray below a rich blue sky, and there was blood to come. It was a beautiful day.

Chapter 13

Mal rode out and met Atlas and the Maidun infantry, come to garrison Forkton. He didn't need to guide them in, the lone hill of Frogshold was impossible to miss, but he'd seized the excuse to spend some time away from it. Despite his best efforts, he'd had a crappy time at Frogshold. The people were a bitterly dour lot, he'd missed Nita and he'd been put off frog meat for life. Two thousand paces from the sea, and the only animals the people of Frogshold ate were frogs from the marshes. No wonder they were so unhappy. Mal had survived mainly on bread. The bread was actually pretty good, and always fresh. The Frogsholders had drained the marshes for a few miles around their hillfort to create several large wheat fields, nicely irrigated by the drainage channels chopped into the fertile peat. It was an impressive feat which should have cheered them up but hadn't. The good bread had cheered Mal up for a while, but by Toutatis he'd had enough of it now.

"Who's this then?" asked Tayden Mottker, chief of Frogshold, when the Maidun forces reached the bottom of the knoll. She'd walked down from the hillfort accompanied by her usual gang of po-faced followers. Her eyes bulged as they flicked up and down Atlas' oversized frame.

"This is Atlas Agrippa, general of the Maidun infantry," said Mal.

"Charmed," said Atlas, holding out his hand. Tayden took it reluctantly.

"Any sign of the enemy?" Atlas asked.

"Depends who you mean by enemy," Tayden replied, looking pointedly at Mal. She was a tallish, strong looking woman of around Mal's age. She had thinning fair hair decorated with shells, washy blue eyes and lips that looked like they were searching for something to suck on. Although there was definitely something of the frog about her, her features somehow combined quite pleasingly and Mal might have found her attractive if it hadn't been for her constant suspicious hostility.

"But if you mean the Eroo fleet, then, no, there's no sign," Tayden said, then followed quickly with: "So you and your soldiers will have to stay down here."

"The infantry will stay here. Mal and I are coming up the hill," said Atlas. "Come on, Mal." Atlas walked past her. There were two ways to the top of the mound: a more gentle road running round and round it for carts, and a steep path that led directly to the top. Atlas took the path.

"All right, but just you two, and you leave your weapons here!" she shouted after Atlas. Atlas carried on, his war axe bouncing on his back. Mal jogged to catch up with him, which actually meant, due to the gradient, trotting daintily on his toes, which was embarrassing. He looked up at Atlas. How did he always manage to look so tough?

As they crested Frogshold by the gates of the hillfort, the view of the ocean opened up and Mal saw them, spread all over the sea. It was like walking into your hut and seeing a million wasps clinging to every surface.

The broad Haffen Estuary, stretching from Dumnonia in the south to the wild land of Kimruk to the north, was dotted with dark ships. They would reach the coast not far from Frogshold in a couple of hours at most.

To the south, he could see the Dumnonian army on the march. Presumably they had spotted the Eroo fleet and were heading to contest its landing. No doubt they'd sent a shout to Maidun which Atlas and Mal had missed as they crossed the marshes from Gutrin Tor. The shout network was fallible, and the marshes between Gutrin and Frogshold were exactly the sort of place where shouts might not reach. That excused the Dumnonians for not alerting them, but not the Frogsholders . . .

There was a clang behind him. Mal spun to see Atlas blocking a sword blow from Tayden with his iron wrist-guard then pushing her away with the palm of his hand. As Tayden staggered back, the big Kushite grabbed his axe from his back and swung it at two guards who'd come at him, slicing through leather, flesh and bone.

Tayden regained her footing and launched herself at Atlas, sword first. Mal ran in, bashed her sword to the ground with his own and drove his hilt into her face. Another woman came in as the chief fell. He blocked her sword, leapt back to face her, but Atlas' axe swung and she was headless.

Tayden and her guard were down, but there were many more Frogsholders watching from the wall of the hillfort. They shouted, "They've killed Tayden!", "Get them!" and other such things.

"Shall we?" said Atlas, nodding towards the bottom of the hill.

"Let's," said Mal.

The two men sprinted down the slope. As he judged his footing, trying and failing to keep up with Atlas, Mal thought. There were, what, five hundred Eroo ships? Probably more. Allowing for supplies, each would be carrying about two hundred troops. Multiply five hundred by two hundred and . . . no, no, he thought. That simply could not be right.

Chapter 14

"Stop that! Just stand still in the middle of the chariot!" Spring yelled. "You're swinging about like a badger's dick! Stop it!"

Dug did not have the temperament for pillion riding. At every bump, dip and corner he'd squat, leap or lean in an attempt to compensate for the chariot's movement. He refused to understand that she could drive the heavy chariot perfectly well and balance out his weight herself without any effort at all, but only if he didn't try to help. It was going to be a relief when they joined battle so she could be rid of him for a while.

It wouldn't be long. The Murkan army was jogging towards them, spread all along the floodplain. They shouted as they ran, bards' horns sounding out. Spring felt sorry for them in their disorganisation. It was such a dangerous and silly way to approach warfare.

The Maidun heavy chariots thundered on with a rumble that made Spring's arm hairs stand on end. They were all a pace apart, with no danger from each others' wheel blades since Lowa had had those removed. Each chariot had a lightly armoured child, small woman or man driving. Tucked in front of each of them was a bow and an arrow-stuffed quiver. Having the heavy chariots' drivers join the fight as archers, rather than just hang about behind the fighting at the beck and call of the mêlée fighter, was another of Lowa's ideas.

Behind each driver was an armoured man or woman armed with a sword, long spear and a large rectangular shield. The shields were Atlas' innovation. Or not innovation, as he'd explained to Spring, since they were a direct copy of the Roman ones. Whatever, they were new to Britain.

So every one of the five hundred chariots was the same, with few exceptions. One exception was Spring's bow, one of Elann's special longbows, almost a pace longer than everyone else's. Dug's hammer was another departure from the uniform. He had a sword in a scabbard like every other chariot passenger, but his hammer jiggled along on his back in an adapted version of Atlas' axe holder. He and Atlas had argued for an age about whether he could take his hammer into battle when he was playing chariot warrior. In the end Dug had conceded to use a sword like everyone else, but then he'd strapped his hammer to his back as well. Atlas had seen what he'd done and scowled, but said nothing.

They were three hundred paces from the nearest Murkan. In theory, Spring was against all sorts of killing, but these were the people who'd slaughtered Miller, Holloc and the others in front of her, who'd thrown her from a cliff, who'd injured Lowa so horribly . . . It was hard not to feel slightly gleeful at the idea of unleashing a few dozen arrows into them. The northerners were sprinting now, yelling, all variously armed and clad. They were brave, she'd give them that, but they looked even more disorderly up close.

Exactly as Spring thought "this is about right", a trumpet over to the right blarted out two short barps and one long *waaaaah*. Spring pulled on the reins and her horse halted.

"Do I jump now?" Dug asked.

"Wait!" Spring shook her head. Why was it impossible for him to remember instructions? Spring would have thought he was going deaf, had he not been able to hear someone offering food at a thousand paces in a high wind. The stop and turn manoeuvre should work brilliantly across the entire light chariot division, unless of course some lunk leapt out early and milled about in the middle of it.

She checked behind. Everyone else seemed to have got it. The drivers had stopped at a stagger, so that each chariot had room to swing around, and the passengers had stayed put. She waited the requisite count, slapped the reins on the horse's hindquarters, pulled the left-hand one and the little animal trotted a semi-circle to rejoin the line, now facing back the way they'd come.

"Now you jump."

"Right-ho!"

"Take care!" she shouted at Dug as he jogged to form a line with the other Maidunites. She could feel the magic today. It wasn't fizzing through her like it had on the day that Zadar had died or at Mallam, but she could feel quiet power flowing into her, which she was sure she'd be able to direct into Dug. He'd be fine. From what she'd heard of his last battle, it was the people around him that she should be worried about. Perhaps her magic would focus his rage a little.

Chapter 15

Ragnall tried once more to talk to Caesar's legate, but Brutus declared that he wasn't interested in Ragnall's "pathetic barbarian attempts to be important to the Romans" and snubbed him again. Brutus then instructed everyone else to ignore the Briton, so nobody would give him any work to do. Purposeless, he left the army camp and wandered inland to the temporary town of the camp followers to wait for Caesar's return. Caesar knew his value and Ragnall consoled himself that being seen in Caesar's inner circle when the general got back would be a pleasing revenge against Brutus.

The first evening he got drunk and shacked up with a sweet-natured Greek prostitute called Helen, which wasn't her real name. From Caesar's bag of coins, he paid her a daily rate not to bring any customers back to her large, comfortable slave-serviced tent, and divided his time between there and the mobile, army-following taverns, where he could listen to the gripes of the legionaries.

Brutus wasn't nearly the leader that Publius had been, everyone agreed. He drilled the men too hard and they disliked him for it. That didn't necessarily matter; hard training wasn't necessarily bad training and good leaders weren't necessarily popular, but so many soldiers of all ranks were wounded in exercises that the structure of each legion was crumbling like a mud wall in a flood. Worse, he had the legionaries rowing ships. That was slave's work, but Brutus argued that there was only enough space for fighters on his boats. The crews' inexperience was proven when a couple of dozen men drowned in two separate shipwrecks during Brutus' ridiculous manoeuvres. Dislike turned to hatred and Brutus tripled his bodyguard. While Caesar had walked among the ranks without protection as if he was one of them, Brutus always made sure there were several stern-faced praetorians between himself and the common soldiery.

Perhaps even more devastatingly for the army, Brutus treated all the Fenn-Nodens as if they were insects to be crushed, whether they were rebelling or not. Many Fenn-Nodens tribes who had been Roman allies stopped sending them food. Several previously supportive towns joined Vastivias' rebellion.

One morning news came that the Armoricans had united and gathered a vast fleet. Everyone was saying that Brutus' ships didn't stand a chance. Consensus was that he should have sailed south and drawn the Fenn-Nodens fleet away. Remove their means of escape and the Romans could wipe out the Gauls that they'd left behind on land and destroy their towns. Instead, Brutus had gathered as many ships as he could in Karnac Bay and readied his soldiers to fill them as soon as the enemy were sighted.

Everyone that Ragnall spoke to thought it was madness, and that the Roman fleet would be wiped out. Ragnall was dismayed. If Brutus went and got the fleet destroyed then the invasion of Britain would be delayed. There was nothing he could do about it, though, apart from wait and hope that Caesar returned in time to put things right.

"They're here, they're here!" Helen shook him awake one morning. She had a croaky, little girl voice. It was one of the things Ragnall liked about her.

"Who's here?" he replied. The night before had been a big one so he wasn't in the mood for any level of cryptic.

"The Fenn-Nodens, in their boats. The Romans have sailed

out to attack them! Come on, you're missing it. All the good places will be gone!"

She was an enthusiastic girl, Helen, in pretty much everything apart from sex, which made her profession seem an odd choice. When he'd asked her about it she'd told him that she'd met a centurion in Illyricum and travelled with him. She'd loved seeing the world, battles in particular, so when the centurion had been killed by one his own side's scorpion arrows, she'd carried on following the army, earning coin in the easiest possible way to feed herself and maintain her two slaves. She never had proper sex with men, though. She was a five-knuckle-shuffle girl who considered occasionally sticky hands a small price to pay for the wonderful sights and fights that she'd witnessed. Besides, whale-blubber soap washed her hands a treat and she was attractive enough that she could still charge good money for her limited service. Nonetheless, she'd been glad to take Ragnall as a permanent client and give her wrists a rest. He demanded nothing from her apart from a place to stay.

Ragnall washed his face and threw on his toga while Helen waited by the doorflap hopping from foot to foot. She'd told Ragnall she liked to watch battles, but he was still surprised by how frantic she was not to miss it.

They headed for the coast along with the rest of the Romans' hangers-on, and many of the friendly Fenn-Nodens who were keen enough on making money to put up with Brutus' insults and attacks.

The crowds were abuzz with excited speculation on the fleet's size and composition, and there was other big news. Caesar had returned. He'd got back late the night before, everyone was saying. Ragnall told Helen he had Roman business to be about, pressed a gold coin into her hand and jogged off, leaving her standing open-mouthed with the crowds streaming around her.

*   *   *

Ragnall found Caesar where he'd expected to, on the western promontory with the best view of the naval manoeuvres below. The praetorians waved him through in their manly way. He paced up to Caesar, annoyed and a little alarmed to see Felix beside him, and said hello.

Caesar nodded to him as if they'd been apart for an hour, not half a year, and returned his attention to the battle. Ragnall hadn't exactly expected a hug, but a smile would have been nice. He'd forgive him, though, since he was probably preoccupied by the imminent death of thousands of his expeditionary force under the idiot Brutus. Although, given the fact that he hadn't tried to intervene, presumably he agreed with Brutus' tactics.

The general looked well. His hair seemed to have stopped receding, or perhaps he'd found a new skull-concealing way of combing it. He was paler than usual, reflecting, Ragnall guessed, all the time spent indoors securing his future with Pompey and Crassus senior, rather than riding about conquering people as usual.

Felix glanced at Ragnall, treated him to an insincere grin, then returned his attention to the maritime manoeuvres below.

One Roman ship had rowed way ahead of all the others, headed for the mass of Fenn-Nodens vessels. The foremost enemy ships were strangely stern-up, since all their complements had gathered in the prows, keen to hurl missiles at the Romans, no doubt. One long, then two short whistle blasts sang out across the waves. The Fenn-Nodens crews redistributed themselves back along the boats, and the trim of each was rebalanced.

"They have some discipline, the barbarians," Caesar noted.

Three hundred paces behind the solo boat, the Roman fleet bobbed about in no apparent order. Some were clashing oars, a couple were heading out to sea. It was a shambles.

In comparison, the Fenn-Nodens ships were whizzing

along on the wind in a well-spaced, regular formation. Their boats were bigger and there were many more of them. They were a stirring sight. It did not look good for the Romans.

"Why is that one Roman boat so far ahead?" Ragnall asked nobody in particular.

"Caesar assumes that they seek to impress him," said Caesar. "He wishes them luck."

"How are the Fenn-Nodens ships keeping such good form?" Ragnall asked, eyes still on the lone Roman ship.

"Each captain arranges his sails so that he's going no faster than the slowest boat. It is not difficult. It is a shame that Brutus does not seem to have had that idea. After we have won this battle, Caesar will have sails added to the boats."

Ragnall looked at Caesar. He did not seem to be joking. He really thought the Romans were going to come out of this on top. Did Caesar know something that he didn't?

The lone Roman boat closed on the Fenn-Nodens. The legionaries on rowing duty pulled harder. Others lifted long wooden poles topped with iron hooks.

"What . . . ?" asked Ragnall.

"Those poles will hook and snap the enemy rigging, rendering the Fenn-Nodens boats immobile," said Caesar. "The legionaries will board the incapacitated vessels and put the lesser armed and lesser trained Gauls to the sword."

The Romans rowed into sling range of the first Fenn-Nodens boats. Stones flew in a graceful arc from one enemy ship, then another and another. It looked and sounded from their perch on the cliff like a sudden, geographically specific hailstorm was striking the Roman boat. The helmsman tumbled from the stern and splashed into the water. Legionaries collapsed. Hooked poles were dropped. Oars fell and swept backward along the hull as rowers raised their arms to protect themselves and others slumped in their seats. The ship lost speed and drifted sideways to the oncoming

fleet. The lead Fenn-Nodens craft, a particularly large ship
with someone who looked a lot like Chamanca standing on
its high prow, struck the Roman craft amidships and
ploughed through it like an aurochs through a rotten gate.
Enemy cheers drifted across the water and up to the cliff.
The sea behind the flagship was strewn with bobbing heads
and waving arms among the wreckage. The heads and arms
quickly disappeared. It was impossible to stay afloat in the
legionaries' leather and iron armour, Ragnall guessed, and
difficult to remove it. Right now, he thought, they'd be on
the sea bed, running out of breath and panicking madly, or
perhaps resignedly cursing their luck. He'd been in a similar
position himself and knew how shitty it was, but this lot
didn't have a one-armed German druid to rescue them. He
was glad to be up on the cliff, safe by Caesar's side.

Another series of whistle blasts rang out. The main body of
the Armorican fleet turned out to sea while the six lead ships
kept sailing for the Romans. Shortly afterwards a second
group of six peeled away and followed the first little flotilla.
  "What are they doing?" asked Ragnall.
  "They are maintaining the weather gauge," explained
Caesar as nonchalantly as if he were a philosopher discussing
the movement of ducks. "If they keep the wind behind or
to the side of their craft, they can manoeuvre as they will
against our slower boats."
  The six Gaulish ships came within sling range of the
Roman fleet, turned ninety degrees like synchronised
gymnasts and sailed in a line along the edge of the Romans,
keeping clear of the legionaries' hooked poles while
unleashing volley after volley of slingstones. As the first six
vessels cleared the edge of the Roman squadron, the second
six turned and engaged. Two more enemy groups were
already on their way. The Roman ships were impotent. The
Gauls had adapted their land-based guerrilla tactics for the

ocean and it was working. Boatloads of Romans were already immobilised. Other ships backed their oars to retreat. Many of them crashed into each other.

All along the shore, Romans watched in silence, apart from where fights had broken out with spectating Gauls who had expressed opinions on how the battle was going.

"Not a perfect start," said Caesar. "Felix, Caesar doesn't like this wind."

"I will see what I can do," replied the druid, shaking his head like a builder assessing a task, "but I'll need five children under the age of ten."

"Children?" asked Ragnall. "Really?"

Felix looked at him with a mixture of disgust and pity in his eyes. "Make that ten children, all under the age of ten," he said.

"Can you do it with five?" Caesar asked.

"Probably," Felix admitted.

"Praetorians! Fetch five children. Quickly!" Caesar commanded.

Chapter 16

Atlas and Mal led four companies of infantry up Frogshold Hill, sending the rest to the coast to take up positions next to the Dumnonians. The Frogsholders capitulated and opened their gates the moment they saw four hundred well-armed Maidunites marching in good order up the hill. Over to the west, the Eroo fleet sailed ever closer.

With Tayden and her retinue dead, Atlas demanded to see the next in charge. There was some debate among the Frogsholders before an ironsmith named Glun was pushed forward. He was short, dark-haired but balding, with a head wider than it was tall. Glun's looks, coupled with his furtive manner, put Mal in mind of a mole. The Frogsholders, guarded by Maidun swords, looked on in churlish silence, other than two babies who cried roaringly despite their mothers' efforts to quieten them.

Glun was not a natural chief. "What do you want? What did I do? Leave us alone," he said, looking at his feet.

Atlas loomed over him and growled. Glun seemed to shrink. "You have a choice, Glun," the Kushite rumbled, "I kill you, or you tell us why you did not warn us about the Eroo fleet's approach."

"You can kill those babies if you like. My hut's next to one of the brats and the nights that me and Shayla have lain awake, just hoping one day that some big African—"

Glun stopped talking as Atlas pulled his axe from its holster on his back. He seemed mesmerised by the weapon's glinting edge.

"What I meant to say was that it was the Dumnonians that made us," he stammered.

Atlas looked at Mal. That was not good news.

"Which Dumnonians?" Mal asked.

"What d'you mean, which Dumnonians? Dumnonian ones. From Dumnonia." Glun was combative again, Atlas' axe apparently forgotten.

"Was it Bruxon, their king?"

"No, definitely not him. I know what he looks like and it wasn't him. It was about twenty of them. They spoke funny. Different from normal Dumnonians. More uppy and downy. They said if we warned you about any ships that came they'd kill everyone. So that's why we didn't. It was Tayden's decision and nothing to do with any of us and you've already killed her. So you'd better leave us be."

"What were you going to do if I'd still been in the hillfort when the Murkans appeared?" Mal asked.

"We were meant to stop you sending the shout." Glun looked at his feet. "We would have tied you up or something . . ."

"You mean you would have killed me."

"They said they'd kill everyone! And look how many are coming!" He pointed at the fleet. It was perhaps six thousand paces out to sea and Glun did have a point. It was terrifyingly numerous.

"All right," said Atlas. "You and every other Frogsholder are to leave, now. Head north then turn west into Kimruk, but keep to the coast to avoid the Murkans and the Maidun army coming south. That's the safest place for you. I daresay you'll be able to come back at some point."

"But we've got nothing ready! We don't know anybody in—"

"You betrayed us," said Mal, "and you planned to kill me. Most Warriors would torture you all to death for that. Atlas is giving you your freedom on the condition that you bugger off immediately. I suggest you take his offer, because his next one is going to be a lot more death-focused."

"No," said Glun, stiffening and staring up at them. "Frogsholders have been on Frogshold for thousands of years. We're not going to—"

Before Mal realised that Atlas was moving, he'd swung his axe overhead and cleaved the angry little man from shoulder to hip. Glun's two halves fell to the ground in a wash of blood.

There was a gasp from Frogsholders and Maidun troops alike. Everyone took a step back.

"What the Bel, Atlas?" Mal half drew his sword. "There was no need to—"

"We do not have time to fuck about," said Atlas, then louder: "All Frogsholders: out, head north then west into Kimruk. I will not ask again. Any Frogsholders still within the hillfort walls in twenty heartbeats' time will never leave."

Mal was still staring at Glun's ruined body. Glun's twitching eyes looked back, his mouth still opening and closing.

"Come on, Mal," said Atlas. "We need to garrison this place with one company and take the others to meet Eroo. Now."

Mal shook his head. "But if the Dumnonians are with Eroo, we should retreat to Maidun or at least Gutrin Tor to meet Lowa with the rest of the army and hold there. There's no way that the infantry alone can—"

"I don't think the Dumnonians are in league with Eroo. Nobody could be that stupid." Atlas wiped his axe on the grass.

"Apart from Glun said—"

"If you were an advance scout from Eroo, would you say you were from Eroo? No, you'd say you were from Dumnonia, so that when we found out we'd fly into a panic. If we believed your story. And Glun said their voices were 'uppy downy'. That sounds to me more like an Eroo accent than a Dumnonian one."

Mal nodded. Atlas was probably right, but Mal was far from convinced. Even if the heavies who'd threatened Frogshold had been from Eroo and not Dumnonia, it didn't mean that Dumnonia wasn't going to turn traitor. Mal had been cheated in a game of bone-dice by a Dumnonian once. He'd seemed like a decent fellow, convincingly and smilingly apologetic for his good fortune. It had been a moon later that Mal had suddenly realised how he'd been tricked. He hadn't trusted a Dumnonian since. Nor played dice, for that matter.

"We'll be wary of the Dumnonians," the Kushite continued, seeing the look in Mal's eye, "but let's not believe that they're the enemy yet." He looked around. "Where's Adler?"

"Here." Adler strode forward. "You want me to ride to Lowa?"

"Yes. Tell her everything that's happened here."

Chapter 17

Chamanca tried to look on the positive side. The skill of the Fenn-Nodens sailors was pleasing. The crews operated like limbs of the helmsman of each ship, responding to commands almost before they were given, pulling and freeing ropes to shift the leather sails into positions that best harnessed the wind's power. As a group, the Fenn-Nodens boats moved in wonderful synchronicity, like dancers from her homeland. That, objectively speaking, was a delight to see. More importantly, as Carden had put it, they were pissing all over the Romans. The Gaulish tactics were working and the Romans didn't appear to have any. Each attack group killed so many rowers that the Romans were increasingly immobile, and, if things carried on like this, eventually the Fenn-Nodens would be able to close in, board and finish off individual ships without too much trouble.

The massive negative, which overrode all the positives, and which she was trying to ignore to prevent her from biting a passing sailor, was that so far she'd done nothing but watch and become increasingly hungry for blood. Not being fed, she could handle. Expecting to be fed and not being fed made her quiver.

"Buck up, Chamanca!" Carden clapped her on a shoulder, almost sending her into the sea.

She narrowed her eyes at him.

Carden laughed: "You look like a cat with a wasp up its arse."

She felt her expression soften. Carden always cheered her up, Fenn knew why.

"I know what you mean, though," Carden looked at the Roman flotilla and shook his head. "It's a bit like being a fairy sitting on the rim of someone's helmet during a battle. You see everything just fine, but it would be great to get involved."

"I agree." Chamanca poked his chest. "You must know exactly how a fairy feels."

As usual, the barbed comment didn't stick in Carden. "Why don't you use your sling on the next pass?" he said, gripping her arm and nodding like a boy encouraging others to play his favourite game. "It's fun! I got five on the last one. Well, four and a half. One of them was on the arm, so I shouldn't count him. But four was still more than everyone else. Bet you don't get more than three."

"Well done, but no thank you. I don't like killing people from a distance. I'll hold until we board them."

"Well, you may have a while to wait. I can see Vastivias' plan. If we can wear them down . . . hang on, look over there!"

Two relatively swift Roman ships were making a break for it, southwards and out to sea. One of them, a good deal larger than the rest with an eagle standard sticking up from the stern, was surely the command ship. Chamanca turned to shout to Vastivias, but he'd already seen them. He spoke to his whistler, who piped out a series of blasts. The helmsman leant on the tiller, the crew pulled ropes, the ship changed course and surged through the waves towards its quarry. The five other ships in their group had performed the same manoeuvre at the same time, and together they set off in pursuit of the two fleeing ships.

Soon she could hear shouted commands from the Roman boats, all on the theme of "row faster". But the rowers were panicking, clashing oars and actually slowing the two ships. Chamanca fancied that she could smell their fear. She looked behind them, where another group of six Fenn-Nodens ships were following in their wake. The rest of the Roman fleet hadn't moved. Very soon they'd be on the two bolters. She gripped Carden's arm and he whooped in delighted pursuit. Her mouth filled with saliva.

Chapter 18

Murkan feet thundered closer. Murkan battle cries rang louder. Dug hunkered behind his shield, shoulder pressed into its centre, and resisted the urge to peek over the top. This new Maidun army relied on good order. In every other army he'd fought in, people just piled into battle. Young and stupid went first with no grouping other than that they'd usually charge alongside their mates, family or neighbours. Most times they got killed quickly. More cautious men like him stood back and looked for maximum impact, minimum danger areas of the battle to join; unless battle rage kicked in and sent them into a frenzy, and then who knew what the Bel happened?

Lowa's army was different. Dug had been impressed by the Maidun army on Sarum Plain against the Dumnonians, but since then Lowa had lifted it to another level of coordination and order. She'd taken the more effective aspects of the British way of fighting – mainly the mobility of chariots and cavalry – and merged them with the unquestioning discipline and controlled fluidity of the Romans. Each person in this line had his or her own exact position, and knew how to respond to a whole range of events as an individual and as part of their unit.

Dug was the exception to this. He knew the theories, had devised a few of them himself, but his Badger infantry company had stayed south with Atlas and Mal and he'd been a late addition to this line of chariot passengers. Lowa had said Spring needed him as chariot crew and that had been that. Nita had put him in between a man and a woman whom he called Thingummy and Wotzit – he hadn't listened when he'd been told their names and had then been embarrassed to ask. He could see that, even though he was a famed Warrior and theoretically a better fighter than any of the chariot-based infantry, Thingummy and Wotzit were pissed off that he was there. They'd probably have been even more annoyed if he'd had his way and brought his dogs with him. He was secretly glad that Atlas had put his foot down. It was good that they were guarding the farm, and that he wouldn't have to worry about them when the fighting started. No, without them, he'd be more able to toe the battle line and try his best not to fuck things up.

He started by not looking over his shield. That wasn't allowed. If there were problems he should know about – a hurled stone heading his way or similar – the line of spearpeople behind the shield holders would tell him. He remembered his first big-ish battle as a younger man, running at the enemy, keeping an eye on the more experienced soldiers to see—

Crump! A Murkan crashed into the Maidun line five shields down. The shield holder held firm, pulled back his sword and . . .

Whump! His own shield jolted as a Murkan whacked into it with an "oof!" A blade crashed down into its upper rim and lodged firm. The shield shook as the Murkan on the other side struggled to waggle his sword free. Dug looked askance at Wotzit. She nodded and they pulled their shields a finger's breadth apart. Dug slotted his sword into the gap, and thrust in and out repeatedly at various angles. It struck several times, there were screams, pressure on his shield loosened for a moment, then came back again, harder. A Murkan woman jumped the shield wall and fell on him. He tried to ignore her and trust the spearpeople to kill her, while he carried on stabbing at foes he couldn't see with his sword. It an odd sort of fighting. He knew it worked, but it didn't feel right.

Arrows whizzed overhead, enemy-wards. All the heavy chariot drivers were now shooting over the shield wall, as were both drivers and passengers from the light chariots, pulled into a line behind the heavy ones. Both types of chariots would be turned, ready for the planned retreat.

Most would be shooting as far as they could, hoping to hit a charging Murkan. The more skilled ones, like Spring, would be shooting high to drop just in front of the Maidun shields, creating a mess of injured and dead there to hamper the Murkan attack.

By Toutatis, he did not like all this regularity. It felt like his hammer was burning on his back. He could feel battle energy humming through his limbs. He suppressed the urge to chuck his shield away, go badgershit crazy and kill everything that came his way. Instead he kept his head down and carried on stabbing between the shields, telling himself that there'd be plenty of time for hammer play when the next phase of the battle began.

Chapter 19

Lowa hoicked and spat on to the splatter of oat-flecked vomit glistening in the grass. She wiped her mouth, straightened and felt a little better. Why they called it morning sickness when it was actually any time of the fucking day or night sickness, she did not know. As a mystery, it was right up there with how Dug had got her pregnant in the first place. Carrot flowers had always worked previously. Mind you, she had been having sex more than ever before. Dug had argued that they needed to make up for the lost years when they should have been together, and she was happy to go with it. It was fun, it helped her sleep and it put her in a better mood in the mornings. And after lunch. And in the early evenings. And quite often in the midmorning, round the back of whatever there was to go round the back of. With hindsight, she should have realised that pregnancy was inevitable.

There were other plants that could stop a baby from developing once conceived, and plenty of druids who knew where they were found and how to prepare them. Lowa had considered using them for about a tenth of a heartbeat. She was queen of a tribe under immediate threat from three armies, so, arguably, it was no time to have a baby and she should have poisoned her foetus. But fuck that, she thought. The little half-her, half-Dug growing in her womb was more important than everyone else put together, herself and Dug included. And if someone called her selfish and irresponsible, never mind. She'd been called worse. She'd been worse.

"Big night?" asked a horseman who must have heard her in the bushes. She bestowed him with her queenliest look, the smile fell from his face and his horse took a couple of paces back.

She rode over to Nita. The square-faced young woman was looking out over the valley. "All right?" Nita asked, a rare note of kindness in her voice. Lowa nodded. She hadn't told her, but Nita knew. Many of the other women had worked it out, as had a few of the more sensitive men. She hadn't told Dug yet. She'd tell him soon, she told herself. He probably knew anyway. He was more perceptive than he looked.

Below them, the Murkans had hit the Maidun line. She'd missed the start of the battle. She could not have picked a worse time to be sick, she thought, then thought, no, at least it was out now and unlikely to recur for a while. Better to chunder semi-privately up here than in front of everybody on the battlefield.

It was a sight. The Murkans were charging the thin shield line like storm waves hitting a beach. But the beach was holding. The Murkan dead were piling up in front of the shield wall and more were dying behind where the chariot archers' arrows were striking home. Murkans were climbing over their fallen comrades' bodies to hurdle the Maidun shields, but the spearpeople were stopping them with pointed efficiency. It was looking good for Maidun.

There were still many more Murkans, though, stretching back along the valley into the distance. With most of the Maidun army sent to meet the Eroo, they were massively outnumbered, twenty to one at least, but thank Danu the notion of battle strategy did not seem to have spread north yet. They still employed the traditional run-at-the-others-and-try-to-beat-the-fuck-out-of-them tactics. Right now, they were running through a rain of arrows to attack a shield wall that was holding. They were brave as mother badgers and no more intelligent. A more precise attack with shields held aloft might have done some damage. It was a relief and a joy that they hadn't thought of that.

"Now?" asked Nita.

"Not quite." She wanted more Murkans committed before she struck. She didn't intend to destroy the Murkans here, indeed that would be difficult with her infantry still off to the south with Atlas and Mal, but she wanted to kill so many of them so quickly that their morale was destroyed. Either they'd head back north, or the force that followed her south to meet the infantry would be shaken to somewhere near its mental breaking point.

A moment later she spotted Pomax and shuddered. She was a hundred paces back from the front line, out of most arrows' range, perhaps half a mile from Lowa. She was cased in helmet and ringmail, but that gait and bulk were unmistakable. By Danu, Lowa had never wanted to kill anyone so much. By the look of what she was up to, the Murkan queen was set to cause her further torment. She was arranging a large group of similarly armoured troops into a shield-protected wedge formation – the one thing that could really fuck up the Maidun shield wall.

Eyes narrowed, Lowa dismounted. She took her longbow from its leather holster on the back of her horse. She chose a long-distance arrow from the quiver and slotted it on the string then drew, aimed and fired. Ten heartbeats later, a man next to Pomax fell. Lowa had missed. Very unlike her. She didn't like to make excuses for herself, but the wind had dropped unnaturally quickly, immediately after she'd fired.

Pomax lifted her arm, middle fingers splayed. Lowa notched another arrow, but Pomax lifted a shield above her head and disappeared among her people. A moment later, Pomax's triangle of troops, perhaps five hundred of them, hoisted their own shields and jogged towards the Maidun line.

"Toutatis's arse!" said Nita. Lowa nodded. Pomax's wedge hit the left of the Maidun line point first, faltered for a moment and burst through. The shield wall was breached.

As was planned and trained for, the nearby light chariots swarmed in to pour arrows into the enemy and plug the hole. The Murkan shields and armour were effective, however, and only a few fell. The rest trampled through a breach that was widening with every heartbeat.

"Sound the cavalry charge!" shouted Lowa.

"Wait!"

Lowa spun to see who'd dared to interrupt her order. It was Adler, Maidun's best rider whom she'd left with Mal to bring messages, heaving her horse to a halt. "Eroo," she panted. "About to land near Frogshold. May be that Dumnonians have turned traitor. Atlas says probably not, Mal thinks they have."

Makka's tits, thought Lowa. The early arrival of the Eroo was a setback, although not necessarily a disaster, so long as they still had the Dumnonians on their side . . .

Lowa looked at Pomax's Murkan wedge, spreading and smashing apart Maidun's shield wall, impervious to Maidun's arrows. Dug was down there. So was Spring.

"How many Eroo?" she asked.

"Mal estimates five hundred ships, two hundred troops at least in each, which makes—"

"A hundred thousand. How far away?"

"If we go now, we might reach the infantry by the time Eroo lands."

"Is there a new reason to suspect the Dumnonians?"

"Soldiers claiming to be Dumnonians threatened the Frogsholders with death if they alerted us to the arrival of the Eroo fleet. But Atlas thinks the soldiers were from Eroo, not Dumnonia."

"Bel's turds." Lowa looked down into the valley. Pomax's wedge was doing well, and other Murkan troops were capitalising. If she pulled her shield wall away now, the majority of them would be routed before they got back to the chariots. Yet retreat they must. She'd wanted to do more damage to the Murkan army, but she couldn't leave her infantry to face a hundred thousand-plus Eroo without archer support.

"Trumpeter," she said, "sound the cavalry charge. Adler, take a fresh horse and go back to Frogshold. Tell them to oppose the landing as far as possible, beware of the Dumnonians, and to retreat to Frogshold hillfort if necessary. We'll be there as soon as we can."

Chapter 20

Before the screams of the fifth child had died away, the wind stopped.

For once, Ragnall had done the sensible thing and not been drawn to watch a nearby horror. He was glad he hadn't. He still had nightmares about the poor Danu's Child.

Felix walked up, flicking blood off his hands, his face split by an even bigger smirk than usual. Unbidden, animal loathing spread from Ragnall's stomach, through his body, along his limbs and into his fingers and toes. He shivered with horror and objection. It was difficult to justify killing children. Had he picked the right cause? Was he on the right side? Yes, yes, he told himself. Under Roman rule, life in Britain would improve immeasurably. It wasn't the aqueducts, the underfloor heating, the waterproof buildings and all the other comfort-enhancing and labour-saving innovations, although those would all be very welcome. No, the main point was Roman law, order and stability. People like Zadar could not exist under Roman rule. In a generation's time, when Roman rule was embedded, no young Britons would ever again have to see their parents, siblings and entire tribe murdered by a despot, as Ragnall had. They would be clean, educated, secure and they would live longer. Their leaders would be elected rather than murdering their way to power. It had to be worth anything to achieve that. He pictured Lowa all doe-eyed telling him that it was OK that she'd killed his family, and him believing her like a chump. That helped. He was on the right side.

"Done and done," said the druid.

"Excellent," said Caesar.

Out in the bay, like a blanket pulled tight, the ripples disappeared all across the water's surface. The proud leather sails of the Fenn-Nodens collapsed and hung like empty scrotums. Their ships fizzed to a halt and bobbed like turds in the baths. Crews ran about, shouting at each other and hauling ropes. All to no avail. There wasn't much you could do in a sailing boat without any wind, other than wait to die.

Chapter 21

"Their sails have lost the wind," said Mal.

"And it's calm behind them," said Atlas.

Stretching back from a line in front of the lifelessly floating Eroo ships to the horizon, the sea was indeed a different colour. Did that mean the wind had died? Mal didn't know. Seafaring wasn't his thing. Atlas, on the other hand, appeared to know more or less all there was to know about pretty much everything.

The change in shade rushed towards them across the water. It hit the shore. Moments afterwards the wind on the hill, previously a stiff westerly, fell so quickly it felt like it was sucked up into the sky above. With the wind gone, there was an eerie, pulsating silence. It reminded Mal of when he'd run a wheel yard next to a busy blacksmith's. He'd not notice the noise, but when it stopped at the end of each working day, the sudden silence was, to him, louder than the day-long beat of the hammers.

"Good," said Atlas. "Unusual, but good. All we need now is for the wind to start up again in the other direction and . . ."

There was movement all along the Eroo fleet. It looked like a swarm of beetles waking and extending their legs as oars bristled from each ship and dipped into the water. The Eroo boats advanced anew, more slowly than before, but they were still coming.

"Bel's beard!" said Mal.

"They are delayed," said Atlas. "That is some blessing,

although the tide will be higher when they arrive and they will be exposed on the beach for less time. Mal, stay here to brief Lowa. I'll talk to Dumnonia, then join the infantry. Tell Lowa that her cavalry and chariot archers will have a clear run to the beach. I'm also going to arrange the lines to defend and retreat if the Dumnonians have changed sides. Assuming that is, that Bruxon doesn't kill me when I see him."

"Well, that's a great plan!" said a chirpy, familiar voice.

Mal spun. It was Maggot, marching into the Frogshold hillfort, ornaments rattling. "But I'd skip the bit about talking to the Dumnonians, because change sides they have. It's not one, but three armies you'll face today."

"Explain," said Atlas.

"Bruxon asked Eroo to invade, you see. Why wouldn't he? Wanted revenge for the defeat at Sarum. He heard that this King Manfrax was a bloodthirsty bastard who'd killed everyone he didn't like the look of on Eroo, so he asked him over here to finish the Maidun maidens and the Maidun menfolk, too."

"The fool." Atlas shook his head. "Manfrax will turn on him the moment he's finished with us."

"Not according to Bruxon," said Maggot, putting a finger to his chin, "because the moment that Manfrax is sitting happy in Maidun, the Romans will arrive. Dumnonia will help the Romans against Manfrax — and those nasty Murkans — and then the Romans will leave the Dumnonians alone. Well, I say alone. They'll sell them cut-price wine and build lovely baths all over Dumnonia, but they won't hassle your day-to-day Dumnonian at all. That's how Bruxon's got it all worked out, anyway."

Maggot's bardish exaggeration aside, Mal could see the Dumnonian logic. He was surprised that Lowa or Atlas hadn't worked out what was happening; or Nita, for that matter. All of these sharp people and none of them had seen the obvious. "Makes some sense," he said.

"It doesn't," said Atlas. "Helping the Romans has one outcome. They enslave you or kill you."

"That's two outcomes," said Maggot. Atlas glowered. "But you are right," the druid continued, "it's almost like Bruxon has been blinded by some kind of magic. Now, who could have done that?"

"What?" said Atlas, grabbing Maggot by his leather jerkin.

Maggot looked at Atlas' big hand, then back up at the Kushite. "Let me go," he said, serious for once. To Mal's surprise, Atlas did.

Maggot straightened his clothes, picked up a bauble that Atlas had torn free and put it in a pocket. "I will go back to the Dumnonians and stop them from attacking."

"How will that help?" Mal asked.

"It will give you time to retreat from there on the beach to here on the hill," Maggot waved his jingling arms, pointing out to the coast, then back to the ground at their feet, "with both Eroo and Dumnonian armies following. By then, Lowa will be on her way with the Murkans in tow."

"How will that help?" Mal repeated

"Why, then you'll all be on a hill surrounded by three armies, each of which would destroy Maidun and deliver Britain to the Romans. Could there be a lovelier place to be?"

"And how does that help?" Mal repeated.

"I never said it would help." Maggot turned on his heel with a jingle of jewellery and jangled out of the hillfort. He was gone before either of them thought to stop him.

Chapter 22

Pomax powered her way through Maidun troops like a short-tempered fisherwoman wading ashore through surf after being told told that her husband is making love to another woman in their hut. She splintered shields with her blade, broke legs with heavy-booted kicks and slashed throats to ribbons with her claw nailed hand. Maidun troops, including some Warriors, took her on solo and in groups. All were left broken in her wake. A few managed to slow her briefly, but none could stop her from her goal, which seemed to be, worryingly for the goal concerned, a young chariot driver named Spring.

She fired arrow after arrow at the giant woman, but all missed. You'd think, she thought, with someone the size of Pomax, that it would be harder to fire an arrow and not hit her. But all her arrows, which would usually skewer a squirrel at a hundred paces, flew wide. So Pomax must be protected by some kind of magic, Spring thought. Annoying. She tried to draw on her own powers to send an arrow through Pomax's magic shield, but none came. She tried to imbue some energy into the Maidun troops who were falling around Pomax by the dozen. No good. She tried aiming slightly off, to see if the arrow-disrupting magic might correct the course, but her shot sailed exactly where she'd aimed it and through the neck of a nearby Murkan.

Pomax kept coming, too fast and too strong to be stopped. Spring finally hit her, on the head, but the arrow ricocheted up off her helmet. The queen of the Murkans ripped off the last of her attackers' faces and ran straight at Spring, light on her feet despite the weight of her ringmail.

Spring chose an armour-piercing arrow and aimed it for her chest. At the last moment, it swerved away from Pomax as if hit by an invisible hand, soared across the battlefield and into the arm a Maidun man who'd had his other arm sliced off by Pomax.

Big badger's shits, thought Spring. She looked for Dug. He was forty paces away, hammer out now, smashing away at Murkan troops in an attempt to re-establish the shield wall. He was needed there. She'd have to deal with Pomax herself or die trying. She put her bow back in its holder on the chariot, screwed her face up, clenched her fists and concentrated on the image of Pomax exploding in a shower of blood and guts.

She opened her eyes. Pomax was walking towards her, smiling. No other living people, Maidun or Murkan, were immediately to hand. Spring breathed out and took her sword from its scabbard. Pomax jammed her own sword into the side of a dead horse, took her whip from her waist and flexed her talons.

Chapter 23

Chamanca spat. "What do you mean 'no oars'?"

"We can read the wind," said Vastivias. "We've been doing it for millennia. We are always back in port before a breeze fails or becomes too great for our boats. We have neither the need nor the space for oars."

Chamanca pictured herself flying at him and sinking her teeth into his neck. "And today?" she asked.

"Something dark is afoot. This wind comes every year at this time and it lasts. It's called Faithful Blow. An ungodly ritual has caused this calm." Vastivias shook his head.

"Or a godly one?" Chamanca suggested.

"You're right. It must be the work of some foul Roman deity. Toutatis would never favour such an indecent scheme. I shall ask him to smite this unwelcome Roman god and bring the wind back to his domain."

Chamanca left Vastivias shouting at the sky and walked back along the deck to Carden. They watched as the crew from two Roman craft climbed into two others. These two overloaded ships rowed either side of the nearest Fenn-Nodens boat, clamped on to it with hooked ropes and boarded. There was shouting, the clash of iron and screaming. Gravely outnumbered and outskilled, the Armoricans didn't stand a chance. Soon the Gaulish crew were all dead or swimming and the Romans were on their way to the next. Similar mini-massacres were taking place all over the bay. The Romans waited until one Gaulish ship drifted away from the rest, then rowed in for the kill. By concentrating their complements into fewer vessels, the Roman boats had become overloaded, gunwales a hand's breadth from the water, but on the dead calm sea it didn't matter.

Chamanca pulled Carden away from the watching Gauls and said quietly: "Two options. Stay here, wait for the Romans and kill as many as we can before they kill us, or swim to shore and live." Several crews on the Gaulish boats nearer to shore were already abandoning ship. Romans with swords were rushing down cliffs and along the beach to meet them.

Carden smiled. "I can't swim. So I've got one option. Or is that no options? If you've got two options and take away one, you're left with zero options. But two minus one is one . . . That's always confused me."

"You can't swim at all? Or do you mean you haven't swum in a while? You don't forget. And it isn't difficult. Maybe you can learn now?"

"Nope. Used to go in the sea as a kid, but never swam. Tried it a couple of times since and sank. Heavy bones, I guess. And heavy penis, of course. Not to mention massive balls."

"I see . . ." said Chamanca.

The Roman flagship and another ship almost as large, both overladen with legionaries, were heading for theirs.

"Well, I guess I don't have any options either." Chamanca took her sling out of her pocket and looked for the nearest bag of stones.

Chapter 24

Spring dropped on to her stomach under the whip's lash. She felt it rip the air over her head. She popped up into a crouch, sword flashing at Pomax's knee. Go low, that's how you deal with the big, top-armoured ones.

Pomax whacked the sword away. Her whip hand shot up in a fist, caught Spring's chin and flung her staggering backwards.

Magic! shouted Spring internally. She needed magic. Why couldn't she find any magic? Dug was just over there! Why couldn't he see what was happening?

The whip cracked again and snapped around her sword arm. She tossed the sword to her other hand, but Pomax jerked the whip at the same moment. Spring's hand clasped air and the sword fell. Pomax pulled. The girl tried to pull back, but the best she could do was stay on her feet as the huge Warrior reeled her in.

"Hello again," said Pomax in her abrasive accent, closing her clawed fist around Spring's neck and lifting her off the ground. Her feet kicked air and her head clouded. Pomax started to squeeze. "I'm going to kill you up close this time, make sure of the job."

Spring wanted to tell her what a silly voice she had, but she couldn't talk. It felt like her eyes were trying to bulge out of her head and everything was very bright all of a sudden.

They closed the gap in the shield wall, but not before many Murkans had swept through it, so Dug was ensnarled in the constant attack and defence of a thick mêlée. A slingstone bounced off his helmet. He ducked a sword swipe, thrust his hammer-point two-handed into a Murkan's face, smashed a shoulder blade with the return stroke. He was glad to have his hammer.

As he dodged, tripped and dispatched another Murkan, something made Dug turn as surely as if someone had shouted his name. In between clashing weapons and roaring fighters, a hundred paces away Pomax had Spring by the neck, holding her a pace off the ground.

Dug roared and ran, shouldering someone, Maidun or Murkan he had no idea, out of the way. Something gripped his legs and he tripped, landing on a dying man who choked out a weakly protesting "ooof". The Murkan who'd brought him down had his legs pinned. His hammer was caught underneath him. As he struggled to free it, another Murkan rushed out of the confusion, sword flashing towards his exposed neck. Dug rolled. The sword smashed into his helmet. The shouts and clangs of battle became suddenly louder, then quieter and his vision fuzzed. He knew the next sword strike could be only heartbeats away. He shook his head, tensing all the muscles he could tense, as if that would help.

Lowa saw Pomax lift Spring. She raised her bow, reached into her quiver, slotted her arrow, aimed and was knocked from her horse by a leaping Murkan. Falling, she drew her sword and drove it into the Murkan's side. She landed hard, sprang up and looked about. Where was her fucking bow? Pomax was holding Spring higher. The girl's kicks were weakening. A large Murkan charged at her, screaming, spear first. Lowa danced aside on to one foot, bounced back on to the other and sliced her attacker's neck open. Two more were immediately on her. These were more skilled. She parried. Desperate to get to Spring, she rushed, dived in too soon and paid for it with a cut to the bicep. She calmed herself, blocked two more spear thrusts, then two more, and looked for an opening. None came.

A thunder of hooves and Nita galloped by, sword chopping into the back of a Murkan neck as she passed. The other, seeing Lowa distracted, thrust at her. Lowa twisted away, brought her sword around in an arc and clanged it into the spearman's iron wrist guard. He barged his shoulder into her. Knocked back, she tripped over his dead friend, fell over, then rolled to avoid his thrust. The spear head gouged into the earth next to her. She chopped through the shaft, leapt to her feet and thrust her blade through the Murkan's ringmail. He fell.

She looked for Spring and saw Nita leaping from her horse on to Pomax's shoulders. Pomax dropped Spring, swung her hand back over her own head, gripped Nita by her chest armour and pulled her over her head. Nita's legs and arms waved as Pomax turned her sideways across her chest, squeezed her and snapped her back as if she was breaking a branch.

Lowa heard a tearing crack as spine and sinew ripped. Pomax dropped the broken woman, looked Lowa in the eye then stamped down on Nita's head with her iron boot. Once, twice, three times.

Spring climbed to her feet and leapt at Pomax. The big woman grabbed at her, but Spring twisted in the air and jammed her sword up and into the underside of Pomax's chin.

Lowa found her bow and ran over. Spring was bent double, coughing and struggling to breathe. Pomax was on her back, gulping weakly, fishy eyes looking sightlessly at the sky. Blood pumped out of her neck around Spring's sword hilt. The point of the sword stuck out from the top of Pomax's head like a decorative iron feather. Nita was lying next to her, body twisted, head mashed into a shining, splintered mess.

Chapter 25

"We should attack now." Bruxon was sure he was right. He stood at the head of a Dumnonian army that massively outnumbered Maidun's. Yes, a smaller Maidun force had beaten a larger Dumnonian one not long before and the Maidun army had been training obsessively ever since, but that previous victory had been down to Samalur's bad tactics and the Maidun cavalry. Samalur was long dead, the Maidun cavalry were somewhere else. Surely they'd be able to devastate the Maidun infantry in a matter of minutes?

"We told Manfrax that we'd let Eroo do all the fighting," said Maggot. "Now, we could cross Manfrax, of course we could do that, but it would be pretty much the same as planting your sword hilt-first in the ground, climbing a tree and jumping arse-first on to it."

Bruxon winced at the vulgar image. "Manfrax will land on a beach thick with hostile, well-drilled troops. No matter Eroo's number or their ferociousness, that will cost them dearly. Maidun still believes that we're their ally so we could surprise them now and Eroo could land unopposed. I swore to help Manfrax."

"You think you'd be helping Manfrax by killing his enemies? Why do you think it is that Eroo have come here? They love fighting and they've run out of challenging opposition back home. Wiping out Maidun before Manfrax lands would be like helping a hungry man by eating his supper for him before he gets back to his hut. I've got a pretty massive imagination, but I bet that if you fought his battle for him, Manfrax would kill you in way that's way, way outside my mind's creative efforts. And, given the blood shake that you shook, he'd have every right to. No, no, I'd avoid the nastiest death in history and stick to your agreement like a puppy sticking to her mum. Follow the Eroo army, build its camps, supply its food. Fight Maidun if Manfrax asks you to, but only then."

"You have a point, but all sense says we should attack. What if Manfrax loses half his army and blames me for it?"

"If Manfrax complains, repeat the terms of the blood shake. He can't deny those. We all know 'em and they're clear. And, if you want a slightly grubbier motive, it will be no bad thing if Maidun roughs up Eroo a little. When Maidun is dead and laid out for the birds, what would be better? A fully intact Eroo standing over her corpse and looking around for the next fight, or a bruised, bloodied Eroo tottering away, looking for a bucket to be sick in and a place to sit for a while?"

Bruxon looked along the beach at the Maidun infantry. From that distance they did look like a pitifully small force. To the west, Eroo ships stretched as far as there was sea.

"All right then," he said. "We hold firm."

Chapter 26

Mal looked north from Frogshold. There was no sign of Lowa, Nita and the chariots and cavalry. A sudden worry about Nita flared into his mind, but he dismissed it. He'd told her he'd rather she wasn't in the army, and she'd told him that she'd rather he wasn't either and that he wasn't to worry about her. If something happened, it happened. Worrying the whole time just made him and everyone around him miserable. She'd told him that she never worried about him, but he knew that wasn't true.

To the south, the treacherous Dumnonian army stretched along the dry spur of land between the marshes and the sea. They showed no sign of attacking. It looked like Maggot had managed to stop them. Mal wondered what the druid's role was in all this. Just a few moons before he'd happily lied to Lowa and the rest of them about Dumnonia and Eroo. Why spill the secret now? What was his game? Was there some new secret?

To the west, the Eroo ships were coming into general arrow range. They'd been within range of Spring and Lowa's longbows for some time. So it was a shame that they had no archers, and that Spring and Lowa were miles away fighting the Murkans. A few fire arrows on to those boats might have produced some lovely results.

All the infantry had were slings and a few stones. The enemy would soon be in sling range, but very shortly after that a very large number of famously vicious and powerful

Eroo troops would be charging up the beach and the Maidun infantry would have the first proper test of its hand-to-hand skills. Given the size of the Murkan fleet, Mal was pretty sure it would also be the last.

Chapter 27

Atlas cast an eye at the Dumnonians. They hadn't moved, but . . . he couldn't trust Maggot.

"Shield wall back a hundred paces! Three lines!" he shouted, jogging back himself.

He could feel questioning looks from the men and women but they were too disciplined to say anything. The looks were deserved. In terms of opposing the landing, moving fifty paces back was idiocy. However, if they stayed so far down the beach it left them horribly exposed if the Dumnonians did attack. Nearer the back of the beach they could, in theory, hold both Dumnonians and the Eroo.

Atlas climbed a dune to get a view. Thirty paces in front, his men and women wedged their shields into the sand to make the shield wall. Two rows formed behind, ready to reinforce and replace front-line troops. All readied their slings and their javelins. A pair of ponies pulled into place the two Roman-style scorpions that Elann had built based on Atlas' descriptions. He was looking forward to seeing them in action, but he wished he had a few hundred more.

The first Eroo ship scraped on to sand. Fur-clad men and women jumped from its side and splashed into the shallows. They tarried, waiting for more ships to land. These were ones that they could have taken with slings, had Atlas not moved the line back. He glanced at the Dumnonians. They were brooding further along the coast, like spectators waiting for gladiators to stop arsing about and start killing each other.

Several Eroo ran forward, screaming battle frenzy. They were killed with slingstones. Atlas was pleased. Discipline was not strong with the Eroo. Maidun's Romanised infantry wouldn't give their lives so easily.

More and more ships beached. There were enough Eroo for an attack now, but still they held, milling about, analysing the Maidun line. A larger ship landed, a ramp dropped from it and a man and a woman were carried ashore. The man stood a head taller than everyone around him. That must be Manfrax, thought Atlas. A king who apparently made Caesar look like a benevolent grandfather. The woman danced a freaky jig, legs frantic, arms pinned to her side. Presumably she was cursing the Maidun army and calling support from Eroo's gods.

Manfrax shouted and ran up the beach, towards the Maidun shield line. The Eroo army howled and followed. Manfrax's running slowed to a walk and his soldiers overtook him as he shouted encouragement. Sensible man, thought Atlas.

The Dumnonians, over to Atlas' left, hadn't moved. Manfrax and his troops were ignoring them, heading towards the Maidun line only. So the Dumnonians were definitely in league with Eroo. Atlas wondered how Maggot was going to stop the Dumnonians joining the Eroo attack – if, indeed, he was.

The Eroo army closed. They were a savage looking rabble, armed with toothed swords, axes even bigger than Atlas', gigantic curving scimitars, hammers with handles like small trees and heads like anvils. These were weapons designed to terrify, thought Atlas, and they'd be effective for a couple of hits perhaps, but after that even the mightiest warrior would weary wielding such weighty weaponry. And toothed swords? Good for cutting wood maybe, but they'd get stuck in armour or shields.

Atlas smiled. The Eroo army had clearly become too used to success and started worrying more about image than function. Carden would have said that they were all shell and no egg. Seeing this lot coming, perhaps the smaller tribes in Eroo had surrendered or fled. The Maidun army would not. They'd teach this horde a lesson in egg over shell.

Thinking of function . . . "Scorpions!" Atlas shouted. Soldiers scurried aside to split the shield wall in front of each scorpion. The shooters whacked chocks with mallets. The scorpions bucked and giant arrows with pallisade-post shafts and ships' anchor heads flew towards the enemy. One skimmed into the sand just in front of the Eroo line and cartwheeled, scattering men and women. The other did what it was meant to. Its laboriously sharpened, pace-wide head hit the throng of Eroo at waist height in an explosion of limbs and blood, punching a gory hole into the leading edge of the charge. The Eroo army faltered, then came on.

Slingshots took down a few and javelins many more before the Eroo army hit the shield wall. There were breaches in a couple of places where the oversized weapons crushed shields and a few Eroo soldiers battered their way through, but the second and third ranks did their work quickly, spitting the insurgents with spears. The Eroo warriors, as Atlas had predicted, swung their heavy weapons only once before the lighter, faster blades of the Maidun army slit throats, pierced stomachs and ruined faces. Breaches were closed in moments, the shield wall held nicely and the Eroo army began to die in large numbers against it.

More and more Eroo ships landed, more and more warriors screamed and shouted their way up the beach to perish on the immovable Maidun line. To the south, the Dumnonians were holding as Maggot had promised. Atlas looked for problems to deal with and saw none. It was going well.

He spotted Manfrax heading southwards and back to the sea. Was he fleeing already? The king stopped at the waterline to wave in a new type of ship, much longer than all the previous arrivals. A rare sense of foreboding filled the Kushite's mind. He tried to shake it but couldn't. He did not like the look of those ships.

Chapter 28

Chamanca stood shoulder to elbow with Carden, slinging stones at the approaching Roman ship. Annoyingly, the Romans had produced some shields, so their missiles weren't having much effect.

"Yes!" said Carden, as a stoned Roman fell from the top of the flagship's sail-free mast and landed on his packed-in fellows below. The lookout had thought he was safe up there. Carden searched for another target, saw none and deflated. "Toutatis's tits," he said.

The Roman boat was twenty paces away. Its oars slowed. A chink jinked open between two shields at the bow and a legionary's eye peeped through. Carden and Chamanca and a few Fenn-Nodens shot for it, but the gap snapped shut and slingstones clacked off shields.

"Do you know what I'd do, given this battle again?" Carden said.

"Have it on land?" Chamanca replied.

"Well, obviously. But, if it had to be on sea – fire arrows."

Chamanca pictured flaming arrows streaking towards the Roman boat. With no sails to set fire to and water all around to soak the wood, they probably wouldn't have been much better than slingstones. "Hmmm," she said.

"And . . ." Carden's prominent brow was furrowed, "a small catapult with caskets of whale oil to fling at the Roman ships and give the arrows something to set fire to."

"That might have worked," said Chamanca.

"Should have thought of it."

"On the bright side, they didn't."

"Ah yes," Carden nodded, "there is that."

In a surprise display of coordinated rowing, the Romans shipped oars on one side and pulled a long stroke on the other. Their ship came around. They meant to go broadside to broadside with the Fenn-Nodens' command boat, to give as wide an area for boarding as possible, but when they came parallel the Roman ship was still ten paces away, its back end bobbing slowly towards the Fenn-Nodens' boat and its bow floating away. They'd misjudged it and Chamanca's assessment of their inept oarsmanship was reaffirmed.

Gaps opened in the Roman shield defence to reveal legionaries swinging grappling ropes. A swarm of slingstones found all but one. The one who did managed to chuck his hook didn't throw far enough and the iron barb splashed into the sea.

"Ha ha!" shouted Carden. The rest of the Fenn-Nodens joined the jeering.

"They are a disgrace," said Vastivias, appearing at Chamanca's shoulder with his warriors Bran and Modaball. They were armed with two cutlasses each. The medium-length, curved blades should, Chamanca thought, be well suited to the tight fighting to come. "When their stern comes round to our gunwale, they will try to board. Instead, we will board them. Bran, Modaball and I will be first on to their boat. Will you honour me by following close on our heels?"

"It would be our pleasure, King Vastivias," Carden bowed.

The Roman ship was around the same size as the Armorican boat, but it had about three times as many people aboard, ranging from fit, superbly trained young legionaries to knarl-faced veterans of a dozen campaigns. The Fenn-Nodens crew were mostly sailors whose closest thing to being in a battle had been seeing brawls in taverns. Most were young men and women, but there were also much older people and several children. Many of then were unarmed, save for their slings. Chamanca felt something like dread seeping into her stomach, not for herself, but for these innocents. Would they have been much worse off under the Romans? Was it fair that they should die in a failed attempt to preserve the freedom of their descendants?

"Follow me." Vastivias walked along his ship, followed by Bran and Modaball. He politely asked some of his people to move, then he leant on the ship's side, and waited. Chamanca looked at Carden. He winked at her. They stood by the Gauls.

The rear end of the Roman ship swung around to the spot where they were standing. The Roman boat was a good pace lower along the hull than the Fenn-Nodens' ship, but it had a raised stern almost level with the Gaulish gunwale. It was lined with shields, which were ready, no doubt, to part and unleash the boarding party.

It was three paces away. Two paces. One pace.

The shields opened. Vastivias roared and flung himself across the gap. The Romans had time only to register surprise before the chief was on them, his cutlasses a hacking whirl. Blood fountained and Romans fell.

Modaball and Bran leapt after him. Bran took a spear thrust to the shoulder and splashed down between the boats. Modaball landed next to his king. A flailing sword found his head and blood sprayed, but he screamed and piled into the Romans, cutlasses chopping in every direction. Legionaries tumbled into the sea. Others backed along the deck, away from the enraged Gauls.

Space opened up behind Vastivias and Modaball. Carden and Chamanca looked at each other then jumped. Chamanca came in on Vastivias' left, mace whacking, blade stabbing. She was aware of Carden's broadsword swinging over on the right and Romans falling. She was also aware of Modaball collapsing, presumably succumbing to his head wound.

Vastivias was next, a sword thrust to the guts.

"Kill them all," he strained to say, "if not today, then—" Blood gushed from his mouth. He toppled.

An order was shouted. The front rank of legionaries tried to back away and regroup, but they were too packed on the boat, and their attempt to retreat made them easier targets. Chamanca and Carden pressed, stepping over bodies. Carden swapped his sword for Vastivias' stout cutlasses. Chamanca's blade pinpointed vital parts of Romans and sliced into them, her mace cracked skulls and blocked sword thrusts. While the Romans were slipping on the blood of their dying comrades, Chamanca was sliding about on the slick floor like a skater and opening more arteries.

She glanced behind. There was empty deck behind her, then sea, then a line of staring Fenn-Nodens faces. The boats had drifted apart and no more Gauls had been able to jump across. They were on their own.

A dagger flashed past her and lodged in Carden's neck. He fell to one knee. Romans closed in and Chamanca flew at them in a fury. Several fell, others backed off and stood looking at her, swords held in defence. None of them wanted to be next to step forward and meet his end. She snarled back at them, panting.

Carden pulled the dagger from his neck and stood up. Blood flowed from the wound in thick pulses.

"Go," he said.

"You go," she replied.

"I'm dead already." She glanced at his neck wound. He was right.

"We'll die together." Chamanca crouched, ready to leap.

"No," said Carden. "Swim ashore. Stay alive. Then kill them all." He raised his cutlasses and ran at the watching legionaries.

The world slowed for Chamanca. A legionary's helmeted head somersaulted up into the air. A sword slid into Carden's side. He gasped. Another blade was buried in his neck. He fell and the Romans charged in, swords stabbing.

Chamanca lifted sword and ball-mace. She feinted. The Romans backed away. She turned, ran to the edge of the boat, leapt the gunwale and dived into the sea.

Chapter 29

Bruxon swallowed. Manfrax's mighty Murkan army, scourge of Eroo, was having as much effect on the Maidun line as a banished drunkard battering on the locked gates of a hillfort. Manfrax's men filled the beach like a rising tide, but the Maidun army held it like a stone wharf. He could see the dark-skinned battle commander, Atlas, watching calmly from a sand dune. Maidun's men and women knew what they were doing. Manfrax's army charged the shields, the shields held, the Eroo died. That was that. Every now and then an attack did cleave the wall, but it was always repelled and the wall reformed like the surface of a pond behind a plunging stone.

Bruxon would have to read this situation well. Even if Manfrax's famously effective army hadn't had quite the swift victory it had expected, then surely its massive numerical superiority would tell and the Maidun shield wall would crumble. However, if Manfrax couldn't break through, if he decided to return to his boats and Eroo, then Bruxon would need a magnificent excuse ready to explain why the Dumnonians had watched the battle rather than joining it.

He looked around. The Dumnonian sub-chiefs looked as worried as he did. There was no point asking that cluster of fools for ideas. Where the Bel was Maggot? He'd know what to do, at least he'd have an opinion. But he was nowhere to be seen. Had he slipped off now he could see that all was lost? Probably. Bruxon had never liked the weasly druid.

The Dumnonian king watched Manfrax. He was at the

water's edge, well away from the fighting, shouting at a ship that was nearing shore. Was he planning an escape?

The ship slid on to the sand in between two other Eroo boats. It was an odd craft, longer and slimmer than the other Eroo ships, and there was something wrong with his perspective, because from where he was it looked like it was crewed by just a few absurdly massive people.

The newly arrived ship rocked over on its side as the crew clambered out. A gasp and several curses went up around Bruxon.

They *were* massive people. Each of them was the height of Manfrax, himself a very large man, then at least half that height again. Despite their height, however, it was their breadth that was so surprising. Relatively, despite their tallness, they were squat. Their limbs were like oak trunks. Bruxon looked about himself. Jaws hung open. He closed his own. Manfrax was gesticulating and five giant figures were following him up the beach. Even from here Bruxon could see that each was thickly armoured, although none of them wore helmets, and each was armed with weapons that made the already oversized swords and axes of the Eroo army look like children's toys. One had a hammer with an iron head the size of a small cart that he – or she, judging by the prominent chest – was carrying with apparent ease. Another had a sword that must have been three paces long and half a pace wide, held casually over one shoulder as if it were made of hollow wood.

What were they? Humans could not be so big, surely? Were they a type of giant bear? Shaved bears with armour and weapons who could sail ships?

"That's just the start," said Maggot. "There are a lot more of them coming."

"What? Where have you been?" Bruxon was partly annoyed with him for sneaking off, but more angry that the druid didn't have the decency to be surprised by the walking phenomena that had the rest of them flabbergasted. The sub-chiefs gathered around Maggot, clamouring questions.

Bruxon held his hand up for silence. "Quiet, everyone quiet." He tried to hide his amazement and eagerness to know where on Danu's earth these . . . people? had come from. He glanced down to the beach. The giants were lumbering towards the Maidun line, Manfrax jogging to keep up. "Maggot, do you know what these . . . arrivals are, and where they are from?"

"They are Fassites, from the island of Fassent."

Various cries of "no!" and "Fassites are a myth!" came from the Dumnonians. Maggot grinned around at all of them in turn, clearly pleased with the attention, and knowing something that nobody else did.

"No," said Maggot, "not a myth. As you can see, they are real. Real, and even nastier than the legends will have you believe."

Chapter 30

Atlas' eyes narrowed.

He wasn't surprised. As a child in Africa he'd seen creatures that would have made the average Briton soil his tartan trousers, so he'd always believed that there were plenty of monsters outside the realms of accepted knowledge that might rear their bizarre heads at any moment.

Shame, though, that such monsters should appear right now, apparently about to fight for the enemy. They were giants. Two-eyed, so not the race of Cyclops who'd built the temples he'd visited on the island of Melita. They could, he thought, be Fassites, a supposedly mythical island-based tribe of giants. Whoever or whatever they were, if they were as effective as they looked, Maidun was in trouble. However, one thing he'd learnt in Africa about giant beasts was that they could be killed if you put your mind, a lot of people and the right weapons to it.

"Scorpions! With me!" he shouted, bounding down the dune. "You lot," he indicated a section of the third rank, "follow me with spears!"

He ran to the place where the giants would hit the shield wall, followed by a couple of dozen men and women, the scorpion crews and their pony-pulled weapons. He slotted his axe into the holster on his back and set about digging a hole in the sand under the tail of one scorpion, to give it a lofted projection. He shouted at the other crew to copy him.

The shield wall and the two ranks behind it stood its

ground as the giants thundered closer, running now, fast as horses, trampling the few Eroo who got in their way.

"Spears ready!" shouted Atlas. Spears went up. "Keep clear of the scorpions!" he shouted to two idiot spearwomen who'd planted themselves directly in front of one of the massive siege weapons.

The giants hit the shield wall like bulls hitting a haystack. Men, women, shields and weapons exploded in all directions. A female-looking giant with a hammer took out a dozen Maidun troops with one swing. Atlas pulled the end of the scorpion round to face her.

"Shoot!"

The shooter knocked the chock. The recoil knocked Atlas off his feet, but he saw the giant arrow smash into the giant's chest as he fell. He scrambled up.

The hammer giant was down. The other scorpion had severed another giant's arm at the elbow. The creature bellowed and ran away down the beach. Spears were pressing in on the other three, poking for gaps in their plate iron armour, but the giants were fast. They danced away from spear thrusts and swathed down whole groups of Maidun soldiers with their swords and axes. They were bare-headed, but they avoided all the spear thrusts that managed to come that high, and dodged the hurled javelins.

Atlas remembered a story from a tribe of desert dwellers whom he'd met on a journey around the east of the central sea. They were a sulky, juvenile lot, whose men resented and subjugated women because their creation story said that the first ever woman had spoiled everything for all men for ever. One of their many legends had stuck in his head, though, about a boy who'd fought a giant.

"Slings!" he shouted. "Aim for the heads!"

Chapter 31

The Murkans were held behind the shield wall again, so it was time to head south and help the infantry against the Eroo. Under archer cover from their drivers and the cavalry, the foot soldiers jumped back into their chariots and the Maidun army left the field. The Murkan soldiers jeered and followed. Maidun arrows thudded into several hundred of them. The jeers stopped, the pursuit petered out and the Maidun army was clear, galloping for Frogshold.

Dug kept asking Spring if she was OK, and she kept nodding that she was. Her throat wasn't so sore that she couldn't talk, but her voice sounded so weird when she did that she didn't want to, and besides, she was too sad. Seeing her tears, Dug droned on as the chariot bounced at a lick along the road, saying that Nita was in a better place, happy in the Otherworld with all her loved ones around, feasting on her favourite foods, probably being provided with a constant stream of idiots to complain about then beat into shape. In fact, Dug said, he wouldn't be surprised if the Otherworld had arranged a whole new rebellion for Nita to . . .

"Oh, shut up!" Spring shouted.

Dug went silent and Spring felt terrible for shouting at him. But he just didn't get it. It wasn't Nita she felt sad for. Nita was dead and that was that. Spring was crying for Mal.

Parents died and it was expected, even, in the case of Spring's father, something of a blessing. Children died and it was a tragedy, a reason to rage against the gods, to do something useful like make improvements in cart safety so the accident didn't happen again, and to lavish more love and protection on remaining children and new babies.

But, she thought, what about someone you'd chosen to be with, like a wife or a husband dying early? Surely you could never be happy again? There was no succour in the idea that it was their time to go, because it wasn't. There was no one to replace them, nothing you could do to prevent similar deaths because there was nobody else similar. When you love someone because you love them, rather than because they're family, and they are killed, surely the only sane response is to go mad? To hate the gods, everyone else, and yourself?

And surely if, as Dug seemed to, you believed that all those you loved were in the Otherworld, living lives of joy in perpetual happiness and waiting for you to appear and get the party started, then the only sensible course of action must be to kill yourself immediately and join them?

She thought about what Mal would be doing right then, as they were driving towards him. Perhaps he'd be watching the Eroo fleet approach, trying not to worry about his wife in the cavalry. She'll be fine, he'd be telling himself. She's with Lowa and Lowa will deal with any trouble. Nita is capable and wise and wouldn't put herself in unnecessary danger and I mustn't worry about her. That's what he'd be saying. Right then, at that moment, Mal thought that Nita was alive. She pictured his friendly face, smiling in welcome when they returned, looking about for Nita, concern overwhelming his happy features when he couldn't spot her. Then hearing the news . . . his face crumpling, collapsing, the happiness gone, never to return. Spring sobbed.

Dug put a hand on her shoulder. She took the reins in one hand and put the other on his.

She couldn't stop thinking about Mal, though. Why do we have to touch each other's lives like this, she thought, when so many unfair and unplanned things happen all the time? The lambs in the field near Maidun didn't appear to give much of a crap when other lambs were taken to be killed and eaten. Why couldn't people be more like that? Why was everything so poignant? She thought back five years, to when she'd skipped into Mal's yard and he'd been so kind, and his wife had helped with − not helped with, ran − the rebellion without which Zadar would never have been toppled. They'd taken Spring in and they'd given her everything and Spring had repaid them by getting Nita killed. If she hadn't gone there, if she'd approached the tavern keeper instead, like she nearly had, then Mal and Nita would probably still be happy together somewhere. They'd probably have left Maidun and started a family somewhere . . .

But no.

Horrible chance had struck. A good woman was dead and a good man's life was ruined. They hadn't beaten the Murkans yet and there was still Dumnonia and Eroo to deal with, and then, if any of them were still alive, the Romans. How many more horrible, unbearable deaths were there going to be?

Chapter 32

The slingstones didn't kill the giants, but they distracted them enough for the Maidun spears to find the gaps in their armour. Two more giants went down, falling on to the corpses of the Maidun men and women who'd died killing them.

The last was the largest, armed with a sword the size of a couple of hut doors placed end on end. One would expect, thought Atlas, that giants would be shaggy and wild, but, this one had neatly cut hair and beardless, smiling face.

If he was smiling now, it was impossible to tell because of the swelling and bleeding from the ongoing barrage of slingstones. He was ignoring the onslaught, though, swiping with his sword, dispatching three Maidun soldiers with almost every swing, hopping about like a barefoot child on an ant's nest to avoid the spear thrusts. He was doing well. There weren't many left to thrust spears.

Atlas took his axe from its holster and appraised the situation. To the south Dumnonians had held. If they were in cahoots with Eroo, why hadn't they attacked? The giants had destroyed a major section of the shield wall, but elsewhere it was holding. Thankfully, few Eroo had come through the raging giants' breach since being anywhere near them was dangerous for all. A giant had smashed one of his scorpions. The crew had reloaded the other one, but were still winding back the twine to prime it. It was taking far too long. He resolved to improve that, or at least ask Elann to find a way.

He grabbed one of the scorpion crew. "When this giant goes down, close the gap in the shield wall."

The man looked at him, his face locked in confusion and shock, but he nodded.

Atlas turned to the giant, who was roaring and looking around for the next person to kill. The Kushite hefted his axe in his hand. It felt light. He charged.

The giant spotted the threat, and lunged with his sword. Dulled by the slingshots, with blood in his eyes, the lunge came too early and thudded into the sand. Atlas checked, leapt on to the giant's blade and used it as a springboard to launch himself. As he flew, he swung his axe two handed, and chopped it with all his might into the side of the giant's exposed head.

The big Kushite stood on the giant that he'd slain and shouted orders. A scorpion arrow blasted back a horde of Eroo charging through the giants' breach. Maidun warriors flowed around the other giants' bodies and the corpses of their comrades to reform the shield wall. When the Eroo army saw the Maidun general standing on the corpse of their fifth giant you could almost see the morale evaporating from them. Atlas wondered if he could give the order to begin shoving the Eroo army back to their boats. If Lowa arrived with the cavalry and chariots, they would start the counter-attack immediately. If she didn't come, assuming the Dumnonians stayed back, the infantry might well be able to do it on their own. He had not expected it to be so easy.

He looked to the Dumnonians again. Maggot, it seemed, had managed to hold them in place. If Eroo retreated, it was very likely that they'd join and help the Maidun army. That would be the clever thing to do . . . he was getting ahead of himself. He had not won yet, far from it.

There were still more ships to land, and only counting the Eroo force already on the beach he was still hugely outnumbered. Although not, he told himself, looking at the dead giants, his holding shield wall and the bank of Eroo corpses in front of it, outgeneralled. Now, thinking of that, where was Manfrax?

Atlas spotted Manfrax at the water's edge, welcoming in a dozen more ships. Ships which looked similar in size and shape to the one the giants had come in.

The first ship beached and five more giants disembarked. Another hit the shore next to it, then another, then more. Giants clambered out of all of them.

Chapter 33

Once she was sure that they were clear of the Murkans, Lowa galloped ahead, flashing across the land. She thundered up the side of Frogshold hill and into the fort's north gate. Everyone was on the west wall. She leapt from her horse and ran to join them, finding the messenger woman Adler looking over the scene.

"News, Adler?" she said. "How goes the . . ."

She stopped talking when she realised what she was looking at. The beach was thick with an impossible number of ships and still more were coming. The Dumnonian army was immobile to the south, but between Frogshold and the sea to the west was a horrific sight. The Maidun infantry were routed, running back from the shore, pursued by . . .

"What the fuck?" she asked.

"Fassites," said a familiar voice. Maggot. "Manfrax has persuaded the Fassites to fight with him."

"But Fassites are a legend." Lowa looked again, hoping that somehow it had been an illusion. No. The Maidun troops were in a long, thick line, the nearest of them about a thousand paces away. The giants were keeping up, in fact overtaking them. She saw two of the huge warriors catch a backmarker and lift him as if he were a puppy. One took him by the feet, the other by his hands, and they pulled him in two in a burst of blood. They threw aside the two halves, both doubled up laughing, slapping their thighs, then ran on. They were as fast as cavalry. She shook her head.

Behind the giants came the massive Eroo invasion force.

"How many?" Lowa asked nobody in particular.

"Giants, I've counted fifty-two." said Adler. "The Eroo — who knows? A lot."

Fuck, thought Lowa. "Atlas?"

"I haven't seen him. He was leading the force on the beach. Knowing him, I suspect he held the enemy back while the others escaped, if he hadn't already been killed."

"OK," said Lowa. Things were not going to plan. New plans were needed. "Any idea how to beat these Fassites, Maggot?"

"Same as you beat anyone," Maggot cocked his head, "find a soft bit, stick some metal in it."

"Thanks, useful."

". . . and," Maggot's eyes bulged hugely, "it so happens some druid or other persuaded them a couple of years back to always go into battle barehcaded, for religious reasons, don't you see? Danu made your body but Bel made your head and he don't like to see it covered. So, although they've skulls that make oxen look brittle-headed and most slingstones'll just bounce off them, an arrow to the face'll slow them right down."

"Good, Maggot, thanks. Adler, how many arrows do we have here?"

"Hardly any." Adler shook her head. "We hadn't planned—"

"Oh yes you had," said Maggot, gesturing over his shoulder with a thumb. On the central road through the hillfort, standing peacefully with no drivers to be seen, were eight oxen and four large carts. The carts were packed with quiver after quiver of arrows and sheaves of bows.

Lowa looked at Maggot. He smiled. She looked at the arrows again, then back to the weird druid.

"You're very deeply involved with all this, aren't you?" she said. "Tell me everything you know. Quickly."

Maggot paused, then said in a rapid staccato voice: "Fresh

eggs taste nicer, the biggest fish have to come to the surface to breath air so they're not really fish, if you feed a dog you've got a friend for life, but if you kick a cat—"

"For fuck's sake," said Lowa. She turned to look for Adler, but found Mal standing there.

"Nita?" he asked.

Five years before she would have lied or let someone else deliver the bad news, but five years of leadership had taught her that if you treated people how you'd want to be treated yourself, you got it right most of the time. She took a deep breath and looked Mal in the eye.

"Nita saved Spring's life but died doing so. Then Spring killed the Warrior who killed Nita – it was the same one who killed Miller."

Mal's face fell.

"I'm sorry, Mal. We'll grieve together when we are done here. When we've killed the rest of these bastards. Now, will you arrange distribution of these bows and arrows, and the manning of the walls to repel three armies?"

He nodded, once.

"Thank you. You'll need to be quick, focusing resources to the south-west at first. I'm going to meet the chariots and the cavalry—"

She kept her instructions brief, then galloped back northwards.

Chapter 34

"Up Frogshold, follow the chariot in front of you, form a circle fifty paces below outer hillfort wall, spike chariots! Bring horses into hillfort!" came the shouted order. Dug repeated the shout to the chariot behind.

"What?" asked Spring.

"Follow the chariot ahead," said Dug. "When it stops, you stop, we get out, I smash a wheel so the chariot becomes an obstacle, we take the horse up to the fort."

Spring nodded. Dug wondered if she knew what the order meant. They were giving up on chariot warfare and preparing for a siege. The horses' role had changed from draught animals to food. So Eroo must have landed successfully, defeated Atlas' infantry and the Dumnonian army on the beach, and the entire remaining Maidun force was piling into the nearest redoubt – Frogshold.

They stopped and Dug smashed a chariot wheel with his hammer. He went to help the charioteers behind disable their vehicle while Spring unbuckled the horse. He wanted very much to stop and look out over the land to work out exactly what was happening, but there were things to do, first of which was to get Spring safely into the fort.

They headed up the hill with the other light and heavy chariot crews, Dug with his hammer in one hand and the horse's rein in the other. Spring had her recurve in one hand, her longbow in the other, with her quiver slapping on her back. There was a press at the gate, so they had to pause and Dug took the opportunity to survey the scene.

Badgers' balls, he thought. The land stretched out huge to the south and east. He could see Gutrin Tor clearly, across fifteen miles of reclaimed fields and marshland. The coastline to the west was fringed with beached ships. Between them and the hill were what must have been the Eroo army, thick on the land and countless in number. South of them, crawling slowly towards Frogshold, was another army. Dumnonia, he thought. So they had turned.

Nearer, at the foot of the hill, were Maidun infantry, running like men and women who'd run a long way but were determined to keep going. As they should be, because three hundred paces behind them, the tail of infantry was being hard pressed by some very large Eroo warriors. Very large – and so broad! Dug had heard they made them big in Eroo, but these were stupidly big. Perhaps, he thought, his eyesight was finally failing. Many people his age were in permanent bad moods because they couldn't see what the Bel was going on most of the time.

He and Spring jogged in through the entrance with a flow of other charioteers and cavalry and their horses. Inside the gates were two loud-mouthed Two Hundred riders screaming at everyone to press on through into the centre of the hillfort. As he jogged, Dug nodded his appreciation. Someone was organising things well. The last thing you wanted in a situation like this was the sort of idiots who stopped as soon as they'd got though a gate and blocked it for everyone following.

There were more screamers stationed along the road, hurrying people along. At the crossroads in the hillfort's centre stood a couple more, handing out quivers and arrows, shouting for those with bows to head left and right to the walls and for those leading horses to carry on ahead. Next to them was Mal, directing it all.

Dug was surprised and pleased to see that Mal had taken the news about Nita so well. If it had been Lowa, Dug would have been among the Eroo, fighting until he was cut down. Mal was doing the sensible thing and contributing more constructively to the battle effort. He was clearly made of stronger stuff.

Spring handed Dug her recurve bow, and Dug passed their horse's leading rein to a woman who already had two others. Dug took a quiver from Mal, and nodded at him, trying to convey condolences and respect in one motion. They had to get to the walls, there was no time for chat.

Mal nodded back, his chin set, his eyes filled with all the sorrow in the world.

On the wall, they were directed leftwards. They jogged along with other archers until they came to a woman directing people to their allotted places, shouting at everyone to line the walls tightly, but not to crowd. Each archer was to have enough space at the palisade to arm and shoot their bows, with a gap left behind for movement and supplies. Dug attempted to pass her by. She put a hand on his chest, looked up, saw who it was and let him go. He took Spring's hand and pulled her with him.

They found Lowa next to the gate, looking out to the south-west, bow in her hand, arrow-stuffed quiver on her back. Dug nodded a greeting, then followed her gaze.

The front-running Maidun infantry had reached the circle of chariots. A gap had been left clear to give them passage. It was hard to estimate, but behind them were perhaps five thousand Maidun infantry, which meant that fifteen thousand more had not made it back from the beach.

Still a good distance away, but hard pressed on the tail of the Maidun infantry were the huge Eroo warriors . . .

"They are giants!" Dug heard himself saying out loud.

"Yup," said Lowa. "Fassites."

Fassites, thought Dug, staring at them, still not quite believing his ears or his eyes. It was like whales had mated with humans and produced offspring sized somewhere between the two species.

"Wow," said Spring next to him. "This isn't good."

"No," said Lowa, "but I'd say they're just coming into our range."

Spring nodded, craning her head forward to peer at them. "They're wearing thick armour, but no helmets, so it'll have to be head shots. Armour-piercing arrows will be best."

Lowa nodded.

On either side of Dug, Spring and Lowa reached into their quivers, plucked out arrows, drew, aimed and loosed. He felt the air vibrate. Those longbows of Elann's were truly amazing. It was just a shame that she'd made only three and that Chamanca had broken one of them. Not that anyone other that Lowa and Spring were capable of drawing them. Dug had tried. He could draw it all the way, but not more than a couple of times before his muscles were spent. Spring had reassured him that it was much more to do with technique than strength.

The arrows disappeared off and the three of them watched. A mile away, a Fassite fell.

"Mine," said Spring and Lowa, at the same time. They glanced a "you're wrong" look at each other, then strung their bows again.

Dug looked at his recurve bow, then back to the rest of the Fassites. It would be a good while before they were in his and everybody else's range.

The Fassites stopped their pursuit well before the range of normal bows, after Lowa and Spring had taken down four of them. The rest retreated out of longbow range. The Eroo army caught up with them, and fanned out to encircle Frogshold.

Dug, Lowa and Spring stayed on the wall by the gate and Dug listened as reports came to Lowa. The Murkan army had arrived and were spread out to the north. The Dumnonians had indeed turned, although they hadn't yet attacked anyone, and their army was occupying the causeways and islands in the marshes to the east. The Murkans and their giant Fassites had the south and west covered. So they were surrounded by three armies, each of which was much larger than their own, more than half of which they'd already lost to the Fassites and Eroo.

"Not what we planned," said Dug.

"Plans only ever last until you meet the enemy," Lowa said.

That sounded good, thought Dug, but it wasn't true. The battle on the plain at Sarum, for example, had gone pretty much exactly according to plan. But they'd been lucky there.

They watched the enemy armies set up their camps as the evening drew on. All around Frogshold, Dumnonian, Murkan, Fassite and Eroo cook fires stretched off into the distance. If you forgot for a moment what it signified, it was rather beautiful.

Lowa stationed watchmen, sent parties to make and light small fires all along the ring of chariots so they might see any attacks in the dark, then they left the walls for the night.

Chapter 35

"We all know about Tans Tali and great Queen Sara," said Maggot to Lowa, Dug, Spring and the others gathered around their fire. He jumped and spun about as he spoke, ornaments jangling, eyeing each of his audience in turn. "But at the same time, hundred of generations ago, there were other great lands, tribes and cities that have since been covered by the sea.

"Think about it!" he cried. "Of course there was other shit going on. The whole world was frozen! All the water that is now the sea was ice, and the ice was sitting on what is now the land. The people walked around, planted crops, raised animals and built their towns on what is now the bottom of the sea. Hard to get your head around! But it's true. And this land was vast. Vast! Dug there is from the north tip of Britain so he knows how big Britain is. Well, the land back then, in the time of ice, was a hundred times the size! Bigger!" Maggot waved his arms in circles.

"And so, of course, there were many more types of animal – loads of big weird ones and weirder small ones, you often see their remains in rocks by the sea – and, here's the clincher, there were different types of people. We know about the halfmen, who got massacred by the humans just after the age of ice, but there were loads more. Little tiny people who ran along on their hands. Hairy people. People with only one leg who could hop over trees. And, of course, giants." Maggot stood on tiptoes, raising his arms high above his head.

"One group of giants was the . . . Fassites! Our friends from today. There weren't many of them, thank Danu, because they are about the most violent, cruel people that ever lived. You think humans are bad? Manfrax? Caesar? Zadar? Kittens compared to the Fassites.

"When the great flood came, like loads of other animals, including us, the surviving Fassites found themselves on a new island. In their case, it was Eroo. Luckily for everyone else in Eroo, the waters kept rising, Eroo was split in two and the island that we now call Fassent was created."

A few people nodded. The mysterious island, to the south of Eroo, was known about and avoided.

"Ever wondered why we know nothing about Fassent even though it's only a bit further than Eroo? 'Cos nobody goes there. And why does nobody go there? Because anyone who does gets killed by the nasty Fassites. So the Fassites stayed secret, known about only in Eroo. They grew in number and the danger from them grew. They had no boats, but, as Manfrax realised, it was only a matter of time before some exploratory idiot from Greece or Rome landed on their shore and the Fassites thought 'oh, look what you can do with wood', built a fleet and invaded the first place they came to, which would have been Eroo, because you can see it from Fassent.

"So when Manfrax had finished shitting all over the rest of his own island, he looked about for a way of dealing with the Fassite problem. Bruxon, the deluded king of Dumnonia, asked him to invade Britain, and Manfrax found his answer. He went to Fassent and stood in a boat twenty paces from shore and shouted his plan to the Fassites. He'd build them boats, they'd sail to Britain and have all the people to kill and all the land that they could ever need. The condition was that they would never come to Eroo.

"The Fassites agreed, and Manfrax set in motion something that was always going to happen when the Fassites got off their island – the next stage of life, in which Fassites kill all the humans, just like the humans killed the halfmen. There are enough Fassites here to be a problem, but now that they know about boats, many more will come. They'll kill everyone in Britain, they will multiply like rats in a deserted grain store, then they will kill everyone else. They may leave Eroo until last, due to their agreement with Manfrax, but I doubt it."

Fire-lit Maidun faces stared dumbly at him.

A familiar voice came out of the darkness: "The question is, how can we kill them before they kill us?" The voice's owner walked into the firelight. It was Atlas.

Spring leapt up with the rest of them, crowding round and asking what had happened. Even Lowa had a genuine-looking smile. On this day of bad news, everyone was over-joyed that somebody they thought had died was alive.

Spring saw Lowa nod to Dug.

"Quiet everyone, quiet," shouted Dug, "let Atlas tell his story."

Atlas told them how they'd killed the first five giants. When the second wave of dozens of them appeared, he'd ordered half the army to hold the shield wall and the other half to retreat. So half the army had fled, and the others had stood to die so that the rest might get away. The giants had struck, then he remembered nothing. He'd woken as the sun was setting and made his way through the enemy camps to Frogshold.

"With skin like mine," he finished, "it is easy to creep through the night."

"Unless you smile!" said a wag.

"I wasn't in a smiling mood," snarled Atlas. She couldn't see him in the dark, but in Spring's mind the wag curled up like a salted slug. Atlas continued: "The immediate question now is how can we beat the Fassites? I cannot see a way. We also face the Dumnonian, Eroo and Murkan armies. Unless the Gauls have upped their challenge or Chamanca and

Carden have pulled off a miracle, the Romans will be here any day, though I fear that they won't find anybody from Maidun left to oppose them."

"I know what we need to do." Everyone turned to Maggot. "The gods planted the idea in my head before I was born and it's grown into a tree. I know exactly what we need to do." Spring thought the use of "we" was odd, for Dumnonia's chief druid talking to the Maidun leaders. He smiled at them all.

"What then?" asked Lowa.

"We send someone to talk to their three kings. That's all I can see. I don't know what he should say. But I know it will work."

"He?" asked Lowa.

"Oh yes, I know who the gods have chosen as our envoy. It's Dug Sealskinner."

Everyone turned to Dug.

"No," said Spring. "Not him. I'll go."

"No, I will," said Lowa.

"Think, Spring." Maggot put a hand on her shoulder.

Spring closed her eyes but she didn't need to. She didn't need to think. She knew Maggot was right, as surely as she knew that she had two feet. Dug had to talk to the three kings. She didn't know how she knew, but she did.

"He is right. Dug has to talk to them. It's our only hope. I think he'll be OK. I don't think they'll kill him," she said.

Maggot smiled sadly at her.

"I'll do it," said Dug, as if agreeing to get the next bucket of water from the well. Thinking of water, Spring had a sudden flash of her nightmares in which Dug was dead and bumping along the bottom of the sea.

"Hang on," said Lowa. "There's no point—"

"I see it too," said Dug. "I'm meant to go. I don't know how I know, but I do. Don't you fuss, it's all going to be all right."

Chapter 36

Grummog had refused Manfrax's summons, so the Murkan force was not represented. Army administration was the excuse, but Bruxon had heard that the northern king was catatonic with grief after the death of his queen, Pomax. His weakness appalled Bruxon. He had physical urges himself, which he satisfied with ambitious, unscrupulous women, but the idea of caring for another person to the degree that their death prevented you from going about your business was utterly alien to him, as perverse as the existence of the Fassites. He suspected that such silly, useless bonds were the preserve of the unintelligent.

He didn't know whether to be relieved or not about the Murkan king's absence. Grummog was a hate-filled man, his character as twisted as his deformed body, and, all things being equal, Bruxon would have been happy never to set eyes on the nasty little fellow again. However, on a practical level, the coordinated planning for three armies was difficult when only two were represented. And there was another reason for wanting Grummog there. He did not want to be alone with Manfrax.

The Eroo king's guards ushered him into an enormous leather tent, but remained outside themselves and insisted that his retinue did the same. So it was to be just him and Manfrax. Bruxon felt fear rise and stick in his throat. He swallowed.

The king of Eroo was sprawled on a fur-covered throne that was more bed than seat. His narrow-eyed druid queen was nowhere to be seen and neither were any of the giants. The Fassites were camped nearer the sea, on the far side of the Eroo camp. Bruxon had not seen them up close. He didn't even know if they could speak.

"Your giants should have remained on their island," he said, sitting with his back straight, hoping that his regal tone would remind Manfrax that they were equals. "They were not part of our agreement."

"Oh, don't fuss yourself," said Manfrax. Bruxon wished that Maggot was with him but he'd trotted off earlier in the day, saying something about "druid business", and Bruxon hadn't seen him since.

Manfrax took a long lug from his wooden beer mug, more a barrel with a handle than a tankard. "The Fassites are lovely people." He wiped his moustache. "Lambs, they are. They do what I tell them to do, nothing more. They won't trouble the brave people of Dumnonia. When Lowa and her army are all dead, they'll return meekly whence they came to go about their farming and their basket weaving. They have no ships, the poor things, and no notion of how to make them, so they won't be leaving their island again without my say-so."

"Well, you make sure that they do stay there!" Bruxon barked, appalled anew at the man's casual appearance and attitude. How could a king deport himself like some drunken adventurer? Manfrax was a disgrace. Why had he let the Eroo army invade?

"Of course," said Manfrax, "there is another army in Britain that we might have a look at, while we've got the Fassites here."

"Is there?" Bruxon sat forward. This sounded interesting.

"With Dumnonia's support, I was thinking we might have a wee trip around Murkan territory after we've dealt with Maidun. After I take Maidun's lands, it'll be a year or two before I'm ready to take a full scale expedition north. Makka knows, it was enough of a hoo-ha getting this one together. But if Dumnonia feeds and supplies my army, the two of us can take the Murkan lands in the next moon or two."

"But what about the Romans? They're in northern Gaul now, by all accounts invincible and about to sail."

"Ah yes, the Romans. Funny that we didn't include them in our invasion plans, especially when your druids have known about their coming for years. It's almost like you hoped the Romans would send me and my fine people back to Eroo, or perhaps even to the Otherworld, Danu forbid?" Manfrax smiled and took another pull on his beer mug.

"We . . . I . . . had no such intention," said Bruxon. "The Dumnonians have no druids: Samalur killed them all. What we know of the Romans we've heard from merchants and bards, just as you have. Nobody could have guessed they'd fight their way through Gaul so quickly."

"And your man Maggot?"

"He's a charlatan. He is a useful advisor, but his talk of magic is an affectation. He is more jester than druid."

"I see. Well, no matter. If the Romans come, the Romans come. The Fassites will show those strutting, feather-headed cockerels just how invincible they are."

"I thought the Fassites were going back to Fassent?"

"Well, maybe we'll keep them here for a while, just until all the obstacles are cleared. Now, get yourself over here to seal our pact against the Murkans. Then we'll plan the details." Manfrax sat up. He pulled his jerkin aside to reveal his broad, well-fleshed chest, and a nipple that Bruxon remembered from Eroo. "Come on then, let's make this official." His jocular lilt had flattened a good deal.

Bruxon tried to remain calm. "Manfrax, this is Britain. I am king here. You are asking for an act of subservience. It was different when I was in your hall on Eroo. I was in your realm, bound by its rules. But I'm sorry, such supplication cannot be contemplated in my own land."

"Really? Stand up." Without thinking, Bruxon did so. Manfrax stood as well. His chest came to the same height as Bruxon's face. Suddenly the big tent seemed very small.

Manfrax reached up with a hand not much smaller than a Fassite's and gripped the back of Bruxon's head. "Thousands of people have sucked my nipple, Bruxon," he said, looking down at the Dumnonian king like a kindly father. "And I can tell when people like it. Usually it's women that enjoy a good suck. Sometimes it's men. And one of those men, my British friend, is you. Don't be embarrassed about it, we all have our desires."

Manfrax pulled his head forward. Bruxon resisted. Wrenching his head to one side, he saw Manfrax's queen, Reena, watching from the corner of the tent. How had she stayed there unnoticed? he thought as Manfrax pulled his head back round. There was no resisting. He stopped fighting and opened his mouth.

Chapter 37

Lowa lay awake in the chief of Frogshold's hut, next to the snoring Dug. They'd made love. Lowa had cried afterwards. Dug had comforted her, then fallen asleep pretty much mid-word. He seemed calmer and more assured than she'd ever known him, not at all concerned about the prospect of walking out to the enemy. It worried her. She liked to be in charge and fully clued up, yet here was something she didn't understand. Something was going on between Maggot, Spring and Dug. She'd questioned each of them. Spring and Dug, she was sure, knew nothing more than their bizarre conviction that Dug would somehow be able to walk down the hill, meet the three kings and save all their lives.

Maggot did know more, she was sure. There was something in his eyes. A sadness that terrified her.

Pressed as they were, armies all around, pretty much certain to die, she did not want to lose Dug. She'd sooner lose everybody else, herself included. She'd decided to tell him that she was pregnant, but then hadn't. She didn't know why. She knew he knew anyway. She just didn't want to talk about it, she supposed. Not with Dug about to face such impossible danger.

She lay in the dark, sick with worry, listening for alarm horns and annoyed with herself for worrying. They said that strange things happened to your emotions during pregnancy, and perhaps that's what was happening to her now. She'd faced certain death before without getting all pathetic about it. Great, she thought. As if swelling up into a giant sow then having to force something the size of a baby out of her vagina wasn't bad enough without the added weepiness.

When dawn finally came, slowly diffusing through the thatched roof's chimney hole, she hated it and cursed and silently pleaded with the sun to melt back into the darkness and let the night last for ever.

Chapter 38

Well, it was a lovely day for it, whatever "it" was, thought Dug as he trudged alone, southwards down the steep side of Frogshold hill. The breeze had returned and was blowing brilliant white clouds across a huge, pale blue sky. The sheep-stripped turf was springy underfoot.

He could feel the eyes of the Maidunites behind him; Lowa, Spring and the rest all watching. Ahead, the three kings of Dumnonia, Eroo and Murkan waited, the Fassites next to them and their armies stretched for Danu knew how far in every direction around them.

"You'll know what to do when you get there," Maggot had said, as if Dug were nipping out on an errand. He had no idea what the druid could have meant, he didn't have a clue what he was even going to open with, yet he felt strangely happy about it. There was a bounce in his step that usually came only after miles of walking on the very finest days.

He thought of Lowa's baby. She hadn't told him, but he knew; he'd seen the same when his wife Brinna had been pregnant with their twin daughters Kelsie and Terry. It was so long since they'd died, but they were still very much part of who he was. He remembered the day that they were murdered by raiders. He remembered falling to his knees and wailing. When he'd been able to think again, many days later, it had seemed that his life couldn't possibly go on. But now, more than a decade afterwards, it didn't seem such a world-ending tragedy, just a moment when his life had changed direction with a jerk. As it had that day in Bladonfort when he'd met Lowa. He hoped that she and baby Dug – he had a feeling it was a boy this time – lived longer and more happily than Brinna, Kelsie and Terry had. It didn't seem likely, given the current situation, but Dug was irrationally optimistic.

He came to what had been a hedge until the Maidun army had retreated through it the day before, and stepped over broken branches. On the other side, grubbing in the churned earth, was a family of badgers – boar, sow and one cub. All three looked up at Dug, then returned to their foraging.

"Now that," he said to himself, "has got to be a good sign."

The badgers made him think of his dogs, waiting for him to come home. The idea of disappointing them sent the first pang of sorrow through him. He felt optimistic for Lowa. For himself, he wasn't so sure.

Grummog, Bruxon and Manfrax were waiting. "Where the fuck is Lowa?" asked the big, bearded king, in a strong Eroo accent.

"Up in the hillfort," said Dug. "And it's Queen Lowa to you."

"Is it now? And who the fuck are you?"

"I'm Dug. Dug Sealskinner."

"I know who he is," spat Grummog from a high seat. "He's a mercenary Warrior. He worked for me for a while. He was a good fighter, but not the cleverest. I got rid of him because the idiot killed too many on our side."

Dug remembered. It was the battle in which both sides had painted themselves blue. "That wasn't my fault," he said.

"Wasn't your fault? I saw you! You were lashing out with that hammer like Makka had got you by the—"

"If you're done reminiscing," interrupted Manfrax, "would

you mind awfully telling us why the fuck we shouldn't feed you to the Fassites right now?"

Dug looked at the three kings, from one to the next. Manfrax leaning forwards threateningly. Grummog oozing hate from his chair. Bruxon subdued, looking at his feet. As if a gate had opened in his mind and a herd of sheep bleating out ideas had run through, suddenly he knew what to say and what to do.

"You, Manfrax," said Dug, "are a torturer who brought misery to an entire land. Worse than that, in your stupidity, you've unleashed the Fassites on the world. They've seen your boats and now they're building their own. They intend to leave Fassent and kill every human in the world, you included."

"That's what you'd like to think, isn't it?" Manfrax said. "But I have a pact—"

"A pact you say? Like the wee pacts you have with the Murkans and Dumnonians? Which of those are you planning to break first?" Dug looked from Grummog to Bruxon. Grummog looked angry; Bruxon, still looking down, reddened. "I see. So, when Maidun is wiped out, you and Bruxon will turn on Grummog."

"We will not," said Manfrax, still smiling. "Although who can blame you, in your desperation, trying to turn friends on each other? That's exactly what I'd do. It's Maidun's only hope. Sorry, my good man, it won't work."

"And when you and your Fassites have killed the Murkans, you will turn on Dumnonia."

"This really is pathet—"

"And then the Fassites will turn on you. Probably before. The few giants here are just biding their time until the rest of them arrive."

"How can you know all this?" Grummog said.

Dug turned to him, "Grummog. You also torture and murder your own. Greed and the love of violence bring you south. You don't care that men and women on your own side will die. You wish nothing for others but suffering.

"And you, Bruxon." Dug turned to the Dumnonian king. "You're weak and you've been used. Not, as you might be imagining, by Manfrax, or even Grummog, but by your advisor, Maggot. Maggot has used you to bring all these evil shits and their armies into one place."

"Now why would he want to do that?" said Manfrax

"You're a scourge, ruining the world. You need to be wiped from the land and forgotten. Maggot has arranged for you all to be here so we can get that done. It won't be long, so if you want to pray to your gods or say farewell to loved ones, now would be the time."

There was silence, then Manfrax began to laugh. Grummog joined in, then Bruxon. Dug stood, watching them. He felt warm and content. It was coming. This was what his life had been leading to.

"Dug – it is Dug, right?" Manfrax said, recovering from his laughing fit.

"That's it. Dug Sealskinner," said Dug.

"You speak for a queen too shy to come to us herself. You speak for an army which I all but destroyed yesterday. Do you know what we're going to do today?"

"I do. You're going to die. All of you."

"We are NOT!" shouted Manfrax. "Right now, we're making shields for the Fassites so they can walk up the hill without worrying about your archers. When that's done, up we'll go and—"

Dug wasn't listening any more. It was time. He was ready. He spread his arms. He turned away from the three kings. He looked back up the hill to where he knew Lowa and Spring were watching. He closed his eyes.

Chapter 39

Up on the wall, Spring knew what to do. She glanced at Lowa. The queen was even paler than usual.

She looked at Maggot, hoping that he'd tell her not to do it. He smiled, but his eyes were full of tears. She nodded, sick in her stomach. She took a long-distance, slim-pointed arrow from her quiver and slotted it on the bowstring. She lifted her bow and drew. She didn't need to aim.

"Spring?" said Lowa. "What are you—"

She loosed. The arrow thrummed off into the sky.

Bruxon was perplexed, and worried. The big northerner seemed strangely calm and confident. He knew things he shouldn't have known. Had Maggot played them all? The notion made some sense, until you got to the part about the Maidun army somehow defeating them. Hopelessly outnumbered and surrounded, it was a matter of when they were destroyed, not if. Any fool could see that.

And now Dug had turned away from them, apparently to show his chest to his friends on the hill. It looked like Maggot-style dramatics. Perhaps the druid had arranged this little show?

Then he saw the arrow, flying down from Frogshold like a diving hawk.

It hit the big Maidun man's forehead and came halfway out the back of his skull. Dug fell back on to the earth, arms out, face up, stone dead.

". . .What the fuck was that?" said Manfrax, with a surprised chuckle.

Bruxon looked about. Everything was the same, apart from the envoy from Maidun had been killed by an astonishing shot from his own side. What was the point of it? Was it a sacrifice meant to bring the gods' help? Was it some sort of display of machismo?

"Somebody clear that shit up," said Manfrax, pointing at Dug's body with half an eye watching for any more long-distance arrows from Frogshold, "and let's get busy – that little gang on the hill isn't going annihilate itself. Are those shields ready yet?"

As soon as the arrow left the bow, Lowa knew where it was going. She knew what Spring and Maggot and Dug had planned.

She watched it fly, helpless. She saw the tiny figure of Dug, standing in front of the kings and spreading his arms. Out of the corner of her eye she saw Spring drop her bow and crumple down into a ball. She heard the girl cry out at the moment that Dug fell.

"No!" shouted Lowa. Tears came. She shook her head. "Nooo!" she screamed to the sky and the gods.

Chapter 40

On the island of Fassent, two hundred and ninety miles from the spot where Dug lay dead, the ground vibrated with a low rumble. The Fassites stopped their boat building. The rumbling became louder; a deep, immensely powerful noise. The vibrations grew until the land was shaking. Boat scaffolds collapsed and buildings toppled. A few were injured and one crushed under a ship, but for the most part the buildings were so lightly built and the giants themselves so robust that the collapse of all the Fassite-made structures on the island was more of an inconvenience than a disaster.

The giants ran then crawled to clear land and sat as the ground beneath them buckled and heaved. Most were laughing – bouncing around was fun. Several started fighting, as Fassites always did when they were enjoying themselves. They were interrupted by a terrible roaring, wrenching thunder from above; much, much louder than the earthquake.

The great mountain, the huge rock that dominated their island, split in half and slowly collapsed. The ground they were sitting and fighting on lurched and folded over on itself, and all the Fassites on Fassent were crushed or drowned as a trillion tons of rock fell into the sea.

Chapter 41

Lowa shook off her numbness and ordered two men to carry Spring to her hut. The girl looked dead but Maggot insisted she wasn't.

"What was that? What the Bel was that?" she asked.

Maggot, for once, looked serious. "I'm sorry. Powerful magic was needed, possibly the most powerful magic that's ever been. Magic works through love and death, and Spring and Dug . . . I am sorry that it had to be Dug. But he has saved us all. Not just us here – everyone. Everyone decent, that is. These armies surrounding us? They're fucked, but it is their own fault."

Lowa looked down from the hundred and thirty pace-high mound of Frogshold. Well outside her own arrow range – she had no idea how Spring had made the shot – a Fassite was dragging Dug's body away from the kings.

"He saved us by going down the hill and dying?"

"Yes," said the druid. He walked away, jangling.

Dug's body was out of sight now. Lowa wanted to scream and rip her hair out, but she forced herself to ignore the pain for now. She had a hillfort to defend and an already much reduced number of Maidunites to save.

It looked like she had a while before the Eroo army or the Fassites were going to move, so she jumped down off the wall, headed out of the gate and began a circuit of the ditch. It had been deepened overnight and they'd dismantled huts to make spikes for its base. She wanted to check that these were all still upright, and that no grass tuft handholds had been left in the fort's wall. She knew it would be fine, but her real goal was to keep herself busy. As she came round to the north, she saw that the Murkans were preparing to attack as well. Was it too much to hope that the Murkan and the Eroo armies would clash and end up wiping each other out while they watched from the hillfort? Yes it was. But perhaps that was what Spring's magic would do?

"Lowa!" someone shouted. It was Maggot, calling from the wall nearby. "Come to me, there is a sight to see!" he yelled. Lowa jogged back into the fort and joined Maggot on the wall.

"Look to the west, out to sea," he said.

She looked. The sea was calm. The only unusual thing were the hundreds of Eroo boats dragged on to the beach and moored off it.

Then she saw it.

On the horizon, stretched across the entire width of the Haffen Estuary, was a line of white, moving swiftly towards them and growing rapidly. Another line developed behind it, larger, then another, then another, each higher than the previous. They were waves, very big waves, moving at an astonishing speed, growing as they approached the shore.

"What the Danu . . ." Lowa asked.

"Fassent fell into the sea. These are the ripples," said Maggot.

The Maidunites teemed onto the wall to watch in silence as the giant waves approached. Lowa looked down. The enemy was carrying on as before, preparing the assault. They did not know what was coming.

The first wave approached the beach, growing astonishingly, towering, breaking. It exploded onto an island near the shore then washed over it. It plucked ships from their anchors, drove them shorewards on a roaring wall of surf and smashed them into the beached boats. The people who'd been on the beach, who'd seen the wave and began to run, disappeared in an instant under the foaming, debris-filled surge. Another, taller wave broke on to the beach. That second one was awesomely, astonishingly huge, but a few waves behind it, perhaps a mile out, was a wall of water that dwarfed the others, overtaking the waves ahead of it and sucking them into itself. It was at least a hundred paces tall, nearly as high as their perch on Frogshold.

"By Danu," said Lowa. "What . . . ?"

"I think we'll be calling it a Spring Tide," said Maggot.

Bruxon strode back to the Dumnonian camp, deeply unhappy. He didn't believe for a moment that the Maidun army was going to slaughter them all, but what Dug had said about treachery had rung uncomfortably true. He'd been a fool and a coward. He should have attacked and conquered Maidun himself, and never even been to Eroo. Because then . . . He thought back to the night before and what he'd done with Manfrax. What he'd done to Manfrax, all while his harpy wife looked on. He'd been overcome by lust and unable to stop himself. He'd sucked his nipple like a starving calf, hands all over him, and then . . . He shook his head. He sickened himself.

Deep in self-abusing thought, he didn't hear the sound until it was a roar. He looked for the source, and saw a towering cliff of water rushing towards him across the flat farmland. He stood, open-mouthed, as it came at him, impossibly fast.

Ragnall Sheeplord was standing with Julius Caesar on the cliff, looking over the Roman fleet, newly swelled by captured Armorican boats, and telling him all he knew about landing an army on the British coast. It wasn't very much. The only coastline he knew well was the Island of Angels, which was on the wrong side of Britain. He'd seen part of the coast near Maidun when he and Drustan had sailed to Rome but he hadn't been paying much attention.

So he was relieved when Caesar held up a hand to silence

him. The general was looking down at the bay with a quiz-zical expression. Ragnall followed his gaze and saw that the tide had rushed out preternaturally quickly and far. Some boats that had been floating moments before were marooned, others were being washed out to sea along channels revealed in what had been seabed.

"What a strange tide . . ." he said.

"It's not a tide," said Caesar. "Finally the British gods are showing their hand. Quick, come with me to higher ground. All of you," he said to everyone nearby, raising his voice but remaining totally calm, "there is a giant wave coming, more or less immediately. Warn everyone, get everyone to high ground."

Men ran off to do his bidding, shouting as they went. As Ragnall and Caesar strode up the hill, the sea returned. It was more like a strangely rapid rising tide initially, refloating the boats and slopping lazily ashore. Then came the waves, like a great swelling at first, then towering and breaking, smashing on the cliffs, rearing up into the bay and crashing down on to ships.

"By Toutatis," said Ragnall. The power was staggering. Luckily for the people on the shore the sides of the bay were steep, so almost all were able to run to safety. The few people who'd been on the ships were not so lucky. Debris from the previous day's battle and the surviving boats was soon indis-tinguishable as the bay churned and rushed, crashing ships against each other and into the cliffs.

When the sea level returned to normal, the ships were gone. The boatsheds around the edge of the bay – everything, in fact, lower than fifty paces up the cliff – was gone. Romans and Gauls alike were staring down at the destruction in slack-jawed wonder, all apart from Caesar. He was looking at his destroyed invasion fleet like a dice player calculating how to react to a good throw by his opponent.

Chapter 42

Dug Sealskinner's feet sunk into sand as he walked up the dune.

He paused when the view cleared over the summit. His broch stood firm by the burbling stream, peaceful as a sleeping dog. Its round stone wall was so solid, everything looked so quiet. But he couldn't see Brinna, Kelsie or Terry anywhere. A knot of worry grew in his stomach. Where were his wife and children?

He jumped down the dune in two huge leaps, sinking knee-deep in sand, like he'd done so many times with his wee girls whooping in his arms. He ran over springy estuarine turf and splashed across the burn's stony ford. Geese scattered out of his way, honking angrily. Geese that should have been fenced into the broch's stonewalled yard . . .

His twin tots ran out to meet him, squealing with joy, sunlight shining in their beautiful red hair. He'd been ready to tell them off for leaving the gate open and letting the geese out, but he couldn't be angry with his wonderful little girls. He crouched to hug them both and saw Brinna standing in the broch's doorway, beaming.

"Now where have you been all this time, Dug? Stop playing around and come in, you great lunk. It's time for your tea."

Dug stood, a girl under each arm, both chattering away with some story about a naughty cow. So happy that tears welled in his eyes, Dug followed his wife into his home.

Historical Note

The reader should bear in mind that this is fantasy novel, not a history text book. If it sparks or adds to an interest in the period, that's great, but you probably shouldn't quote from it in a history exam.

Having said that, the Roman stuff is pretty accurate. The descriptions of Rome, all the main Roman characters with the exception of Felix, all the politics and all the battles mentioned in Clash of Iron do tally with history books. Caesar really did have a comb-over, he and Clodius the Beautiful did have those adventures with pirates, Licinius Lucullus did have his slaves dig through a mountain to irrigate his fish tanks and people did call Clodia Metelli "Lady Copper Coin", but only very carefully because the revenge I've described that she had on a man for leaving copper coins by her beside is also true. One thing I found researching the Romans is that there's no need to make up stories about them.

Caesar's rampage through Gaul is accurate too – or at least the book more or less tallies with his own diaries. I haven't made up any of the individual campaigns or battles, but I have shaped them a little to suit the story and omitted a couple in order to keep this trilogy to just three books. It's estimated that out of five million or so Gauls alive at the beginning of Caesar's campaign he killed a million of them and enslaved a million more – something to bear in mind if you feel I've been a bit unfair with my recreation of his character and portrayal of the Romans.

The characters and tribes in Britain and Ireland are pretty much entirely fabricated because the ancient Brits didn't write and any oral histories were obliterated by four hundred years of Roman occupation which began a hundred years after Dug and Lowa's time. There are descriptions of tribal groups from the time in history books, and even some names of individual people, but as these are uncertain I have taken the liberty of completely ignoring them. The technology – weapons, wheels, towns and so on – tallies more or less with what historians say but, again, I have taken liberties because the history is so uncertain.

The books and sources I used are too numerous to list in full, but here are the books which were most useful, and which I'd recommend to anybody who wants to learn more about the period.

Baker, Simon. *Ancient Rome: The Rise and Fall of an Empire*. London: BBC Books; reprint edition, 2007.

Caesar, Julius. *The Conquest of Gaul*. London: Penguin Classics; Rev. Ed., 1982.

Carey, Brian Todd, Allfree, Joshua B. and Cairns, John. *Warfare in the Ancient World*. Barnsley: Leo Cooper Ltd, 2005.

Cunliffe, Barry. *Iron Age Communities in Britain: An account of England, Scotland and Wales from the Seventh Century* BC *until the Roman Conquest*. London: Routledge; 4th edition, 2009.

Goldsworthy, Adrian. *Caesar*. London: Phoenix; New ed., 2007.

Holland, Tom. *Rubicon: The Triumph and the Tragedy of the Roman Republic*. London: Abacus; New Ed., 2004.

Jiménez, Ramon L. *Caesar against the Celts*. Boston: Da Capo Press; reprint edition, 1996.

Pryor, Francis. *Britain* BC: *Life in Britain and Ireland*

Before the Romans. London: Harper Perennial; New Ed., 2004.

Sage, Michael M. *Roman Conquests − Gaul*. Barnsley: Pen & Sword Military, 2011.

Acknowledgements

While I was writing this book, my wife Nicola had a baby. So while she was going through the later stages of pregnancy, then staying awake most of the night to nurse our son, I was whinging about things like the difficulty of finding yet another way to say "he hit him with his hammer." So massive, colossal, on-my-knees-and-waving-my-hands-above-my-head thanks to her for putting up with me and supporting me. Thanks also to my excellent editor, Jenni Hill, for being so spot-on with edits and encouraging me through my pathetic bouts of insecurity, to all at Orbit for putting together such good-looking books and marketing them so well, and to Richard Collins for a diligent copy-edit. Much gratitude to my agent, Angharad Kowal, at Writers' House, without whom none of this would have been possible, and a huge thanks to my brother Tim for his invaluable plot suggestions. Finally thanks to our son, Charlie, who hasn't done much yet other than surprise me (a) by being such a happy little boy and (b) by making my heart burst with love.

Look out for
REIGN OF IRON

Age of Iron: Book Three

by

Angus Watson

Caesar's soldiers have murdered, massacred and pillaged
their way through Gaul and loom on the far side of
the sea, ready to descend upon Britain – with them are
an unstoppable legion of men twisted by dark magic.
Somehow Queen Lowa must repel the invasion, although
her best general is dead and her young druid powerless.
She faces impossible odds, but when the alternative is
death or slavery, a warrior queen will do whatever it
takes to save her people.

EVERY EMPIRE HAS ITS DOWNFALL.

orbit

extras

orbit

meet the author

Nicola Watson

Angus Watson is an author and journalist living in London. He's written hundreds of features for many newspapers including *The Times*, *Financial Times* and the *Telegraph*, and the latter even sent him to look for Bigfoot. As a fan of both historical fiction and epic fantasy, Angus came up with the idea of writing a fantasy set in the Iron Age when exploring British hillforts for the *Telegraph*, and developed the story while walking Britain's ancient paths for further articles. You can find him on Twitter at @GusWatson or find his website at www.guswatson.com. Find out more about Angus Watson and other Orbit authors by registering for the free monthly newsletter at www.orbitbooks.net.

introducing

If you enjoyed
CLASH OF IRON
look out for

A DANCE OF CLOAKS

Shadowdance: Book One

by David Dalglish

The Underworld rules the city of Veldaren. Thieves,
smugglers, assassins . . . they fear only one man.

In book one of the Shadowdance series, Thren Felhorn is
the greatest assassin of his time. All the thieves' guilds of the city
are under his unflinching control. If he has his way, death will
soon spill out from the shadows and into the streets.

Aaron is Thren's son, trained to be heir to his father's criminal
empire. He's cold, ruthless—everything an assassin should be.
But when Aaron risks his life to protect a priest's daughter from
his own guild, he glimpses a world beyond piston, daggers,
and the iron rule of his father.

Assassin or protector; every choice has its consequences.

Prologue

For the past two weeks the simple building had been his safe house, but now Thren Felhorn distrusted its protection as he limped through the door. He clutched his right arm to his body, fighting to halt its trembling. Blood ran from his shoulder to his elbow, the arm cut by a poisoned blade.

"Damn you, Leon," he said as he staggered across the wood floor, through a sparsely decorated room, and up to a wall made of plaster and oak. Even with his blurred vision he located the slight groove with his fingers. He pressed down, detaching an iron lock on the other side of the wall. A small door swung inward.

The master of the Spider Guild collapsed in a chair and removed his gray hood and cloak. He sat in a much larger room painted silver and decorated with pictures of mountains and fields. Removing his shirt, he gritted his teeth while pulling it over his wounded arm. The toxin had been meant to paralyze him, not kill him, but the fact was little comfort. Most likely Leon Connington had wanted him alive so he could sit in his padded chair and watch his "gentle toucher" bleed Thren drop by drop. The fat man's treacherous words from their meeting ignited a fire in his gut that refused to die.

"We will not cower to rats that live off our shit," Leon had said while brushing his thin mustache. "Do you really think you stand a chance against the wealth of the Trifect? We could buy your soul from the gods."

Such arrogance. Such pride. Thren had fought down his

initial impulse to bury a short sword in the fat man's throat upon hearing such mockery. For centuries the three families of the Trifect, the Conningtons, the Keenans, and the Gemcrofts, had ruled in the shadows. Over that time they'd certainly bought enough priests and kings to believe that the gods wouldn't be beyond the reach of their gilded fingers either.

It had been a mistake to deny his original impulse, Thren knew. Leon should have bled out then and there, his guards be damned. They'd met inside Leon's extravagant mansion, another mistake. Thren vowed to correct his carelessness in the coming months. For three years he'd done his best to stop the war from erupting, but it appeared everyone in the city of Veldaren desired chaos.

If the city wants blood, it can have it, Thren thought. *But it won't be mine.*

"Is that you, Father?" he heard his elder son ask from an adjacent room.

"It is," Thren said, holding his anger in check. "But if it were not, what would you do, having given away your presence?"

His son Randith entered from the other room. He looked much like his father, having the same sharp features, thin nose, and grim smile. His hair was brown like his mother's, and that alone endeared him to Thren. They both wore the gray trousers of their guild, and from Randith's shoulders hung a gray cloak similar to Thren's. A long rapier hung from one side of Randith's belt, a dagger from the other. His blue eyes met his father's.

"I'd kill you," Randith said, a cocky grin pulling up the left side of his face. "As if I need surprise to do it."

"Shut the damn door," Thren said, ignoring the bravado. "Where's our mage? Connington's men cut me with a toxin, and its effect is...troublesome."

Troublesome hardly described it, but Thren wouldn't let his son know that. His flight from the mansion was a blur in his memory. The toxin had numbed his arm and made his entire side sting with pain. His neck muscles had fired off at random, and one of his knees kept locking up during his run. Like a cripple he'd fled through the alleyways of Veldaren, but the moon was waning and the streets empty, so none had seen his pathetic stumbling.

"Not here," Randith said as he leaned toward his father's exposed shoulder and examined the cut.

"Then go find him," Thren said. "How did events go at the Gemcroft mansion?"

"Maynard Gemcroft's men fired arrows from their windows as we approached," Randith said. He turned his back to his father and opened a few cupboards until he found a small black bottle. He popped the cork, but when he moved to pour the liquid on his father's cut, Thren yanked the bottle out of his hand. Dripping the brown liquid across the cut, he let out a hiss through clenched teeth. It burned like fire, but already he felt the tingle of the toxin beginning to fade. When finished, he accepted some strips of cloth from his son and tied them tight around the wound.

"Where is Aaron?" Thren asked when the pain subsided. "If you won't fetch the mage, at least he will."

"Lurking as always," Randith said. "Reading too. I tell him mercenaries may soon storm in with orders to eradicate all thief guilds, and he looks at me like I'm a lowly fishmonger mumbling about the weather."

Thren held in a grimace.

"You're too impatient with him," he said. "Aaron understands more than you think."

"He's soft, and a coward. This life will never suit him."

Thren reached out with his good hand, grabbed Randith by the front of his shirt, and yanked him close so they might stare face-to-face.

"Listen well," he said. "Aaron is my son, as are you. Whatever contempt you have, you swallow it down. Even the wealthiest king is still dirt in my eyes compared to my own flesh and blood, and I expect the same respect from you."

He shoved Randith away, then called out further into the hideout.

"Aaron! Your family needs you, now come in here."

A short child of eight stepped into the room, clutching a worn book to his chest. His features were soft and curved, and he would no doubt grow up to be a comely man. He had his father's hair, though, a soft blond that curled around his ears and hung low to his deep blue eyes. He fell to one knee and bowed his head without saying a word, all while still holding the book.

"Do you know where Cregon is?" Thren asked, referring to the mage in their employ. Aaron nodded. "Good. Where?"

Aaron said nothing. Thren, tired and wounded, had no time for his younger son's nonsense. While other children grew up babbling nonstop, a good day for Aaron involved nine words, and rarely would they be used in one sentence.

"Tell me where he is, or you'll taste blood on your tongue," Randith said, sensing his father's exasperation.

"He went away," Aaron said, his voice barely above a whisper. "He's a fool."

"A fool or not, he's my fool, and damn good at keeping us alive," Thren said. "Go bring him here. If he argues, slash your finger across your neck. He'll understand."

Aaron bowed and did as he was told.

"I wonder if he's practicing for a vow of silence," Randith said as he watched his brother leave without any hurry.

"Did he lock the outer door?" Thren asked.

"Shut and latched," Randith said after checking.

"Then he's smarter than you."

Randith smirked.

"If you say so. But right now, I think we have bigger concerns. The Gemcrofts firing at my men, Leon setting up a trap...this means war, doesn't it?"

Thren swallowed hard, then nodded.

"The Trifect have turned their backs on peace. They want blood, our blood, and unless we act fast they are going to get it."

"Perhaps if we offer even more in bribes?" Randith suggested.

Thren shook his head.

"They've tired of the game. We rob them until they are red with rage, then pay bribes with their own wealth. You've seen how much they've invested in mercenaries over the past few months. Their minds are set. They want us exterminated."

"That's ludicrous," Randith insisted. "You've united nearly every guild in the city. Between our assassins, our spies, our thugs...what makes them think they can withstand all-out war?"

Thren frowned as Randith's fingers drummed the hilt of his rapier.

"Give me a few of our best men," his son said. "When Leon Connington bleeds out in his giant bed, the rest will learn that accepting our bribes is far better than accepting our mercy."

"You are still a young man," Thren said. "You are not ready for what Leon has prepared."

"I am seventeen," Randith said. "A man grown, and I have more kills to my name than years."

"And I've more than you've drawn breaths," Thren said, a hard edge entering his voice. "But even I will not return to that mansion. They are *eager* for this, can't you see that? Entire guilds will be wiped out in days. Those who survive will inherit this city, and I will not have my heir run off and die in the opening hours."

Thren placed one of his short swords on the table with his uninjured hand. Holding it there, he met Randith's gaze, challenging him, looking to see just what sort of man his son truly was.

"I'll leave the mansion be, as you suggest," Randith said. "But I will not cower and hide. You are right, Father. These are the opening hours. Our actions here will decide the course of months of fighting. Let the merchants and nobles hide. *We* rule the night."

He pulled his gray cloak over his head and turned to the hidden door. Thren watched him go, his hands shaking, but not from the toxin.

"Be wary," Thren said, careful to keep his face a mask. "Everything you do has consequences."

If Randith sensed the threat, he didn't let it show.

"I'll go get Senke," said Randith. "He'll watch over you until Aaron returns with the mage."

Then he was gone. Thren struck the table with his palm and swore. He thought of the countless hours he'd invested in Randith, the training, the sparring, and the many lectures, all in an attempt to cultivate a worthy heir for the Spider Guild.

Wasted, Thren thought. *Wasted*.

He heard the click of the latch, and then the door creaked open. Thren expected the mage, or perhaps his son returning to smooth over his abrupt exit, but instead a short man with a black cloth wrapped around his face stepped inside.

"Don't run," the intruder said. Thren snapped up his short sword and blocked the first two blows from the man's dagger. He tried to counter, but his vision was still blurred and his speed a pathetic remnant of his finely honed reflexes. A savage chop knocked the sword from his hand. Thren fell back, using his chair to force a stumble out of his pursuer. The best he could do was limp, though, and when a heel kicked his knee, he fell. He spun, refusing to die with a dagger in his back.

"Leon sends his greetings," the man said, his dagger pulled back for a final, lethal blow.

He suddenly jerked forward, his eyes widening. The dagger fell from his limp hand as the would-be assassin collapsed. Behind him stood Aaron, holding a bloody short sword. Thren's eyes widened as his younger son knelt. The flat edge rested on his palms, blood running down his wrists.

"Your sword," Aaron said, presenting the blade.

"How…why did you return?" Thren asked.

"The man was hiding," the boy said, his voice still quiet. He didn't sound the least bit upset. "Waiting for us to go. So I waited for him."

Thren felt the corners of his mouth twitch. He took the sword from a boy who spent his days reading underneath his bed and skulking within closets, often mocked by his older brother for being too soft. A boy who never threw a punch when forced into a fight, never dared raise his voice in anger.

A boy who had killed a man at the age of eight.

"I know you're bright," Thren said. "But the life we live is twisted, and we are forever surrounded by liars and betrayers. You must trust your instincts, and learn to listen to not just what is said, but what is not. Can you do this? Can you view men and women as if they are pieces to a game, and understand what must be done, my son?"

Aaron looked up at him. If he was bothered by the blood on him, it didn't show.

"I can," Aaron said.

"Good," said Thren. "Wait with me. Randith will return soon."

Ten minutes later the door crept open.

"Father?" Randith asked as he stepped inside. Senke, Thren's right-hand man, was with him. He looked slightly older than Randith, with a trimmed blond beard and a thick mace held in hand. They both startled at the dead body lying on the floor, a gaping wound in its back.

"He waited until you left," Thren said from his chair, which he'd positioned to face the entrance.

"Where?" Randith asked. He pointed to Aaron. "And why is he here?"

Thren shook his head.

"You don't understand, Randith. You disobey me, not out of wisdom, but out of arrogance and pride. You treat our enemies with contempt instead of respect worthy of their danger. Worst of all, you put my life at risk."

He looked to Aaron, back to Randith.

"Too many mistakes," he said. "Far too many."

Then he waited. And hoped.

Aaron stepped toward his older brother. His blue eyes were calm, unworried. In a single smooth motion, he yanked Randith's dagger from his belt, flipped it around, and thrust it to the hilt in his brother's chest. Senke stepped back, jaw hanging open, but he wisely held his tongue. Aaron withdrew the dagger, spun around, and presented it as a gift to his father.

Thren rose from his seat and placed a hand on Aaron's shoulder.

"You did well, my son," he said. "My heir."

"Thank you," Aaron whispered, tears in his eyes. He bowed low as behind him the body of his brother bled out on the floor.